the BEST MEN

USA Today Bestselling Author
SARINA BOWEN
#1 New York Times Bestselling Author
LAUREN BLAKELY

TROLIVER  BOOKS

YES, HE DEFINITELY GOT MY DRUNK TEXT

MARK

*T*he first time I met Asher St. James, he was twenty-seven minutes late. The second time, he spilled his drink on me. I'd like to think the third time will be a charm, but I highly doubt it.

Only this time, it'll be all my fault.

I've behaved badly. And now I must pay the price.

Asher isn't even my biggest problem. As I make my way up Lexington Avenue on a warm May evening, I prepare to give my mea culpa. The one I have to deliver any second now to, count 'em, three people.

My baby sister, her groom, and his *superhot wingman*.

Groan.

Did I actually call Asher *that*?

Maybe it was just a bad dream.

Grabbing my phone from my back pocket, I click on the group text once more, wishing for the five hundred and seventy-ninth time that last night's string of single-malt-fueled messages would go the way of a fax machine and just disappear.

But they're all still here. For digital posterity.

As I cross Fifty-Seventh Street, I pass a garbage can and seriously consider chucking my phone in it. Too bad throwing away the instrument of my own mortification won't do the trick. Nothing except a time machine will erase the drunk texts I fired off last night somewhere between midnight and regret o'clock.

Also known as the hour the scotch took over all my decision-making.

Thanks a fucking lot, liquor. You're a pal.

Have I mentioned I'm still hungover? I have the remnants of last night's Very Bad Decisions and a dull headache that aspirin won't cure.

I deserve it.

My head pounds, but the clock is ticking on my sister's engagement dinner so I keep trudging uptown. Three more blocks till I have to eat crow.

The crosswalk sign on Fifty-Ninth Street tells me not to go.

No shit, sign.

Stopping at the curb, I picture the three of them waiting for me at the nearby sushi joint. And I rehearse my apologies, one at a time.

First, Hannah. All big blue eyes, freckled nose, and small but growing belly bump.

Hey, my second-favorite person in the world. I wish I could say someone hacked my phone last night, but that was me with the all caps text: **'I SWEAR YOUR HASTY MARRIAGE WILL TOP A BUZZFEED LIST OF BAD IDEAS THAT ALSO INCLUDES CRYSTAL PEPSI AND MULLETS. AND I SHOULD KNOW. I'VE TRIED ALL THREE.'**

I'm so sorry. Your nuptials are nothing like mine, or that bad haircut I had in high school, and getting married to Flip is a great idea.

At least, I hope it is.

It damn well better be.

As for the guy my little sis is marrying, I'll have to apologize to him next. They're madly in love. And even though I'm still privately horrified that he got her pregnant three months after they met, I'll man up and apologize.

Hey, Flip, I deeply regret saying that your marriage will fail harder than Bear Stearns and Lehman Brothers. And also for saying that grown men don't call themselves "Flip."

My analogy game was on point last night, scotch be damned. But my behavior wasn't.

Which means I'll inevitably turn to Asher, the groom's best bud, the guy who was twenty-seven minutes late the first time I met him. He'd delayed the start of game night six months ago—the one my sister had arranged so we could all meet, back when she and Flip had just become an item.

Then Asher had sauntered in. Yes, he *saunters,* with his too-toned-to-be-real frame, and too-floppy-to-be-anything-but-a-shampoo-model hair, with his *so sorry I was late, but I found a puppy shivering outside the building so I had to take him to the local rescue* apology.

Of fucking course.

He couldn't be that good-looking and just be late. He had to be late with style *and* substance.

The second time our paths crossed, they literally crossed. He lifted his glass of champagne right when I entered the dining room for my sister's dinner party, and my chest ran into his arm, dousing me in bubbly.

With a lopsided grin, and the kind of cocky confidence that only a former pro athlete can pull off, he proceeded to unbutton his shirt, take it off, and offer it to me in front of everyone.

I declined, while trying not to stare at his eight-pack. Obviously, I wore my champagne-soaked button-down all through dinner.

I'm not taking another man's shirt.

And, so, Asher, I didn't mean it when I called you Flip's superhot wingman, or referred to your body as annoyingly perfect.

His abs are truly perfect. Nothing annoying whatsoever about that washboard.

But still, as I reach the door of the restaurant, I remind myself to apologize thoroughly and sincerely. To proceed like I didn't mean all the things the liquor unleashed from my thumbs last night.

Like I'm not completely panicking over my little sister's

sudden engagement. And her just-announced pregnancy to the guy she started dating in December.

Like I'm not at all terrified her shotgun marriage will go belly up, beached-whale style, just like mine did.

And like I'm not attracted to the wingman who irritates the hell out of me, the guy I also maybe, kinda, sorta would like to see naked.

Nope.

That shit will stay locked up tight. Where it belongs.

I straighten up, open the door, and walk inside.

"May I help you?" the hostess asks with a gracious smile.

It's tempting to ask her to put me out of my misery. But I give Flip's name instead. Well, his real name.

"I'm here for the Phillipe Dubois party," I say.

"Fantastic. They just arrived," she says. "You're all so punctual."

Great. I'm always on the dot, and this time they beat me to it by showing up earlier. Could this night suck more?

I follow her to the back of the restaurant where the superhot wingman is hosting a small but chic engagement dinner. He'll have invited all their old prep school friends, with their boat shoes and suntans, and names like Carlisle Bancroft.

And, yup, the first guy I spot inside the room has whales on his tie. Called it.

The second guy is Flip. The welcoming smile slides right off his face when he sees me. My gaze swings from him to Hannah, who's standing arm in arm with her groom-to-be. My sister's expression doesn't chill, though. If anything, she's eyeing me with concern.

And then there's Asher St. James. He's leaning casually against a chair, his hair flopping theatrically across his forehead, a cocktail glass in his hand.

For a quick second, I wonder if it's possible that he didn't even see the texts. The thread was full of engagement party planning stuff. He's probably too busy chatting up famous athletes and models to bother with my drunken rants.

A man can hope.

But the exact moment he registers my arrival, that hope dies. Asher doesn't frown at me, though. It's worse than that. So much worse.

A corner of his handsome mouth tilts up. And he smirks.

That's when a chill enters my body. Because it's go-time. No more rehearsals, just three awkward apologies.

Slowly, I cross the room toward Hannah, Flip, and Asher. One of them is frowning. One looks worried. One looks smug.

The answer is, yes, this night can suck more.

2

THE SLIDING SCALE OF HOTNESS

ASHER

*A*nd here I thought engagement parties were dull.

This one might have been, in spite of the fact that I'm throwing it. My opinion of marriage rituals is ambivalent at best. But here comes the bride's brother slinking through the door, looking like a kid who's just been caught putting a snake in the teacher's desk. A venomous one.

So this party just got a whole lot more interesting.

Ever since meeting Mark several months ago, I haven't known what to think about the buttoned-up banker with the midnight blue eyes. He's always struck me as mild-mannered and carefully inoffensive. Like a striped tie, or a white dress shirt. I'm sure he owns both. In multiples. If he has a car, I bet it's silver.

He works at a Wall Street bank, for fuck's sake, doing something with math or spreadsheets. "He's in derivatives," Flip once said, and I'd shuddered because the word made me think of failing out of calculus class in college.

Sometimes, though, if you get a few drinks in a guy, the truth comes out. That's what happened last night, I suspect. A little after midnight, when Flip and I were out on the balcony of his apartment, smoking a couple of Cubans I scored off a client, both our phones started pinging with drunk texts from the mild-mannered banker.

I should probably feel guilty for reading them. It was immediately obvious to both of us that Mark had only meant to text his sister. The four-way group text had begun only yesterday, as a quick way for me to plan this spontaneous engagement party, and Hannah was the last one to weigh in with an exclamation-laden (*I can't wait for the party!!!*) reply.

But did Flip and I stop reading? Not on your life. That text thread was a box of delights.

In the first place, I was fascinated to learn that Mark opposes his sister's wedding. Most men would be over the moon to welcome Phillipe "Flip" Dubois III to the family. My friend is both loaded and head-over-heels for Hannah. He's a good man, and she'll never want for anything.

He owns a full-floor condo on Park Avenue, a Mercedes E-Class, and has a membership at Maidstone. Material wealth aside, I'm here to tell anyone who asks that he cried actual tears of joy when she told him she was pregnant.

But all that's not good enough for our boy Mark, I guess. He wrote—in shouty caps, no less—that the marriage was **DOOMED LIKE THE TITANIC. I'M AFRAID FOR YOU ON THAT FLOATING DOOR.**

Now that's just dark. Besides, it's not even a good metaphor. Everyone knows there was plenty of room for Leo on that thing. The MythBusters even proved it.

The whole ugly blowup was, however, entertaining. The next five minutes will not disappoint, either, since our buttoned-up Wall Streeter now wears the abashed look of a man who's about to do the right thing and apologize to his sister and her fiancé.

I should probably walk away and give them some privacy. But I think I won't.

"Hannah Banana," Mark says in a rough voice as he approaches. "God, I'm sorry. I didn't mean any of it."

His sister grabs him into a hug. "Yes, you did, Marky Mark.

You meant every last excruciating thing, including the mullet comparison. And I forgive you anyway."

"Thank you." He groans, sounding relieved. "I just don't handle change all that well."

"Gosh, you think?" she asks. "I know we just sprung this on you. The baby. The wedding."

He grunts in acknowledgment as he hugs his sister. "How can I ever make it up to you?"

She pulls out of that tight hug and looks up at her brother. "Hold that thought. Because I do have a favor to ask a little later."

"Anything. Whatever you need. But I do need to apologize to your fiancé," he says.

"Good. I'd appreciate that," she says, patting his arm.

Mark obviously left the rep ties at home tonight in favor of a dress shirt in a deep blue color that makes his eyes pop. I'm such a sucker for eyes. And he's wearing a very sharp pair of glasses that accentuate instead of hide them. His glossy dark hair is cut in an attractive style that works with the whole boss man look he's got going on.

Fine. If I'm being objective, he looks good tonight. Hot, even. I've always thought so.

But he's still a stuck-up banker who doesn't like my BFF. And now he's got to grovel for Flip anyway.

This should be fun.

Slowly, Mark turns toward my friend, his expression chastened. "Flip, man, I'm sorry. There was no excuse for the lack of faith I showed last night."

"Damn right," Flip says, posting an arm around Hannah and lifting his strong, waspy chin in defiance. "I've never given you a *single* reason to doubt my good intentions toward your sister."

God, where is the popcorn when you need it? Mark's jaw is flexing. I can practically hear the arguments forming in his brain —most of which center around my friend's inability to use a condom correctly.

Flip and Hannah didn't mean to get pregnant three months after they met. It's all good, though, because by the time that plus sign showed up on the pregnancy test several weeks ago, they were already planning a future together.

"I'm sorry," Mark says again, even if his teeth are practically clenched. "It's just been sudden. I worry."

Flip rubs Hannah's shoulder. "I know it seems fast, but we're very happy. And we chose that wedding date next month partly for your sake."

Apparently Mark's high-pressure job makes it hard for him to get away, but he's free for the second half of June. "Thank you," he says, rubbing the back of his neck. "I'll be honored to attend."

His sister grins. "Go get a beer, Mark. Just stay away from the whiskey."

"Good idea," he says. "Thank you."

Mark turns and reverses course toward the bar in the corner. I'm about to follow him when the waitstaff begins carrying in an array of sushi rolls arranged on wooden boats, and also thinly sliced bites of ahi and hamachi served on elegant little dishes.

As a party planner, I've outdone myself.

"Mister St. James?" the manager says, touching my elbow. "Please let me know if you need anything at all."

I survey the generous spread of food and my stomach rumbles. "This looks terrific. I really appreciate the way you arranged this so quickly for me." Everything came together in a flurry, Hannah announced her pregnancy a few weeks ago, and last weekend, Flip proposed. Now, here we are.

"My pleasure, sir." The man gives a slight bow, and I return it, as I learned to do on an extended trip to Japan a few years ago. "If you need anything more, don't hesitate to ask."

Pleased with both him and myself, I turn back to the party and take a plate off the top of the stack. Then I hand it to Hannah. "The bride-to-be should start, right? If that's not a tradition, it should be. Step right up, Hannah. All this sushi isn't going to eat itself."

Then I move out of the way so that my guests can have first dibs on the spread. My drink is empty, though, so I head for the bar and another Asahi Super Dry.

That's where I find Mark, elbow on the bar, drinking . . . "Is that orange juice, Banks? How's your hangover?"

"I'll live," he says. "But I suspect drinking tonight is probably not in my best interests."

"I have to agree with you there," I say with a chuckle. "Unless you really enjoy apologizing. I know I enjoyed *watching* you apologize."

He gives me a dark look, but doesn't bother to respond. Understandable. That comment was more for my amusement. Which, let's be honest, a lot of things I do are.

But there was one *I'm so sorry* I definitely wanted a front seat to. I clear my throat. "I noticed I didn't get one."

"An apology?" Mark snorts, furrowing his brow. "Unless *you're* going to the chapel after knocking up my sister, I don't think I insulted you."

A laugh bursts from my chest. "Something no one will accuse me of. Ever."

"Then we're all good," he says.

I give an easy shrug. "Sure, sure. I guess I don't require one. After all, you did say I was hot. Nothing to be sorry for there. You're absolutely right." Then I flash him a grin. A damn good one, and I know how to give them. Though, as a rule, I don't flirt with straight men. Waste of time, right? But why did Mark say I was hot? Where did that come from?

But the loose-lipped texter is hard to read. He's shooting me an *I-can't-be-bothered* look. Damn. Mark Banks must kill it at poker. He has some impressive bluffing skills. "That was *just* the whiskey talking," he says evenly.

I scoff-laugh. "Right. Of course. Whiskey often goes on and on about levels of hotness."

"Like I said, you can't trust the words of a single-malt scotch," he says.

Hmm.

So that's how he's spinning this. Well, two can play that game. "You may be right. It is hard to trust the liquor, so I better refresh my memory to make sure I got it all correct." I stop, grab my phone from my pocket, and whip it out, sliding a thumb across the screen.

Mark cuts in quickly. "There's no need for that."

Ha. Now I've rattled him. I clear my throat, and read aloud my new favorite text message ever. *"Also, what is the deal with your friend with the hair?"*

I glance up from the phone, tilt my head. "You noticed my hair. So sweet," I say, giving a shake of the locks.

"It's impossible not to. It enters the room before you do."

"Allow me to continue. *Why is it so floopy . . . wait . . . floppy . . . nope . . . it's floofy. His hair is floofy.*" I look up. "Is floofy even a word?"

He answers my question head-on. "Yes. It's a combo of poofy and fluffy."

Well, he's a worthier adversary than I expected. All the more reason to keep going. "My hair is not poofy, Banks. It's shaggy. But we're not even at the best part of your epic rant." I inhale deeply, savoring what's to come. The piece de resistance.

He knocks back his orange juice, and kudos to the man. He's taking the text message reenactment like, well, like a champ.

I brandish my phone, savoring every single second. *"Anyway, whose hair looks like a shampoo commercial? Who takes off his shirt at a dinner party? Who has a body that annoyingly perfect? He's not even real. He's like a fucking comic book hero in those graphic novels I used to read. Here he comes . . . FLIP'S SUPERHOT . . . WINGMAN! Asher, with his stupid hair and stupid lips and ridiculous body. Who even looks that good in real life, Hannah? No one. Just no one."*

There's more, but really, I need to bask a little longer in the glow of compliments. I tap my lip. "You're right, Banks. I do not at all require an apology for this ode to me. In fact, I ought to give you a thanks," I say, bringing a hand to my heart. "This made my week."

"You're welcome," he snarls.

I should let him off the hook now, and circulate a bit here at the party.

Yet I can't just drop it. Everything I thought I knew about Mark Banks is suddenly in question. Is he the fun-phobic banker I thought I knew? Who is this guy who invents words to describe my hair, and has deep thoughts about my abs?

I'm pretty sure straight guys don't refer to other dudes as superhot.

Which makes me wonder if he's not as straight as I thought.

Maybe I can get him to clarify. I tap my phone one more time. "I do have one last question about this description—*superhot wingman*. That must mean there are levels of hotness. So, Banks. Tell me. Where does the scale start?"

This is when he'll back down. Talk in circles. Run away. I'd be willing to bet my sexy new Nikon on it.

Mark takes a breath, meets my gaze head-on. "Yeah, St. James. There are definitely hotness scales for, well, lots of things. Starts at basic hot. And, to be honest, *lots of things* are basic hot. Like, for instance, when someone can do square roots in his or her head, that's *basic hot*."

I blink. What the hell? He's talking math now?

Mark continues, counting off on his fingers. "Superhot comes next. That's, like, knowing all the openings in chess, and their variations." He lets out a low hum that kind of rumbles past his lips, like he thinks that's the height of seduction.

I scratch my jaw, trying to figure out where he's going with this.

"Then you have extra hot," he continues, all smooth talker like he's the slick trader in a movie featuring a bunch of sharks on Wall Street. Or wait, is it wolves? "And that's understanding probabilities. Example—in any group of twenty-three people, there's a fifty percent chance that two of them have the same birthday." He taps his temple.

My brow knits. I part my lips, but words are hard to find. Because I think he just danced a whole math-word circle around me. I tap my chest. "Did you just compare me to a mathematician?"

He pushes his glasses higher up on his nose. "Stay with me, St. James. I said *superhot* was the person who could play chess. *Extra hot* is higher math. That's the highest level of hotness."

"I'm not even at the top of your hot scale?"

"It's a sliding scale," he says, lifting his juice and finishing it. "Anyway, like I said, lots of things are hot. A double play to get out of a bases-loaded jam, buying Apple stock in 1991, a chocolate molten lava cake with vanilla ice cream. Doing math for fun. I could go on. My remarks mean nothing, because many, many things are hot, and you just shouldn't trust whiskey."

Holy fuck.

Mark Banks, mild-mannered banker, just twisted my tongue with his hotness sliding scale of mental math. Even if he backpedaled his way out of that jam. Even if he did it with a whole lot of smoke and mirrors.

He did it.

And that's just *hot, hot, hot.*

The highest level on the Asher St. James scale.

But he's still the guy who doesn't like my bud.

And he still dresses like my dad.

So I'm not about to bend, even if he won't admit he wants to run his fingers through my so-not-floofy hair.

At least, I thought he did.

But now, I'm not so positive after all.

Dammit.

So that fishing expedition gave me nothing.

And yet, I toss out the bait one more time, swiping up on the thread. "But there is one thing that I keep tripping on." I clear my throat, adopt his sexy, rumbly voice. *"Asher, with his stupid hair and stupid lips and ridiculous body. Who even looks that good in real life, Hannah? No one. Just no one."*

I lift my gaze from the screen. Mark simply stares at me with those dark blue inscrutable eyes. "Yes, Asher?"

If there's something wrong with my mouth—and no one has ever complained about it before—I have to know. "How are my lips stupid?"

3

DOUBLE SCREWED

MARK

ecause they make me think about things I don't have room for in my life. Like this inconvenient attraction to my sister's fiancé's best friend, who relishes goading me.

But I can goad back. I didn't get my promotion to VP by having zero game.

I know how to negotiate, and I've got a plan to shut this conversation down once and for all, then stuff this lust in a suitcase and tuck it away in an attic.

And never unzip it again.

"Let's make a deal, St. James," I offer.

"Okay," he says, tentatively.

"How about we forget I ever said that, and in exchange, I'll help you make sure you didn't ruin Hannah's night?"

He jerks his gaze away from me, gesturing to the guests milling about behind us. "I'm celebrating their engagement with a great party. On twenty-four hours' notice, no less. How would I have ruined her night? She loves sushi. Also, I might add, when I learned she was pregnant, I threw a party. You threw a fit."

Time to put him in his place *and* help Hannah.

I cast my gaze toward the server passing by, carrying a tray full of yellowtail rolls on the gleaming silver plate. "But sushi," I whisper. "Especially species of fish high in mercury . . . is on the verboten list for pregnant women."

"Wait." Asher's jaw comes unhinged, and for the first time ever, the cocky cavalier playboy is off his game. "Did I . . . really just throw an engagement party where the bride can't eat any of the food?"

"Seems you did," I say. "And I figured you knew and would have ordered some cooked fish or edamame. Or I would have said something sooner."

"Fuck, fuck, fuck," Asher says, then jumps off the stool, waves over the manager, and quickly gives a request. "Big favor, Hiroki, but we've got to pivot and serve something cooked right away. Some of my guests are staying away from raw fish."

"Of course. We'll get some avocado rolls, shrimp tempura, and edamame out right away," the man replies, then heads off to the kitchen, and just like that, Asher St. James saves the day.

No wonder he irritates me.

Too smooth.

Too handsome.

Too . . . just everything.

"How did you know that?" he asks when he returns, sounding begrudgingly impressed. "Do you moonlight as a midwife?"

I laugh, in spite of myself. "No. I have a kid, as you may recall. We discussed her at game night, when I said she prefers Chutes and Ladders to Scrabble. And I made sure her mom didn't eat raw fish or drink too much coffee when she was pregnant."

"How is Rosie? She was a total delight the time I met her with Hannah at the coffee shop," he says, remembering her name as easily as he remembered the manager's.

"Hi Marky Mark!"

I turn to find a college friend of Hannah's sidling up to me. "Hey Yasmin!" Finally, someone I actually know at this party. I've never been so happy to see anyone in my life. Now we can stop talking about Asher's mouth, for fuck's sake. "How's the art market?"

"Bangin.' I'd ask you about your job, but I wouldn't understand the answer. So, tell me about your daughter instead. How's your little cutie-pie? What's she up to?"

My chest squeezes with happiness, as it usually does when I talk about my favorite person in the universe. "Learning to read, doing both karate and T-ball. Her other skills include keeping me on my toes, and trying to wiggle out of brushing her teeth. She's just finishing kindergarten."

"T-Ball! That is totally adorable," Yasmin says in her cheery voice. "And how's Bridget? I haven't seen her in ages."

My shoulders tense. This is the seriously un-fun part. When I tell people I'm not with Rosie's mom anymore. "We're recently divorced," I say plainly, keeping emotion out of my voice.

Which is somewhat easy to do. I'm not heartbroken about my split. For many reasons.

What I am is bitter. But nobody wants to hear that from a twenty-seven-year-old divorced man.

A hand flies to Yasmin's mouth. "Oh, I'm so sorry. I had no idea."

"It's fine," I insist. "Don't worry about it." I give her a huge smile to show I don't care at all. And I won't. Eventually. That's what people tell me, anyway.

Even if signing my divorce papers made me feel like a giant fucking failure.

And even if my baby girl cried like she'd never stop the first night my ex stayed at her new man's apartment.

"Now your daughter is getting a cousin!" Yasmin gushes, shifting gears maybe for both our sakes'. "That is so exciting."

"Totally exciting," I repeat, and I can practically feel Asher's smirk even though I'm not looking at him.

"Well," Yasmin says brightly, "I think I'll go and congratulate her again." She gives me a peck on the cheek and then beelines for Hannah.

I look into my empty juice glass and wish scotch were in there.

"Here," Asher says, thrusting a bottle of beer in my direction. "I'm sensing you need this."

"So I can entertain you some more?"

"No," he says quietly. "Dude, I had no idea your divorce was official. How long ago did that happen?"

"Last month," I mutter. "Although we've been separated for a year."

He frowns. "So . . . you got divorced the same month that Hannah announced her pregnancy and right before she got engaged?"

"Yup."

He toys with the label on his beer. "You know, your freak-out is starting to make a little more sense to me. No wonder you let whiskey drive the bus last night."

I bark out a laugh without meaning to. He's right, though. My sister is having a shotgun wedding, just like I did six and a half years ago after getting my college girlfriend pregnant. And look how that turned out.

Asher St. James isn't getting that story, though. No thanks. Or any stories. Earlier, I could hear him fishing for clues about my sexuality. I'm bisexual. I'm not conflicted about it. My family knows.

But my drunken text rant was over-the-top embarrassing. There's no way I want Asher to think that I was hitting on him. Like his ego needs any more stroking.

More guests come through the door, and he hurries off to greet them. I watch him go. Well, fine, I admire his ass in those trendy, close-fitting pants. Still, Asher is everything I'm not. He's the life of the party. He was a professional soccer player; now he's a top photographer of athletes and models. He's sporty and artsy and smooth.

So damn smooth. Like his clean-shaven face that I bet would feel so good . . .

"Mark!"

I drag my eyes off Asher's hiney and find my sister and Flip marching toward me. "Yes, Hannah. How's your party? I heard they're bringing out some vegetarian rolls, by the way." I give her a wink.

"That's amazing. Who could eat, though? I'm just so excited to see everyone!" She's beaming and fanning her face with excitement. That giant rock on her finger hardly looks real. She sent me about fifty pictures of it yesterday, and I assumed the camera angle was exaggerating things.

But, nope. Rosie's marbles are smaller than that thing.

She puts her hands on my chest, and the sparkle almost blinds me. "Mark, one of the reasons I was so happy for Asher to plan this party tonight is . . ." She stops, her smile growing bigger, like it's about to unleash a secret she's been holding in all evening. "Ever since we were kids, I always knew I would want to do *this*."

Ah, I sense a moment coming.

Hannah isn't dramatic, per se. But she does like to do things up. Why go hiking when you can go bungee jumping? Why go to a wine tasting when you can do mustard canning? Proof of her get-out-and-go-for-it approach is that she met Flip at a candle-making class in Brooklyn that she signed up for at the last minute, and that's why *you just need to try new things, since life is full of moments, and you need to be ready to receive them*. Her words.

I'm not a moments guy. But I love my sister, and I owe her, so I go along with it. "And what is *this* exactly, Hannah Banana?"

Her eyes twinkle brighter than her diamond. "I've always imagined when I got married . . . that you'd be my best man." She practically squeals the request.

And whoa.

That's definitely a moment.

I didn't think I'd be part of her wedding party, being a guy and all. I figured Yasmin would be her maid of honor. Bet she is, and I'll be standing with Hannah's college bestie.

"How many attendants are you having, exactly?"

"Just you."

That's all she says. But the way she says *just you* conveys the meaning. This matters to my sister. We're twelve months apart in age. We're good friends and always have been. We rely on each other.

I clear my throat, square my shoulders, and treat the request with the gravitas it deserves. "Yes, of course. I'd be honored."

I pull her in for a hug, trying to wrap my head around how I went from the worst brother to the best man in twenty-four hours, but hey, *it's one of life's moments.* As she squeezes me, Asher sails behind her, moving next to Flip. My skin prickles. He's everywhere, and I can't get away from him.

When Hannah and I break the embrace, she locks eyes with Flip, then gives the quickest of nods. Like she's giving him permission.

They've definitely got something planned.

Flip pivots, claps a hand on his wingman's shoulder. "Asher, we've been best buds since our first year at Lyceum du Lucerne when we had the brilliant idea to try out for the ski team and I broke my leg instead of making the cut. But you carried my tray in the caf for eight weeks. You're my guy. You've been there for me through everything. It'd be an honor if you'd be *my* best man."

I groan inside. No fucking way.

I bet it's not easy to surprise Asher St. James, but judging from the size of his hazel eyes—wide AF—Flip just did it.

And for the first time all night, I've got a sinking sense that Asher and I are feeling the same damn thing.

I don't want to be "the best men" with that guy.

But it'll be fine. It'll all be fine. What's the big deal anyway? Asher was always going to be at the wedding. Who cares that we're the best men? It's not like we have to pick balloons and boutonnieres together.

Probably all we'll have to do is stand opposite each other at the wedding. And right now, since Yasmin waves a hand high above her head. "This calls for a pic!"

She ushers the four of us together, and thank fuck she has the good sense to put the bride and groom in the center as she snaps a few shots of the wedding party.

When Yasmin lowers her phone, Hannah grabs my arm, and thrusts me next to Asher.

"Let's get a pic of the best men, too," my sister says.

Where is an escape hatch when you need one?

The answer is—nowhere close enough, especially since Asher throws an arm around my shoulders, and that is not fair.

Arms on shoulders are not supposed to send my mind spinning with thoughts.

My jaw clenches.

"Say cheese, Mark. You're not getting a root canal. You're going to a wedding," Yasmin instructs.

"And I promise I don't bite," Asher says, in a volume just for me.

Biting.

That's not helping.

I manage a sliver of a smile.

I probably look like I'm posing for my office headshot. Sidenote: I hate my office headshot. I also hate the existence of office headshots.

Ten endless seconds later, Yasmin is done. "I'll send them to you, Hannah, and you can send them to the guys."

There's no need for that, but I keep my mouth shut on that front. Asher lets go, then says, "It wasn't *too* painful," then he heads off, probably to charm more guests.

And I suppose it wasn't that bad.

And being the best men together won't be either.

How long does wedding stuff take? Two days? Then I'll be free of the object of all this weird, misplaced lust.

I move away from the center of the party, when Hannah grabs my arm, Flip beside her. "Just one more thing," she says.

I turn around. "Sure."

"The wedding is going to be a small one, and I'm already asking our friends to drop everything to come to it next month. So . . . remember that favor I said I needed?" she asks, rocking back on her heels.

Flip puts a protective hand on her waist. And I try not to hold it against him.

"Of course, Hannah," I say. "What can I do for you?"

"It's about the wedding. We're going to be pulling this off at warp speed, right in the middle of your MTA next month."

"Right, I do appreciate that." MTA, or *mandatory time off*, is a requirement for all securities traders who run more than a billion dollars of risk for the bank. For two weeks, you're not allowed to step foot in the building, so your books can be marked to market by someone else.

It's meant to root out fraud. But it's really just the best scam ever. Two weeks of paid freedom. If I ever meet the genius who devised MTA, I'm probably going to kiss him, because MTA is extra hot.

"We're going to do a glam little destination wedding in Miami," she says. "It was Asher's idea, actually."

Of course it was his idea.

"But some of us don't have Wall Street jobs with MTA." She rolls her eyes playfully. "And I want to use my vacation days for my honeymoon. So I was hoping you would fly down there a few days early and check out all our vendors. The caterer, the DJ. That kind of thing."

"Sure?" I rub the back of my neck, trying to picture how this would all work, since I'm not, well, a wedding planner. "I'm not that familiar with Miami, though."

"You won't have to be," Flip says. "Asher will be there to help you."

Wait. Did he just say what I think he said? "Asher and me?" I choke out, hoping I got it wrong.

But Flip nods. "Yup."

"*Just* Asher and me?" I ask, in case Flip arranged for a wedding planner to join us in Florida. Preferably a little old lady who carries a small white dog everywhere she goes—they'd be the perfect cock-blocking pair.

"Asher doesn't have a shoot that week, so it's no problem for him to fly down and help out," Flip continues. "He's the one who found us this sweet venue. A client of his owns a mansion on the beach. You two can be around to tell the equipment rental people where to set up. The tent. Chairs. Stuff like that."

LAUREN BLAKELY & SARINA BOWEN

"O-kay," I say slowly. My mind whirls while I try to think of a good reason I can't do this, because I can't be alone with a guy I'm stupidly attracted to. "If I don't have Rosie that week. Let me do some checking."

Hannah holds up her phone. "I already texted Bridget to invite her to the wedding. Maybe she'll bring Rosie down with her, so you can go early and help me."

"Who knows if Bridget is free, though? I bet she's busy. Probably has a wine show."

God, I hope she has a wine show. A wine anything.

But who am I kidding? My ex loves Hannah. She loves Florida, and used to complain in the early days when we couldn't afford vacations.

She'll take to this trip like a calico to catnip. I'm so screwed.

When I open the door to my apartment on West Sixteenth Street, my phone pings. I click on the notification.

It's the dreaded group chat.

And Hannah has dropped in pics.

Nope. I'm not going to look.

I stick to that mantra the whole time I get ready for bed. I don't so much as glance at those photos as I give Blackbeard a couple scratches on the chin, or while my one-eyed rescue cat watches me brush my teeth from his favorite staring spot on the bathroom counter. *Weirdo.*

I let the tap run lightly for a few seconds so the orange beast can drink straight from it, then I turn it off. And I still don't look.

My willpower holds out until I flop onto my mattress, just before I take off my glasses. I leave them on, though, for one moment too long.

That's all it takes to peek at the last photo.

And, damn. That easy smile. That casual pose. That fucking arm around me.

Yup. He's annoyingly perfect, and I'm double screwed.

22

4

THE DA VINCI OF UNDERWEAR

MONDAY, A MONTH LATER

ASHER

I gaze at my forty-two-inch monitor, putting the finishing touches on a photo campaign I shot for UnderKlad.

Translation: I'm staring at photos I've taken of the ripped bodies of professional athletes who model underwear on the side.

I love my job. So much.

"Hey Lucy," I call. "Did we hear anything from FLI today?"

"Negative," she yells back from her desk across the studio.

Okay. That's a setback. I'd really been hoping to land a sweet gig with the most influential sports organization in the whole entire world. They told me I'd hear back from them ten days ago.

For the first few days, I'd thought maybe the contract got lost in the mail. Now I think they gave it to someone else.

I'll be pissed off if they did. The whole campaign was my idea.

But I'm not going to let it kill my vibe today. Whistling along with the Citizen Cope track playing on my speakers, I adjust the color balance of the final shot. Then I deepen the shadows, so that the hockey player's eight-pack comes into sharper focus. And, wow, it's perfect now. You can almost taste the tiny beads of sweat on his torso.

Yummy.

"I will be known as the fucking Da Vinci of underwear," I say to myself as I tap save on the project file.

"You are already," my assistant says from her desk at the other end of my studio space. "But if you don't leave now, you will also be known as the Da Vinci of showing up late. *Again.*"

I whirl around in my chair. "Late? For what?"

Lucy blinks at me from behind her round glasses. "Don't tell me you've forgotten to check the schedule again."

"But I thought I was free today before I take off tomorrow for the wedding," I whine. "I swear the calendar said so."

She winces. "Check again."

"Lucy! What did you do?" She probably snuck something onto my calendar. *Hell.* All I want to do is finish these edits, wipe my own drool off the monitor, and then reward myself with a long lunch of mussels and frites. "Just tell me—what am I almost late for?"

"Your fitting at Angel Sanjay."

Shit. I open up my calendar and there it is—an appointment at the designer's showroom, beginning in forty minutes. "This fitting—it's for the wedding, right?"

"Of course," she says. "You asked me to book you and a Mark Banks in for, quote, Miami-style beachy wedding attire."

"Sure, sure," I babble. The best men need to match their suits. And if I'd let Hannah's brother pick the clothes, we'd probably end up in some 1955 seersucker disaster.

So this appointment was my idea. But I know it wasn't on my calendar three hours ago.

Oh, boy. Lucy and I are quite a pair. I'm told that I function as about three quarters of a real adult. Lucy also seems to operate at seventy-five percent. But between us, we're good for a person and a half. So I figure I'm still ahead.

Plus, even though she dresses head to toe in navy blue Talbots, and her aura doesn't exactly scream fashionable photographer's assistant, real talent, though, is telling it like it is to her boss and I need that.

My business has taken off these last couple of years, and before I hired Lucy, I struggled to keep my own calendar.

That led to some regrettable screwups. Just ask my ex-boyfriend. Garrett hated the way I was often late for our dates and all the times I was double-booked, or jet-lagged. It had been a huge transition from the life of a professional athlete in Europe to running my own small business here in New York.

But I wanted Garrett to be happy with me. In a great leap of faith, I'd decided to ask him to move in with me.

I made reservations at the Kimoto rooftop lounge in Brooklyn, left early. But then a truck jackknifed on the Williamsburg Bridge, leaving me stranded for forty-five minutes in an Uber.

When I finally arrived, Garrett was waiting at the corner table in front of the sweeping city views, a designer cocktail in hand. I gave him a big, hopeful smile, fingering the copied key to my apartment that I had for him in my pocket.

But the moment he spotted me, his expression shuttered. The moment I sat down, he said, "Asher, I can't do this anymore."

"There was this truck! It will probably be on the news tonight. Seriously—"

He'd shaken his head. "It's not about tonight. I met someone else."

That was not what I'd expected. "What? Who?"

When I'd pressed him for details, the breakup turned even worse. He'd met a lawyer, who worked as in-house counsel, and took every weekend off in East Hampton.

"That's what you want? A lawyer?"

"What I want is someone who's not a hot mess," he'd said bitterly.

That was the low point. Even though I knew he was gone for good, I needed a change. So, the very next week I hired Lucy. I couldn't afford to be known as a hot mess. It had already ruined my chances with Garrett. I wouldn't let it ruin my business.

Since then, my bookings are up. Screwups are down. But I'm still lonely. Garrett's Instagram is full of pics of him paddle boarding in the Hamptons with his lawyer.

I know I shouldn't look. That's just dumb.

"Asher!"

My head snaps up, and Lucy is standing next to me. "Google says it's a forty-three-minute trip via the F-train. Or forty-eight minutes if you take the ferry. I suppose you could chance it in a cab."

"No cabs," I bark. "Why am I always running late? Wait. Don't answer that!"

I shove my keys and my wallet into my pockets. But where is my phone? "When will I see you? We still have to go over the Commando upload. That's happening next week."

"Go already." She gestures toward the door. "Call me from Miami. I'll upload the Commandos while we're on the line together. Until then, go get sunburned and enjoy the wedding. Take some Instagram photos. Find a pool boy to hook up with."

"While that sounds fun, this isn't really a vacation."

"You'll find a way to make it fun," she insists. "Oh! And don't forget that *An Arranged Marriage* premiers on Webflix tomorrow night. It's on the calendar that you never check. So don't come crying to me if you forget to tune in."

"There's got to be a TV in that mansion that can stream from my laptop," I say, ransacking my desk for my phone.

"Asher, your phone is in your shirt pocket," Lucy says. "I can see it from here."

"Oh, fuck. Thank you. Bye!" I give her a wave as I trot past her desk.

"Call me about the Commandos!" is the last thing she says before I run to the stairwell. Even if the trains are on time, it'll take at least fifty minutes to make it to Manhattan and to the designer's showroom on West Thirteenth.

I've got forty.

Shit.

5

CAPTAIN FILTHY MIND

MARK

*S*ome parents are chill when their kids play sports. I am not one of those people. Especially when my little cupcake hits a double in T-ball.

"Go! Go! Go!" I shout as Rosie runs her butt off to second, while pigtailed Alba rounds third base, determination on her little face as she races home. When she reaches it, my daughter's best friend jumps up on the rubber and her teammates join her, shouting with glee. Rosie cheers from second base, a bundle of energy.

"Yes! Go Firecrackers!" I thrust both arms in the air, shouting the loudest.

"A little excited, Mark?" The question comes from Alba's mom, Valencia, standing next to me at the edge of the field in Chelsea Park.

"I can't ever sit during softball games," I say.

Her long, brown hair swishes against her olive skin. Valencia pats my arm affectionately. "And I love that about you. Though, you were just a touch louder last week when Rosie hit a homer."

She has me there. I shrug sheepishly. "What can I say? I've got a fanboy in me and I'm not afraid to show it. I'm going to let you in on a little secret, V," I tell her. "I had zero game as a kid. Team sports were not my friend."

Valencia feigns shock, her big brown eyes going wide. "You? Nooo. You don't say."

"Is it that obvious?" I ask the woman who's become a good friend over the last few years. She and her wife live in our building over on Sixteenth Street, and since our kids are friends, we became buds. A few months ago, we signed the girls up for the Firecrackers together.

"Yes, Mark. I can still recall your shudder when I suggested you join our co-ed frisbee league."

I shudder involuntarily. Again.

She laughs. She often does at my expense, which is fine by me. I kinda feel like I can relax with her and her wife—they know how shitty the last year has been for me, and it's nice to let down my guard a little with someone. All day at work, I have to keep my game face on. I don't bring my personal life into the office—not at the water cooler of Wall Street.

"Fine, fine. I'm man enough to admit I'm a better spectator than participant." I raise a finger in my own defense. "But I'm excellent at the treadmill, the StairMaster, and running solo in the park."

"And I'm woman enough to know I will never invite you onto my frisbee team, since I want to win," Valencia says.

A few minutes later, the game ends on a Firecrackers win, and Rosie runs over to me, a tiny brunette ball of energy. She lands in front of me, dirt kicking up as her pink cleats hit the edge of the softball field. "Did you see my double, Daddy?"

"Did you hear my shout, Rosie?"

With a serious stare, she says, "Everyone heard it, but I like to make sure."

"That's my girl. Checking and double checking. Yes I saw it, and all I have to say is watch out, New York Comets. You're going to be the new slugger for the city's best Major League Baseball team," I say.

She high fives me. "Yes! But I'd actually rather play on a girls' team than a boys' baseball team," she says, matter-of-factly. "Or maybe I'll play hockey someday too. We're going to see the Bombshells next fall. Mommy is taking me."

"Ooh, I love them," Valencia chimes in.

"You and your wife have a crush on the goalie," I say to her as the kiddos return to the field to pick up their bats and gloves.

"We have good taste in our crushes." Valencia gathers her purse as I snag Rosie's backpack from the bleachers behind me. "Gimme. I'll take that for you."

"You don't have to do that. I can bring it along with me."

She shakes her head, emphatic as she grabs Rosie's bag. "You're not taking a *Peppa Pig* backpack into Angel Sanjay's showroom. I will not allow it."

I let her have it. "Thanks again for taking Rosie to dinner with you so I can go to a . . . *best man fitting*," I say, my tone a little heavy.

"On a scale of one to tax audit, that sounds like you're looking forward to it?" Valencia asks with the lift of a well-groomed eyebrow.

"If you think trying on clothes is fun," I say, groaning in over-the-top misery. "I don't. Especially because . . ."

Because of Asher St. James. It's impossible to explain in a rational way how difficult it is for me to keep my cool around him.

Tomorrow begins five days with him, including the travel day. The dread is strong in me now.

She shoots me a concerned look. "Are you okay, Mark? You look like you swallowed a grapefruit. Do you hate trying on clothes that much?"

The tension in my chest cranks tighter. "The other best man and I are polar opposites. But even that's generous. It's more like we're poles of poles of polar opposites. I'm not sure how I'm going to survive the next week."

Or the pent-up lust that rears its head when I'm around the former soccer star. But I keep that tidbit all to myself.

She hums, like she's deep in thought. "Is he hot?"

"Yes," I answer immediately. "But also smug."

She laughs. "Then when you return from Miami, maybe you'll need to do something fun. A little self-care in the form of dating again. You should finally let me set you up with my friend Gwen from my Zumba class. And if you're not into her, then the creative director at my agency is smoking hot, too. Josh has got the whole cute nerd vibe working," she says, waving a hand in front of my face, gesturing to my glasses. "It's a smorgasbord out there for you, Mark."

"Possibly," I mutter. "I'll let you know when I'm ready."

But will I ever be? This past year, I've been concentrating on Rosie. She took the divorce hard. I've just wanted to be there for her, not running around dating strangers. I don't have the time. Bridget and I had agreed to parent fifty-fifty. But she has a job with her new wine merchant beau that requires travel.

So guess who does at least two thirds of the parenting? This guy.

That makes dating tough. But even if it didn't, the prospect of dinner and drinks with someone new sounds equal parts exciting and horrifying. The last time I dated, I lived in a dorm.

Although I'm definitely eager to get back in the sex saddle.

It's been a while.

A long, long while of just me and my hand.

If dirty thoughts were an origin story for a superhero, I'd be Captain Filthy Mind. But there's a big difference between entertaining my long list of sex wishes alone at night and going out and getting them.

What would Asher do if he knew I had a spreadsheet buried on my laptop, with nearly a hundred lines dedicated to various fantasies?

He'd laugh his ass off, that's what.

Good thing that sucker is password protected.

"When you're ready, I'll be your matchmaker," Valencia says as Rosie rushes over, Alba by her side, the bats, balls and gloves all neatly sorted.

"We cleaned up, and now I'm ready for a burrito with my bestie," Rosie announces.

"And fro-yo. Can we go to that new shop?" Alba asks.

"Yes! We have to try the pineapple-mango-coconut cake flavor."

"With Gummi Bears and Sno-Caps on top," Alba adds, intensely serious, and I have a feeling they've been planning their dessert all day. Goals.

Then, before I can remind her, Rosie remembers her manners and turns to Alba's mom. "Thank you for taking me with you to dinner."

"And thank you for taking care of Blackbeard while I'm gone, too," I tell Valencia.

Rosie lifts a finger, all six-year-old bossy, as she sometimes is. "He gets two-thirds of a cup of cat food a day. That's sixty-six percent of a cup. Well, almost sixty-seven."

With an eyebrow arch, Valencia stares daggers at me. "This is your fault, Mark. All this mathing."

I hold up my hands in surrender. "I happily take the blame."

I say goodbye to my friend, then my kid and hers, and hoof it several blocks south to the designer's showroom.

Fashion is not my thing. Shopping for my own suits is a bit like changing cat litter. A necessary chore.

Just like this outing with Asher.

That's what this outing is—just another task. This mental trick works just fine until I reach Thirteenth Street, where my gaze lands on a tall, toned, ridiculously good-looking guy jogging down the block.

Effortlessly.

Looking really fucking good, and yeah, it's a good thing Rosie isn't here since I'm thinking about item 2B on my spreadsheet.

Focus, Mark.

Asher stops in front of me, looks at his wrist. "Damn, I impress myself. Forty minutes. Made it exactly on time," he says, sounding insanely pleased.

I lift a brow. "You're congratulating yourself for making it on time? Do you pat yourself on the back when you remember to brush your teeth, too?"

He shoots me a mega-watt smile, all gleaming teeth, and perfect lips. "Maybe I do, Banks. Maybe I do."

"To each his own," I say, as Asher eyes me up and down.

"I had no idea you owned anything other than your Wall Street uniforms," he remarks, his gaze traveling over my navy-blue polo shirt and jeans.

"Well, it's laundry day. Dieter, my valet, is brushing and steaming my wardrobe this afternoon. Straightening the pinstripes. You know."

A wrinkle appears in the center of Asher's forehead. "You're kidding, right? Nobody is really named Dieter."

"The second you think that, you run into someone named Dieter." I take a beat. "That's a mathematical probability."

Asher looks doubtful. "Sounds more like coincidence. Admit it. They're one and the same," he says, dragging a hand through his hair. I try not to follow the path of his fingers, but dammit, my gaze strays for a fraction of a second.

Probability of me making it through the next hour without thinking about 2C on my fantasy spreadsheet? Captain Filthy Mind says five percent.

So I return to his first question, answering it finally. "And yes, I own seven polos, five T-shirts, and three pairs of jeans. I don't wear suits to my daughter's softball games."

That brings a smile back to his face. "I didn't know your kid liked sports."

"Of course you didn't. You don't know me." And that came out snappish.

Asher rolls his eyes, like *can you believe this guy*. "I'm well aware of that."

Why am I such a dick around him? Just because I can't handle this inconvenient attraction? *Man up, Banks.*

I redirect my attitude. "Rosie loves softball. And she wants to try hockey too," I say, aiming to inject more goodwill in my tone, and also to talk about anything besides clothes, so I don't mention how good he looks in that tight not-a-T-shirt, not-a-polo, I-have-no-idea-what-it's-called, but it's short sleeve and just the right amount of snug to show off his pecs, and his biceps . . .

And that's not helping.

We head inside, and I hope this fitting ends mercifully fast.

6

A COUPLE OF HIGH-NET-WORTH FLAMINGOES

ASHER

*A*ngel Sanjay's showroom is on the first floor of an old meatpacking house. The place is newly done up in riotous colors from the old wooden floors to the industrial rafters. A vintage neon sign advertises double-breasted suits, alongside a mannequin wearing a navy blazer over a tie-dyed tuxedo shirt. There's even a Triumph motorcycle parked beside a captain's chair.

Beside me, Mark whistles softly. "Now, I don't think we're in Target anymore, Toto."

Chuckling, I take in the staid leather furniture and the brightly colored men's shirts. "Not even in the same country. This place is basically the love child of Ralph Lauren and a Parisian bordello. Isn't it great?"

Mark's face says that he does not, in fact, think this mash-up is great. But he doesn't get a chance to say so, because the designer himself strides toward us, his smile wide, his dark curly hair shining in the retail lighting.

"Asher! It's great to see you again." He leans in and kisses my cheek. "So sorry that we couldn't get you in here last week. I was in Milan. Then seeing family in New Delhi. Returned last night."

"And back to work the second you landed," I say. I shot an ad campaign for him last year. He was fun on the set and easy to work with. "Thanks for fitting us in. This is Mark, the brother of the bride. When I realized that Mark and I needed matching menswear for the wedding, you were my first and only call."

"Radical!" His dark eyes dance as he shakes Mark's hand. "My guy upstairs will fit you with whatever you need. But let's give him some direction. This event is in Miami, right?"

"Right," Mark says. "It's a beach wedding, but fairly traditional. The bride is wearing white."

"So we'll need some color," I add.

"But not too much color," Mark says quickly.

Angel just grins. "Okay, fabric first. Linen, perhaps? What is the groom wearing?"

"Hold on," Mark says. "I have it in my spreadsheet." He starts tapping the screen of his phone.

"Spreadsheet?" I laugh. "You're joking."

Mark gives me a withering look. "Spreadsheets are no joke, St. James. Here. Look."

Sure enough, there's a photo of a straw-colored wedding suit pasted into one cell, a white shirt in the next, and a white bowtie in the third. A wedding dress claims the fourth.

"That's lovely," Angel says. "Very tasteful and nearly monochrome. I like it. But we're going to need some contrast on you two."

"Right," I agree, glancing around the busy room. My eye lands on a suit near the window. And maybe I'm an asshole, but I can't resist. "Something like this," I say, striding toward the mannequin in a snappy salmon-colored linen suit and matching bowtie. "Here's some contrast."

"No," Mark says, looking like his head is about to explode. "Not on your life. It's our job to be invisible."

I gasp. "Not possible, Banks. This face is never invisible."

He actually rolls his eyes. "Stop it. I know this is just a negotiating strategy. You start with something outrageous so that when you suggest something more reasonable, I'll just agree to it immediately. Oldest trick in the book."

Angel claps one of his long, slim hands over his mouth and tries not to laugh.

He fails.

Honestly, I'm a terrible negotiator, and that tactic would never occur to me. But the truth is that I wouldn't actually upstage Flip and Hannah by dressing us like a pair of high-net-worth flamingoes.

"This may come as a shock to you, Asher," Angel puts in. "But I don't stock unlimited inventory of the salmon suit."

"Oh. Shame," I say, taking the out that he's offering me. "Maybe something in a steely blue or dove gray, then?"

"Let's see what we can find," Angel says.

Mark is flustered.

I'm a bad man. Because I'm enjoying his discomfort immensely.

We're upstairs in the private fitting area. It's one room, flooded with natural light and outfitted with the grandest three-way mirror I've ever seen. A curtain hangs in the corner, where you can go to change, if you're feeling modest.

But I'm not feeling modest. Rarely am. And there's nobody here but me, Mark, and a young fitter with sharp, bird-like features. He's busy bringing us various suits, shirts, and ties to try on.

So I don't bother with the curtain in the corner. I simply strip right here in the center of the room whenever bird man hands me a new shirt or pair of pants.

Poor Mark has claimed the changing area for his own. And he keeps peering around the edge of it, checking to see if I'm decent.

Or—and maybe this is crazy talk—he's checking out my ass. Or my abs.

That can't be it. But wouldn't it be fun if it were true? I don't waste my time crushing on straight men. But is he totally straight? He did send that fantastic text about me. And the idea of getting Mister Spreadsheets all hot and bothered is pretty irresistible.

"How do we feel about lettuce?" the fitter asks, carrying in a suit in a spring green color.

"It's great," I say at the same moment as Mark says, "No, thank you."

I turn around, wearing nothing but a pair of trousers in dove gray. "What's wrong with lettuce?" I demand of Mark.

"I like it in a salad," he grumbles, peeking out from behind the curtain, his gaze stopping on my chest for a second before he looks away. "That's where it belongs."

The fitter turns on his heel and departs with the green suit.

"Look," I say, crossing my arms and flexing my pecs. Mark's eyes skid predictably around the room. And I've got to know if *something* is going to be a problem for him. I look the man straight in the eyes. "Is it too gay for you? Is that the issue?"

"No, that is *not* the problem. Not at all," he thunders, stepping out from behind the curtain, holding up a stop sign hand. "Trust me. You don't get to make this into a character assassination just because I don't want to look like a freshly picked artichoke at my sister's wedding. I don't want Hannah to regret anything. Ever. I don't want her looking at the photos five years from now and thinking *I made the wrong choice.*"

Either this guy really loves his sister, or he really can't stand bright colors. Or me. "Look, I love Hannah too. And your sister gave me carte blanche to choose. She said right to my face —*Asher, I trust you with the color scheme. You have impeccable taste.*"

Mark's head snaps back. "She said that?"

"Of course. I'm sure she'd say the same of you, no? In my opinion, she's lucky to have two hotties like us in all those wedding photos." I wiggle my eyebrows a little, because I'm fourteen years old inside. Just ask Lucy.

Mark sighs. "But what's wrong with the gray gabardine, or whatever the guy called it? The fit worked on both of us. And it looks . . ." He flaps a hand in my direction. "Just fine."

"Banks, I like to shoot a little higher than *just fine* when I buy a suit."

"It looks *good*, okay?" His face reddens, then his voice dips, a touch rumbly, when he adds, "Especially on you. That color works a hell of a lot better on you than me. I'm being generous here."

"He's right," our nervous fitter says, entering the room. "The dove works well on a blond, with your golden undertones. We could liven things up with a splash of color in the tie," he adds. I didn't catch his name, which is unusual for me. "The gray could look quite sharp. But I have one more idea for you gentlemen." He hangs a garment bag on the rack and unzips it. "These just arrived from Italy. The fabric is a finely woven linen. The color is steely blue. I can picture this with a floral tie in a deeper blue, and a white shirt."

The moment he pulls the jacket from the bag, I already love it. The color is interesting without being bright. The summery fabric makes it festive, but not ostentatious. "Mark, please don't reject this until we try it on. I think the man is onto something."

"Okay," my grumpy companion allows. "Fine."

Five minutes later, we stand side by side in front of the mirrors. Mark is scowling, which means he likes the suit and doesn't want to say so.

"Wow," I say. "This totally says Miami wedding, no? I think our helper even got the bowtie right on the first try." It's a deep-sea blue with flowers ranging from salmon to wine red. And we're wearing suspenders in the same deep red shade. They add color in a subtle way. "It's perfect."

Mark grunts an acknowledgment.

"Tie the tie, maybe?" I say. "Don't you want to see the full effect?"

"Don't need to," he says. "It's good."

He's been reduced to single-syllable words. I'm not sure what to make of that. I turn to him anyway and reach for the bow tie that's draped around his neck. I hold one end of it up to his cheek. "This color makes your eyes pop."

His face is flushed, and his eyes widen. He's even more flustered than he was earlier. I brace myself for a rejection.

"Okay," Mark mutters. "Good. Let's go with this."

Then he takes a step backward, and I end up holding the bowtie, which slips smoothly from his neck, the way it would if I were undressing him on purpose.

"Yup, done," he babbles. "We can go now."

I'm staring at him, the silk tie clutched in my hand as my imagination runs wild. That flushed face is the same one he'd have after a half hour of relentless kisses. Those bright eyes would darken with lust . . .

"Excellent choices, men," Angel says, stepping into the room. "And look at that—you'll barely need any tailoring. The shirts are perfect. The jackets work. And my guy can hem those trouser cuffs this afternoon, Mark, and we'll have everything messengered over to your place by evening."

"Good, good," I say, tearing my eyes off my fellow best man. "I'm glad we could do this so easily. Let me grab my credit card."

Angel waves a hand toward the hallway. "I'm running off for drinks with a fabric designer. The front desk will take care of everything you need. I've already explained your tight timeline. Great to see you. Nice meeting you, Mark. And enjoy Florida."

"Oh, I will," I agree.

Mark does not, though. He just smiles awkwardly and then thanks Angel for his help as the fitter pins his pants for hemming.

Once he's gone, Mark disappears behind the screen. And I undress slowly, trying not to think any lustful thoughts about a man who hates me, and yet is somehow my travel companion for the next five days.

I haven't explained the sleeping arrangements to him yet. That ought to be fun. "What's next on your spreadsheet?" I call out, carefully removing my new shirt.

"I thought we'd go over it on the flight tomorrow," he mutters. "Unless you're just making fun of my spreadsheet. In which case, fuck you."

"Oh my," says the fitter, appearing in the doorway. "Is this a bad time?"

"No, no," I say grandly. "Don't be fooled—that's our love language."

Mark snorts from behind the curtain.

"Can I give you these things for the wrap desk? And my credit card," I say to the fitter.

"Of course," says the obsequious man. "Let me just hang everything on a special trolley, and I'll have you out of here in no time."

Mark's arms appear from behind the screen, holding perfectly creased trouser pants, the shirt and jacket neatly on the hanger.

"Thank you, sir," the fitter says, carrying the clothing to the rolling garment bar as carefully as if they were priceless artifacts.

I deliver my clothes to him as well. "Thank you for your help today. I didn't catch your name."

"It's Dieter," he says. "And serving you was my pleasure today."

A thunk sounds from behind the curtain, and Dieter rolls out of the room with the trolley, leaving me with my jaw unhinged.

"Holy shit," I whisper. Then I dart over to the curtained corner and peek inside. "Did you hear . . . ?"

Mark did indeed. Shirtless, he's leaning against the wall, hands pressed to his face, laughing silently.

I lose it too. Laughter shakes me. But I'm not too incapacitated to notice that a half-dressed Mark is a lickable Mark. He's got a slimmer frame than I do. A runner's build, all lean muscle and smooth skin. My eyes take in the details, the grooves and divots of his abs, the cut of his arms, the tease of a happy trail.

I stop laughing when I notice his fly is open, revealing a tight pair of red boxer briefs with a generous bulge behind them.

Red. Our banker has red underwear. It's like waving a flag at a bull. I'm going to be picturing him in nothing but those for the rest of the week.

Just shoot me.

7

FIRST CLASS VIRGIN

TUESDAY

MARK

*a*fter spending all that time in close quarters with Asher, I have a new theory—that he moonlights as a stripper.

Who the hell is that comfortable showing so much skin?

And another thing.

I'm going to need a whole new approach to dealing with him.

For instance, I know plenty of words that contain more than one syllable. But around Asher and his so-damn-charming ways, I'm reduced to speaking like a caveman.

When we finally escape the close confines of the fitting room, spilling out onto the street at rush hour, I shove the thoughts of his abs, and arms, and V-cut far from my head.

I pluck at my navy-blue shirt. "Just a heads-up. Tomorrow I'll be wearing another polo. Call it . . ." I wave a hand airily, like he'd do, ". . . polo number two. So, if you find yourself shirtless again, just let me know, and I'll pack some extras for you." I hook my thumb eastward, and confirm the pickup plan for tomorrow. "On that note, see you in the morning. Bright and early."

He studies me for several long seconds. "Bright and early," he repeats, and the smooth, suave guy sounds a little bit flummoxed, too.

Score one for the nerd.

That night, I do some light bedtime reading on the science of why stuff works, like elastic waistbands in underwear and the bendy metal in a paperclip. Yup, that's my armor to gird myself against all those errant sex thoughts.

It does the trick, too. It's like my brain is conducting a clean install, free of Asher St. James.

I've got this.

The next morning, I'm no longer a hot, bothered, turned-on mess.

I wake up a new man. While the sky is still dark, I shower—cold, of course—and get dressed for the flight in a gray polo and khaki shorts.

I dry off my hair, hang up the towel, and then head to my bedroom to zip up my suitcase. The task is complicated by the orange fluff ball in it, staring at me with one eye. I could have named him Orange Beard, but that's not a thing. So Blackbeard it is for my orange cat. "You can't come with me, dude. Plus, the belly of a plane is no fun for a mammal," I say, lugging him out of my carry-on.

He protests with a beleaguered meow, clearly annoyed that I disrupted his travel plans.

"The kitty wants to go to Florida," Rosie declares from the hall then bounds into the bedroom to scoop up the creature from the floor and pepper him with kisses. "Valencia will take good care of you," she says, then sets him down.

We head to the tiny kitchen that's about the size of a broom closet. "Only three more days before I get to go to Florida too," Rosie says, then yanks open the fridge and grabs a yogurt.

"Lucky you," I say, as I grab one too, still wishing I didn't have to head to Miami so early.

But hey, I can do this. My new Zen outlook means I won't be bedeviled by 6B, or 7C, or 9D, and definitely not sixty-nine.

As Rosie dips a spoon into her yogurt, she says, "Do you know what I like most about yogurt?"

"That it's not eggs?" I ask drily, lifting one brow.

"Yes! Yolks are so gross, Daddy," she says, and I offer her a hand to high five.

"That is proof you're my kid. Forget the numbers stuff. Detesting eggs is evidence of the power of genetics."

Once we finish, my phone bleats with Bridget's ringtone. So it begins.

You'll get through this, Banks. You made it through English lit class, too.

When I answer, Bridget's weirdly cheerful voice sing-songs, "Hey Mark! I'm here for the little cutie." As if trading our kid back and forth like a tennis ball is just a super-fun time.

Her upbeat attitude grates on me. Her life *is* a super-fun time, I guess. She has a new man, Morgan, and a new apartment that's nicer than the one we shared in this building, before I moved to another unit.

Whenever she shows up, I gird my loins and smile, so I don't poison our child with my bitter attitude.

"We'll be downstairs in three minutes, Bridge," I say, as I check the time. God, I hate saying goodbye to my baby girl. Every single time, it sucks.

I end the call, scratch Blackbeard behind the ears, then grab our bags, and hold Rosie's hand as we head down two flights of stairs. Outside it's a warm June morning on our tree-lined block. Even though my rent bill here in the Flatiron District makes my eyes bleed despite my decent Wall Street salary, I can't imagine living anywhere else in the city. I can walk Rosie to school a few blocks away, and that's one of my favorite things to do.

With a squeeze of her little hand in mine, I remind her that I'll call her every night.

"You better! Eight forty-five on the dot. That'll be thirteen hours and fifty-five minutes from now," she says.

"Show-off," I say with a laugh, ruffling her hair as we reach my ex-wife.

Bridget tucks her chestnut strands behind her ears. "Hi Mark. Looks like you're ready to get a suntan and relax on the beach."

That's *not* what I'll be doing, but I don't bother to correct her.

I'm civil to Bridget. I don't look forward to seeing her, though. Not because I'm heartbroken. I'm not. Our marriage grew lackluster over the last few years. But I did what was expected of me. I got the highest paying job I could find, and I stuck it out.

She didn't, though. And I'm angry. I'll always be angry.

Even if we didn't marry *for* love, I *did* love her. We married because it was the right thing to do once she was pregnant. I stayed with her because loyalty matters. You should do what you say you're going to do.

Like show up on time.

As Bridget takes Rosie's hand, a sleek black town car pulls over to the curb. The hair on the back of my neck prickles. Before anyone opens the door, I know, I just know, that it's Asher. He said he'd grab a Lyft and swing by, but of course he can't just arrive in a white Nissan from a ride-share app. He has to do everything with style. My jaw ticks while my pulse spikes. Because even though it kind of irritates me, I also kind of like the town car.

Story of my life with him.

The back door swings open, and Asher unfolds himself from the car, and . . . *fuck me.*

He looks so damn good in vacation mode. A tight, cool blue, short-sleeve button-down hugs his arms, and he's got it tucked into trim shorts. He whips off aviator shades.

Of course.

"Good morning, Mark and you must be Bridget," he says, introducing himself to my ex, then turning his gaze to my kiddo. "And it's good to see you again, Rosie the Slugger."

My daughter beams. "You heard about my double too?"

She sounds utterly enchanted.

Know the feeling, kid.

"I hear you're a superstar on the softball field, which is all kinds of awesome." He bends down to her level, his eyes locked on hers. "But have you taken up football yet? Or soccer, as Americans call it? You need to think about soccer, too."

"I have been thinking about it. I want to try it."

I motion to Bridget, lower my voice. "He used to play in Europe. Premier League."

"Oh," she says, sounding intrigued. "That's like the major league in Europe."

"Yeah, that's the one," I say, and for a second, I sound a little impressed even to my own ears.

Bridget shoots me a curious look, like *how do you know all this?* But I don't share with her.

I know because I do my homework. After I met Asher, I looked him up online. Read his Wiki, checked out his stats from six years as a striker. Fine, I even watched a highlights reel.

Including a short interview with a French TV station after his team won the championship, and his face was shining with sweat, his hair slicked back, his jaw covered in a short beard. He looked elated as he talked to the reporter in French.

No clue what he said, but it sounded hot coming out of his mouth.

". . . And when you score a goal, it's the best feeling ever. Bet you like it more than a home run," Asher tells Rosie, and he's a magician too, casting a spell on my little girl.

"I bet I do too," she says, then spins around. "Daddy, can I try soccer?"

Yup. Abracadabra.

"Sure, cupcake," I tell her, then lift her in my arms, and give her a big hug.

Then, I say goodbye to Bridget, toss my carry-on in the trunk, and slide into the car, onto the cool leather seats.

Asher joins me, the door clicking closed behind us, the partition rolled up. He deals me a sly smile, gesturing to my polo. "Did you bring me one just like that? Please say yes."

And it's on. My strategy locked down. "Of course. We can

practice our matching looks before Hannah walks down the aisle. Every day, we'll look like twins."

There. Twinning is so not sexy.

"Good. *Practice* is so important," he says, lingering a little on that word as the car peels away, and it's just us now.

Maybe if I'm lucky, there will be a chatty, little old lady next to us on the flight. Preferably one who knits and wants to tell me how to make an afghan the whole plane ride down to Florida.

I'd listen to every detail as it'll take my mind off my traveling companion who speaks French, and looks good when he sweats, and says words like *practice* in a smoky voice.

When I was a kid, I used to count down the days on the calendar before the trips we took to Cedar Point, the amusement park a couple hours from where Hannah and I grew up in Columbus, Ohio.

I still love checking items off a list, and marking the X, since it's rewarding. Once we're past security, we've chopped an hour and a half off this trip already so that's some progress.

Along the way through the terminal, Asher fiddles with his phone more than I'd expect a grown-up to do.

That's fine. It keeps us from talking.

When we reach the boarding area, there's no line at our gate. "Perfect. I'm going to see about an upgrade for us," he says.

I jerk my gaze to him. Is he speaking French again? "What for?"

"Well, you don't *want* to fly coach, do you?" He says that like it's preposterous.

I've never flown anything except coach. But it's not like I want to say, *hey I'm a first-class virgin.* "You don't have to spring for first class. I'm fine," I say, assuring him, since I'm not flashy. I don't need extras. I also have literally no clue what I'm supposed to say to a guy who wants to upgrade me, too.

Asher claps me on the shoulder, curling a hand over my

muscle. "Banks, I might be an asshole sometimes. But I'm not a total ass."

Tension blankets my body from the feel of his hand on me, and it's joined by heat sizzling under my skin. Great. Just that touch and I'm lit up. "I'll bite. How are you not a total ass?" I ask, trying to focus on what he's saying, not how I'm feeling.

With a playful glint in his eyes, he says, "I'm not going to upgrade just myself. And I'm not going to fly coach if I don't have to," he says, then grins mischievously. "And I don't have to. Ergo, *we* don't have to either."

Wait! This is brilliant. This is an out. Three hours to escape from this rampant lust if I can wiggle away from his offer. "You should definitely do it, Asher. Live large. Enjoy yourself. But listen, I'm completely fine in coach. I sleep on planes anyway, so it's not a problem for me to just crash the whole time."

That's a lie. I hate sleeping on planes. Your head falls to the side, your mouth lolls open, and you look stupid. But he won't want to upgrade someone who's just going to snooze the whole time.

"That sounds miserable. You'll sleep better in first class."

I try harder, upping my negotiation game. "Save the miles for yourself, and you can upgrade again the next time you go to Fiji or São Paulo or wherever."

Asher shrugs. "This is why I have credit card miles in the first place."

I want to find a reason to say no. Because him spending points on me—or money in the form of points—makes me uncomfortable. It's a little too close to everything I'm trying to avoid with him. Nonetheless he's already striding toward the gate agent, flashing the kind of smile that can probably charm the underwear off anyone, man or woman, in seconds.

His eyes stray to her name tag. "Hi, Karina I see your upgrade list has just enough room for two more."

I roll my eyes so hard I nearly pull a muscle.

"Why, yes it does! Let me get you all situated."

"That would be fantastic."

47

A few minutes later, he wheels around, waggling his airline app like it's the spoils of war. "And we're in 3A and 3B."

I wince, but do my best to show my gratitude. "Thanks. If I can repay the favor sometime, just ask."

"Huh. Like you'll help me with all those spreadsheets I've been dying to make?" he counters, zinging me once again.

This time I take the bait, and return to my deal-with-the-hottie approach. "Aww, you're so sweet. Talking our love language."

That makes him laugh. "And I believe the retort to that is . . . *fuck you.*"

Just like that, my mind is right back where it started.

Thirty minutes later, I slide my messenger bag under the seat in front of me, and park in a first-class seat for the first time.

It's cushy, and spacious, and wow—this is a whole lot swankier than coach. Plus, the flight attendants treat us like kings, offering hot towels and asking if we need anything. This is a different country up here, and I love it more than I'd thought I would.

I'm a little bit like a kid at Christmas as I run my hands along the armrests and stretch out my legs.

Asher's lips curve into a grin. "So you're a first-class virgin, Banks?"

It's that obvious? I swallow past the dry patch in my throat. "Yes. Thank you. That was really nice of you," I say.

But nice hardly covers it. Asher's flair is as ridiculously sexy as his body is annoyingly perfect.

And I have more than one hundred hours to spend with him. Time to strap in and buckle up.

8

YOU POSH FUCKER

ASHER

*M*aybe I can put Mark out of his misery for a few minutes.

The guy seems to swing between discomfort and deadpan humor around me. I get it. I'm *a lot.*

And he's a little awkward by nature.

So to ease the tension once we're airborne, I smack his arm gently. "Look, Banks. I've been meaning to tell you something."

His dark blue eyes flicker as his defenses go up. "Let me guess. You hate my shirt. My shoes. My haircut."

Actually the whole neat, trim haircut he has going on is sexy in a let's-mess-it-up-already way. "No. It's this." I take a deep breath, like I'm prepping to say something hard. "This isn't easy to admit. But I'm going to do it anyway. I had a mullet once, too."

A laugh bursts from him. But then it fades, and his eyes turn suspicious. "I think you're fucking with me."

Oh, you have no idea how much I wish you were into that . . .

The way his skin flushed in the dressing room yesterday makes me wonder, too. Makes me want to go fishing again about his red briefs, and his one-syllable speech whenever he's near me. But now isn't the time. Not when we're stuck in the air with literally no escape. So I return to that drunk text, when he'd said he'd had a mullet once upon a time, and I share my story.

"In my fifth season in the Premier League, we were playing great. So, naturally, none of my teammates got a haircut or shaved. Superstition and all," I say, then drag a hand across my clean-shaven jaw, like I'm remembering those days. His irises follow my hand, almost like he's wondering what I'd look like with a trim beard.

Hot, Banks. I looked hot.

"Anyway, we won the championship, and a few days later, I cut my hair in a mullet just to fuck with my teammates."

Mark smiles and it's easy, relaxed. Maybe the first one I've seen from him like that. His body language seems to shift, too. "Pics or it didn't happen," he counters.

Interesting. Mark's a challenging one. "I'll find something on YouTube for you. I promise," I say, then make a beckoning gesture for him to serve up the goods. "Your story now, since I can't picture you as anything but the guy with the banker's cut."

"My mullet was part of a Halloween costume when I was thirteen. There was a contest at school, and I wanted to win."

"What was the prize? A calculator?"

"No. A chess set."

"Kind of the same thing, isn't it?" I tease.

"Not at all."

"And so you dressed up as . . . a guy with a mullet?"

"I went as Rob Lowe. In his '80s, brat pack mullet days," he says, and I stare at Banks, counting the similarities he shares with the actor. Dark hair. Captivating blue eyes you can't look away from. Carved jaw. A boy-next-door sex appeal. Put a pair of black glasses on the movie star, and you've got my traveling companion. "I can see that. Circa 1984," I say, but Rob Lowe was and is hot in any era.

"Thanks," he says, and a tiny smile seems to tug on his lips as he shrugs. "But I didn't win."

"Whatever did you do about the chess set?" I tease.

"I got a used one at Goodwill. It was missing a knight. I made one out of a pink ceramic pig salt-shaker that my mom had," he says, a determination in his voice, and there's more to that story. Something about who he is, and I want to know more.

But right when I'm about to ask another question, a statuesque flight attendant with serious Gisele Bündchen vibes stops at our row.

"Hello, Mister St. James, it's so wonderful to see our frequent fliers again. Would you care for a mimosa? Coffee? Tea? Or anything else for you and your . . ."

She trails off as her eyes drift from Mark to me and back.

Oh, this is rich.

I laugh, but Mark gapes, and there's that familiar shade of fire engine red again, creeping up his neck.

"You can just call us the best men," I say to her. "And a mimosa sounds great. Mimosa for you, Banks?"

He shakes his head whip fast. "I'm good. Thanks," he says, like there's sand in his throat.

A few minutes later, my drink arrives, and I savor it, relaxing against the leather seat. My eyes are just beginning to feel heavy when Mark says, "Wouldn't now be a good time for our battle plan?"

"Sorry?" I take another sip of fresh-squeezed orange juice and sparkling wine. "Is that a movie?"

In answer, he turns his laptop to face me. "Our battle plan— for getting the wedding sorted out. I've listed everything we need to do, with deadlines. And I've color-coded it for priority."

"That's a spreadsheet," I say sleepily. "I'm not good with spreadsheets."

"It's a list," he insists. "Everyone is good with those."

I'm pretty sure both Lucy and my ex would disagree. But I keep that to myself. "Are we going to divide and conquer? That leaves more time for the swimming pool."

He blinks. "We have about the rest of the week to plan a wedding. It has to be perfect. I doubt I'm getting any sun unless it's during the ceremony on Saturday."

Well, shit. I'm as eager as anyone for my bestie to have a great wedding weekend. But I never thought that meant I'd spend the whole time busting my ass. "But there are people for that. Your sister already hired some vendors, right? A tent? A caterer? It's all handled."

His eyes narrow. "What? You can't just *depend* on people like that. We have to check-up on all of them ahead of time. We can't drink beer on the beach and hope the catering truck rolls up the driveway on Saturday like they said they would."

Not beer, I argue privately. When I'm in Miami, I prefer a nice rosé. But Mark's searching stare lets me know that the cork isn't coming out of that wine until he gets some satisfaction.

And not the fun kind.

I let out a groan. Just a small one. And I mentally put my wine glass back in the cabinet. "So show me this list."

Mark gestures to a terrifying-looking chart on the screen that makes my head spin. "Okay, Column A is the contact name. Column B is the phone number . . ." His tone turns more animated, like this column stuff turns him on. Hmm. What does turn him on? And why the hell do I want to know?

I focus on the horror on the screen.

He's collected the email address, the business hours, and physical address for every single contact. So at least they'll be easy to find.

". . . First, after we drop our stuff at the house, we can measure that patio for the tent, to make sure my sister and I ordered the right one. And then I thought we'd swing by the florist."

"Give me a task," I argue. "This will go faster if we split them up."

With an intense stare from behind those black glasses, Mark scrolls through his list. "Well, a lot of this stuff I need to see with my own eyes. But I guess you could call the officiant."

I bark out a laugh. "That's it? Are you sure you're willing to trust me with this one alone? Wow, Banks. I know I have a reputation for being kind of a mess. But I can probably be trusted to make a couple phone calls without fucking it up. I could record them for you to review later."

While I'm sunbathing.

"Hey." His blue eyes fly to mine, and his tone gentles. "That is not what this is about. You run a damn business, right? I'm sure you're single-handedly dazzling clients from sunup to sundown." His scowl is back before I can even say thanks for the compliment. "But this is my only sister's wedding. Her *only* wedding, I hope and pray. And I have less than four days and a lengthy list of sins to atone for."

"Oh." I blink. "So this is about those drunk texts? You want to make sure everything's perfect, because then it doesn't seem like you hate the idea of this wedding?"

He slumps in his chair. "Yes and no. I want to do this for Hannah. She already knows that, though. We spent every night these last two weeks at my kitchen table, working hard on this stuff."

I hadn't known that. When I'd asked Flip if he needed any help with the wedding, he'd just said *Hannah's got it. You already did your thing by getting us this house, man. But I wouldn't say no to some good cigars.*

And it turns out Mark's been stepping up all the way as the best man to the bride. Got to admire his devotion.

"She knows I'm all in," he continues. "But I need this wedding to be perfect for her. She needs a better start than . . ."

"Than what?" I prod.

"Than I got." He waves a hand dismissively. "Never mind."

"Never mind?" Like I could let that go? "Banks, tell me. Did you have a wedding disaster? Is that it? The tent collapsed, or the caterer poisoned everyone?" Maybe his own wedding was like one of those BuzzFeed lists of everything that can go wrong.

It would explain the hell out of this spreadsheet.

"Not exactly," he says in a low voice. "I got married at the City Clerk's office. Bridget's parents were our witnesses. Then we all went out for pizza because Bridget craved carbs the entire time she was pregnant."

"Pizza," I repeat stupidly. "That sounds grim."

"It was actually really good pizza. Serafina on the Upper East Side? Have you been?"

"Oh, that place. Yeah. Everyone who works there is model-hot too." I chuckle. "But don't distract me, Banks. I want to hear the rest of this story."

He sighs. "It *was* grim. Not the pizza—the occasion. I got my college girlfriend pregnant during my senior year—her junior year. We had no money and plenty of student loans, of course. We got married. I finished school, but she didn't. Rosie was born during finals week. I started my finance training program two weeks later."

"Damn." That's some drama. "And now you're divorced."

"Yup. I spent the last six years trying to make it work. Trying to do the right thing. And then last year she said—*I'm in love with my boss, and I want a divorce.*"

"Whoa." We sit quietly for a moment while I absorb this truth bomb. No wonder Mark has been prickly. His life is blowing up.

And now I get it. "You think Hannah and Flip are just going to repeat your disaster, right? That Flip is going to bail on her?"

"I have PTSD, I guess. It's nothing against Flip. Not really." His voice drops. "Those two were different from the start. More in love. More ready to make big decisions. But would it have killed them to take it a little slower?"

I grin up at the ceiling. "Yeah, I've got some whiplash too. It feels like only last week that Flip was saying, *I met a girl.*" I'd be a liar if I said their whirlwind romance hasn't ever given me pause. A year ago, we were planning our next clubbing trip to Ibiza. Now Flip is looking at paint chips for the nursery.

The flight attendant reappears. "Gentlemen, can I bring you a slice of quiche, and some breakfast pastries?"

"Yes please," we both say simultaneously. "And I'll take one of those mimosas too," Mark adds, sounding sheepish. "If that's still on offer."

"Of course, sir. One moment."

I pull Mark's laptop off his tray table and onto my lap. "Okay. I think I get it. This wedding has got to be perfect for Hannah and Flip. They need some good juju."

"You probably think it sounds dumb," Mark grumbles. "But everyone looked at my marriage as a huge risk. Like they were waiting for us to fail. My mom cried when I invited her to come to my civil ceremony. And they weren't happy tears."

"Did she say you were ruining your life or some shit?" I got this speech myself when I chose art school in Spain over a degree from Cambridge.

"Well, no. She was mostly upset that she didn't get to make her ham and noodle casserole with potato chip topping for the reception. But she wanted a traditional wedding, not at City Hall. Oh, and my father cited this statistic about young marriages failing more frequently." He's quiet for a beat. "Guess he called that one."

Mark sounds resigned, but I need to address something more pertinent first.

"I'm still stuck on the casserole," I admit. "Did you say *potato chips?*" I try to keep the horror out of my voice.

But I fail.

"It's less disgusting than it sounds," he insists. "My parents are super traditional. They don't understand why Hannah and I like New York. Not a day goes by when my mother doesn't warn me with some big-city crime stats. They honestly think everyone should be happy in the suburbs of Ohio."

Yikes. "They'll love me then. The queer guy who's going to ask the caterer if we can add ceviche to the menu." I'm craving all of Miami's delights. Sue me.

Mark snorts. "The queer thing would be no problem for them, but the ceviche would be a deal-breaker. Hannah made sure to add pigs in blankets to the cocktail menu, because my mom thinks you can't have a party without those."

Interesting. I file Mark's comment about his parents away for safekeeping as I scroll down the spreadsheet a little farther. "This is very thorough. We can hit most of these places tomorrow. We could even visit the florist first. It's not far from the house. I know where this address is."

"Thank you," Mark says softly.

"No big." I hand the computer back, because our breakfast is arriving. "Quite the spreadsheet. What do your parents do for a living?"

"Dad is an auditor. Mom is a librarian."

And the background to the Mark Banks picture fills in a little more. "That kind of explains a lot."

He rolls his eyes as a beautiful plate lands on his tray table—china, of course, followed by silver utensils. And a mimosa in a crystal flute. "Wow. Thank you," he says to the attendant, and his reaction to first class is adorable. But best for me not to think of him that way. It's adorable in an I-can-understand-the-other-best-man-a-little-better way. That's all.

"My pleasure." She puts the same in front of me.

"How are we feeling about first class now, Banks?" I ask after she's gone.

He spreads a real linen napkin across his lap. "It will do, you posh fucker."

Now I'm laughing too hard to take a sip of my drink. Just wait until he sees the car I rented, and the mansion my friend lent us for the wedding. His nerdy little head might blow off.

I can't wait.

9

I KNOW HOW TO HANDLE A STICK

MARK

I *survived three more hours with the superhot posh fucker.* Maybe I'll get that printed on a T-shirt as a souvenir from this trip. All I have to do is make it through the next few days.

Can't be too hard.

Especially since everything is going our way. No line at the car rental, so Asher's finishing the paperwork as I answer some texts.

Valencia: Question. When Blackbeard swats me, that means he's biting the hand that feeds him?

Mark: No, V. It means he likes you. It's his love language.

But thinking of Asher's remarks from yesterday makes me stop and reverse course as I tap out another reply.

Mark: Or maybe it means he's just a cat.

Valencia: Got it. He's a feline. Ergo, a cocky jerk. But so handsome. I just can't stop petting him.

I'm not going to touch that one, so I say thanks, then check out the texts from my parents.

Mom: I've never been to a mansion before. Do you think the kitchen will have a casserole dish? Or should I bring my own?

Mark: Mom, you won't need a casserole dish. The wedding is catered. You're just going to relax and enjoy everything.

Dad: Mark, there have been eight hundred recorded shark attacks in Florida since 1845. Please stay out of the water.

Mark: Thanks! I'll bear that in mind.

I've learned to humor my father. My mother? Not so much. If she attempts to serve a casserole at Hannah's gourmet wedding, I will have to do some kind of ninja stunt to make it disappear.

So I have that to look forward to.

As Asher peels away from the counter, I close the text app, and we leave the cool lobby and cross the parking lot. Along the way, he scratches his jaw, his eyes twinkling. "One thing I wanted to mention."

Why do I think he's setting me up again? Oh right, since it's his favorite pastime. "You didn't really rent a car? You ordered a surprise helicopter to fly us to the . . ."

My joke dies when we arrive in front of a sleek ruby-red car that gleams like a just-polished fire truck.

The hood of the swank Porsche 911 convertible catches Asher's reflection, and my too cool, too charming, too good-looking traveling companion grins at the vehicle like a most satisfied man.

I look up at the rental company's lit sign above the parking space for confirmation of what I already know. In brightly lit all caps it reads: ASHER ST. JAMES.

This guy.

He does everything big.

"Are you kidding me right now?" I gesture to the wheels. "Do you do anything the ordinary way? Or is your whole life super-size?"

"We're in *Miami*, Banks. What else would I rent? Or wait. Are you worried about your hair getting messed up?"

"Nah. I was more concerned about you. I don't want it to affect your next Pantene commercial."

With a laugh, he tosses the keys up and down in his palm. "Want me to take it back? Get a Subaru instead? Or how about a hatchback? Something with room for groceries and your chess sets in the back?"

I burn a little inside. This guy doesn't understand that not everyone gets a shot to be Mr. Big Time. Some of us live in a different reality.

And, fine, I'm annoyed that he can get my goat better than my sister did when we were kids.

Yet nothing about being with Asher feels familial.

Everything feels . . . tingly.

Even this car.

We both move at the same time. And we both move in the same direction—right to the driver's side of the candy-apple wet dream of a car. In fact, we get there at nearly the same instant. But Asher reaches for the door handle first.

In a flash, I picture exactly what I want. It's not on my spreadsheet. It's not sex. It's just a taste of *this* life. *His life.*

I grab his hand, curling mine over it to stop him.

His grin burns off as he turns to meet my gaze, his nostrils flaring ever so slightly. Maybe from the feel of my hand on his?

A dangerous hope ignites inside me—the wish that I could turn him on.

But I doubt that's possible. A guy like him wouldn't want anything to do with a guy like me.

And I should take my hand off his. I really should. But I don't.

I also don't ask for what I want.

I *tell.*

"I'll drive," I say. Firm and clear.

Asher's face registers my command in slow motion. His hazel eyes twinkle, then his lips crook into a curious grin. "Be my guest, Banks."

At last, I let go of his hand so he can take it off the car handle. When I do, he presses the keys into my open palm, and heat curls through my body from that barest touch.

I swallow roughly, wanting this second to last a little longer, and wanting to escape from it too.

But it ends, as all good things do. We toss our carry-ons into the trunk, then crisscross, Asher heading to the passenger side, me back to the driver's side.

Once I sink into the beige leather seat and adjust the mirrors, I groan. "Fuck. I can't drive this car."

Asher chuckles. "Aw, really? You can't drive a stick shift? God, the jokes I could make right now."

Go ahead and make them, pal. I think you'd be surprised.

"I know how to handle a *stick*, man. I'm talking about the rental agreement. We'd have to add my name to it. Or insurance won't cover it if anything happens to this hundred-thousand-dollar car."

His face goes slack with horror. "Oh dear. That sounds awful." He lowers his voice to a stage whisper. *"Taking a risk."*

"It's not about the risk. It's about the major pain in the ass that would result from an accident."

"I wouldn't want you to have any pain . . . *there,*" he says, taking the joke to its inevitable, tawdry conclusion.

But I barely hear it. I've got a bad case of car envy. So I wave my hand toward the lobby of the car rental. "Can we just go add my name? Or do I have to beg?"

He taps his lip, all serious. "Hmm. Not a bad idea." Then a smile takes over. "Just fucking drive. Of course I put your name on the rental agreement."

I pull back, my brow creasing. "You did?"

"Yes, I did. That surprises you?"

"That you'd let someone else drive? Yes."

Asher just gives an easy shrug. "The last thing I am is a control freak, Banks. Sometimes I like to drive . . . Sometimes I like to be driven," he says, then leans back against the chair, and shuts his eyes, letting those words linger deliciously in the space between us.

Like he's taunting me with their double meaning.

Good thing his eyes are closed, since Captain Filthy Mind takes over. My brain goes haywire, images flipping through it at rapid speed.

Control. Giving up control. Wanting it. Letting go of it.

Him pinning me down on the bed. Me pinning him. And then taking. Just taking what I want from him.

I rake my hand through my hair, trying to clear the fog from my brain by zeroing in on the basics of driving.

Keys. Ignition. And one more thing.

I turn around, reach into the back seat for my messenger bag, and grab my prescription shades. I switch them out, then turn on the engine, and the car roars to life with a sexy purr.

As I back up, I return to the last thing he said. "Glad you added my name, since I definitely like to drive," I say, since I can't quite resist.

Asher doesn't answer.

Just smirks.

And off we go.

We cruise past Miami's collection of man-made islands along the MacArthur Causeway, the robotic voice on the Waze app directing us to Star Island.

It's a good thing I'm driving, too, because Asher gets sucked into a call with his assistant. From what I can gather, she's supposed to be uploading some photography for a client.

"The folder is called Banana Hammock Twenty-one," Asher says.

I glance quickly toward the passenger seat. Is he joking right now?

"What? You have to have fun at work. No, Lucy, not you. Please write this down. The subfolder with the finished edits is called *Final*. I'd also like you to supply *Alt*, in case the merchandiser doesn't agree with my choices. But that's it. Those are the *only* two they need. Uh-huh. Right. By cocktail hour, okay? Thanks."

"Banana hammock?" I ask when he hangs up.

"It's for Commando," he says with a shrug. "The swimwear company."

Waze interrupts him with, "Turn left in one mile."

The bay hugs the bridge as boats zip through the blue waves. It's possible I might be driving above the speed limit. It's also possible I like it.

I half want to be annoyed by Asher's flash, but this car is—holy fuck—fun.

So much of the last six years have been the opposite. Work, parenting, trying to prop up a marriage.

But very little fun, and even though he drives me crazy, Asher is the definition of fun.

Maybe that's why I told him my wedding story on the plane. I want him to know why I am the way I am—wound a little tightly.

Okay, maybe a lot.

Asher isn't, though. And I can't help but wonder where the hell he came from. "What do your parents do? Are they around?"

"Yes. Sort of. They're divorced. Have been since I was in boarding school. They're both remarried. Dad's third marriage. It's . . . whatever. I'm not close with either of them," he says, offhand. "They both do something with money. International finance or what have you." I catch a quick glimpse of him as I turn off the causeway. He strokes his chin. "Does that make them bankers like you?"

"I'm not a *banker*," I scoff. "Please. I'm a trader."

"But you work for a *bank*," he says slowly.

"Well, sure."

"If it quacks like a duck . . ."

I snort. "Trading and banking aren't the same, no matter what the sign on the building says."

"Enlighten me," he insists.

"A banker borrows at one percent and lends at fifteen percent and plays golf on the weekends. A trader is out there in the choppy water." I gesture vaguely toward the sparkling ocean beyond the bay. "Trying to buy low and sell high and keep the water out of his nose before the hurricane arrives."

"In other words—and it shocks me to learn this about you—the job is *risky*."

"All the time," I agree. "One bad day can end your career. So you have to be the kind of guy who never has that kind of a day."

"And how do you do that?"

I shrug. "You just have to be smarter or more ruthless than everyone else who's out there trying to eat your lunch."

"So you can either outmaneuver or out-nerd the other guy," he says with a chuckle.

"Exactly. On a good day, you can do both."

Waze speaks up again. "Your destination is two hundred feet on the right," the app announces, and I turn into a driveway that makes my jaw fall to the other side of the bay.

"Are you kidding me?"

Hannah showed me pictures. But in person, this mansion is insane. A massive, gated entrance sprawls across a driveway that's probably made of gold bricks.

Details first, though. I gesture to the sheltered keypad at the gate.

"I've got the code in my phone," Asher says, grabbing it from his shorts pocket. "Someone likes long passwords," he mutters as he swipes the screen, then finds what he's looking for. He starts to read it off. He must think better of it, because he unclicks his seatbelt, reaching across me to tap in the code. His chest rests against my right arm and his body stretches along mine.

I. Don't. Move.

I just try not to inhale his scent.

But I can't stop. He smells like rainwater and a summer breeze and all my fantasies, and I want to touch him so badly. My runaway brain rattles down the tracks as I picture dropping my mouth to his neck, licking his throat, sucking on his earlobe.

My breath catches on that image.

He freezes.

He noticed the hitch in my breath.

He totally fucking noticed.

Please don't say anything. Don't tease me over that. I don't think I can handle it.

But the squeal of the gate saves my ass as Asher settles back into his seat without a mention—just a casual, "There we go."

I pray I'm not going to sport wood when I get out of the car.

With a loud, final wrench, the gate stops rolling, and I drive past it. A few seconds later, it rattles closed, sealing us in.

When I cut the engine, I have no choice but to gawk.

It's a *palace*, sprawling at the top of a short hill. And it does take my mind off matters south of the border. "Wow," I say, and I breathe a sigh of relief.

Hannah will be ecstatic, which is all that matters. I grab my phone, send her a quick text.

Mark: You're gonna love it. This place is stunning!

She replies right away.

Hannah: Eep. Show me pics!

Mark: Stand by.

Once I switch back to my regular glasses, we leave the car in the driveway, and Asher types his code into another lock box on the mansion's spacious front porch.

Then we're heading inside the air-conditioned home worthy of Madonna or a Super Bowl-winning quarterback, and I snap some shots for Hannah. The marble floors. The vaulted white ceilings. The entire glass wall in the living room overlooking the glistening bay, with boats bobbing in the distance on the placid water.

And a pool in between that's bigger than my New York apartment.

I'm itching to jump in the water that practically glitters under the sun. I head for the sliding glass door and step onto the mosaic tiles that surround the pool. Beyond that, I catalogue the terrace—where the air-conditioned wedding tent will go—and the emerald-green lawn that stretches into the distance.

Then my eyes stray to something I didn't notice before. At the edge of the pool sits a little cottage. "Oh. Nice pool house," I say, turning to Asher.

He's watching me. No, he's *staring* at me. Yet he doesn't seem to have heard. "St. James? Hello? Did the zombies get you?"

Asher blinks. "Sorry, what?"

I point outside. "Is that a pool house?"

"Not exactly. It's a guest house. That's where we're staying."

My gaze snaps back to the guest house. Suddenly, my brain is a computer server that just overheated. Warning signs flash on my personal dashboard.

He did *not* just say that. There is no way he said that. That cottage is maybe ten square feet. Not literally, but it might as well be. There's no way my desire for him can fit inside it. *With him.*

Best to double check. "We are?" I croak out.

With his thumbs hooked into his shorts pockets, he rocks back on his heels, and just nods. "We are."

Newsflash: Getting through the next few days is going to be *too hard.*

In every sense of the word.

10

MAYBE IT'S THE POLO SHIRTS

ASHER

*M*ark spins around, and something like wild fear flashes in his blue eyes. "But . . . this is a goddamn *mansion*. Why would we stay out *there*?" The question comes out with no space between the words as he gestures wildly toward the guest house.

But I'm having a mental breakdown of my own. For the last three minutes I've been trying to get used to a shocking new idea.

Mark Banks is hot for me.

I don't know how I missed it before. Maybe it's because I don't know him that well. I hadn't learned to read his particular brand of stammers and scowls. And long, lingering stares.

Or maybe it's the assumption I made about his marriage to a woman.

Actually, maybe it's the polo shirts.

Or prescription sunglasses.

But there's no mistaking what just happened outside in the car. When I invaded his personal space, he shivered like a teen girl watching the *Twilight* movies. His eyes dilated. His breath hitched.

I am shook.

And now he's waiting for me to answer him. Those unhappy blue eyes are pinched behind his sexy, hot-nerd-style glasses.

Wait. What was the question? Oh, right. "That whole wing in the mansion is reserved for your parents, Flip's parents, and the bride and groom. Some of your sister's college friends too," I say, my voice clipped.

Maybe I sound like a dick right now, but my head is too busy exploding. I need a moment to gather my thoughts. So, bag in tow, I walk off, circling the edge of the pool.

I head to the guest house, unlock the door, and immediately claim the larger bedroom.

He'd expect me to, right? Mark thinks I'm an arrogant fuck.

Or, wait. I honestly don't know what Mark thinks of me. His attitude suddenly hits me in a completely different light.

He wants me. And he's struggling with it.

I sit down on the edge of the bed and try to think. I don't have any sexual hang-ups. I'm thirty years old, and I've been gleefully, and successfully, chasing men for half my life.

But not everyone is me. And I don't just mean that they don't have my looks or my athleticism. Not everyone is comfortable with all the things they want.

If there's one thing I know, it's that Mark is *not* comfortable with his attraction to me. It could be that he's curious and inexperienced. It could be that he isn't out. Or maybe it's neither of those things, and he just finds it inconvenient to lust after the best friend of the guy his sister is marrying.

This doesn't change anything, right? Who cares if he gets stirred up every time I get close to him?

I rise from the bed, flip my suitcase open, and head into the bathroom to brush my teeth. This doesn't matter. It isn't important to the next four days.

When I look in the mirror over the sink, though, I see my own flushed face staring back at me. Evidence that I kind of dig the hot nerd vibe Mark has going on.

But we're in Miami, where everything is sultry.

We're together in this tiny house that suddenly feels even tinier.

We're alone on this gorgeous property.

I've got to keep my mind off Mark's attraction. I can't dwell on the way his pulse throbbed at his throat when I got a little too close to him.

And I sure as hell can't spend time wondering what it would be like to peel that polo shirt off him and put my tongue all over that lean chest.

When I leave my bedroom a couple minutes later, Mark's waiting in the tiny living room, cracking his knuckles, all fidgety.

Hell. He's struggling. But I don't know if it's a big deal—something he can barely even acknowledge—or just an ordinary case of inconvenient attraction to someone you don't actually like.

I'm not going to say anything. If he wants to avoid the subject, then so will I.

"What's the matter?" I tease. "Is the bed not soft enough for you, Goldilocks? You want mine?"

Mark mumbles something that sounds a lot like *fuck off*. But then he exhales heavily, gestures around the bright little room, and says, "This is fine. It's no problem. I just didn't realize we'd be staying here instead of in the house."

"Good, good," I say crisply, since I don't want to dwell on our close quarters either. "So what do you say we grab some fish tacos and then head to the florist?"

"Right. Yes," he says, rising to his feet. "Let's do that."

"Excellent. I'd like to pick up a bottle of wine for later too." *But not because I'm going to ply you with rosé and hit on you. Nope. No sir.* ". . . And then we'll hit the florist and check off item 2A on your spreadsheet."

That red hue returns to his cheeks.

Weird. Do errands get him hot?

No. It's still me somehow. I recognize that look from Angel's showroom too. When he was undressing me with his eyes. It's the same look he had in the car when I stretched across him. And the one he wore, too, when he covered my hand with his thirty minutes ago and told me he wanted to drive.

I take a deep breath and ignore it. "Come on, Banks. I'm not getting any younger." I head for the door, where I step out and then turn around to make sure he's following me. "P.S.—this time it's my turn at the wheel."

His pupils widen, and here we go again.

Fuck.

Ignoring this attraction won't be easy.

It gets a little easier when we hit the road, with the wind in our hair. I turn on the radio, and EDM blasts from the speakers.

Mark immediately changes the channel, surfing until he finds NPR.

I snicker. But I let him get away with it. The MarketWatch guys are giving a financial rundown. "The S and P is up twelve points in blah, blah light trading. The US Ten-Year Note is blah, blah, blah, blah. A big company bought another big company, and for some reason that matters."

I'm paraphrasing.

Mark pulls out his phone and makes a call. "Hey, Brett. How'd the yield curve react to the CPI? Eh, okay. I hope you hedged out those futures. Right. Sorry. Yeah, I'm sure you're tied up. But before I go—rook to A4. Later."

He hangs up, and I attempt some casual conversation.

"What's a CPI?"

"Consumer price index. It's a measure of inflation. The bond market hates inflation."

"Don't we all. And what's A4?"

"Oh, a chess move. It was my turn."

It takes me a beat to understand what he meant. And then I snort. "Who were you talking to? I thought it was a co-worker."

"It was. Brett is my work husband. And we play chess too."

There are so many things I need to unpack in that sentence. "Your work husband?"

"Sure. Just because it's Wall Street doesn't mean you can't have friends. Especially if they play chess."

"But you don't have a chess board here in the Porsche, Banks."

He points at his temple. "It's right here. I've been stewing over this move, because he's kind of got me cornered."

I'd like to get you cornered.

"Huh. Is playing chess without a board anywhere on your scale of hotness? Because it totally should be." Oops. That just slipped out.

For the briefest of seconds, his lips curve up in a grin. "Maybe," he grumbles before changing the topic. "Where's this taco place?"

"Coming up."

Maybe I'll make my own scale and just call that move *chili pepper hot.*

———

Lunch is fine. I barely taste the food. And Mark wears those shades the whole time, so I can't see his eyes. I don't know what he's thinking.

Not that it matters, I guess.

Then we're off to the florist, where we learn that they don't have the salmon blush roses Hannah requested, but they have *peach* blush roses instead.

Apparently this is a problem, because Mark's lips thin. "Could I see one, please?"

"Right away, sir." The young man behind the counter disappears into the back and returns a minute later with a . . . flower. *Christ.* I care about aesthetics, probably even more than most people. I like art, and I love photography. But flowers are *all* pretty, and a rose is a rose is a motherfucking rose.

Shakespeare was right.

Mark picks up that flower and inspects it like the future of humanity, and maybe even his precious inflation index, too, hangs in the balance. Then he sets it onto the scratched wooden counter and aims his phone at it.

"Whoa!" I say, holding up my hands to stop him. "Are you sending that to Hannah?"

"Of course," he clips.

"Well don't just plop it down there and expect her to approve. Allow me." I pick up the stem, where the thorns have already been carefully removed. And I hold it close to my face. "Take the picture now. She'll be able to see the scale and the hue this way."

"Good idea," he says, aiming the camera at me.

At the last second, I pull an underwear model face, a *come hither* look, tongue caught between my teeth. Like Jamie Dornan for Calvin Klein.

Click.

I expect him to roll his eyes. And maybe he attempts it.

But mostly he scowls. Hard. Then he swallows roughly.

It's fascinating.

Suddenly, it's me who doesn't know where to look. I can't look at Mark, because I don't want him to know how much this blows my mind.

Maybe the guest house *is* too small. At least we have separate bedrooms.

Mark's phone chimes with a text. "The peach will do," he says.

"Thank *goodness*," the florist says, clapping his hands together. "We're going to make everything beautiful, Mister Banks. You don't have to worry at all. We'll see you Saturday morning, right on time."

"Excellent," my companion snaps. "We're counting on it."

The florist looks a little terrified. So, after Mark turns to walk away, I linger there beside the counter for a moment. "Thanks for making Hannah and Flip's arrangements. I'm sure they're going to be amazing."

He beams. "You're welcome. It's our pleasure."

Now that he's smiling again, I follow the other best man out to the car.

He's waiting in the driver's seat, that sneaky fucker.

This time, I just hand over the keys.

PROVEN BONER KILLERS

MARK

*P*ools are proven boner killers.

Studies show that not only is shrinkage real, but that cold water is the number one source of it.

So in the scheme of things, a dip in the pool is a good idea this evening. Especially since Asher's not around right now.

I dive in and cut through the cool water, swimming to the shallow end, then turning around. Exercise always settles me, and after a full day vibrating at maximum do-not-ogle-your-travel-companion levels, I need a release. We've hit all the necessary errands: the florist, a visit to the valet company, and a chat with the manager of the string quartet. Plus, Asher called the DJ to set up a meeting for tomorrow.

I swim laps for thirty minutes as the sun slopes toward the other side of the sea. Once I feel like I can survive another day with the man who makes me hot, bothered, and thoroughly annoyed, I climb up the steps at the shallow end, head toward the iron table where I left my glasses, and put them back on.

When I turn around, I'm grateful for the scientists who proved the power of pool water since Asher has appeared, looking all sleep-tousled and sexy with his messy hair.

But it's not the hair that has me grabbing my towel and wrapping it around my waist, stat. It's his bare chest on display since he wears only shorts.

Do you even own a shirt, I want to ask. But that's just gonna unlock a conversation that'll crank me back up to sixty-nine on a scale of one-to-ten.

With a yawn that tells me he just got up from a nap, he flaps a hand in my direction. "You don't wear prescription goggles when you swim?"

"No. I don't."

"Can you still see?"

Weird question. "I can see well enough. Why? Were you doing a shadow puppet show that you thought I missed?" I sit at the table.

"No. But I'll add that to the evening entertainment schedule. I was just curious what your vision is," he says, flopping onto a lounge chair a few feet away, pinning me with his gaze once again. "I'm curious about a lot of things."

Dude. Join the club.

But I don't think we have the same curiosities, nor are we operating at the same levels. Asher St. James is at an all-star level in the bedroom, I suspect, and I'm trying to get a job as a bat boy.

"It's twenty eighty. And eighty is a number that's only good when it's your ROI."

"Or the number of goals a great striker racks up over two years," he quips.

"You had sixty-two goals in six years," I say, before I think the better of it. *Shit.* He's obviously going to know I'm into him now.

His eyebrows rise to the sky. "Impressive, Banks. Very impressive. I was a good striker. But not great." He sits up straighter. "You looked me up?"

Pretty sure all the crimson in Miami is visiting my face right now, but I've got to play this cool somehow. I shrug, adopt my best casual tone. "Yes, because that's the kind of guy I am. I do my homework, St. James. I like to know who I'm dealing with."

There. He won't think my interest is about him now. It's just how I am.

He chuckles, a playful glint in his eyes. "And so do I, Banks. So do I."

He goes quiet. That's rare for him, but he's busy studying me, like I'm the curiosity now, and his gaze unnerves me. So much for the unsexual swim.

Time to take this conversation to safer ground.

Something completely innocuous.

"And how was your nap, Sleeping Beauty?" I ask.

"Invigorating. You should try them sometimes." Of course he naps. Of course he enjoys them.

I shrug. "I don't nap."

"Not even on planes?" He lifts a brow in question.

Crap. "That's not really a true nap," I say evenly, since I'm not going to let him catch me on a technicality.

"Why does that not surprise me? Both that you don't nap, and that you have a definition of what constitutes a nap," he says.

But I'm done with this topic.

Adult sleeping habits.

Adult sleeping arrangements.

And adult desires.

Dancing around it is tricky, though. A part of me wants to tell him I'm bi. Just get it off my chest. But what's the point? Hell, even Brett from the office doesn't know yet. It just never came up. For the last seven years, I've lived, for all intents and purposes, as a straight-passing man. I haven't even touched a guy since college. Though I do remember those days of experimentation fondly.

Quite fondly.

"In the mood for some dinner?" Asher asks, shifting gears too.

I picture dinner out on the town, and I'm not sure I want to grab grub with him again.

That's not because it would look like a date. I don't care what strangers think of me. But because it might *feel* like one, him and

me out at night, sitting under an umbrella in this tropical destination with other couples around us, wearing skimpy clothes,
sipping cocktails, touching each other.

All that desire on display.

Then we'd leave together, walking through the doorway here
after dark. There'd be that awkward moment when we're in the
living room of the guest house together, about to go our separate ways.

The moment when we could smash into each other and
finally, fucking finally, touch.

My skin flashes hot at the thoughts flickering before my eyes.
I adjust the towel, making sure it's strategically placed. And I
muster my best casual voice. "Let's order in. What have you got
in mind?"

"How about Mexican?" he asks. "There's this place I know
with great tamales."

"Sounds great," I agree, and when I scan the scenery, it's
about as damn sexy as going out. The water glistens in the
fading sunlight. Soon, the sky will darken. Temptation is
hemming me in from every direction.

When Asher orders, I pick up my phone for a distraction. A
note from Valencia pops up on my screen.

Valencia: Excuse my manners from earlier! I also meant to ask
how's the hot best man?

I sneak a glance surreptitiously while the superhot best man
chats with the restaurant. This topic isn't entirely distracting,
but maybe I can just will away the desire by declaration.

Mark: Still smug, still hot, but I've got it under control.

Valencia: Then don't forget tonight! You know what premiers
on Webflix. I demand a recap after you watch.

Mark: Oh, right! I'm so there!!!

That's what I need. Some TV distraction.

Although I'm not sure this show will have the right effect on me. Valencia and I are a little obsessed with checking out the spin-off of *Archibald Lane*, a period piece that was all the rage on Webflix last year. The show was good, but there was one particular storyline I glommed onto, and it included a smoking-hot kiss that made it to the top of my spreadsheet. 1A.

The kiss continues, supposedly, in the spin-off.

I promise her a full review, then put my phone down.

When Asher hangs up, he meets my gaze. "Food will be here in thirty," he says, and is it just me, or do his eyes drift down my chest, lingering there, right there, on my pecs?

I want to do the same to him—to give him a long, lingering eye fuck. But doing that also terrifies me. I take risks with gobs of money every day. I have iron balls when the market is volatile. When it comes to men? My risk tolerance is at the level of a CD. Better yet, a savings account earning .01 percent.

"What did you order?" I ask, since that's the savings account question, and that's how I'm playing things tonight.

"Mexican. It's spicy. I didn't ask if you like spice. My bad," he says, cocking his head to the side like he's studying me once again. "Do you like spice?"

His words say one thing, but his tone says *do you like sex and would you like it with me?*

Or am I just hoping he's going fishing again? Maybe it's more than hope, especially since his hazel eyes glimmer with something that feels a lot like rabid curiosity.

"Yeah, I do," I tell him, and just like that, I'm vibrating with lust once again.

A feeling I already tried to get under control.

But it keeps slipping away from me.

Twenty-nine minutes later his phone buzzes. "Bet it's the restaurant," he remarks, but when he slides open the screen, a line digs into his forehead. "Shit," he murmurs.

I straighten my spine. "What's wrong?" Better not be something with the wedding.

"It's the DJ. Tomorrow's all booked up," he says. "He'll try to see us on Thursday."

I grimace. "That's too far away."

"I know, but we'll figure it out," he says, right as his phone beeps again, and he heads off to greet the delivery guy. Where he'll probably strike up a conversation, memorize the guy's children's names and tip fifty percent.

Pink streaks paint the sky when Asher returns a few minutes later with dinner, and a bottle of wine. I don't touch the wine, but the food is good.

And when we're done, the sky is dark. The moon is casting silver light across his face. I look at the time. Eight-forty. Perfect. I don't even have to tell him I'm cutting out early to watch a sexy-as-fuck TV show. I've got the kid excuse.

"I should go," I say, gesturing to the cottage.

"Do you have an inflation index to adjust?"

"Yes, St. James. I'm magic with inflation. I can make it disappear." Just like inconvenient boners. "I need to call Rosie. I promised I'd call her every night at eight forty-five," I tell him.

"See you in the morning."

I leave the pool and open the door to the guest house, a little relieved. I made it through the first day in Miami with the sexiest man I've ever known.

And he has no idea I'm thinking of him naked.

I'd call that a win.

I VOLUNTEER AS TRIBUTE

ASHER

*I*t's a dick move to give Mark a hard time for turning in early. I've been hoping to find a reason to head inside and watch my show. I have a reputation as a party boy to uphold. The Miami hotspots are just about to start their engines for the night. But I have a hot date with a nineteenth century bad boy poet and the lord who loves him.

So I watch the house as Mark moves around, pacing the tiny living room while he says good night to his little girl. Eventually, he disappears into his room. The living room goes dark. And then—like a child—I legit count to a hundred before finally getting up and carrying my wine glass inside the house.

But, seriously. I've been waiting for *An Arranged Marriage* for months now. I must witness the hotness between Lord Oliver and Sir Trevor when they're allowed more than one kiss. The trailer was full of meaningful glances and doors swinging shut at just the wrong, torturous moment. I'm so there.

At 8:59, I'm sitting on the bed in my room, clicker in hand, streaming my laptop onto the bedroom TV. The show kicks off with a carriage ride through London, a conniving duchess and the death of the lord's uncle, all in the first seven minutes. And by the time Ollie and Trevor plan a secret rendezvous on a London rooftop, my tongue is practically hanging out.

Gah! Their plan is foiled at the last minute when the duchess detains Oliver on false pretenses! And poor Trevor is left, candle in hand, gazing at the gently lit rooftops of a CGI'd London, feeling certain that he's been stood up.

Trevor, my man. I'm sorry. I know how this feels.

On a goddamn rooftop too. It's like they know me.

Laughing to myself, I hit pause on the show. Can't wait to find out how the drama unfolds in the final twenty minutes. But the sparkling water and the rosé I drank at dinner means I have to pee. I head into the john to take care of business, walking past the screen door, and the gentle sound of the bay lapping against the island. I love the way Florida smells—like salty air and palm trees. If I didn't love New York so much I'd consider living here, among the modeling agencies and the excellent nightlife.

In the minus column, there are hurricanes and alligators. But hey, nobody is perfect.

When I turn the sink off after I wash my hands, a swell of music comes through the wall, or maybe the open window. Mark is watching TV too.

But hang on. That's a *familiar* swell of music.

And it's followed by the *clip-clop* of horse hooves, like the sound they make on ye olde London's cobblestone streets.

Hold the phone. Could Mark be watching *An Arranged Marriage*?

My stomach shimmies with amusement. This is rich. I wonder if he knows what this show is about?

Mark is a very smart man. He's much smarter than I am. So the odds that he doesn't know what he's getting into are small.

Which means something big, big, *big*.

Mark is either a fun-loving, super open-minded Wall Streeter from Ohio with a thing for sexy period drama, no matter the storyline. Or, he, like every queer man I know—the fun ones, anyway—cannot *wait* for Lord Ollie and Sir Trevor to bone down.

Standing in my bathroom like a dingus, my ears strain to hear what's on Mark's screen. But now, everything is quiet.

Whoa. Was the whole thing my imagination? It's entirely possible. Let's face it—I have a thing for him. An attraction. A curiosity. I'm a little stuck on this man. I don't know how it happened either. He's certainly never encouraged me. But the more I get to know him, the more attractive he becomes.

A *banker*. Or a trader—whatever he calls it. And with a kid. Fuck me.

But now I have to know.

In stealth mode, I leave my room and step into the living room. But I hear nothing out here. So I slip out the front door and circle the guest house. Mark's room has a sliding glass door, just like mine. It's pathetically easy to position myself in a way where I can see his laptop screen.

And there's Lord Oliver, frantically penning a message to Sir Trevor, who's about to set off on a journey to the colonies.

There, also, is my hot banker, lying against the pillows with his knee cocked, and an arm propped up over his head. He's wearing basketball shorts and a thin T-shirt that hugs his frame . . .

The screen freezes, and the sound cuts off.

I stop breathing.

A long moment glugs by with only the beating of my heart as the soundtrack.

"Well?" Mark asks drily. He doesn't even turn his head. "Are you just going to stand there like a creeper? How worried should I be right now?"

"S-sorry," I sputter. "It's not what it looks like."

"Really?" He tosses the clicker onto the quilt as he finally turns to me. "So you're *not* watching me from outside the door? I've seen horror movies with scenes just like this."

My face is on fire. But if I slink away now, it will only get weirder. So I square my shoulders and take a step closer to the door. "Can I come in?"

"I'm guessing I can't stop you, so . . . sure?"

I slide the screen door open and step inside. He doesn't move from the bed, though. He just watches me with amused blue eyes. There's something sturdy about his character that I find refreshing. He's unflappable.

And I dig it.

"Look," I try. "I just heard your show through my open door. So I stepped outside to see if we were watching the same thing. I'd been working on a theory about you, and this seemed like a harmless way to investigate. I wondered if you were a fan of Lord Oliver."

He actually rolls his eyes. "Is that the secret pass phrase? *Hey man, are you a friend of Lord Oliver's?*"

Our gazes lock. His gives away nothing. My crush is seriously formidable. Not for the first time, I wonder if he plays poker.

He should.

I run a hand through my hair—then stop. That's always been my tell. "Look. It's none of my business. I just thought you'd want to know this show is about to get gayer than a kick line in a pride parade."

"Thank you."

That's it. He doesn't even blink.

For once in my life, I don't know what to do or say. I've literally got nothing. "Right." I gulp. "Thanks for sharing."

Mark snorts. And something in his expression slips. "Is that a requirement? That I spill my guts to you?"

"No," I say quickly. He's right. Of course he is. I cannot figure out how to stop being a dick where Mark is concerned. "Never mind. Sharing is, well, not easy for some people."

Then he snarls at me. Actually snarls as he sits bolt upright in bed, staring hard at me. "You don't *know* me, asshole. You think I'm just an uptight banker. I could be anyone. I could be a guy who has always known he was bi, and couldn't wait to take that out for a test drive. But then he got his ungrateful college girlfriend pregnant and is now an overworked single dad who knows everything there is to know about *Peppa Pig* but who has been off the market so long he has no idea when he'll ever relieve some of this unbearable tension since he doesn't know how to find some willing, non-creepy single dude with good hygiene to sixty-nine."

Holy wow.

I'm still trying to take that in when Mark swings his legs off the bed and stands up. Suddenly, we're eye to eye. His are angry. "We don't all have a big, loud life on four continents. But here you are, interrupting my show! For what? To say *Aha! I knew it?* That's just rude. My entire sex life for the past year has basically been replaying the Troliver kiss over and over while I got myself off. So, thanks for busting in here to satisfy your own curiosity."

"Jesus." His blue eyes are on fire. "Sorry. But . . ." The image of Mark stroking himself has lodged right in the center of my brain, making it hard for me to finish sentences. So I manage to say exactly the wrong thing. I raise my hand into the air and pull a total Katniss. "I volunteer as tribute."

Mark blinks. "What? You're teasing me right now? *This* is when you decide to do that again?"

"No. No, no, nope." I shake my head. "I tease you a lot. I know. But this time, I'm serious. We could, uh, have a little vacation fun. Totally harmless fun." I'm practically babbling right now.

And I don't babble. The last time I was this flustered was five years ago when a bull ran onto the field mid-match during a game against Barcelona. For the long moments between the bull's invasion and the ref's whistle, I couldn't decide whether to run down the ball or cover my balls.

This is almost exactly the same situation. I can't figure out if I should dive to safety through the screen door, or start stripping off my clothing like a go-go dancer who's late for his shift.

I prefer the second option.

THIS COULD BE THE BIG ONE

MARK

I cannot believe the words coming out of this man's mouth.

"There's no such thing as totally harmless fun," I say, sounding just as uptight as the duchess from the show. But I don't do well with surprises.

And Asher St. James propositioning me definitely falls into the *surprise* column. He can't actually be serious. Nothing he does is serious.

So I soldier on. "That's a terrible idea, anyway. We're here to throw a wedding for Hannah and Flip. And also?" I have to address the annoying bleat coming from the other room while we've been arguing. "Your phone is ringing."

"What?" He's gazing dreamily at me with those beautiful hazel eyes. Maybe he's drunk. That would explain a lot.

It makes no sense for Asher to proposition me. He probably gets more sex than the entire Brooklyn Bruisers team after a playoffs win. He doesn't want me.

I don't need that kind of pressure, honestly. While I'm looking forward to someday exploring the dude side of my bisexuality, it hasn't happened yet. Except for some making out in college . . .

The damn phone squeals again. "Your phone," I repeat, crossing my arms like the uptight fuck he thinks I am. "It keeps ringing."

"Oh," he says, giving his head a shake. "So I should go answer that."

I don't bother agreeing with him. I just wait.

"You should play poker," he blurts out.

What?

I don't get a chance to ask what that means, because Asher seems to shake himself out of a reverie. "Right. Phone. Later." He leaves through the screen door, sliding it shut behind him.

And now, it's silent again. My laptop screen is still frozen with Lord Oliver's hand clutching the quill. I should press play and pretend like none of this ever happened.

As if I did not make a speech that somehow mentioned *Peppa Pig* and sixty-nine in the same breath.

As if Asher did not offer me a pity fuck.

And as if I sure as hell didn't *turn him down*.

Seriously. That did not just happen.

I throw myself on the bed, push my face into the pillow, and groan so quietly that there's no chance in hell he can hear me. And I lie there for several minutes, trying to think calm thoughts, with zero success. Example: I'm still losing that chess game to Brett.

Losing is a theme this week.

The only thing I did right today was make Rosie laugh at bedtime.

There's a knock on the bedroom door—the interior one that non-creepers would use.

"What?" I mutter from the pillow.

The door opens. "Um, sorry. Trust me, I really, *really* didn't want to knock on your door right now. But we have a situation."

I roll over. "What kind of situation?" I'm already imagining the worst. "Is Hannah okay? Is Flip?"

"No. It's not *that* kind of situation. But our DJ just bailed."

"What?" I sit up fast. "Why? I'll kill him."

Asher hands me his phone, where there's a voicemail. And I tap the play button.

"Dude," says a stranger's voice. "Look, I was on for playing that wedding on Saturday. That address looks *righteous*. But my buddy just called. He found some sunken treasure off Bimini, and we gotta fly, man. You only get one shot at treasure. This could be the big one, ya know? I gotta go and meet my fate. You be well, yeah?"

Click.

"Fuck!" I shout. "He had four point nine stars on Yelp!"

"I know," Asher says, rubbing the back of his neck. "It's a blow."

I grab my phone off the bedside table. "Let's start googling. Which half of the alphabet do you want?"

"Actually, I have a better idea. There are a couple of clubs where I know people in town. I'll drive us to one of them and we'll see if we can't hire the DJ for Saturday—or else hire one of his friends."

I can't think of a better solution. And Asher seems to have a plan as he rattles off details about DJ Drake.

"Okay. Let's go. But I'll drive."

"Fine. I'm going to change. Meet me out front in ten?"

"I'll be there."

———

Miami twinkles magnificently as we cross the causeway again in the dark. Warm, salty air blows past my face. But I am not relaxed.

It's still sinking in that I just turned down sex with Asher St. James. But that was so far outside my comfort zone. I've been with one person for *seven* years. I don't even remember how first kisses work. There's no way I could pretend to be cavalier about his offer. I'd probably go in for the kiss and break his often-photographed nose or something.

Where is my sex spreadsheet when I need it? But I know for

certain that none of the items on my sexual to-do list read: *Make fool of self while naked with a professional athlete and underwear model.*

Strangely, Asher is quiet in the passenger seat. He doesn't seem drunk at all, though. I might have been wrong about that.

So, what the hell was he thinking? And why did I shut down the conversation before I got to hear more?

Because he was flip about it, I guess. And because I was angry that he'd extracted a truth about myself that I'd chosen to protect.

Not that it's a state secret. My family knows, and they don't care. My ex has always known. I've been out to her from the start. Valencia is aware too. But that's the whole list.

Now that I'm single again, it's more relevant. But divorce is humiliating. I haven't discussed my sexuality with other people in my life, because I'm a little sensitive about people's speculations about my marriage. Sometimes a guy needs some time to sort himself out in private.

And everything with Asher St. James is very exposed.

Including my attraction to him.

Waze tells me to turn left, and that my destination will be in one hundred feet.

I do as told, and pull into the parking lot, then check out the colors on the sign. Another thing that's very, very exposed?

The clientele at this club. There are all manner of toned, tanned hot guys in twos and threes outside. They're smoking, laughing.

Kissing. Letting loose.

Suddenly, I'm aching to go inside, and that desire has nothing to do with finding a new DJ.

I want to let loose for once in my damn life.

I want to get out of my head.

No—*I need to.*

14

I DON'T WANT TO DO THE CONGA

ASHER

*W*ell, ouch. Mark's rejection stings.

But I know how it is. Rejection is part of life. Rejection is an opportunity for growth. Rejection is merely God's way of saying: *That was the wrong attack on the ball, you dingus.*

Fine. I'll find another opening, and I'll redirect.

But first, we're going to hire a DJ and save this wedding.

In the parking lot, I slam the passenger door with a resounding thud, the music from the club seeping out before we even reach the entrance.

As we walk toward Edge neither one of us says a word, just like on the drive over.

I'm still trying to untangle the math problem of Mark Banks, so I can give him what he needs. So I can solve his equation.

Possibly with my tongue.

But I'm getting ahead of myself as the music grows louder, the electronic beat pulsing in the humid air. The neon sign above the entryway greets us, blinking bright in the South Beach night, and crystal clear. The name of the club flashes on and off, each letter cascading through red, orange, green, blue, and so on.

Above the door, a rainbow flag with a triangle on the side billows in the breeze.

"So, you do know this is a gay club?" I ask.

Mark turns his head to me. "It is?" His delivery is so perfectly deadpan, it could go in the dictionary as a usage example.

"Just making sure you were aware," I reply. He gives me a searing look, and it turns off my snark spigot.

Mark is the only man I know who can make me half-speechless.

"The neon rainbow signboard was kind of a clue," he says, then grabs the door. "And since you just established I'm a friend of Lord Oliver, I think you know now I'm all good with that."

But not with me?

Patience, I coach myself. It will happen in good time. *And why the hell not?*

The doors swing open, and a couple of guys spill out onto the sidewalk. A Latino guy in tight white shorts has his arm wrapped around a toned Black dude in a crop top. Behind them stream more men in barely-there clothes, and I'm suddenly overdressed in my shorts and button-down shirt, but at least my clothes are relatively tight, and show off my arms. Mark sticks out like, well, like a straight guy in khaki shorts and another one of those god-awful polos.

I bet those red briefs I caught a glimpse of in the dressing room were a fluke. It probably was laundry day, and those were from his . . . I dunno . . . Halloween costume drawer.

Bet he has on navy-blue boxer briefs.

Bet I don't care, I don't care, I don't care.

Except, I'm dying to know.

Mark follows me through the door and into the club as we make our way along a dark hallway to a ticket counter. Dance music pounds, and a host with a white feather boa around his neck and silver skyscraper boots on his feet flashes a smile. "Hey there, hotties. There's a twenty-dollar cover charge tonight," he says to me.

"We just need to see DJ Drake about an event," Mark says, coming up right by my side, and taking over.

Okay. That's how he's doing this.

But really, we should pay the fee even for a quick meeting.

The man with the boa gives Mark an *aren't-you-cute-you-preppy-straight-guy* smile. "It's still twenty dollars to get past me, hottie," he says sweetly, but firmly.

I grab my wallet, and reach for my card. But before it's even open, Mark slaps two twenties on the counter and says thanks.

"Drake is on his break for ten, so he's in the green room." The host points polished silver fingers behind him. "Go that way, then past the main dance floor, and turn down the hallway, and it's at the end."

With a crisp nod, Mark's off, stalking down the corridor. Like he can't wait to get this over with.

"You didn't have to pay for me," I say as the music grows louder and we turn into the main dance area.

I expect an eye roll. A zinger. Instead, his gaze lands square on me. "I know."

And he leaves it at that. Just an *I know*. Like he's fucking Han Solo.

And it's just like when Harrison Ford said it to Carrie Fisher. It was ultra-hot then, and it's ultra-hot now as I follow Mark Banks into a gay dance club in South Beach.

My world is officially topsy turvy. I've been to this club before. I've even partied with Drake. But I'm not in charge this time, it seems, as Mark Banks leads me through throngs of men, weaving past bodies, and muscles, the smell of sweat and cologne and the promise of sex potent under the dark purple lights of the dance floor.

We reach the green room and find Drake slouched on a leather couch, flicking aimlessly on his phone. A sleeve of tattoos covers his right arm, a dragon tail intertwined through the mouth of a skull.

The second his gray eyes land on mine, he pops up from the couch. "St. James! How's it hanging? How the fuck are you? When are you going to Ibiza again to party with me and my man?"

I give him a quick hug. "The answers are to the left, great, and not soon enough. How's Axel?"

"The best," he says, with a dopey grin befitting the newlywed. Then Drake slides his gaze to my confusing companion. "I'm Drake."

He extends a hand to Mark, and they shake.

"Mark. Brother of the bride." He's all business.

"Tell me what you need, Mark," Drake says, catching on fast.

"We need you on Saturday at noon. Daytime wedding. No Macarena. No chicken dance. No 'Hello' from Adele, since it's not a love song. Nor is 'Stay With Me' by Sam Smith, no matter how much the ladies love him. Or the dudes. I don't want to hear the conga, or do the conga. Also, no Coldplay whatsoever."

Before I can even say *who would play Coldplay at a wedding*, Mark adds, "Brett's DJ played it at his wedding at Tavern on the Green and it killed the mood."

No, Mark. Tavern on the Green killed the mood.

But I don't correct him, because he continues his wedding song diatribe that's inexplicably turning me on. "'You Send Me' by Sam Cooke for the couple's first dance. So, if you can do all that and show up an hour early, and stay till six, I'll pay your regular rate, plus a twenty-five percent premium if you agree now."

Drake blinks, dollar signs in his eyes. "Someone knows what he wants."

You're telling me.

"Will that work for you?" Mark asks, and he is not a three-martini lunch guy. He doesn't schmooze. He just fucking throws down. And it's getting me hot under the collar.

Or hotter.

"Yes," my DJ friend says. "Anything for a friend of St. James."

Mark and Drake finish the details, exchange numbers, and then I say goodbye, telling him to send my love to Axel. We head back down the hallway, the music thumping louder with each step.

Bodies come into view on the dance floor. Hips swiveling. Arms tangled, legs intertwined, and pelvises grinding. My eyes

LAUREN BLAKELY & SARINA BOWEN

gobble it up, the press of skin, the lips colliding, the preludes to fucking.

But I'm not the only one staring. From the looks of it, my companion is drinking it all in too.

When we reach the dance floor, since we have to cross it to leave, he stops, grabs my arm, and tips his chin toward the bar.

"Drink?" If he doesn't want to leave yet, I am here for it. I'm here for a lot of things.

Mark nods.

Yeah, baby. "Hey, Banks? Who's the driver?"

"I was going to order a soda," he yells over the throbbing music. *"I wouldn't drink and drive."*

"Yeah, I know. But how about *I* order a soda and you order whatever you want. A soda. A Shirley Temple . . ." His eyes narrow, so I rush on. "A shot of Jack. A kilo of heroin." I wink. "If you feel like letting loose, I'll drive home. Your call."

Something shifts behind his eyes when I say *letting loose.* His expression is still intense. And determined. I'm lost in that hungry blue gaze when he abruptly turns away, slicing through the crowd toward the bar.

Mark edges his way past guys in leather, guys in dresses, guys in nearly nothing, and he's totally unfazed. Maybe he's even, dare I say, in his element?

I hurry to keep up.

When I reach his side, Mark has already captured the bartender's attention with his Jedi skills. The man behind the bar puts one LaCroix on the bar. And? A shot glass of tequila.

Then? Mark hands *me* the soda.

It's so on.

And when he tips the shot glass back and downs the liquor, I see it. The heat in his eyes, followed by that hitch in his breath. I can't hear it over the music. But this time, since we're inches away, I can *feel* it. His breath ghosting near my neck. The low hiss of a murmur. And, I let myself feel it, too, in my body as I fully enjoy the possibility of him.

Oh yes, I want you, Mark Banks.

Because it's not math, and it's not logic.

And I am not a math person. I'm all about instinct. Instinct on the field from my playing days, and instinct behind the lens now as a photographer.

I don't operate according to lists or numbers, columns or rows.

I go with my gut.

And my gut, which has a direct connection to my favorite body part, knows that Mark Banks wants what I offered.

Desperately.

There's no mistaking his interest.

So there's a *reason* he said no.

And my gut has the answer.

Actually, my cock has figured this one out. My interest in being the car Mark takes out for a test drive simply wasn't clear enough for the hot nerd who lives in his head.

The guy doesn't know how to listen to his body.

So I'll show him with mine.

15

DIRTY DANCING IS NOW ON THE LIST

MARK

*T*he tequila burns going down.

But it also burns off more of the noise in my head. The did-he-mean-it-didn't-he-mean-it seesaw my mind has been riding for the last hour.

Or maybe this place has worked its dark and dirty magic. So many of my own fantasies are unfolding in front of me. Other men living out loud, putting their desires on the line with each other.

I haven't made space in my life for the things I crave. But maybe I can have some of those things. Just for tonight.

But I *might* need one more drink to get there.

Like he can read my mind, Asher mouths *want another?* the second I set down the glass.

"Yes," I say.

"I'll get this one," he says, then turns to the bartender, motions for a second shot with his left hand, and sets his right hand on my back.

Oh, fuck.

In a hot second, I go up in flames.

We're facing the bar, and his hand slides across my lower back, and there is no way *that* should feel like the promise of dirty things to come.

But it does. Oh yes, it does.

Sparks fly everywhere. Along my skin. Under my skin. Ten thousand fires start in my goddamn cells.

He doesn't take his palm off me either. He travels his fingers across the fabric of my shirt, and I can't move.

My body lights up from this simple touch. He says nothing, doesn't even meet my gaze, and I'm grateful for that.

I just need to exist in the thrill of this contact a few seconds longer. I swallow roughly, let out a low and smoky sigh. I doubt he can hear me, but that doesn't seem to matter. He knows what he's doing to me.

I stare at the liquor bottles behind the bar, but I can barely see anything, and it's not because of my twenty-eighty vision. My world is simply narrowing to his hand exploring my back. Asher slides his palm around me, traveling to my hip, covering it with his hand, sending another jolt of pleasure through me as the shot arrives.

"Here you go," says the bartender.

Yeah, here he goes, all right.

I don't even grab the glass yet. I just stay like this, since it's the best I've felt in ages. Curling his hand tighter, Asher grips my hip, hard and possessively. I groan under my breath. My God, how will I withstand reenacting a single Troliver kiss when a simple touch already turns me on this much?

Somehow, I manage to reach for the tequila and knock it back, then put the glass on the counter right as Asher circles the pad of his thumb over my hip bone.

"Oh hell," I mutter, dipping my face for a few seconds, then meeting his gaze.

He licks the corner of his mouth, stares wickedly at me, then parts his lips like he's about to say something.

Before he can speak, I jump off the cliff. "Dance with me."

His grin is filthy and makes my cock throb. "I thought you'd never ask," he says, and with his words, the last remaining smidge of nerves turns to ash.

I step toward the dance floor first, and he's right behind me, his hand on my back again, and it's borderline possessive, like he's signaling to everyone else that I'm here with him.

We weave past patrons—they're bumping and grinding, kissing and shaking—and find a spot near the edge of the dance floor.

In a heartbeat, he moves closer to me, his body swaying to the slow and sexy beat of the music. He looks good on the dance floor.

I'm not a dancer, but I don't think I need to be. This isn't a team sport. It's one-on-one, and I can do that. I mirror him, my hips swaying, shoulders grooving.

Asher stares at me, mesmerized.

There are only inches between us, and that seems like too much. I edge closer, my thigh brushing against his.

"*Yes*," he murmurs, but I can't hear his words. I can just make out the shape of my new favorite one on his lips as we dance, slow and sensual.

His hands are back where he seems to like them—on my hips —and it's probably a prelude to how he wants me, and that's fine by me.

Everything is just so fucking fine right now.

I don't touch him yet. I'm still not quite sure what to do with my hands, but I'll figure it out soon.

As our thighs touch, our knees graze too, and we're danger-ously close. But not quite close enough. I want to erase that last bit of distance.

I take chances every day at work. Iron balls and all.

I lift my hands, and finally put them where I want.

On him.

Then he's the one looking blissed out as his eyes float closed. I take that as my cue to explore him more. My hands coast down his arms, traveling over his smooth skin, hot from the club, covered with the faintest sheen of sweat.

I like his sweat.

I want more of it.

I get closer, my right thigh wedging between his legs as my hands travel up and down those strong arms. His eyes open and he stares like he can't get enough of me.

Of the way I'm touching him.

It's illogical to think I'm any good at this.

But logic has left the club.

I don't need to be rational right now.

I can be ... impulsive.

And Impulsive Mark listens to Captain Filthy Mind, who says to just grind against the superhot wingman.

Here I go.

As I press my crotch against his, we dance in a whole new way.

And it is insane.

We become all these other guys in the club, and I'm finally having what I want.

This wasn't even on my spreadsheet. I never put dirty dancing on my list.

But already, this is the sexiest thing I've ever done in my life, as our hard cocks rub together through our clothes.

It's mind-bending.

It's circuit-frying.

It's so fucking good, I hardly know what to do next.

I just don't want to stop.

So I don't.

I dance unabashedly, shamelessly, with a man in a club in Miami.

For the next few songs, our bodies collide, hands, limbs, arms, legs. But soon, it's not enough at all.

I have to have more. I rope my hands around his neck, then bring my mouth to his ear, my jaw brushing along his as I go, electrifying me. He hauls my crotch closer to his, letting me know that whatever I'm going to say he's already given me his yes.

But he speaks first. "Mark," he says, loud enough for me to hear. He hardly ever just calls me Mark.

I pull back. "Yeah?"

"I wasn't teasing you in your bedroom. Not one bit. I was dead serious. Still am."

I needed that. "Good. I'd like to change my answer then."

Then I show him my yes.

I smash my lips to his, and my world ignites.

Colors burst, my brain goes haywire, and my entire body thanks me for giving in at last. He tastes incredible, and I feel amazing.

Every. Fucking. Where.

It's like my world has turned inside out as I kiss Asher St. James on a hot, sweaty dance floor in South Beach, music thrumming though my bones, pleasure humming in my cells.

And the best part of all this is that I know he wants this too. That I'm not fucking up too badly. The way his hands roam up my arms, strong and confident, says he wants what I have to give. The way he kisses me back, fevered and hungry, drives me on.

So do his hands that travel to my ass, curling over my cheeks as he jerks me against him. All my nerve endings fire at once in a loud *snap-snap, pop-pop* in my head. There is just too much happening in my body at once. It's a complete overload of the senses as we kiss harder, more desperately, our cocks pressing against each other.

I can't get enough of his mouth. His body. And I need so much more. The kiss grows more urgent, hotter, hungrier as our tongues skate together.

Nothing about the way he kisses me says there is a single thing wrong with my lack of experience.

Everything about his touch says he wants to experience more of me.

As he deepens the kiss, my hands rope through his shampoo model hair that I want to tug and yank, then let go of while I travel down his body.

And just like that, I'm ready.

I wrench apart, panting, horny, and dead set on the next thing on my list.

2A.

"Let's get out of here."

We leave in seconds flat.

16

ARE MY LIPS STILL STUPID?

ASHER

*Y*ou know that saying: *It's always the quiet ones?* Yeah, that. To my utter delight, Mister Spreadsheets is the best kind of sex fiend.

The eager kind. All that heat in the club, the way we rushed through the door, how we stumbled into my bedroom, kicked off our shoes, we are both raring to go.

At the edge of the bed, I jerk him against me, intent on dropping my mouth to his in a slow, languid kiss since I plan to show him just how fantastic my teasing can truly be.

From kissing to everything else.

But I stop, because I've wanted to do *this* for a long time. I reach for his glasses, gently remove them, set them on the nightstand.

Wow.

Mark without glasses is sexy in a whole new way. Those eyes shimmer with lust, and a touch of vulnerability.

Wait. No. *Nerves.*

But I know how to ease those, so I grab at the collar of his awful polo. "Of all the colors in the world, you chose gray? I hate this shirt," I say, with a grin, returning to our favorite way to communicate.

"Those are pretty intense feelings for a shirt, St. James," he fires back at me.

I have a lot of intense feelings right now. Most of them involve getting him naked. "But I bet I don't hate the way you look *out* of it. I liked what I saw tonight."

"At the club or at the pool?"

"Both, Banks. Both."

His grin is stupidly adorable. "Just take it off."

Tugging at the waistband, my fingers travel under the fabric. Mark shivers.

I roam my hands along the grooves of his abs, savoring his reaction, his shudders.

I jerk it off him, up and over, and *yes*.

My breath comes fast as I stare at him again, admiring the smooth skin, the cut of his lean muscles. Sliding my hands along the expanse of his pecs, my skin heats.

"So much better," I mutter.

He lets out a low groan and then just trembles all over from my hands on his chest. It's heady, this power, knowing I can arouse him in every way I want.

I travel back down his body. When I reach that happy trail that makes me very happy indeed, I slide my thumb along the dark hair. His hands shoot out and curl around my hips as he mutters, "*Fuuuck.*"

As he grips me tighter, I dip my face to his neck, licking a line along a pulsing vein. His chest rises and falls as another harsh breath falls from his lips.

I'm going to make him lose his mind, and he wants this delicious torture. I drag his earlobe between my lips, sucking on it, then nipping him.

"Ohhhh," he mutters, like nothing has ever felt better.

Mark Banks is a ticking bomb about to explode. I let go to see what's in his eyes. To read him.

But Mark is rocket fast as he grabs my face, hauls me closer, and kisses me deeply.

His moan is dark and dirty, like he's going to die of desire. That noise makes my dick even harder. But it also raises an important question.

One I simply have to ask.

I break the kiss.

"Are my lips still stupid?" I ask.

"Shut up." He goes to kiss me again, but I weave out of the way.

"Are they?"

"Yes, they're still stupid." He takes a beat. "Stupid hot."

"Good answer." I coast my hands down his chest, unbutton his terrible khaki shorts. "By the way, I can't stand these either."

"Just take them off. Just take everything off. Maybe you won't hate me so much."

"Maybe I won't," I say, but I definitely don't hate him.

He's growing on me. A lot.

I take him up on his offer, stripping him . . . and *shut the front door*.

Orange.

Tight.

Briefs.

Am I hallucinating? Or is this my lucky week? I have such a thing for a hot pair of underwear. "I had this nightmare you were going to have on navy-blue boring boxer briefs," I confess as I gawk at the sight of my banker nearly revealed. Yeah, I have no more questions about Mark Banks. Everything is clear.

"I'm full of surprises," he says.

I'll say. "And this is my favorite kind." I cover his bulge, and we both groan at the same time. "But, as much as I like these . . . I need them off."

I reach for the waistband, but he's faster. In the blink of an eye, Mark shoves down his briefs.

I heat up everywhere.

"Oh, fuck me," I groan as his cock springs free.

That preview I got in the dressing room had nothing on the real thing. He's long, thick, hard, and already leaking at the tip.

I wrap a hand around his shaft, and lust charges down my spine.

"Oh God," he rasps, and then his hands are everywhere. They're all over me. Traveling up and down my chest, and grabbing at my waist like he has to hold on or he'll fall apart.

I suspect something else about Mark too. I've done the math on how young Mark was when he got married. Twenty-one.

Which means . . .

As I fondle his cock, I ask a direct question. "Have you ever been with a guy before?"

He shrugs. "Barely. And when I did I wasn't even old enough to drink," he says, on a breathless shudder.

Holy hell. This is not just a treat. It's a *privilege*. I'm not merely his idle curiosity. I'm his first time with a man?

Now there are two of us trembling with eagerness. I want to say something witty and clever, but I've got nothing except the truth. "I'll make it good for you," I whisper.

His lips curve into a cocky grin. "You know what would be good for me? If you shut up and got undressed too."

I laugh, then we're both working fast to get my clothes off, and when I'm wearing nothing, too, I slam my body to his, our cocks rubbing together as I take over the kiss again.

Mark tugs me back to the bed, falling down onto the mattress, making sure we don't separate. His hands race along my back, my arms, down to my ass. Like he's determined to explore every inch of me.

I climb over him, pinning him down. Staring at him. "So maybe you did want me," I tease, keeping up the mood, since it seems to unlock him.

"You know I did." He grunts.

He is just a man on edge. I let go of his wrists and the second I do, he sits up, reaches for my cock, and wraps a hand around me. Pleasure skids down my spine. But the way I feel right now is nothing to the way he looks. His eyes heat as he strokes me, brings a thumb over the head of my cock, wiping off a drop of liquid arousal.

"Taste me already. You know you want to," I urge him on.

With just a breathy nod, he brings his thumb to his mouth, sucks off the taste of me. "Mmm. *Yes.*"

Have I ever seen anything sexier than Mark Banks right now?

The answer is no. Those gorgeous eyes roll back into his head, and he unleashes a hungry groan.

When his thumb slips from his mouth, his gaze locks on mine.

I lean over him, plant a soft kiss on those lips, then pull back. My instincts haven't led me astray so far with Mark, so I toss out a question. "What do you want to do to me?"

I'm pretty sure he wants to touch *me* right now, more than he wants to *be* touched.

"I've got a long list," he says, and it's like the admission frees him.

Maybe it frees me a little bit too. My plan to tease with exquisite sexual torture falls to the wayside entirely. I give the man what he wants.

Me.

I fall down on my back, park my hands behind my head. "Then do whatever you want to me. And start at the top of that list."

17

THE FULL PROOF

MARK

*T*hat's going to take a long time.

The man has no idea. Seven or eight years of pent-up curiosity is nothing to sneeze at.

I straddle Asher and dip my face to kiss his neck. Inhale that rainwater and summer breeze scent that's now mixed with a little sweat from the dance club. My God, he's so much better than my fantasies.

I can't believe I'm actually indulging in them right here, right now, mere hours after I ached to do this to him in the car.

Where do I even go next? I just want my mouth all over him. *Everywhere.*

I roam my lips down his neck, along his throat, across his chest. Tingles slide down my spine as I go lower, closer to that washboard I have definitely dreamed of.

His moans and sighs urge me on.

As I flick my tongue along the ladder of his abs he writhes under me, letting loose a sexy *yes.*

That makes me smile. But even as he breathes out hard, I still have to know if I'm doing this the way he wants.

I lift my face, swallow past the nerves, then ask, "Just tell me if you want something different, okay?"

Asher's eyes are hazy already. "Just keep doing that," he rasps out.

I take the man at his word.

And since he's been so bluntly honest with me tonight, I ought to do the same. "I've never done anything more than kiss."

His smile lights up my world. "But you want to?"

"So much," I say.

"Good. Then don't stop," he says, then smirks before he finishes with, "*Please* don't stop."

Damn him. He's making this so easy for me. He's making me feel so good about telling him my secret wishes.

I return to my mission, traveling down his chest, kissing and licking, flicking my tongue along his annoyingly perfect abs. I half can't believe I'm actually doing this. But I'm also keenly aware that I don't want to fuck this up as I come face-to-face with both my greatest fear and my greatest fantasy.

I want to drive him wild, but I don't know if I can. Only, it's not in my nature to shoot for second best.

Just go for it, Banks.

I slide down between his legs, and I lick the crown of his cock, tasting a man for the first time in my life.

Oh, yes. This is better than first class. Hotter than a sexy red sports car.

Asher lets out a growl.

I take that as a *keep going.*

I draw him in deeper, and he tastes so good. Salty and musky, and like a validation—*yes, you always knew you liked dudes. Now you are just getting the full proof.*

And I want the full proof.

I try to relax my throat, and take more of him.

But . . . that's a lot.

I gag slightly, then let go.

"You don't have to take it all," he says, his hand wrapping gently around the back of my head. "Trust me. It feels so fucking good, what you're doing."

I just nod since I don't want to talk anymore.

I want *to do*. I want to know his body and know myself too. To understand if everything I fantasized about for the last several months is as good as I think it is.

I return to his cock, and go again, drawing him deep, as much as I can.

His hips jerk. His breath shudders. I relax my throat, and then I just . . . suck. And I focus on him.

His sounds.

His noises.

The curses and grunts.

I don't try to lick long stripes up his shaft, or work him over with some wild new technique I researched online.

I just give it my all.

I slide my hands along his thighs, and do what *I'd like*, what *I'd want*.

He curls his fingers through my hair. "That's so good, Banks. So fucking good," he murmurs. Then he bucks his hips, like he can't hold still.

Holy shit.

I'm making a naked Asher St. James lose his cool in the bedroom.

Another hand comes down and he holds me tightly, and this is not easy. I am definitely going to need a lot of practice. But I will sign up for all the classes, please and thank you.

I would like to master sucking a cock, because already, I'm an eager student at my novice level. And he seems a very willing teacher as he murmurs words of encouragement, like . . .

Yes.

More, yes, fucking more.

Don't stop.

I don't plan to.

18

THE BLOW JOB DEPARTMENT

ASHER

*T*here is zero finesse in the Mark Banks blow job department and I don't care. He's sucking with absolute enthusiasm, like he wants to blow my mind.

And it's working. Electricity crackles in my body, lust sizzling up and down my spine.

With my fingers roped tight in his hair, I want to fuck his mouth, but I'll save that for another time.

If there's another time.

I've no idea where this is going except to my favorite place right now.

With his lush lips stretched around my shaft, he sucks me like he's all in. I'm going to give him a medal for determination and for making me feel like a king.

That's what he does with those lips and that tongue and that intensity. My balls tighten. "Fair warning. I'm going to come really soon," I murmur. "So if you want to stop . . ."

He shakes his head. That doesn't surprise me at all. When Mark Banks wants something, he goes for it.

He sucks with fervor, his hand wrapped around the base of my shaft as he goes to town with his mouth.

I am such a lucky bastard right now.

Pleasure blasts through my cells as my orgasm arrives on the scene. "Yessss. Coming," I groan as my vision blurs and my whole body lights up as I come down his throat.

He takes it all, with loud, wet slurps that are ridiculously sexy.

Kind of like everything he did tonight.

"That was . . ." I pant, unable to finish. This is my favorite kind of speechless.

Then, Mark pops off my dick, and when my pulse starts to settle, my eyes land on his face. Lust-drenched is a good look on Mark. His hair's all mussed up from my hands. His eyes are shining with . . . satisfaction.

Yeah, this is what he wanted. To make someone else feel amazing. Well, mission accomplished.

"Do you think Lord Oliver liked Sir Trevor's mouth as much as I liked yours right now?" I ask.

He blushes, and this is the first time the red in his cheeks has come with a smile. "At least as much as the bad boy poet liked sucking off Lord Ollie."

"Get up here," I tell him, and he climbs over me, pinning me with his arms.

"Now get that mouth on mine and tell me again how much you liked sucking my cock."

With a laugh, Mark brings his lips to mine, gives me a firm kiss. "You're such a greedy fucker. You want a blow job *and* praise?"

"You wanted to give me one," I point out.

"I didn't hear you protest," he says, and this is the *you posh fucker* Mark, the *I like to drive a stick* Mark.

The Mark who lets down his guard every now and then.

I like this side of him. A lot.

"So, I guess I fit your requirement for some willing, non-creepy single dude with good hygiene to sixty-nine?"

Pretty sure I know the answer, but I'm ridiculously hopeful for a big, fat yes.

He flops down next to me, doesn't even crack a grin.

"You'll do."

"Fuck you," I say with a laugh.

"Aww, there you go again with our love language."

"Fuck you, fuck you, fuck you," I add.

Finally I get a smile. "Yes, Asher. That's on the long list."

A flash of heat rushes through my body, headed straight for my dick. I want *that*. Badly. "Sounds like a great list." I kiss the corner of his lips. "Along those lines—*say it.*"

"Say what?"

"How much you loved sucking my cock." I run a finger across his lips. "Say it again."

He scoffs.

"C'mon," I goad.

"Why?"

"Because the word cock is so fucking hot on your lips," I tease him.

He crooks his lips in a devilish grin. "Then why don't you suck *my* cock?"

"I will."

Then I move down his body, giving him the same delicious treatment. Kissing his pecs, licking his oh-so-lickable abs, and settling between his legs.

Time to indulge in my favorite treat.

I slide my hands under his thighs, haul him close, and then finally . . . I tease him.

I taunt him with my tongue and my lips.

Kissing his inner thigh. Sucking on his balls. Flicking my tongue along his shaft.

I reduce him to a panting, hot, babbling mess as he mutters curses and then curses me.

And finally, I give in, taking him deep, sucking him good till his hands are roped in my hair, and he's holding on for dear life till he comes.

So damn loudly.

His groans last forever and make me very happy.

After I let go, I drop next to him and drag a hand through my hair.

"I knew you wanted to run your hands through my so-not-floofy hair. It just took me a little while to realize you wanted to do it while I was sucking your dick," I say lazily.

With a laugh, Mark shoots me a look. "It's so floofy."

19

DISNEY WORLD FOR HORNY ADULTS

WEDNESDAY

MARK

I wake up reluctantly. When I become aware that it's awfully bright in this room, I bury my face in a soft, unfamiliar feather pillow. Somewhere nearby, my phone vibrates. I ignore it. The cotton against my skin is too soft. And the ocean breeze against my naked body is too soothing.

As I drift here in partial wakefulness on the comfortable mattress, I slowly realize a few crucial things that ought to be alarming.

This is not my bed.

I'm not wearing underwear.

My body feels heavy with sexual satisfaction.

My eyes fly open. And the first thing I see is the muscular back of an ex-professional soccer player, and miles of his golden skin.

I let my gaze travel lower to a tan line that begs me to run a finger across it. And below that, the most impressive bare ass that I've ever had the pleasure of sharing a bed with.

Okay, yup. Last night happened. And it's all a little hard to take in.

I blew Asher St. James. And he liked it.

Then? He made me see stars.

But do I panic? No way. I'm not a guy who panics. I'm the man who doubles down when the ten-year note breaks out of its trading range. I'm the dad who calmly bandages the cut on his daughter's finger while her mother freaks out in the other room.

This is no cause to freak out. I'm living my best life right now. Yup, that's a cliché. But now, I know why the saying exists. For moments like this.

I roll over, fully awake. And so is my cock, now that I'm ogling Asher. I slip a hand down my bare stomach, the same one Asher traced with his tongue. And I wrap my hand around . . .

My phone vibrates again.

Ugh. That call could be important. We have a million errands scheduled this morning.

I slide my loose body off the bed, grab my glasses and put them on, then hunt down my phone in the pocket of my discarded khakis.

Hannah's calling, so I swipe to answer. "Morning." My voice is rough with disuse.

"Mark! How's Miami?" she trills.

If she only knew. "It's great," I manage as Asher rolls over with a groan.

And, wow, that view. His famous hair is messy from me running my hands through it. And that toned, biteable body is spread out on the sheets.

I step into the living room, so I can't get too distracted. And so that Hannah won't hear whatever it is that Asher says when he wakes from a night of impulsive sex.

"Miami is great," I repeat. "It's like Disney World for grown-ups." *Horny grownups.*

"That's great, Mark. You deserve a vacation."

"I do," I agree. I deserve this moment of reckless fun and mayhem. I have two more kid- and job-free days in the sultry sun. And I'm going to live it up.

I glance out of the guest house window. A young man stands maybe twenty feet away, a pool skimmer in his hand. His T-shirt says *Bobby's Pool and Spa*.

And he's staring at my naked body with a funny little smile on his face.

Oops.

I walk quickly into my bedroom and shut the door. "What's up, Hannah Banana? Everything okay with you? Any cold feet?"

"No way." She laughs. "But feel free to send me some more drunk texts about my life choices. That was very entertaining."

I scrub my face with my hand, but I'm smiling at the same time. "I'm trying to cut back. Does Flip still think I hate him?"

Her hesitation is revealing. "Hate is a strong word. Wary is more like it."

"Fuck. I'm sorry. He comes from a different world, you know? But that's not his fault. And it's not necessarily a bad thing. I let it bother me when I shouldn't have."

"It'll be all right," she insists. "We'll laugh about it one day. How are things with Flip's superhot wingman?"

"Fine," I say briskly, offering no further details. But my neck is probably turning red.

"Good."

And it's good, too, that my baby sister can't see me right now. Eventually—some night in the distant future—I might confess last night's fling to Hannah. But we're definitely not talking about it now. First of all, because she'd ask a lot of questions that I can't answer. Like—will it happen again?

I hope so. After all, we're sharing this tiny house for a couple more nights. That seems like the obvious timeframe.

But also, it's a distraction. Hannah sent me to Miami to make her wedding special. And I don't need her worrying that I'm too punch drunk to fulfill my duties.

"Hey, Mark? Thanks for checking in with the florist yesterday."

"No problem. They're going to do a good job. Today I'll check on the caterer. I want to look every vendor in the eye before Saturday, so they know I'm paying attention."

"Thank you. I *really* appreciate this. Today I'll be busy staring at my phone, hoping the dressmaker finishes her alterations in time for me to make our flight tomorrow."

"I'm sure she will," I say soothingly. I find a fresh pair of underwear and step into them. And I follow those with a pair of shorts. "I'd better run. I've got things to do."

Like Asher St. James. If I'm lucky.

"Go, go!" she says. "Taste those appetizers! And do me a favor? Hide all the casserole dishes in the kitchen of that house."

"You got it. I won't let you down."

She signs off after a little more chatter about the dress.

I tiptoe into the living room, but the pool boy is gone, and Asher is brushing his teeth. So I head into the kitchen to start the coffee, but Asher has already done it.

And that's where the panic finds me—as I stand in front of the coffee maker, mug in hand, waiting for the pot to fill. I breathe in the hopeful scent of coffee, wondering what the hell Asher will say when he comes into the kitchen.

Hey, Banks. That was a fun time. Thanks for the BJ. Nice knowing you, but I'm going back to hooking up with the rich and famous now.

Okay, he's too suave to actually say that. But if he doesn't want a repeat, he'll probably be distant. Cool, even. He might suggest dividing and conquering today's activities, just to make his point clear.

It could be so awkward.

This right here is *exactly* why I never let on that I'm attracted to him in particular.

And I'm still trapped in this tiny house with him for at least three more days. Just him, me, and the memory of my mouth on his cock, and the sounds he makes when he comes.

I'm still staring at the coffee maker when he pads into the kitchen. I don't turn around, though. I need to put on my game face first.

But he doesn't give me a chance. He comes up behind me, presses his bare chest to my bare back, and kisses the nape of my neck softly.

Fuuuuuuck that's nice.

"Good morning," he says huskily.

"Isn't it?" I reply.

"I'd hate to interrupt the mind meld you're having with the coffee pot, Banks. But I thought we should plan our day. The caterer is this morning, no?"

Setting the mug down, I turn around. And there he is, at point-blank range, all floofy hair and tanned smirk and sleepy hazel eyes. My heart spasms, like I won some kind of hookup lottery last night. "You *do* want coffee, St. James? I didn't suck off some kind of monster, right?"

He barks out a laugh. "Of course I want coffee. I made it, didn't I? And guess what—your poker face is good, but everyone has a tell."

I successfully fight off a smile. "No way. I have no tells."

"Yeah, you do," he says in a low, guttural voice. "It's right here." He lifts a hand to my throat, which is strangely sexy. Then he strokes a thumb across my Adam's apple. "This jumps when you're turned on."

He drops his hand and leans down to kiss my throat instead.

Check, please. I just want to shove him back into the bedroom and have my filthy way with him.

Instead, the coffee pot dings, and Asher straightens up. "Outta the way, Banks. We have to drink coffee and sample crab cakes." He moves me to the side and picks up my mug to fill it. "There's no time for whatever is running through your mind right now. We have a wedding to throw. It has to be perfect for Hannah! Not one detail out of place."

"Are you quoting me back to me?" I ask grumpily.

"Just telling you how it is." He shoves the mug into my hand and reaches for a second one. "Get out your spreadsheet. Let's see what's left on it."

About ninety-nine more wickedly dirty things.

Oh, wait. "Which one?" I mumble.

He pokes my belly. "What do you mean, which one? Is there more than one wedding spreadsheet?"

"No," I say quickly.

His coffee mug stops on the way to his mouth. "Hang on. What's the other spreadsheet?"

"Nothing." I take a gulp.

Those hazel eyes narrow. "You use spreadsheets a lot, right? For any kind of list?"

I shrug indifferently. My poker face is tight.

Asher's gaze drops to my throat, and I gulp. "Banks. You mentioned a list of things you'd like to do to me. Do you keep it on a *spreadsheet*?" The corners of his mouth twitch.

"Spreadsheets are very convenient," I mutter.

"Huh." He struggles not to laugh. "Break it down for me. If you were going to keep a spreadsheet for sex, how would that work?"

I sigh. "The rows are for the action, and the columns are for body parts. If you're going to laugh, just make it quick. We have a busy day planned."

"I'm not laughing." He takes a slow breath and masters himself. "You gotta do you, Banks."

"That's why the spreadsheet exists. Because me doing *me* was all I ever got."

He bursts out laughing. "Okay. I see your point. And kudos to you for giving new meaning to the word *spread*sheet. Do I get to see this thing?"

"Only if you're nice."

"I'm very nice," he says, ghosting a hand over my ass before withdrawing it quickly. "But we need some rules."

"Rules. Okay. Tell me." But what I really mean is *stop talking and kiss me more.*

"We get the work done first," he says. "Because I don't want to rush next time. I want to play with your body. Show you things I can do to make you writhe and moan, harder and hotter than you did last night. Want to spend some time doing," He lowers his voice, leans into me, and whispers his plans into my ear. My head pops.

I actually moan into my coffee mug. "Not fair. That's 9A, 9B and 9C."

A smirk comes my way. "So *that* body part will get *a lot* of action, if I'm doing the spreadsheet math right."

"You are." Because him plus touching me equals all the *O* columns.

Asher steps back. "Was that nice enough?"

"You whispered dirty things in my ear just to get me to show you my spreadsheet?"

He lifts the mug to his lips, and says *yes* with his eyes, then takes a drink.

"Good move, St. James. You're learning a thing or two about negotiation," I quip, as I head to my room and snag my laptop.

Less than a minute later, we're seated at the kitchen table, and for the first time ever in my life, I let someone into my fantasies. I never did anything like this with Bridget. True, I didn't have a detailed list back then. Though I doubt that's the reason I didn't reveal them to her.

But now I'm compelled to share this with him. It's not just necessary, but important. After I tap in my password, the first seven digits of pi, I click it open while Asher scrubs a hand across his jaw.

He's silent as he stares at the screen.

For several long seconds, he's frozen with that hand on his face. Maybe a minute.

He can't think I'm too dirty?

Or too . . . type A?

Lowering his hand, he turns to me in slow motion, his eyes registering Vegas-slot-machine-payoff glee. He curls that hand around the back of my neck. "You filthy fucker."

His lips come down on my mouth and he spears his tongue with mine in a hot, dirty kiss that tastes like coffee and the promise of morning sex.

When he breaks the kiss, he rubs his palms together, glancing at the time on the computer.

In a flurry, he points to the cells.

This one, please. And that one, I absolutely call dibs on that. When I do this one, I will make you forget how to trade bonds, or stocks, or piggy banks, and when we're doing this, all you'll be saying is don't stop, don't stop, don't stop.

My throat is dry. I can't speak. I don't want him to stop talking.

"Let me tell you something, Banks. I don't know how your probability curves or equations or what-have-you work, but the probability of us getting to as much as we superhumanly can in four nights," he says, then points to the screen again, and drags his index finger past all my dirty gifs and porn clips, "is only going to work if we get started really fucking soon."

"Yeah. Good. That."

He cracks up. "You and your one-syllable words when you're horny."

"Your fault."

"And I take the blame," he says, emphasizing the short sounds. But then his excitement drains away. He's dead serious as his eyes laser in on mine. "But we need to finish that list of rules, Banks."

I square my shoulders, and use his original words. "Rules for . . . *harmless vacation fun.*"

That's the biggest rule of all. This *will* be harmless. I don't have room in my life for anything more. And even though I don't know Asher well, I'm confident he lives every day of his life by that motto, *harmless fun.*

"I'm game for anything on here. So let's pick your *top* fantasies," Asher says. "And they'll keep us busy for the next four nights."

But that's not quite right. My convertible days are numbered. "I'm jetting Saturday night right after the wedding. I'm taking Rosie to Disney World on Sunday when it opens so we need to hit the road."

"In a minivan?"

I roll my eyes. "Dude. No. There are just two of us." I don't tell him I rented a Subaru.

"Okay, three nights then. Tonight, Thursday, and Friday."

I clear my throat. "Did you forget about the existence of mornings too?"

He chuckles. "I like the way you think. Morning and evening. Hell, add in an afternoon handy J for me as well. Wait, make it a double. You can have one too," he says, light and breezy.

That's his style, spontaneous and spur of the moment, but I'm a planner. "Consider it done. But after Friday night, it's over."

He lifts a shoulder in a half-shrug, his eyes saying *not quite*. "Mark, did *you* now forget about the existence of mornings? Don't give Saturday morning the cold shoulder when you can give me your hard cock instead."

I laugh, and I definitely don't mind his carpe diem attitude when it comes to sex. Still, I've gotta do me. "Then we're done on the wedding day," I repeat, for emphasis. "New York is not an option."

It can't be. There's a reason for my unfortunate celibacy, with Bridget handing me the majority of the parenting, I don't have time for more. Rosie's at home with me most nights, and that's the way I like it. I can't imagine bringing hookups home. *Hey, cupcake. After you fall asleep, Daddy's gotta take care of 11A and 11B with his Tinder date.*

Pass.

New York sex spreadsheet tabs are out of the question.

"Got it, Banks." Asher smiles at me. "I didn't think it was anything more. And that's fine by me."

Of course it is. Asher screams *the good times guy*. Has he ever even had a relationship? I don't know, and also, I can't care about that. We are in agreement on all the points. This is a win-win.

"That's what I figured. But it's good to be on the same page. But there's one more rule."

"Hit me up."

"We keep this quiet. Between us."

He snorts. "I was going to post it on my Insta, but now that you've laid down that law, I'll just write it in my diary instead."

"I mean, no Flip. No Hannah." I don't want my sister thinking she can't trust me with the most important moment in her life because I'm distracted by dick.

Asher's eyes go introspective, like he's weighing something for a few seconds. "My stupid lips will be sealed," he says, a little coolly.

I'm tempted to ask if there's a problem, but maybe I imagined the tone, since it's gone seconds later when Asher swirls his finger at the screen, points to 11B and 11C, then gives me bedroom eyes.

My dick jumps.

Why didn't I put *bedroom eyes* on my list? But hey, I've always liked bonuses, so I'll take that as an extra.

"Banks, we've got an hour till we meet the caterer. We have just enough time for a shower."

I'm already up and stripping off my clothes.

———

Sometimes when I watch porn, Logical Mark argues with Dirty-Minded Mark. Would that position truly work in the real world? Does water make matters harder or easier?

I have nothing to argue about right now as the rainfall shower beats down my body, and Asher St. James crowds me against the tiled wall, wrapping a hand around my hard shaft.

When he grips me, I shudder. When he slides his hand up and down, I moan. And when his other hand cups my balls, I grab onto his shoulder.

"FuckFuckFuck," I mutter.

With a sexy laugh, he drops his mouth to my shoulder, and nips. "I lied when I said I didn't bite."

His teeth on my skin feel crazy good too. Go figure.

As he strokes me, all I *can* figure is I am officially a sex fanatic. I fucking love everything. I want everything.

Water sluices over my skin, and I peer down at his hand stroking my shaft. Talk about dirty dreams coming true.

The temperature in me shoots higher than the water. I burn everywhere under my skin and this feels so good. But it would be better like this . . .

"11B," I murmur.

"You dirty man," he whispers with an approving rumble. My cock jerks in his hand as he pushes his body against mine, grips our dicks at the same time.

Words can't find the path from my brain to my mouth.

I can't even utter *nothing has felt this good*.

Grunts are all I can manage.

Ungh.

And *ohhhh.*

As he jerks us together, he watches my face, my mouth, my throat. I don't think anyone has ever stared at me during sex before, like my every reaction thrills him.

Asher stretches an arm to the soap dish, grabs a lube pack. I didn't even notice him bring it in here, but then, I did set a land-speed record to get in the shower.

He rips it open and I have no idea if he's going to explore my ass or . . .

"Finish us off," he growls, then he grabs my palm, drizzles some lube in it, and guides my hand to our dicks.

I won't last more than thirty seconds.

But I don't think he cares. The second I wrap a hand around our cocks, pleasure twists in me.

And I learn something brand new—two dicks are better than one when jerking it.

As my body overheats, I take over the double hand job, my fist flying up and down our lengths, fast, determined.

And fueled by him.

His mouth hangs open, and he braces his hands on the wall behind me. "Fuck yes. So good. Want to come on you."

Done.

Consider it done.

My orgasm steals all my brain cells. I come so goddamn hard in my hand, shooting on his abs.

"Yes . . ." He grunts and he's right there, seconds later, painting me.

11D. That's where my fantasy has always ended. On finishing. That's all.

But my reality gets better.

Letting go of us, I step closer and cup his face under the water, then capture his lips with mine. I try to tell him with my kiss that I can definitely stand him now.

———

After I get dressed, I meet Asher at the door of the guest house. He doesn't even bother to bust my chops about my shorts. They're navy.

"Question for you, Banks," he says, focused. "About your single-malt-scotch-fueled *text fest.* Remember that one?"

I groan. Here we go again. "I thought we'd already clarified all the points in the text."

He claps a hand on my shoulder as we walk past the pool, toward the house. "*Nearly* all. And they're all in the *I was right* column," he says, clearly delighted to poke and prod me again. But admittedly, I like our new style of poking and prodding, since it involves the use of body parts. "But there is one more little thing I wanted to address, since we sorted out the *blow job* hair and the *stupidly hot* lips last night." He draws a deep inhale. "You referred to me as, and I quote . . .*like a fucking comic book hero in those graphic novels I used to read.*"

I don't bat an eye. "Yes, Asher?"

He taps his chest. "If I'm Superhot Wingman, what's *your* superhero name?"

I stifle a laugh. "And why do you think I have one?"

"You do, Banks, you do. Do you want me to play dirty to get it out of you?"

Playing dirty sounds like a great game. "I mean, if you think that'll work," I deadpan.

I bet it works. I bet it works so well.

Asher stops at the sliding door, grabs the back of my neck, and plants a scorching-hot kiss on my lips. Jesus. This man can kiss. When he breaks it, his lips are inches from mine, and he drags a thumb along my jaw. "Soooo."

My head is a daze. "Captain Filthy Mind," I mutter, since his kisses are my truth serum.

Asher laughs, and even his laugh makes it sound as if he's just had sex. "Perfect. So fucking perfect." As we resume our pace, he says breezily, "And by the way, for a split-second yesterday when I mentioned we'd hit errand 2A, I thought tasks got you all hot and bothered, but then I realized 2A wasn't an errand. It was . . . *me*. And now that I've seen the world's greatest list, I can confirm 2A was *you* putting your mouth all over me."

Oh, he's good.

Then Asher adds, "For the record, 2A was excellent."

His eyes flicker with that big charm the man breaks out anywhere and everywhere, using it on the designer, the gate agent, the florist.

And on me.

I kind of wish I were immune, but his charm is coming at me full throttle now. I simply nod my thanks as I try to fight off a smile, so he doesn't know what his compliment just did to my stomach—made it flip.

"What are you smiling about, Captain Filthy Mind?" he asks, as we near the front door of the palace.

"Lunch. You know, Cubanos and all," I say, offhand. "Just thinking about Cubanos."

"Yes, same for me," he says, then he stops me in the doorway and kisses the corner of my mouth. "Sandwiches," he repeats, and it sounds like he's keeping my secret. That he knows I wasn't thinking about ham and cheese.

I have a secret about him too.

Asher really likes kissing me.

When we reach the car, he smacks my ass. But before he gets in the driver's seat, he says, "Wait." Then he grabs the waistband of my shorts, tugs it back, and peeks. "Mmm. Purple."

A tingle rushes down my spine. "Guess you like *some* of my clothes."

"Seems I do."

But we aren't talking about clothes anymore.

20

I'M A FAN OF EGGPLANTS

ASHER

I've always understood that a match can hinge on one single play. One well-placed feint or one perfect kick can change everything.

So I shouldn't be too surprised by how much has changed between Mark and me in the past twenty-four hours.

Still, it's hard to reconcile yesterday's tensions with the mood in the convertible as I cross the causeway toward the city. Mark whistles to himself as he takes in the scenery. He looks like a new man.

I take a subtle glance at him, and I swear he looks more relaxed than I've ever seen him. I'll take the responsibility for that, thank you very much.

"Stop," he says without turning his head.

"Stop what?"

"Stop sneaking glances at me. Keep your eyes on the road, St. James. You can admire me later."

Maybe subtlety is overrated. Instead, I plant a hand on his muscular knee and stroke it. The crisp hair feels good under my hand. "It's going to be a long day," I murmur, keeping my eyes on the road as instructed.

"It will be if you keep doing that."

I let my fingers inch up his thigh.

"Asher," he groans.

With a quick, cocky smile, I release him. My phone is trilling, and it's Lucy's ringtone. "Mind if I answer that?"

"Let me help," Mark says, and then he hits a button on the console to bring the call in through Bluetooth.

"Thanks. Hi Lucy. You're on speaker."

"Asher, I'm calling to tell you that you have an appointment with the caterer in twelve minutes."

"*Right*," I say heavily. "Thanks for that timely update."

"There is no need for snark," she says crisply. "You rarely make appointments this early in the day, so I didn't check."

Mark gives a little snort from his side of the car, but I ignore him.

"Anything else?"

"There's something on the Twitter I thought you should see."

"Okay, something good? Are you monitoring the Commando hashtag? I think the new campaign went live at midnight." I'd meant to look at this myself this morning.

But a sexy banker distracted me.

"Well . . . you know I don't look at the Twitter all that often. So I can't really say. But it's on that trendy board."

"Trending?" I guess.

"Right. Just like I said. The brand is trending together with hashtag eggplant. I just thought you'd want to know."

"Eggplant . . ." I say slowly. That doesn't make a whole lot of sense. "Okay, Lucy. Thanks. I'll check it out."

She rings off. But of course I'm sitting in Miami traffic. "Mark, would you mind . . ."

"On it," he says, tapping his phone. A moment later, he chuckles. "It is trending with the eggplant emoji. I'm afraid to ask why."

"Not as afraid as I am," I mutter. "Is there a link?"

"Um, yup. Hang on."

The car inches forward, and the silence from the passenger

seat is worrying. Then Mark makes a strangled noise. "Well, hello to *you*, sir. That's an impressive bulge."

"Isn't that the point of a Commando?"

"Well, this isn't how I wear mine." He waits until I stop at yet another red light, and then he turns the phone to face me. My lungs seize up in horror. It's a well-lit, well-composed shot of one of the hockey players who'd modeled the tight-fitting bathing suits.

But he's sporting a comically oversized erection.

"I mean, I wouldn't consider myself a size queen," Mark says. "But you can't help but stare."

"That was . . . it's . . . shit! That was a *joke*," I sputter. "The guy put his water bottle down there while we were warming up on the set. I took a pic to amuse him."

I poke the console where my connection to Lucy is still onscreen. And I seethe while it rings.

This could cost me business. People have no sense of humor when their brand becomes a punchline on Twitter.

"Lucy!" I shout when the connection is made. "You uploaded the wrong folder! There's a pornographic shot in there somehow. Find the real shot of the suit in peacock blue and get it over to them right away. We have to fix this."

"You know, I did think that one was a little over the top," she muses. "But pea*cock* blue . . ."

"Please," I beg. "Fix this. And then we'll work on my apology."

"Of course, Asher. I'll call them to say that the best file is coming."

"And was there any word from FLI?"

"None."

Of course there wasn't. Who'd hire a hot mess like me? "Thank you. Text me when this is fixed."

I hang up and let out a huge sigh. "Honestly. I love taking photos. I'm good at it. But the business part of running a photography business is killing me. I know I didn't put that photo into the deliverable file."

Mark makes a sympathetic noise. "Is Lucy a temp? Maybe she needs to move on."

"I'm not firing her," I grumble. "I should have done the upload myself. Aren't I supposed to be turning left somewhere?" It would be just my luck to get us lost right now, too.

"*The turn is two hundred meters ahead,*" Mark says, reading from my phone's GPS. He arches a brow. "Meters, St. James? Too posh for American measurements?"

"I bought the phone in Switzerland," I say. The restaurant sign comes into view as I take the turn. "Are we on time?"

"Simmer down." Mark places a palm on my thigh. If I weren't so tense, I'd enjoy that. "We're actually five minutes early."

"Thank fuck. I'll use the time to grovel to the world's most successful bathing suit manufacturer."

———

Thirty minutes later, I'm still not over it. All the canapes and tiny quiche and ceviche we've tasted ought to have soothed the beast within.

But they didn't. I blew it with Commando. The artistic director I got on the phone was apoplectic, and I don't blame him. All I had to do was deliver some excellent photography, and I couldn't even hand in my homework without a catastrophe.

Mark pokes me in the hip, and I realize the French chef has asked me a question. And I missed it.

"I'm sorry," I mutter. "You were saying?"

"*Et zees* are *les entrées*. The duck confit and *le steak*. *Les aimez-vous?*"

I force myself to focus on the two little plates a nervous waiter has placed in front of us. I lift the piece of steak to my mouth, and it's butter-soft. And the bite of duck in a cherry reduction is perfect. "*Délicieuse. Formidable.* But what will you have for our vegetarian guests?"

The chef waves his hands like nothing could be less important. "*L'assortiment de légumes,*" he says. "It will be perfect." He kisses his fingertips like a TV character.

But, hell, if I came to a wedding and was stuck with a couple of tiny quiches, a mini spring roll, and a few vegetables, I'd sad. "Could we do a little more for our guests who don't eat meat?" I ask. "Perhaps a pasta or a risotto?"

His bulbous nose wrinkles. "Pasta. So *bourgeois*. The vegetables will be beautiful. The most beautiful vegetables in Miami."

I hesitate since I suspect the vegetarians want more than pretty beans, and I want to argue, but he's the chef. "Okay."

"Hold on," Mark says. "A vegetarian option is in our contract. And we have approval power over all the dishes. Page four, item six," he says, flipping through what must be contract pages on his phone. "Asher wants something more for the veggie crew. How can you help us?"

"Euh . . ." The older man rocks back on his heels. "We could do a couscous. Very Moroccan. Chickpeas, bell peppers. Very edgy. With aubergine. You Americans call it eggplant."

"Ah, I'm a fan of *eggplants*." Mark pokes me in the ass cheek when he says this, just in case I don't get the joke. "But no butter, right? This dish should be vegan."

"Pas de beurre?" The chef looks scandalized. *"Non?"*

"No," Mark says firmly. "Page four, line . . ."

"Pas de beurre," the chef repeats heavily. *"Quel dommage."*

Triumphant, Mark turns to me. "Will that do, Asher?"

"Yes," I say quickly. "Thank you. We really appreciate this."

"It will be a beautiful wedding," the chef says. "You two will make a handsome couple. I will see you on Saturday at eleven."

"Thank you," I say brightly, smiling at him. I don't risk a glance at Mark. "We will see you there."

"And now I must go and prepare my restaurant kitchen," he says. *"Au revoir."*

"Au revoir, et merci pour tout ce que vous avez fait."

This burst of French gets the attention of the two men. The chef smiles at me, which means I've won him over. So I can check that off my list.

But Mark's eyes also widen. I put a hand on his back and guide him toward the door.

"You didn't have to do that," Mark says as soon as we're outside.

I stop short and turn to him. "You mean . . ." I swallow hard.

"Speaking French? Or touching you in public? I wasn't trying to embarrass you."

Mark squints at me. "Nah, I liked the French, and you can touch me all you want. But Chef Garnier has to fulfill his contractual obligations. That's his issue to correct, and you don't have to apologize. I get that it's your style—you like making people happy. But all we owe that guy is a timely check and basic civility. Flip is paying him a small fortune for taking this job on short notice, right?"

"A large fortune," I admit.

"Right," Mark says. "So you can hold him to his obligation without apologizing. It's quicker if you don't bother turning everyone into a new friend. Just saying." He shrugs, and walks toward the car. "Oh, and I'm driving now."

But winning people over *is* important. When I played football, I didn't gain the acceptance of teammates and fans by being an asshole. I pulled that off by giving a good word to everyone, and as one of the few out guys in the sport, I needed that tool at my disposal. But I tuck Mark's comments away in a drawer, since his bossy style back there is winning over *other* tools—mine.

I follow him in slow steps, climbing into the passenger seat as docile as a well-trained Labrador Retriever. "That's so hot," I say, closing the car door with a sigh.

"What is?" He adjusts the mirrors.

"The way you handled that guy. With the contract right there on your phone."

"Oh, it wasn't." He starts the engine. "I didn't think he'd have it memorized. So I just winged it."

He just winged it. *Oh, baby.* I chuckle. "It's even hotter now, handsome. Do you have, like, a trainee I could steal to run my life? I need a keeper."

"You're fine, St. James. We all have different talents. Mine is negotiation. Yours is charm. Now tell me how to get to the cake place."

Fine? I'm fine? "You mean big charm, right?"

"You and your need for compliments," he says.

"You and your need to leave quickly. Turn right from here. Coco's Cakes is two miles down this road." The wind rustles through my hair, and it calms me. "Seriously, though, did it freak you out when he thought we were a couple?"

"No. Why?"

"Well . . ." This is a tricky topic. He was so adamant that we not tell Flip and Hannah that we're fooling around. And, sure, that's probably the right move. But it made me wonder how Mark would handle it if they knew. "Let me ask you this—are you out to anyone?"

"Sure," he says easily. "My parents, my sister. Some college friends? I don't even remember at this point."

"Your ex-wife?" I'm prying now.

"Oh, sure," he says with another shrug. "But we never talked about it. She didn't want me to."

"Wait, what?" I hear this like the screech of tires on a road. "She had a problem with it? And you *married* this woman?"

"Easy," Mark says. "That's not how it was. She knew I was bisexual, and she didn't care. Maybe she even thought it was sexy. But then she got pregnant. We got married. Our lives took a turn for the . . ." He's quiet for a second. "We both sacrificed a lot. Neither one of us sowed any more wild oats, right? So we had, like, a stiff upper lip about it. We didn't discuss the things that we'd given up."

"Like hot single dudes."

Mark gives me a smoldering look before he answers, "Yeah, like hot single *anything*. She hated it when I pointed out anyone else's attractiveness. *Hated it*. So I just didn't talk like that. I kept my feelings about Luke Evans to myself. Along with my thing for Anna Kendrick."

"Huh. I don't have a thing for Anna Kendrick, but I take your meaning." And I definitely have a thing for Mark Banks. It grows stronger by the hour.

But I'd better rein it in. The week will be over in a blink.

Tonight, though, is going to be amazing. I'm going to clear out a dozen items on this man's sex spreadsheet.

And that will just be the appetizer.

21

MY FIRST SEX ERRAND

MARK

*M*aybe someone switched bodies with me last night, since this hardly feels like my life. Asher and I eat Cubanos at a sidewalk café by the beach. Ocean waves gently lap the shore in the distance, and pop music saturates the warm air.

With a napkin, Asher wipes the remains of his sandwich from his lips, then says, "Just as good as I imagined they'd be."

"Same here," I say, as I ball up a napkin.

He runs a finger across the top of my hand. I shiver. "Mmm. Too many errands," he murmurs.

"I know," I say.

"But now that we've had our lunch detour, it's time to hit the bakery," he says.

We rise, weaving through the early afternoon crowds, chatting about lunch, and Miami, and beaches. "You've been to Miami before?" he asks.

"Sort of. Sure. But only on business. I never go to the beach. I'm always in a conference room."

"Jesus," he murmurs. "I'm going to have to stage an intervention."

"I think you already have," I insist, and he smiles.

The moment is so easy. So normal. Us, surrounded by tanned bodies in the sunshine.

But then, this whole scene must be normal to him. Going out. Dancing through life. Seeing men in New York whenever he wants.

I wince at the thought.

"You okay, Banks?"

Of course he noticed. He notices everything about me.

No way am I letting on that my mind meandered to his romantic life. Nope. I don't want to know anything about it or how I fit, since this thing between us is *not* romantic.

It's a fling. Just Cubanos and sex and errands.

"I'm all good," I say, and we resume our path to Coco's Cakes.

Amidst the scent of sugar and frosting, the tanned, curvy baker slinks up to us, all hips and shimmery body lotion, the swell of her breasts visible in a halter top.

Normally, I'd sneak a peek. But I'm on a mission, checking off tasks as I count down to sex o'clock. Only a few more hours till I can get this man alone.

"And this is the tropical coconut cake your sister hand selected," Coco says, then slides between us at a tiny white wooden table, nibbling on the corner of her lips. "It tastes so decadent. Try it. It's like a delicious explosion on your tongue."

Asher chuckles, taking the fork from her. "Good thing I like explosions on my tongue. And I believe my friend Mark was saying the same thing last night."

Shaking my head, I hold in a laugh. He nudges my foot under the white table, like I didn't know what he meant.

"Yes, Asher, I said *that*," I reply.

"Try this one then," she says to me. "The frosting is so rich and creamy."

"I love it nice and thick," Asher says, laying it on, well, thick.

And making it very difficult not to laugh as I try the frosting.

It's sinful, and I tell Coco as much.

"So you definitely like the taste?" Asher asks me, his tone dripping with sex.

So much that my dick sits up and takes notice, hardening in my shorts. "Yes," I say, since why waste words when I am so damn ready to be done?

"It's orgasmically delicious," Coco chimes in.

Now I'm *only* thinking of orgasms, and I'm at a loss as to what to say to the baker, and why I'm even here.

But Asher's not. "Thank you again, Coco. The cake is great. We'd love a Saturday morning delivery as planned. And now we need to go," Asher says abruptly. He grabs my hand and tugs me up, and we leave in seconds flat.

"We didn't get to finish . . . the whole thing," I point out, but I'm not even sure what I needed to do in there since my mind is filled with rich and creamy thoughts.

"Finish what, Banks? The cake was amazing. Your sister picked it out. And I want to get you the fuck out of here and do bad things to you," he says on the streets of Miami, teasing at the bottom of my T-shirt, sending a fresh wave of goose bumps down my arms. "You don't always have to negotiate. Sometimes, it's quicker if you don't," he says, using my words from earlier. "Then, you can just leave, so you can get to the good stuff in life."

And . . . he has a point. Asher insists on enjoying things, and that's not a bad way for me to live for the next few days. When I return to New York, I'll return to my way—*complete* control.

"What's the good stuff?" I ask, as his hand curls over my ass as we walk.

This man is into touching me in public, and I like it.

He whispers in my ear. *14C, 17B, 22F.* Why the hell do we have to see the officiant now?

Errands hate me.

An hour that lasts a lifetime later, we're done with the officiant, and I rush down the steps of the office building.

I race to the car, and take the driver's seat. I will speed home now. I will engage the turbo thrusters or what-the-fuck-ever. I don't care. "Let's go," I call out, since Asher's ten feet away, and why are his feet made of molasses?

Sauntering, Asher takes his sweet-ass time, then gets in the car like we're sitting on the porch in the summer, frittering away the day. As he shuts the door, he flashes me a smile. "Got somewhere to be?"

I groan in misery. The sun is dipping on the horizon, and I want to return to the mansion and get naked with him. Screw, and then order dinner, and screw, and then swim, and screw. "Yes. In bed. With you. Now."

I enter the address, hit *go* on Waze, then pull away from the curb.

A block later, Asher gestures lazily to a side street. "Take a right."

I point at the concrete ribbon in front of us. "Dude. That's wrong. The GPS says go straight."

"Just turn right."

"No, that's *not* the most direct route." I'm horny as fuck, and it's all his fault.

"Trust me. I'm not wrong about this."

I huff out a breath. "You are."

He drapes an arm around my shoulder, squeezes. "If you know what's good for you, turn here."

"This is *not* good for me," I grit out, but I listen.

"It is, Banks. It *is*."

I turn, and he points to . . . a freaking CVS.

Flicking the signal, I pull into the lot. "Seriously? Do you need shampoo? Shaving cream? Deodorant? Is that what can't wait?"

His lips curve into the smirkiest smirk of all time. "And to think I was going to tell you. Not sure I will now."

When I park, he gets out of the car, tips his forehead to the pharmacy. I follow him, because of course I do. He's where I want to be.

Asher strides through the air-conditioned store with

purpose. He does everything with purpose, and he's hell-bent on passing the gum aisle, the aspirin row, the lotion shelves. Till he turns down . . . *oh* . . .

Oh, yes.

This is the best errand of my life.

Asher doesn't even look at me. Just swaggers down the aisle to the condom display. When he stops and reaches for a box, all the air evacuates my lungs as reality hits me squarely in the chest.

I'm going to have sex with a hot man.

This hot man.

I don't know if we'll do it tonight. Or tomorrow. Or the next night. But it's happening. It is on. I can barely breathe, I want it so badly.

Want *him* so badly.

My face goes up in flames as I stop next to him, catch a faint hint of that rainfall and summer breeze smell. What does he smell like when he's fucking?

Don't know, but I'm going to find out.

I nearly sway. I may topple over from desire and turn into a puddle on the floor of CVS.

He turns to me, steps closer, brushes his jaw along mine, dips his mouth to my ear. "Like my errand now, Banks?"

My bones melt. "Uh-huh."

As he pulls back, he locks eyes with me. His flash with dirty deeds. "Some of your list items require lube."

I say nothing because if I tried to speak, all I would do is croak.

"Now, do you think it's a good idea we . . . *came* here?"

It's the best idea ever, I want to shout.

But there's no way I can speak without sounding like an overeager teenager who just discovered his first X-rated video. I simply nod, though I can't hide the smile that's taking over my face.

I, Mark Banks, am on a sex errand.

My lips twitch and they don't stop.

"Ah, so errands do get you hot?" Asher teases.

I tug at my T-shirt. "A little."

He stares at my neck, then his eyes sweep down my body, landing at my crotch. "A lot."

I just nod several times, giving in. "*Yeah. A lot,*" I say, and I'm in a trance.

But a question hangs over my head. How exactly are we doing it?

Like I did last night when I asked him to dance, I dive into the deep end. "Asher," I ask, in front of the extra-large condoms, since that seems fitting. "What you said in the car yesterday about not being a control freak. Were you alluding to . . ."

Asher laughs. "Yes, I was."

And I *should* know how to do this. This is a negotiation, after all. But I have no clue how *this* works.

Something else nags at me, though. I don't know exactly what I want in bed either when it comes to . . .

So I'm quiet because I don't want to say the wrong thing.

Maybe sensing I need him to handle the conversational reins, he takes them and speaks again. "Let me help you. Do you want to know if I'll top or bottom?"

Just hearing him ask the question fuels me. I *have* to know. I have to say those words to him. "Well? Will you?"

He strips away the teasing from his tone. "Like I said yesterday, I'm good with anything. What about you? Do you want to fuck me or do you want me to fuck you?"

Images of us tangled together flash before my eyes. I drag a hand along the back of my neck. I am lava. "All of the above. I think."

He brandishes the box of protection. "Then we really should buy these right now. And some top-shelf lube."

"We should," I agree, as he reaches for a bottle. There's an issue though. "Trouble is, I don't think I can move for a while."

He smiles slyly. "So you really do like my big charm?"

I like it so much, it's frying my brain cells. I'm a starving man at an incredible feast. Asher's offering me everything and anything, and I can pick and choose at the buffet of his body.

"Sometimes," I say, lying and he knows it.

He leans in and I expect him to say *all the time*. But he doesn't. Instead, he whispers, "*Je te veux tellement.*"

I don't know French. But I have a feeling that means something like *I want you*.

It also means he's figured out his French turns me on.

"Same," I mutter.

He brushes his lips along my jaw, stopping at my ear, taking his time with each word, letting them last. "*Alors, prends-moi et fais de moi ce que tu veux . . .*"

What the hell did he just say? I try to repeat it in my head, to make it stick.

I pull back. "What was that?"

His eyes glimmer with taunts. "Bet you'd like to know."

I simmer. "You multilingual fucker."

His gaze drifts down my body again. "*Je te l'ai déjà dit, Banks. Tu peux me faire tout ce dont tu as envie.*"

Once more, I try to press the words into my brain. Memorize them.

Then he waggles condoms and lube. "I'll buy these, and you can meet me at the car."

Asher turns and walks away, leaving me with my erection, my filthy thoughts, and my white-hot desire for the other best man.

A minute later—who am I kidding? It takes five for my dick to settle to walkable levels—I make it to the car.

Aviator shades on, Asher leans against the hood, cool and casual, tossing the keys in his palm. "Want me to take the wheel?"

"Yes."

I spend the rest of the drive in Google translate, ignoring messages and notifications, desperately trying to unlock the puzzle of what he said.

I plug in every possible combination of sounds and words, and finally, when we pull up at the house, I'm pretty sure I've got it.

Pretty sure, too, I might pounce on him in seconds flat.

He cuts the engine, and I follow him inside, driven solely by my desire to get his clothes off, stat.

When we reach the pool, I clear my throat, take a stab at translating that line of French he spoke to me back in the store, the one after the *I want you* bit. *"Then, pin me down and have your way with me . . ."*

Asher turns around, a throaty rumble escaping his mouth, approval in his eyes. "Well done, Banks," he says, and I stalk over to him, peel off his shirt, toss it on the concrete, then run my hands along his smooth, sun-kissed skin.

This is where my hands belong.

I grab his face, bring my mouth inches from those lips I want to devour, and solve the rest of the French puzzle. *"I already told you, Banks. You can do anything you want to me."*

He smiles, slow and pleased. "Have me, Banks," he whispers.

In a flurry, I push him down on a lounge chair, rip off my glasses and shirt, and slam my body to his.

I'm not thinking about spreadsheets or lists or items.

I'm not thinking at all.

I'm doing.

Him.

I kiss him ravenously, grinding my crotch against his, our hard-ons thumping together through our shorts. His hands grab my ass, and he jerks me closer to him. I need to get this lust out of my system so we can slow down and spend all night naked.

I break the kiss, panting. His eyes are fevered, his hands gripping me tight. He's as wound up as I am. I try to catch my breath, and as I do, words just spill out. "You're so fucking sexy, Asher St. James. It's insane how much I want you."

His hand slides up my back. "Same here, so just fucking get naked and rub your dick against mine."

I dive back in for one more hot, filthy kiss that knocks all my senses out of whack. I can't wait to strip off the rest of our clothes.

I rise up to my knees, unzip my shorts, when the sound of the door opening hits my ears.

"Mark? Are you here somewhere?"

My sister's voice has the same effect on me as the time someone from work convinced me to do the ice bucket challenge. Instant deep freeze. In five seconds, I've got my shorts zipped again, shirt on, and I've sprung into a standing position. And I set another land-speed record today—this one for time to deflate. Less than thirty seconds.

"Oh, hell," Asher mutters. "This can't be happening. Flannah is a day early."

Flannah?

I don't even have time to react to that ridiculous nickname as my sister steps outside, her smile as wide as the bay. "My God, this place is amazing! Everything is so great!"

"Yup, terrific," Asher agrees, and you'd have to have had your tongue in his mouth a moment ago to hear the irony in his voice.

Hannah flings herself at me, and I hug her as a reflex.

But what if she'd shown up about five minutes later? Or even three? *Christ*, that was close. "H-hey Banana," I stammer. "You're, uh, about fifteen hours early."

"Isn't it amazing? My dress was ready right after we spoke! So Flip called the charter company and asked them if the jet could be ready by four-thirty. And here we are! I texted you before we went wheels up."

Must have been one of the many texts I ignored when I was playing crack the code on Asher's dirty French talk. "Here you are," I repeat, patting her back. "It's great to see you."

The sound Asher makes might or might not be a snicker. I can't even look at him right now. If I did, my embarrassment would etch itself across my face.

God, if we'd been alone a few minutes longer, we'd have been buck naked on that chair, rubbing off and trying to fuse our tongues together.

We would have *never* lived it down.

"So . . ." Asher clears his throat. "What are we going to do with this extra time together?"

"I have so many ideas," Hannah says.

I'll bet *zero* of them match mine.

22

HARD-ON CHUTZPAH

ASHER

*T*he lady wasn't kidding.

About five minutes after we help carry their luggage up to the largest suite, Hannah opens up a crate to reveal fifty miniature glass and brass lanterns, plus a bevy of crafting supplies. She sets up shop in the huge, white living room, with the three of us as her minions. "Mark, please cut each ribbon to exactly sixteen inches."

"Sixteen. Got it," he says, because she definitely asked the right man to do the right job.

"Asher, tie them into a bow, please. And Flip, you can add one of these tea lights that I'm unpacking. After this job is done, we'll move on to the Jordan almonds and the goodie bags."

Great. I have to get through almond bagging before I get my hands on Mark again. That also means I *can't* give Mark the lingering glance I crave. My face would give me away to Hannah. I might as well rent a billboard with six-foot letters reading: I WANT YOUR BROTHER TO BANG ME RIGHT FUCKING NOW.

After fifteen minutes of hard labor and zero eye contact, I

put some jazz on the stereo speakers and raid the beer fridge, then grab a soda for Hannah.

"The room looks like the wedding aisle at Michaels exploded," I point out, as I seat myself on an armchair across from the happy couple.

"Wait. How do *you* know what the wedding aisle at Michaels looks like?" Hannah asks, a smile lighting her sweet face.

"Woman, a photo shoot can go sideways in a million ways. Ask me sometime about the dozen plastic tiki torches I bought to get just the right flickering light for a Halloween shoot."

Mark's amused eyes lift to mine for a split second before darting away again.

He's avoiding me too. We're in the same room together, but he's on the opposite side of the space, in an armchair that I swear he chose for its distance from mine.

But now I can't help staring. My eyes dart over to where his muscular legs are propped onto a leather footstool. And the open collar of his shirt gives me a view of his neck—and the smooth column I traced with my tongue not so long ago.

I rein in a whimper.

"So how are you taking this change?" Flip asks me.

"Hmm?" I drag my gaze off Mark. "It's uh . . ." Wait. I have no idea what Flip is talking about. "This change," I repeat.

My friend tilts his head, studying me. "You seem distracted."

"No! Just tired . . ." I protest. *From twenty-four hours of sexual tension and sexual release.* ". . . from a long day of running wedding errands."

"He won't ask you to be the photographer, will he?" Flip asks. "Garrett?"

I blink. Now I'm sure I've missed something. "The photographer?"

"At his wedding," Flip says gently. "I just asked you if you saw the Instagram announcement and you nodded."

"Right," I say quickly. But inside, I'm reeling. Garrett is getting married? Already? "Of *course* I'm not taking wedding photos for him. He wouldn't want me to anyway. That's not my thing. And that would be super awkward."

"That's your ex?" Hannah asks, tying a satin ribbon around the last little bag of almonds.

"My ex," I repeat dully. "We broke up a while back. Actually, it was only eleven months ago. But who's counting."

"Oh, ouch," Hannah says.

I am very busy not looking at Mark, because I don't want to know what he thinks about that. And I'm also very busy not looking at Instagram, just for confirmation. It's probably a cheesy photo. Two guys in preppy clothes on a golf course somewhere, looking snazzy and well-organized as they plan their future together.

Ick, right? Who needs that? I wouldn't be any good at it either. I'm much better as a sex concierge—my role for the next few nights.

Still . . . something isn't sitting right.

When I look up from my glass, three people are still studying me. Maybe because I'm tapping an anxious foot against the sleek marble floor at the tempo of machine-gun fire in a mobster flick.

So I stop doing that. There's nothing to be anxious about. I'm just staring down a long tunnel of lonely nights in New York while my ex gets married and my best friend starts his life as a husband and a father.

Yeah, I'd really like to steer this conversation away from me and my ex. "Speaking of photographers, I talked to Simone, and she's all set for Saturday. She'll get shots of you getting ready, Hannah. The candids you want," I say. "Let me just reply to her text from earlier."

Since I already texted Simone and she's all good, I yank my phone out of my pocket and text Lucy. *Any word from FLI?*

Nothing, she replies immediately. *Sorry.*

Yeah, me too. They must have gone with another photographer.

I didn't *need* that job, but I wanted it. Not only would it have been fun, but it would have been very distracting.

After I close the text app, I raise my face. Mark's peering at me again, but his expression is unreadable. So much so that I

143

wish Hannah were yawning and ready to hit the hay so I could just ask Mark if he's still onboard for tonight's festivities.

"Guys, it's Wednesday," Hannah says, setting aside her crafts. "You know what that means?"

"Hump day!" Flip announces with a chuckle. "I'm surprised Asher isn't out hitting the nightclubs right now." He gives me a knowing smile, and I try my best to return it but I'm pretty sure I fail.

"No, it's our new *game night*," Hannah says firmly. "Let's start with a few rounds of Wits and Wagers. And after Mark crushes us, we'll switch to a bloodthirsty game of Scrabble. Who's in?"

"Me!" Flip raises his hand.

"I'm in. I just need to call Rosie to say goodnight," Mark says, shoulders hunched, like he doesn't want to play either.

Hannah reaches into a shopping bag and pulls out the travel edition of both games. She's going to be the greatest mother in the world, I bet. She's always prepared. And Flip will probably be a great dad, because he's good at everything he tries. Mark will probably rule the world with his spreadsheets. And I'll still be a fuck-up, hot mess, living gig to gig and hitting the clubs until I'm eighty-seven years old.

These thoughts brought to you by my ex announcing his wedding on Instagram.

It shouldn't bother me.

Yet it does.

Our game of bloodthirsty Scrabble takes a million years, but it might be drawing to a close soon when Hannah snags a triple-word score on *chutzpah*, and Mark counters with *whizbang*.

They are a fierce family. Fiddling with my tiles, I rearrange them until . . .

Ha!

Not even sure this is a playable word, but fuck it.

And fuck exes.

And fuck their engagements that I don't care about anymore

tonight, or hell, at all. What I really want is to get my hands on Mark again and soon. So I've got to do my part to end Scrabble.

Setting the tiles one by one on the board, I spell a word off *chutzpah*.

And maybe send a message to him as I play . . . *hardon*.

I sneak a glance at Mark.

His lips twitch.

His expression is no longer unreadable. He's an open book as those eyes swing to me, then away. He fights like hell to rein in a grin.

I want to wipe off that grin with a hot, searing kiss.

"Dude, that's not a Scrabble word," Flip puts in.

I arch a brow at my buddy. "But are you sure?"

Flip grabs his phone and asks Google as Hannah leans in to read his screen.

Perfect timing. I meet Mark's gaze, and his baby blues are filled with dirty wishes. *I got you, Banks. I am going to take care of those filthy desires.*

"It's not a word. *Hard* is, though, and Asher can leave it at that," Hannah offers, always the helpful one.

"So is *boner*," Flip says, which is not helpful.

"Thanks. I'll just whip out the extra *boner* letters in my pocket for that," I say, spelling *hard* instead.

Gets the point across.

Flip hauls Hannah in for a peck on the cheek. "We *could* play dirty Scrabble," he murmurs.

Yes. Do that. Elsewhere.

Her eyes flutter closed as he kisses her jaw, and that gives me another chance to catch Mark's attention. I lift a brow. He lifts one in return, and *that*—just knowing he's still up for us—makes me, well, harder.

This game must end soon, or I'll combust. Florida is known for strange occurrences, right? I'll wind up on that Twitter feed people make fun of. *Florida man erupts from sexual frustration, leaving behind only a pair of Andrew Christian underwear and one testicle.*

Okay, that's dark. But this is the same state where a man

recently set an alligator on fire while trying to shoo it away from his inflatable chair with a cigarette lighter.

Another eon later, the game mercifully ends. Hannah wins. Mark comes in second, Flip is third, and I'm last.

I could probably have played better, but my concentration is shot. As we put the game away, all I can think about is Mark's mouth on my *hard* cock. And his hands on me too. And, fine, his *hard* dick in my ass.

And Hannah still hasn't retreated to their room.

I'm here, waiting in this mansion, wanting to escape to the guest house. Basically, I'm a living, breathing sex spreadsheet tonight while the minutes tick by slowly. As they chat, I drink some wine and try not to stare across at Mark the way a hungry cat stares at a fish in a sealed aquarium.

Finally, as midnight approaches, Hannah puts a hand on her growing belly and yawns. "I should get to bed. We'll put in a long day tomorrow, right boys?"

I'm on my feet as quickly as if someone had pulled the fire alarm. "Good point. Let's get some Zs." I stretch my arms over my head for effect.

Flip gives me a curious frown. "Right. Are you guys staying upstairs too?"

"No, we're in the, uh, guest house," Mark says, his eyes on his shoes. "Our families will get those rooms upstairs. There's one for your parents and one for ours."

"Ah! That was nice of you," Hannah says. She crosses to her brother and hugs him. "Night, Mark. Thanks for your hard work."

I'd like him to thank me for my hard work in, say, about an hour.

"Oh, it's nothing," he says. "Anything for you." He sounds a little guilty.

Wait. Did I misread those dirty looks at the end of the game? What if Mark is about to give me some kind of speech about responsibility, or keeping promises, or something like that? What then?

Well, God made tongues for a reason, and mine can be very convincing.

Mark stands too, his overhead stretch more legitimate than mine. It's punctuated by an actual yawn. His shirt rides up a few crucial inches, and I catch a glimpse of the shadow of his happy trail against his lean abs.

My mouth actually waters. I'm in danger of pouncing on this man. The bottle of lube is still wedged in the pocket of my shorts, where my hand pats it now, just to make sure it's safe and sound.

"Night, guys," Flip says. "I should probably lock up, right?"

"Right," Mark says. But his eyes are on me. "We'll get out of your hair." He actually licks his lips.

Oh, boy. So maybe he's still onboard. I head for the sliding glass doors, reaching them in a nanosecond.

Mark stops to say goodnight to Flip, and to show him how the outside lights work. "These are pretty bright. You'll probably want to shut them off to sleep."

"Good point," Flip says. "See you for brunch tomorrow?"

They make a plan while I stalk toward the guest house. The lights go out on the swimming pool. Freedom is close at hand!

But then Hannah's voice rings out once again. "Oh! Hey— Mark! How did you like the first episode of *An Arranged Marriage*? I didn't get to watch it yet. But I know you couldn't wait."

"Oh," he says, sounding strangled. "It was . . . yeah. Real good. Lots to unpack there. Let's talk tomorrow."

Move it along, kids. Unpack it all tomorrow.

"Okay. Night," she says again.

I swallow a chuckle, and then the door snaps shut. But Mark doesn't follow me across the patio. I turn around and squint, looking for him while my eyes adjust to the dark.

Inside the house, more lights flicker off.

That's when I spot Mark, with his glasses already off. He's standing by a pool chair. *Our* pool chair.

Maybe to retrieve the box of condoms we left there. It's a good thing nobody saw those.

But no. Wait. He's removing his shirt.

I'm riveted.

By his body *and* his boldness.

This is hardly the Mark I thought I knew. This isn't even the Mark from the dance club last night. Or the shower this morning. This is the next level Mark, daring in ways I didn't expect.

Ways I like a lot.

As his shirt falls to the chair, I'm suddenly less eager to leave the pool deck. On silent feet, I cross back toward him. I'm dying to ask what he's up to. But I'm mindful of making any sound that Flannah might overhear.

As soon as I get close, though, Mark reaches for my shirt and tugs it over my head. A moment later, it's gone. I have so many questions for Mark right now, but I start with one.

I lean toward the heat of his skin, and whisper into his ear, "What gives? The guest house is more private."

"Maybe," he breathes. "But outdoor sex takes up quite a few rows on my spreadsheet. How quiet can you be?"

For a second, I just blink at him. I'm supposed to be the experienced one here. But this man keeps surprising me.

And I'm done with questions.

"Not that quiet," I admit. "Not if you're fucking me."

His eyes go *molten*. "That's tomorrow night," he rasps. "Right now, I want you naked in that pool. Just be Really. Fucking. Quiet."

Like I need to be told twice.

Mark and I both shed our clothes near the edge of the pool. He's naked a hot second later, his prick already hard for me. Wearing nothing but a serious frown, he stalks along the edge of the pool, looking up at the house. When he's standing near the deep end, he points upward, toward the only lit room. It's on the second floor.

By silent, mutual agreement, we both move toward the shallow end. There's a bench there, and a ledge with cupholders in it, in case you want to bring your cocktail into the pool.

Me? I only want to bring my cock.

And Mark's.

He sits down on the edge of the pool, arms flexing in the

moonlight as he lowers himself into the water. Rivulets slide down his firm chest as he settles onto the bench.

I slip into the water. But I don't sit beside him—not when I can straddle him instead. Who does he think is running this show, anyway?

Mark lifts his chin, looking me right in the eye as I settle onto his wide-stretched thighs. Our cocks line up, and even that first, paltry contact makes me have to hold back a groan. The only sound is the water lapping against our heated bodies, and the distant hum of a motorboat out in the bay.

We regard each other for a long beat.

"I thought that game would never end," I whisper.

"Same." He reaches up and sets a hand in the center of my chest. Wet fingertips tease me lightly, leaving goose bumps in their wake.

Nggggh. I'm raring to go. But I also like this little staring contest we're having.

"You have an ex who's getting married?" he asks suddenly.

Fuck, I don't want to talk about that. "Apparently." I lean in and scrape my whiskers against Mark's. The friction, the water rushing past my cock, the scrape of Mark's chest on my nipples . . . A man can't really think too well. I tongue his earlobe. "Kind of hard to remember his name right now," I whisper. "And I've got better uses for your tongue than talking about him. Like, I want 77C and D tonight, and 33A tomorrow."

"I'm all in," he says, and then I show him better uses for our mouths.

Mark lets out a horny grunt and grabs my ass with both hands. And I slide my body down his until I can plunder his mouth with my greedy one. Until our cocks line up and gyrate together.

This is exactly what we need. A slow, dirty grind. Wet kisses and even wetter bodies.

If Flip or Hannah decided to take a midnight stroll, we would be caught in a heartbeat. I fucking *love* the riskiness of this. But even more, I love how much Mark loves it. He is a goddamn study in contrasts. Nerdy banker. Spreadsheet maker. Skinny-dipper.

Sometimes, getting to know a guy makes him less interesting. But not Mark Banks. His slippery, questing hands light me up.

And I can't wait to see what else he'll do next.

23

ANVILS AND TELEPHONE POLES

MARK

*T*here's no cell in my spreadsheet for the way I feel right now.

Asher was right—the sheet *is* a piss-poor way to describe all the things I'm feeling, and all the things I want. There aren't even words for the way the water caresses my body, making me tingle everywhere. Or the way Asher's kisses taste. Like heat. And need.

Getting into the pool was the best idea I've ever had. And it turns out that a swimming pool isn't actually a boner killer after all. I'm on fire, and mere cold water could never extinguish it.

My brain is full of static as Asher climbs off my lap. "Come on," he whispers. "Out you go."

I take a drunken glance at the house. It's dark and quiet. I should probably be shocked when Asher guides me down onto a chaise lounge again.

And I should be even more shocked when he says, "Hands and knees."

But I'm not shocked. I'm just . . . *consumed* with want.

I sneak another glance at the house. The chair Asher chose is blocked by a potted palm. So if someone does wander by, only eighty percent of my dignity will be shredded.

And I'm too drunk on lust to care.

I do as I'm told. Suddenly, a cool hand wanders up my inner thigh. A muscular knee presses between my legs. It's almost rude, the way he's spreading me open.

Yup. There should be a spreadsheet cell for nudging my knees apart like he owns them. Hell, I might need a whole new tab for the way he's manhandling me right now.

I wait for the snick of the lube bottle, but it never comes. Has he lost it? I lift my head to look around when suddenly his thumbs spread my ass cheeks apart, and a hungry tongue traces my rim.

My head falls forward as a hot gasp escapes my chest.

But I lose his tongue immediately. And then one of his hands reaches around to clamp over my mouth as his chest covers my back. "Quiet," he snarls into my ear.

I nearly come on the spot.

He's braced me with strong arms against his body. My dick is as hard as a telephone pole. And the hiss of his voice in my ear is the sexiest part of all. "Banks. If you make any more noise, I'll have to take you inside."

I nod in agreement.

Releasing his hold, he kisses a slow path down my back. I'm vibrating with anticipation as he spreads me apart slowly again. And I stop breathing when his hot mouth finds my hole.

It's . . . outrageous how good that feels. Slick and dirty. I press my face against my arms and try to breathe instead of moaning. But when he snakes a naughty hand between my thighs to tease my balls, I have to bite my own wrist.

And it doesn't stop. He licks and teases and tortures me until I'm a damn mess. Until I'm so hard it hurts. But the moment I reach down to try to rub my aching cock, he gives me a single, sharp slap on the ass.

Then he grabs my arm and pulls me up off the chair. "We're going in," he whispers. Or maybe I only hear it in my head as he grabs our clothing off the deck and shoves it into my arms, along with my glasses.

I follow him at a fast clip into the house, where he closes the door behind us and orders me onto his bed.

Asher disappears for a moment. I hear water running as I haul the comforter off the king-sized bed and lie spreadeagled on the sheet. My heart is pounding like I've run a half marathon, and my cock is heavy like an anvil between my legs.

I've never felt more alive than I do right this second.

"Roll onto your side, baby," he rasps as he returns to the room. "Bend your knee."

I look up, and there he is in all his muscular glory, and he looks voracious. God, I'm a lucky man. Loopy with desire, I arrange my body the way he's asked as he sinks onto the bed in front of me. He opens the lube bottle and pours some into his hand. My eyes practically roll back in my head as he reaches around to press the pad of one thick finger against my hole.

"Breathe," he says.

And I do. But I'm so willing it doesn't even matter. I bear down on that slick finger and groan with pleasure. The invasion is unfamiliar and it stings a little. And it's still exactly what I crave.

"Jesus, Banks." Asher makes a low noise of approval. "You're magic."

"More," I growl, as I shift to my back.

"Patience," he whispers. Then he leans down and kisses the place where my thigh meets my body. It's unexpectedly tender, and I shiver from head to toe.

That's when he swallows my dick in one shocking, well-practiced motion.

My back bows, and I let fly a string of curses. My skin breaks out in a sheen of sweat as Asher gives me a sturdy suck. And when he releases me a few moments later, I practically howl from the loss of his mouth.

"Easy, Banks," he murmurs. "I'm not done with you yet."

And he isn't. As I sprawl on the bed, spread open and panting, he teases my crown and then takes me into his mouth again. His tongue is wicked and weighty against my shaft.

I press my shoulder into the mattress and groan. All my nerves are jumping with electric anticipation. And when I glance down to see Asher's blond head bobbing between my legs, it's almost more than I can stand.

Tonight, I'm living someone else's life—some fun guy's dream. A secret hookup in balmy Miami. With a guy whose sense of humor I've come to appreciate as much as I enjoy his sculpted shoulder muscles and the too-long golden hair at the back of his neck.

I reach down and run my fingers through it, and Asher moans.

That's another thing my spreadsheet could never capture—this strange bubble of intimacy we've created in the tiny guest house. There's no cell for the way his soft hair sifts between my fingers. Or the wickedly hot view I get next as he tilts up his chin to look me in the eyes.

"Fuuuck," I whisper as he gives me another suck. "You're killing me."

His naughty finger slides farther into my channel. I can't even sort out the sensations anymore. There's the pressure in my ass, and the pleasure on my cock.

Then he strokes a place deep inside me, and I feel a kind of dark, intense pleasure that's completely unfamiliar. And I hear a low, desperate moan that probably comes from me.

"You like that, Banks?" he murmurs.

My answer is a tangle of curses and gibberish.

With a chuckle, he moves his mouth away from my cock and kisses my stomach instead.

"More," I beg.

"You'll get more." He strokes my prostate again and I arch off the bed with pleasure. "You ever do this to yourself?"

Well I *thought* I had. I've plugged myself while I jerk off. The pressure was nice. "It's not the same," I murmur.

His laugh is wicked. "Can you take two fingers?"

"I'll take whatever you give me."

Asher groans. "Careful what you wish for, hotshot. Aren't we taking the list one item at a time?"

"What list?" I grunt. I'm ready to throw the damn thing overboard. Lists aren't real life.

This is real life—the press of his finger into my body, and the fizz of longing pounding in my veins. I want this beautiful man with the smart mouth and crooked smile. I want this night to never end.

Sadly, his magic finger disappears. I lie boneless on the bed, listening to the sound of the lube bottle opening again while my heart thrums with anticipation.

Next comes the sting as he penetrates me once more. I'm expecting his mouth on my cock again too. Asher is a slick lover. He has all the moves. I don't like to think too hard about all the men who've come before me—all the living he's done while my life took a long nap.

This is the most fun I've had in years while I'm just a notch in his belt.

But those worries fall away as he hitches himself up my body and kisses my chest. That crazy hair of his tickles my chin as well as my nipples. And I clamp a hand around the back of his neck and ask my body to stretch a little farther. The burn is already easing off. He scissors his fingers and I groan as he brushes my spot again.

Yes. This. More, says the drumbeat of my heart. And I'm still waiting for his mouth to torture me again.

And it does—but not in the way I'm expecting. Asher rises up, one strong arm wrapped around my thigh, and then he sinks down onto my chest for a kiss. I moan against the unexpected assault of his tongue against mine. The kiss is an erotic multiplier, heightening every sensation times ten. I'm a forest fire, and I don't want to be put out.

When I gaze up at Asher in the dark, I'm astonished to see my own wonder mirrored back at me. Those bright eyes bore into me, like he's never seen anything so interesting in his life.

I'm greedy for him. I want more of his kisses and more of his artful touch. Just *more.* "Fuck me," I demand. "Do it."

He goes still. "Aren't we saving that for later?"

"No," I insist. "I'm on a deadline here. And you've got just what I need."

He blinks. "A hard dick, and good hygiene?"

Hell, the way I feel about Asher is so much more than that. But I haven't got any idea how to explain it. I'll never forget this night. I'll never forget him. And I'd never want to.

But that's too many words for a guy who's addled by lust. So I crane my neck and kiss him roughly instead. Our teeth click and our whiskers scrape and our tongues clash.

He moans, and I feel it in my balls.

I reach up and artlessly rub his chest. I don't want to stop touching him.

Ever.

24

THE JOY OF DICK

ASHER

I'm stalling. And I'm not sure why.

Maybe it's because Flip would kill me if he knew I'd deflowered his fiancée's brother's ass.

Maybe it's because I've never been anyone's first time.

Maybe—and this is not my favorite theory—maybe I'm not sure I really deserve the way Mark is looking at me. Like I'm a superhero. I'm basically Iron Man right now. Just ask my dick.

Mark weaves his fingers into my hair and tugs. "St. James," he says against my mouth. He kisses me so hard that I think that's the end of the sentence. But then he adds, "Fuck me now. Pound me right into the bed."

In answer, I let out a horny groan and hump his thigh. Because I'm eloquent like that.

"You're wasting time," he whispers. "And it's not like we have lots of it."

Of course he's right. This perfect moment won't last. They never do. I untangle myself from Mark and reach for the condoms. "You're sure about this?"

"Deathly."

I get busy suiting up. And when I turn back to the bed,

kneeling between Mark's thighs, he tucks his hands behind his head, lifts his chin, and gives me a look that says *what are you waiting for?*

God, Mark Banks could break me. He knows what he wants, which is sexy as hell. And he's not afraid to ask for it.

He isn't the boring man I mistook him for a few months ago.

Hell, he's not who I thought he was yesterday morning when we got on that plane to Florida.

He's so much more, and if he floored me in all the best ways yesterday, that's nothing compared to how he's affecting me now.

I'm utterly stunned to discover who he is and what he wants.

It's a big fucking deal to be someone's first.

That's why I was stalling. For him, but truly, for me.

I want to give him something he's never felt before. The most intense pleasure ever. I want to make this so out-of-this-world for him that he never regrets the night I walked into his room when he was watching that show.

And hell yes, I can fucking do that.

Iron Man didn't shirk away from his mission. I won't lose sight of mine—making this moment worth it for him.

In every single way.

Including one really fucking important way.

Words.

"Just tell me if it hurts. Tell me if you want to stop," I say, since that's the stark reality of sex. Not everyone likes it every way.

"I will, but . . ." His blue irises flames at me as he reaches for the lube, squirts some on his hand, and then coats my covered cock. ". . . I can't do that till you're in me. So just get in me," he rasps out. "Or do I have to beg?"

My entire body shudders, a wave of pleasure jolting through me. I can't remember the last time I ever felt this . . . restless about sex.

But that's the wrong word entirely.

I've never been this *thrilled.*

My body buzzes with excitement as I rub the head of my

cock against his entrance, my breath staggering past my lips the second I make contact.

A tight gasp comes from him. He pushes up on his elbows, his eyes wild as he watches my face, then as his gaze drifts down to where we connect.

His fearlessness spurs me on.

I grip his knee, pushing his right leg up, making this easier for him as I breach him.

"Oh fuck," he grunts tightly, his breath hitching.

I know what he's feeling. The first stirring of pain that's not quite pleasure yet. "You good?"

Mark won't want me to ask if it hurts. He probably won't care anyway if it does. He'll make it through those inevitable seconds of pain that always ebb away till everything feels just right.

That's where I want to get him.

"I'm good," he mutters. This guy knows his body, knows his needs, and he reaches for my arms, locking his hands tight around my biceps.

I sink in deeper, pleasure twisting through me as his gorgeous body hugs my cock.

"Fuck, you feel incredible," I rasp out since I can't *not* tell him. Can't *not* share.

He feels so fucking good, it's mind-blowing. The tightness, the heat. Most of all, the way he trembles under me.

"More," he urges, a husky, needy plea.

I dip my face, and capture his lips with a hard, wet kiss as I ease in all the way.

"You got me?" I ask as I pull back, meet his eyes.

He just nods a few times, lips parted, breath hot. His grip on my arms is almost too rigid, like he's holding on.

In that space between pleasure and pain.

And so, I give him what he needs. My man is such a sucker for kissing. As I let him adjust to all these brand-new sensations in his body, I kiss him again. Hungry, greedy kisses that he deserves, and with each press of my lips, he relaxes under me. Welcomes me inside.

His hands relent their death grip on my arms. Then he sinks back down, his head pushing into the pillow.

His eyes pin mine.

"Fuck me hard now," he says, and I unleash a carnal growl.

Mark Banks isn't intimidated by a single thing between the sheets, and I am so into him.

"Gonna make it so good for you," I tell him as I start to move, pumping my hips.

"Good for *us*," he corrects.

He has no idea how good he is for me. But then, I didn't know that he'd be good for me either, and I'm discovering so many things as I introduce Mark Banks to the joys of dick for the first time. Top amongst those? I thought I was the teacher and he was the student, but that dynamic fell by the wayside some time ago.

We're just two men in bed. Two lovers who want to make each other feel incredible.

Experience is irrelevant right now when I know, beyond a shadow of a doubt, that all we both want is to experience each other like this.

Mark slides his hands up and down my chest, like he's looking for a place to put them. At last he settles on my hips, anchoring them there.

And then I deliver exactly what he asked for. Because when a man tells you what he needs, you damn well ought to give it to him and give it good.

As I thrust, adrenaline spins higher in my cells, and I ask in a dirty growl, "You want it hard, Mark?"

"I do," he grits out.

"You want me to pound you into the mattress?"

He pushes up again, his face meeting mine, inches away. "Nail me."

"With so much fucking pleasure," I say, and then I rise up between his thighs, push his knees to his chest and I pound the fuck out of the other best man.

We are nothing but groans and grunts.

The world narrows to the slap of flesh, the beads of sweat, the moans as we fuck.

It's the thing I never expected to happen between us. But strange things do happen in Florida. Like this kind of sex. Wild, passionate, bold.

His eyes squeeze shut, and his mouth falls open as he reaches for his cock.

No way. "I'll get you there," I demand as I take over, wrapping a palm around his thick shaft, my hand flying. I give him everything he asked for.

Turns out it's everything I want too.

The vein pulses in his neck, like an orgasm beacon. His features twist with that relentless press of delicious agony. He pushes up, wraps one strong hand around the back of my head, and crushes his lips to mine for a few delirious seconds before he lets go.

Then rasps out the sexiest words ever . . . *"Fuck yes."*

He shoots all over my hand and his stomach. And my whole body overheats, my brain a static haze of bliss as I follow him there with a heady rush.

Panting, I fall onto his chest, his release smearing all over me. "Holy . . ."

I can't even finish the thought.

And I'm not sure I should say what I'm starting to think: *Was that as good for you as it was for me? Because you are the best adventure I've ever had in bed . . .*

That wouldn't even be post-orgasmic hyperbole.

It's just the truth.

A few minutes later, we're in the shower, cleaning off chlorine and climaxes.

I'm still not sure what to say, because too many thoughts are bumper cars in my head. *Does it hurt? Did you like it? I mean, I know you liked it, but did you like it as much as . . . the other sex you've had? And are we still on for tomorrow night too? And, holy fuck, how did I not notice the first time we met how fucking sexy you are? Or how much I'd relish being your first?*

I keep that all to myself and try to focus on the safest way to ease any post-sex weirdness he might feel.

"So, sliding scale of hotness for fucking you," I muse, as I run the soap over my chest one more time while he rinses his hair. "I'm going with ultra-hot."

He just smiles, a little drowsily. "Sounds about right."

I turn off the shower, and when we've dried off, I usher him back to my bed, pull up the comforter, and glance at the clock. It's past midnight, and I'm too blissed out to do much more than yawn and plant a kiss on his shoulder.

"Hey, Banks," I murmur.

"Yeah?"

"I've been meaning to ask you something."

He tenses, and I run a hand down his arm. "Why is there a fifty percent chance of two people in any group of twenty-three having the same birthday?"

"You really want me to answer that now, St. James?"

"Mmm. I do," I murmur. "I think it might help me sleep."

"You sarcastic fucker."

I drag him close, kiss the back of his neck and drift off.

25

GOOD MORNING TO ME

THURSDAY

ASHER

*A*s the light streaks through the window in the morning, I'm still basking in the after-effects. My helpful brain conveniently replays the reel of the night before—Mark's throaty groans, the heat of his body, the smell of his skin. A potent mix of chlorine, of all things, and his endless desire.

Mine too.

In fact, I'd like to go again right now.

I flip over in bed, all ready to tug that warm body against mine, when I'm met by . . . nothing.

Cool sheets.

A silent room.

And an empty bed.

I rub my eyes and push up, hunting for him. His glasses aren't on the nightstand. His phone is gone.

I listen for noise. The shower maybe? The hiss of the coffee pot?

But the guest house is eerily still.

Did he return to his room after we conked out post-shower?

My chest tightens. Swinging my legs out of bed, I pad to the bathroom, take care of business, and brush my teeth.

Then I wander past his room to sneak a peek, but the door's cracked open only an inch. I can't see in.

But why do I care if he crashed in his room?

Because . . . I do. I just do.

My thumping heart needs to settle down, though. It's only *sex*.

So what if he took off after he got off? I've been there, done that. Hell, it's pretty much been my MO for the last decade. And it ought to be de rigueur for this tryst that's ending this weekend.

I head to my bedroom when the main door creaks open.

A shirtless Mark strolls in, hair a mess, glasses on. His eyes sail down my body, stopping point-blank on my dick.

"Good morning to me," he says, with an appreciative hum.

And my dick shows off how much I like Mark Banks by getting harder. Fucking exhibitionist.

Good thing he's checking out my junk, since the smile I'm wearing is too much. Don't entirely want him to know I was stupidly worried he took off for his own room late last night. "But mornings are better in bed," I say casually as I turn into my room.

He'd better follow me.

I flop down on the bed. Waiting.

When he turns into my room, he stops in the doorway, dips his head. Mark looks a little shy, and a lot happy.

My chest warms. Hmm. Must be from the sunlight.

Leaning against the doorjamb, he scratches his jaw. "Since my parents arrive later this morning, I was busy hiding the casserole dishes," he says, pointing at the sprawling house. "Like I told Hannah I would."

"Are they stashed anywhere I should know about? Under the couch cushions? Just so I don't sit on one."

A smile curves his lips. "No. I hid them in the pool shed."

"Explain."

"Mom loves to clean too. And vacuum. So if I hid them in a

linen closet or the pantry in the house, she'd find them. She'll open all the cupboards and doors, so I had to put them in the one spot she wouldn't look. With the pool chemicals."

"Your brain is a very busy place," I say.

"And then I spotted a pelican. I took a picture of it and sent it to Bridget to show Rosie. She likes animals. My daughter, that is," he says, and for the first time ever, Mark sounds like he's rambling. Mark is not a rambler.

"That's adorable," I say, because sending bird pics to his kid is cute. But I don't think he's telling me about his kid so I'll think he's a good dad.

He's waiting for me to make the next move.

Ah, hell.

That's why he's shy right now. He's got that morning-after *was-it-good-for-you* look in his eyes.

And I've got the answer to soothe his worries. That's a heady feeling, too—knowing you can give someone what he needs. "Are you just going to stand there looking incomparably sexy in those basketball shorts and nothing else? Or are you going to get your fine ass back in bed? No one expects to see us for a while. After all, I have an excellent track record for not showing my fabulous face till brunch. And everyone probably assumes you're off solving algebraic equations in that pretty head of yours while jogging ten miles on Key Biscayne."

"Please. I do differential calculus when I run." He slides back into bed.

My brow knits as I pluck at the waistband of his shorts. "What the fuck is this? Get naked. Now."

"Are we fucking again?" He sounds eager. It's a good sound.

"Not yet. Emphasis on *yet*. I just want . . ." But I'm unsure if I should fully articulate what I truly crave right now. A little more time with him. "Just want you naked in bed with me."

"Twist my arm." He shucks off his shorts and underwear, and that's what I like to see. All this skin. All these muscles. All of his body that I want again and again.

But I should be a good sex tutor, make sure my straight-A student is holding up. "Are you sore?"

He shrugs. "A little. But I'm good with it."

That's pretty much his mantra in bed, I'm learning. He's good with everything. He wants everything. He's open to all of the above. Funny, how I thought I was the only one among us with no hang-ups. Seems we're both that way. I run a hand down his hip. "Good. Glad you're . . . good."

"And you?" he asks cautiously.

I get it now. Why he's all tentative and this side of shy. Grabbing his ass, I haul him against me. "I'm excellent. Last night was incredible."

He fights off a smile. "Good. That's good."

Mark's not into swoony words, though, so the better way to let him know how I feel might be like this. "So, the pool shed. Is that on your list? Do I need to bend you over the pool pump and fuck you there tonight?"

His eyes glint. "No. That's what I'll do to you."

"Bet I'll love it. You banging me among the pool chemicals and casserole dish stash has got to be top of my wish list," I say, and we both burst into laughter.

That feels good too.

I stretch out on the sheets, parking my hands behind my head. "By the way, it's nice that you did that for Hannah. It's cute the way you look out for her. How you want everything to be good for her."

"She's been my best friend pretty much my whole life, so I try to look out for her, take care of her however I can."

"I like Hannah too, but . . ." I say, drawing out the last word.

Mark shoots me a *don't-you-dare-say-shit-about-my-sister* look, which is all kinds of endearing. "But what, Asher?" The question comes out as a challenge. One that says *don't cross me about my family.*

I raise a finger to make a point. "But I have one bone to pick with her."

"Yes?" he asks, still cool.

"Why didn't Hannah tell me you were bi six months ago when I met you?"

Mark laughs, letting go of his steely veneer. "Because it's personal. We keep secrets."

"But it's not really a secret. You did let me pretty much feel you up all over Miami yesterday."

"You weren't complaining," he tosses back.

"As if I would. I fucking loved it. But my point is, why keep it from me?"

He meets my gaze. "Because it's personal, and you know what I mean by that. It wasn't for her to share."

"But it would have been *useful* to me," I say, a little tease in my voice.

Mark props his head in his hand, stares at me like he doesn't quite believe me. This guy is a physical manifestation of the word skeptical. "How would it have been useful?"

I shrug lazily as I yawn. "I could have chased you in New York. So I could get you under me sooner. Or me under you."

"Somehow I doubt you'd have done that."

I might have then. I won't now. He laid down the law yesterday about New York benefits, and there'll be no extension of them. Which is fine with me for so many reasons.

Still, he's wrong about my interest in him. It's been brewing for some time.

"You think it took a dance club and one mere day of sexual tension for me to develop an interest in you?" I counter.

He says nothing.

Oh, ye of little faith.

Scoffing, I reach for my phone on the nightstand. Clicking open my text app, I show him where I saved the stupid lips text thread he mistakenly sent me.

He groans in misery. "And that proves what? That you just wanted to lord it over me?"

I look at the drunken confessional. Read the series of texts again. Let the buzz whip through me one more time. "They delight me now like they did then," I confess.

"You sentimental fucker," he says, elbowing me.

"Yeah, yeah. Hang on. Look." I make good on my promise to show him the pics of my mullet days.

"Wow." He cracks up, and I like that sound.

But now I have another question. "I bet you've got something saved on your phone about me. Like one of my underwear modeling shots. Come on. Admit it," I say, riling him up.

He rolls his eyes. "My God. How much stroking does your ego need?"

I wrap a hand around my dick. "Baby, it's not the ego that needs stroking. Although the ego is directly connected to my cock."

"And you want me to stroke that?"

"You know you want to," I say, but I'm undeterred from my true mission. I'm determined to know how long he's been into me. I'm greedy like that. "Anyway, you looked me up. You knew my pro stats."

"I told you I did my homework," he says, but we both know he's lying.

Good thing I've learned how to extract the truth from him.

"Tell me," I whisper as I cover him with my body, press my lips to his, and give him a soft, tender kiss. He murmurs under me. A sexy sound that turns into a long, low, groan of pleasure. And then, it begins—the melting of Mark Banks. I can feel the shift in him. The way his body responds, how he lets go of his constant need for control, how my kisses unlock him.

It's crazy to think that a kiss can do that, but mine seem to have that effect on this man. That's a gift—one I don't want to deny.

I skate my mouth along his jaw, under it, kissing my way down his neck, across his Adam's apple. Then I slide my thumb over his morning stubble, and give him one more slow, sleepy kiss that tastes like sunshine and shared secrets.

When I pull back, his eyes are hazy. "You know I looked you up," he whispers.

"Tell me why."

His jaw tightens. "Why do you think?"

"You had a thing for me," I say, taking a guess.

I really want to be correct on this count. I like being right almost as much as I like driving fast cars and drinking expensive wine.

But not at the same time.

"If by 'having a thing for you' you mean I thought you were an arrogant dick, then yes," he says, in that dry tone he's mastered.

I scoff-laugh. "Then why bother looking me up, Banks?"

His eyes travel purposefully down my body. "Because you were a superhot arrogant dick."

Emphasis on *were*.

I really want to ask if he *still* thinks I'm a smug bastard. But I kiss those lush lips instead, indulging in as much of him as I can get. When I break the kiss, I press on, since these fun and games are just that—fun. "So what do you say, Banks? What's on your phone? What's your equivalent of me keeping the best text thread ever?"

He heaves a sigh. "Stupid fucking picture," he mutters, without meeting my gaze.

That gets my interest. "You saved a picture of me?"

He shuts his eyes, like this pains him.

Maybe I should relent, but I can't back down. Another kiss. Another sweep of my lips along his jaw, across his collarbone, up to his ear. And I whisper again, "What picture did you save?"

His body twists deliciously under me, his hands roping around my back, gripping my ass. "The one from the engagement party," he grits out, vulnerability in his tone.

I pull back. "Yeah?"

"Yeah."

"Show it to me."

"Why? You were there."

"Don't you get it? I want to see it for the same reason you have it," I admit.

For once, Mark Banks loses his poker face. In its place is a smile.

The grin doesn't retreat as he reaches for his phone, swipes his thumb on the screen, clicks around. He shows me the picture of us from that night. I whistle in appreciation of the two hot guys in the shot. "Look at that. You're scowling. I'm grinning like a cocky asshole."

Mark snorts. "Yep. It's our . . ."

He trails off before he says *our love language*.

But I know that's what he meant. I was going to say the same thing.

Maybe because the moment's getting too heavy, too intense, he shifts gears. "So, you were kind of checked out for a bit last night. Does it really bother you that your ex got engaged?" Mark asks the question evenly, in the same tone he used to talk to the chef, the florist, the officiant.

But I understand him better now. This is not a business question he's asking me. It's personal, and important to him. He shared the story of the demise of his marriage with me, so I crack open my recent history.

"We were together for a year. I was about to ask Garrett to move in with me and he told me he met someone else. The rest is history."

"Wow. That sucks."

It did. But I'm not entirely sure the brief bout of self-loathing I wrestled with last night was about Garrett after all. Hearing that news reminded me of the grade my ex gave me in the relationship department—an F. "He didn't think I was a very good boyfriend."

Mark meets my gaze head on. "Are you a bad boyfriend?"

I scratch my jaw, unsure how to answer. "Maybe?"

"Did you cheat on him?"

I scoff. "No. I don't cheat."

"Did you steal from him, insult his family, treat him badly, ignore his wants and needs, or root for the Boston Red Sox in front of him? Wait. Make that *at all*."

I laugh, deep in my belly. "I didn't do any of those things. Especially the last one."

Mark nods, like a lawyer pleased with the line of questioning for his expert witness. "And the day you were going to ask him to move in with you, he told you he met somebody else and was into some other guy?"

I squirm a bit from the reminder. But is it the memory of Garrett that's bugging me or the fact that I don't necessarily want Mark to think of me that way? "That's what happened."

Mark seems to mull this over for several seconds. "Sounds to me like the problem wasn't you, Asher. It sounds to me like the problem was him."

Then he turns my tricks on me. My daring fling straddles me and roams his mouth along my neck. In seconds, his lips erase all thoughts of anyone else.

As he kisses his way down my body, he murmurs, "The problem definitely wasn't you."

He stops talking when he takes my cock in his mouth, and treats me to a fantastic morning blow job.

Just like that, I'm not thinking about the past—only the deliciously sexy present. I intend to enjoy every second of it since it's going to end very soon.

Two hours later, I am officially an expert on wedding tents. Add that to my resume after an hour with Ramon in the late morning, surveying the expanse of lawn past the pool.

"It's going to look great," I tell the man from Dream Tents.

"Like the wedding tent of *your* dreams," he says, and I hate to break it to the mustached man, but I definitely don't dream about wedding venues.

Even ones that come complete with air conditioning, a wood floor for dancing, white tables, a DJ stand, and firefly lights flickering under the roof. Although it might be perfect for sneaking off to later for an outdoor tryst with Mark.

Or wait. Is that an indoor boink?

Hmm. I'll have to ask the brainiac if tent-fucking qualifies for the indoor or outdoor cells on his fucksheet.

Either way, I might have an item to add to his to-do list.

Which is getting longer rather than shorter.

Ramon tells me his crew will start setting up this afternoon and it'll take a day. I thank him for his time, stride around the pool, then stop in my tracks at the trio emerging from the mansion.

Like father, like son.

The man in horn-rimmed glasses with a thick head of dark hair must be the one and only elder Banks.

And I know where Mark gets his sense of fashion.

His father wears polos too. I glance down at my burgundy shorts that fit so well they could be tailored.

Note to self: Take Mark shopping someday.

Wait, there is no someday. So there's nothing to take him shopping for. I strike that idea from my agenda.

Besides, the here and now is too much fun.

His mom wears a straw hat and khakis, too. Maybe they have a family crest in khaki. She even wears a polo shirt. It's white. Because of course it is.

I stop at the deep end of the pool, shamelessly listening.

His mother peers at the sky. "Are you wearing sunscreen? Melanoma is an epidemic in Florida."

"Mom, I'm always wearing sunscreen," Mark says as I near them.

"But you have to make sure it's a particular kind of sunscreen," his father puts in. "Especially in Florida. Everything's much more dangerous here. Did you hear about the lightning strike last week? June is the deadliest month for lightning in Florida, so we have to be vigilant."

"I will keep an eye out for lightning," Mark says, and somehow, in some way, I bet Mark will find a way to be a lightning ranger.

"It might even hit that red car in the driveway. Please tell me you got insurance on it. Those things are dangerous. I heard about them blowing up."

"Mom, it's a different make of car that blows up. One with a faulty electrical system," Mark says as they near me, and he meets my gaze, his eyes saying *I told you so about my family.*

She waves a hand airily. "My point exactly. You have to be very careful with everything."

"Mark opted into the insurance. And he's quite an excellent

driver," I say to Mark's parents, who snap their gazes to me at the same time.

"You must be the lovely Mrs. Banks," I say to his mother, extending a hand. "Your daughter is wonderful and my best friend is madly in love with her."

She beams at me. "That makes me so happy to hear."

"And it's a pleasure to meet you, sir," I say to Mark's dad, shaking his hand too.

"And you as well," his father says.

"This is Asher St. James," Mark cuts in, finishing the intros. "He's . . ."

My rabid desire to tease the hell out of this man rises up, and I sincerely hope Mark's struggling with the urge to introduce me as *the guy who banged his brains out last night.*

"The best man too," Mark adds, and those four words come out in a rush.

I ask Mark's father if he heard about the crocodile fire, and that keeps his parents riveted as I show them the pool, and we dissect the best strategies to avoid dangerous reptiles.

When they're standing at the edge of the lawn, debating the ideal time to swim, I step closer to Mark, tip my forehead to his parents, and lower my volume. "I understand everything about you now."

He rolls his eyes and mutters, "Fuck you."

Funny, but I understand that, too, and what it does to my chest.

Squeezes it.

But I stay focused on winding him up, speaking in a barely audible voice, just for him. "You wanted to tell them, didn't you? That I'm the guy who made you come harder than you ever have before?"

He swallows roughly, a shudder moving through his body before he collects himself. "Yes, Asher. That's exactly what I wanted to tell my parents about you. *By the way, I got laid last night by Flip's superhot wingman, and it was epic.*" He turns to face me, his blue eyes shining with heat. "And tonight I'm going to fuck him."

"I'm holding you to that," I say, then cross over the grass to join Mark's parents. "The view is stunning, isn't it?"

"Gorgeous," his mom says.

"Mrs. Banks, would you like me to take a picture of you and your kids for your family mantel back home?"

Her eyes light up. "Would you?"

We round up the bride, then I call Mark over, and Flip joins us too. I take pictures of the five of them with his mom's cell, the bay shimmering behind them.

When I show his mother the shots on the phone, she brings her hand to her heart. "Those are some of the best pictures anyone has taken of me. You can't even see my crow's feet."

I shoot her a questioning look. "What crow's feet, Mrs. Banks?"

She dips her head, smiling as she pats my shoulder. "I like you."

"Want to see the goodie bags, Mom?" Hannah asks, then she corrals everyone else into the house.

It's just Mark and me again at the edge of the pool. "I won them over," I say to him.

"Was that your goal?" There's doubt in his tone.

"Yes."

"Why did you want to? To show you could do it?"

I shake my head. "No. For Hannah. But mostly for you."

I leave him with that thought as I head off to join Flip.

Mostly, I go so I don't tell Mark anything more.

Like . . . *I wanted to win them over because I want your parents to like me.*

I just do.

26

WET T-SHIRT CONTESTS

MARK

"*D*addy!"

The sound of my little girl's voice has me dropping the knife next to the wedges of cheese. Flip and Hannah did some shopping, and I agreed to set out a spread for everyone to nibble on for lunch.

But now Rosie is here, running through the gourmet kitchen, arms outstretched. "I LOVE Florida!" she shrieks.

Oh, boy. Someone has excess energy to burn off. I grab her just as she's about to collide with my thighs. And I lift her up and whirl her around while she shrieks again.

"Turn it down a notch, Rosie," Bridget begs. I stop whirling and catch sight of my ex in the doorway. She looks bedraggled.

"Long line at the rental car place?" I guess. *Sugar on the plane?* I mentally add. Bridget never used to have trouble saying no to our daughter. But everything is a little haywire this year since the divorce.

"The longest," she says. "Then I got lost looking for the causeway."

"Sorry," I say, and then mentally kick myself. It was Hannah's idea to invite Bridget to the wedding along with Rosie. My sister has this romantic idea that Bridget and I will someday become best friends and the happiest co-parents on the planet.

I don't see it. Divorce doesn't usually work that way.

"Is there a pool?" Rosie asks in my arms. "There has to be a pool. I brought all of my bathing suits. And Mama got me a dress for the wedding! It's purple. It's the kind that whirls. I need to go swimming."

"I need some brie on crackers and a tall glass of wine," Bridget puts in.

"Fine," I say. "You finish the board. There's fruit and sausages left to cut. My parents could also use some food."

"Fun times," Bridget mutters. My parents aren't her biggest fans this year.

But that isn't my problem. "I'll take Rosie for a swim."

"Go," she mutters. Then she grabs a crumble of aged gouda and pops it into her mouth.

I leave the kitchen without a backward glance.

Fifteen minutes later, I'm holding Rosie in four feet of water. We're both wearing swimsuits and sunscreen. It's a bright, sunny day, and I have forgotten to be irritated by my ex. And I like this kind of forgetting.

"I really shoulda brought my water wings," Rosie says.

"You don't need them," I insist. Rosie should learn to swim. There aren't many places to learn in Manhattan, though. Just a couple of public pools with limited hours, and very few swim lessons.

But here, we're in a gorgeous private pool. No time like the present.

"Okay, I'll swim," Rosie says. "Just as long as I don't have to put my face in the water."

A deep, manly chuckle comes from behind me on the pool deck. *Asher.* The sound of his voice is like a second sun heating the back of my neck. But I'm a little busy here, so I don't turn around.

"I think you're old enough now that I can share the secret to swimming," I tell my daughter.

She perks up. "The secret?"

"Yup." I kick my feet, and I swim us both into the deep end. "There's a secret way to keep all the water out of your nose and mouth like magic. All you have to do is blow bubbles."

"What? I didn't bring any bubbles."

"Not the kind of bubbles in a bottle. We make our own. Watch." I allow myself to sink partly into the water, until my chin is submerged. And I blow a stream of bubbles out of my mouth.

Rosie watches me with a smile on her face. "I can do that."

"Show me."

She leans down until her lips are touching the water. Barely. And she burbles out a few bubbles.

"Good!" I say. "That's it. But you don't have to be so careful. This really is magic. So long as you're pushing air out of your body, no water can get in. Watch." I sink my whole head under— holding her up above the surface—and blow bubbles for a good fifteen seconds before coming up again. "I want to see you blow all the bubbles. If you're brave and you make it work, there's a bowl of watermelon in it for you."

"Seedless?" she asks, because my kid is a fearsome negotiator.

"Seedless," I agree.

She squints at the surface of the water for a moment. "All right. I'll try."

And maybe it *is* magic. Because I'm teaching my kid to swim, and it's working. Fifteen minutes later, Rosie can put her whole head underwater like a champ.

But she would like a steady stream of praise for her efforts, please. "Mama, look! Daddy, watch! Grandma, See?"

From their spot under an umbrella, my parents assure her that she's a swimming genius. So does Bridget. Hannah and Flip get in on the cheerleader action, too, as they stroll out to the pool from the house. "You're a dolphin now, Rosie," Hannah calls as she grabs a chair.

"My cousin will be too," Rosie answers, and Flip sets a hand on my sister's belly as they sit.

"And now you can do that bubble magic and kick at the same time," I tell my kiddo. "You swim to me, and I'll catch you."

"Swim from where?" she demands.

"The wall? The ladder?"

She wrinkles up her nose. Dubious. She clings more tightly to me. "I don't think so. Maybe another time."

"Bridget?" I call. "A hand, here?"

"I'm not wearing a suit," my ex says, a glass of rosé in her hand as she stretches on a lounge chair in shorts and a tank. She's not going anywhere.

"Grandma? Grandpa?" I say to my parents. But they're both close to dosing in their chairs.

"Why are we the only ones in the pool?" Rosie asks. "The pool is the best place in Florida. Except for Disney World. So, this is the second-best place."

I'm with her on the pool being the second-best place. Right after Asher's bed. And speak of the devil, Asher stands at the edge of the deep end. "It's a shame I'm not wearing a suit, or I'd swim with you two."

"Yeah. Shame," I agree with a smile. *But it didn't stop you last night.* My brain offers up a visual of Asher, naked, grinding on my lap in the shallow end.

Asher turns to walk away. But then he bobbles, and one foot slips over the edge. "Uh-oh." His arms come up suddenly. "Oh God." He flaps his hands uselessly.

Rosie shrieks as Asher falls ass-first and fully clothed into the deep end.

Wait. Did a professional athlete just fall into the pool by accident?

He pops up, beaming, a clear sign it was a hoax. He did that on purpose, something I like all too much. "Hey, guys," he says. "Nice day for a swim. Anybody need an extra pair of hands around here?"

Rosie needs a minute, actually. She's giggling so hard that if I weren't holding her up, she might actually drown.

"Let's play catch," Asher says. "Anyone have a ball?"

"N-no!" Rosie laughs.

"Fine," he says with a shrug. "Catch-the-kid it is! Toss 'er over, Banks."

"Great plan," I say. "On a count of three. One . . ." I swing her through the water. "Two . . ."

"Daddyyyy!" The shriek is so high-pitched that it almost breaks the human sonic barrier.

Spoiler: I don't throw my child at my hookup. I wait for her to calm down, and then I ask her if she wants to swim to Asher.

He holds out both his hands. "Betcha can't kick this far!"

He's four feet away. Tops. His designer T-shirt is clinging to his ripped chest. Are wet T-shirt contests a thing for men? They should be.

"Bet I can!" Rosie sticks her face in the water and kicks so hard I have to twist my body out of harm's way. She reaches Asher a split second later. "Did it!"

"Again," he says, effortlessly turning her around with tanned hands. "Swim to your dad now."

I back off a few feet, and we carry on like this for a while with Rosie swimming farther and farther distances until she's panting and exhausted.

"Watermelon," she gasps. "You promised."

"And you earned it." I lift her up onto my shoulder and wade toward the stairs. "Thanks for the help," I say over my shoulder.

Asher smiles at me.

I'll thank him properly later.

Or improperly.

I can't wait.

I'm toweling Rosie off in the guest house entryway when Hannah flops down next to Asher in the lounge chairs many feet away. "You are such a goofball! I totally thought you were falling into that pool."

"Well, I *did* fall in," he says. "It's just that it wasn't an accident."

"Well played, St. James. You have such a way with kids. I can totally see you teaching a child to swim someday."

My blood stops circulating. Because I can see it too. Any kid would be lucky to have Asher in their life. He's better at living in the moment than I'll ever be. He'd be the *fun* dad.

But the next thing I hear is a very uncomfortable chuckle. "Don't hold your breath, Hannah," he says. "That's not the kind of thing that's anywhere in my future."

"You never know," she chirps.

But it sounds like he does know. And he doesn't want kids.

I guess that should have already been obvious to me. His lifestyle is full of late nights and travel.

And it's not like it matters, right? Not to me.

Even if I'm starting to wish that it did.

27

MY ROOMMATE IS BUSY

ASHER

"*I* cannot *believe* you're getting married in two days. How far we have come from our days in school, talking smack about girls."

"My smack talk was more sincere," Flip says, elbowing me from a few inches down the terrace railing where we're standing together, looking at the moonlit bay.

"That must be why you're the one marrying a woman."

He snorts. "Must be."

My smack talk was all pretense, of course. I spent the first part of high school—or upper school, as we called it in Switzerland—wishing girls were interesting to me. And then at some point, I realized I'd rather kiss the captain of our football team.

When I'd finally confided this to Flip, he'd looked utterly appalled. My heart had bottomed out, terrified that Flip was about to recoil with disgust at my sudden revelation. "*Armieux? He's a smug wanker. We can find you a better guy than that.*"

Flip has been my wingman ever since. And the fact that he's taking himself off the market this weekend is still a little shocking to me. In less than forty-eight hours, no less.

There's nothing like a Cuban on a humid night. The cigars

we're smoking right now are part of the wedding gift I'd bought him. The scent of the smoke makes me feel wistful. And I couldn't even tell you why.

Flip. *Married*. With a baby on the way. It doesn't seem real. I honestly thought we'd be single forever together. I'd just gotten comfortable with the idea that relationships weren't right for people like Flip and me.

And about a half hour later, he met Hannah.

So, this is it. My last night with my single bestie, since tomorrow is the Friday night rehearsal dinner. Which means that'll also be my final night with the hottest nerdy single dad on the planet.

Spending time with Mark has been an unexpected pleasure. I hadn't expected him to be so much fun. I'd never expected to actually *like* the guy. A hookup, sure. I'm easy. But after this is done, I think I'm going to miss him.

And I don't normally miss hookups.

Although the whole wedding thing is probably just getting to me. Watching two people tie their lives together forever makes you think about all the big questions in life.

Next week, I'll probably put this all behind me, right? I'll be back to having deep thoughts about the EuroCup final, and whether or not I can order naan bread with my Indian food without developing a gut.

"Hey, let's go have a whiskey," Flip says, out of the blue.

"Sure, man. I could run to the liquor store."

"No—I meant let's go to South Beach. Just the two of us, for old times' sake. One more time to that place on Collins. With the models?"

"That's every place on Collins." I take a surreptitious look at my smartwatch. "It's ten-thirty already. It will take us a half an hour to get there and park, though. You sure you're up for a late night?"

Flip snorts. "Who *are* you? Ten-thirty is, like, lunchtime for you. Am I right?"

The man has a point. But I'm not willing to admit it. "Just

want you to get your beauty sleep. Those wedding photos are forever."

"Uh-huh." Flip taps the ash from his cigar into the bay. "Look, I have a couple things to discuss with you."

"What are they? We can just talk here."

He shakes his head. Then he grabs my arm and tows me toward the window of the house. It's all lit up inside, and we're looking in at the giant den.

Where Mark Banks is currently passed out on a huge L-shaped sofa. His daughter is asleep beside him, too, her head on his arm, her cute mouth slack.

It's really freaking cute. Like, ridiculously so. My heart warms in an unfamiliar way as I gaze at them.

"See? Your roommate is busy right now anyway," Flip says.

And I stop breathing. What is he saying exactly? I'll admit nothing. But I brace myself for questions.

"Come have a drink with me," is all he says, though. "I'm pulling the best man card on your ass. This is it. This is my hour of need."

"Sure," I say, turning away from the window. "Of course. Whatever you want."

On the way out the door, I send a text to the sleeping hottie as surreptitiously as I can.

Forty minutes later, we're seated in a bar on Collins designed to look like a smug wanker's private library from the Victorian era. A buxom model in a maid's uniform pours us each a glass of Macallan and charges me one hundred dollars. Plus tip.

"Now, what did you need to discuss with me?" I ask after the first sip.

"Couple things," he says, reclining against his wingback chair. "The first one is that I want you to be the baby's godfather."

I cough on the next sip and scorch my lungs with peaty scotch. "Really? Me?"

"Why not you? Who else would I ask?"

"Mark Banks," I say immediately. "He's the obvious choice."

"But I'm asking you," Flip says, setting his glass down on the marble-topped table between our matching chairs. "Besides, it's a ceremonial job, Ash. A figurehead position. Nothing is going to happen to Hannah and me. You get to be the fun uncle in this situation. It's your forte."

The fun uncle. He's right. That's kind of my role in life. "I'm honored, Flip. Thank you."

"No, thank you." He picks up his scotch. "Now, speaking of Mark Banks . . ."

Uh-oh.

He stares hard at me with gray eyes. "What the hell are you doing, dude?"

I consider playing dumb. But dumb isn't a good look on me. "It's a little harmless fun between consenting adults. Since when do you care who I bang?"

He runs a finger around the rim of his glass, and then looks me right in the eye. "He just got out of a six-year marriage. The guy is kind of a mess."

"Not really," I argue as a reflex. Does Flip know all the details on Mark's marriage, how his wife checked out, left him for her boss, how she wiggles out of time with their kid? Does he know, too, what I've been able to figure out in a few days—that Mark wasn't in love with Bridget? At least, not recently. Maybe not ever.

Flip sighs. "But I see the way he looks at you. That's the only reason I guessed that you've been polishing his sword."

"How does he look at me?" I ask, fascinated.

"Like he's a college freshman and you're a case of cold beer."

"So? I'm really not seeing the problem here."

"You're a player, Ash. Are you trying to prove that his drunk text was right about us?"

"His drunk text said I was superhot," I remind him. "So, sure, I'm okay with proving it."

"You know what I mean," Flip says. "I just think it's dangerous to toy with him. Hannah will kill me if you break his heart. And every family gathering from now until eternity will be really fucking awkward."

"I'm not breaking anybody's heart," I promise. "Show me a heart I've broken."

"You don't stick around long enough to actually break 'em," Flip corrects. "You bruise them a little and move on."

I bristle. That's not true. And even though I'm supposed to be toasting Flip's health and his marriage right now, I open my mouth to argue. *Is that really what you think of me?*

But a different question comes out instead. "Do you think my hair is too floofy?"

Flip looks at me like I've grown an extra head. "I'm sorry . . . *what?*"

"Never mind."

We sip our scotch. I'm still sore about Flip asking me to leave Mark alone, though. I know I'm not doing anything that man doesn't want me to do.

And *beg* me to do, damn it.

Flip couldn't possibly understand the inner workings of Mark Banks. My roomie told me to my face that he isn't looking for more than a hookup. It's going to be fine.

I sneak another look at my watch. Eleven-thirty. I can still make the most of tonight. For maybe the only time ever, I'm the one itching to put the fork in a night out with my bud.

Guess there's a first time for everything.

28

I DON'T SNORE

MARK

*O*ut the window, the night sky is blurry. Silence engulfs me as I glance around the unfamiliar room. Yawning, I rub a hand along my chin, then hunt for my glasses.

What day is it?

What the hell time is it?

Spotting my glasses on a marble coffee table, I grab them and put them on.

I'm in the tennis-court-size den of the mansion, and all the lights are out. One glance at my clothes tells me I conked out on the cushy couch.

In my defense, your honor, this couch is mighty comfy.

Except for . . . this book under my thigh. I reach for it—one of Rosie's early reader books, about a sporty girl.

Like the kid who's snoring softly next to me.

How long have we been sleeping?

No idea.

I stand and scoop her into my arms. She murmurs something, then drops her head to my chest. I carry her up the stairs and to her room, next to Bridget's. My ex's door is ajar but it's dark in there. Bridget loves her sleep, and will get plenty more of it when I take off with Rosie Saturday night and my ex does . . . whatever.

But . . . so what?

It suddenly strikes me that I'm tired of being tired of Bridget. I've got my kid, and my work, and my life in New York, and Bridget can just do her thing. I don't care so much anymore.

And that feels good.

I lower Rosie onto the twin bed. She doesn't wake up once, so I don't bother to tell her to put on jammies or brush her teeth.

Leaning down, I kiss her forehead. "Love you, cupcake," I whisper, then leave, padding barefoot along the hall and back down the stairs.

The sleek modern clock on the wall ticks past eleven-thirty. Everyone's asleep, but my thoughts veer to one person only.

Is Asher in the guest house, alone and waiting for me? Going for a dip, hoping I'll join him? Drinking a whiskey poolside, looking ridiculously sexy as he waits for me to ravage him?

I'll take all of the above, thank you very much.

But when I slide open the glass doors and walk past the water, the pool is dark and quiet. My gaze flicks to the chair by the potted palm this time. A white-hot image flashes before me of what he did to me on that chair last night, but that's chased by other images too. Yesterday, walking around the city so comfortably together. This morning in bed, talking like it's just what we do. Even playing in the pool with my kid.

Which is stupid. Just stupid to think of.

Best to focus on sex.

Maybe he's waiting in bed for me.

That possibility puts a spring in my step, but when I open the door to the guest house, it's empty and dark. I try to shrug away the disappointment.

It's fine.

I'm here for my sister anyway, and today, I helped her with wedding stuff. That's the point of this trip.

After I brush my teeth, I head to my room. A pang in my chest twinges as I pass Asher's room, which is so, so dumb.

It's just the sex I'm missing.

That's all.

In my room, I get undressed, then slide into bed and grab my phone from the nightstand. After I unlock it, my text notifications rain down on the screen.

Brett: God, will you please come back from vacay because I'm sick of getting picked off by Ryan at Chase.

Better news: Options got clobbered for a minute and I covered your short in September volatility. You're welcome. And even better news (for me), knight takes rook.

But seriously, I hope you're having fun. If you're not, go find some fun. Get a sunburn. Get laid. Or I will never share my list of the best secret spots in the city for pork buns ever again.

Damn, I can't believe I left that rook exposed. I guess my mind hasn't been on chess.

Mark: One, you can't resist sharing your finds so I call bullshit on your threat. Two, I'm definitely enjoying it.

Brett: Define "enjoying." It better not be that you read some new how-stuff-works book while watching the market.

I snicker. I haven't even opened a book since arriving at Disney World for Horny Adults. And I'm not going to tell him exactly how I'm whiling away the hours.

Mark: Clubbing, Brett. I've been clubbing.

It's the truth, but he'll never believe me. I click to Valencia's text next.

Valencia: Did you know Blackbeard likes to smell my hair? As I tell Zoe, my coconut shampoo is definitely catnip, since it drives her crazy too.

Mark: I guess if I ever want to turn on my cat, I'll know the trick now.

I'm about to shut down the app when I spot a text at the bottom of the names. And fuck, if it doesn't make my heart leap.

Asher: Captain Filthy Mind . . . or should I call you Sleeping Babe? (Incidentally, you're still smoking hot when you're snoring because now I know all the dirty thoughts running through your dreams are about me.) Alas, duty calls. The groom has corralled me for a drink. I'll be back a little after midnight. But I have my heart and dick set on 33A . . .
—The superhot wingman

And my chest officially flutters. From the nicknames, from the message, from the everything. I'm fucked now in a whole new way.

Especially since I know I shouldn't respond.

But I do anyway.

Mark: I don't snore.

Then I get out of bed, head to Asher's room, and set down my phone on . . .

I stop in my tracks as the thought finishes, hitting me hard . . *my side of the bed.*

189

Well, it has been my side for the last few nights.

When in Rome, and all.

I take off my glasses and slip under the covers, picturing 33A. And B. And C.

But apparently, hitting multiple list items in a twenty-four-hour period, plus parenting, plus managing *my* parents, and seeing my ex, tires me all the fuck out. I close my eyes. Just for a minute.

I see the surface of the swimming pool behind my eyelids. I hear Asher's laugh, and Rosie's giggle. I float along the surface.

The door creaks somewhere in the corner of my mind. I flip to my side, but don't open my eyes.

29

A LITTLE APPRECIATION HERE

ASHER

*T*here's no hot sleeping dad in the den when I return. The house is dead quiet. So I head toward the guest house where a light burns in the living room.

Mark isn't on the couch, though.

And he's not in his bed.

Hmm.

I find him in the last place I look. But it's also the best place. He's in *my* bedroom, lying on his side of the bed, possibly reading a book. Huzzah!

"Hi honey, I'm home," I say. And then I want to kick myself. I can hear Flip's voice in my head, telling me it's dangerous to toy with Mark.

I'm not, though. He knows the score. He laid down the rules. I merely agreed to them, since they suited me. No one gets hurt. Everyone gets off.

"Mark?"

He doesn't stir. My hookup is sleeping.

I tiptoe into the room and circle the bed. His dark eyelashes touch his cheeks. I switch off the lamp, but as my eyes adjust to the dark, I still admire him in the moonlight. Asleep, he looks younger than his twenty-seven years.

Quietly, I unbutton my shirt and then toss it onto the chair. Then I remove my slacks. And, why not, my underwear. Retracing my steps, I slip into bed behind him.

His skin is warm and smooth against mine. I take a deep breath of Florida nighttime air and Mark's shower soap. It's a potent combination if there ever was one. Then I press my lips to the back of his neck and lay down a soft, openmouthed kiss.

"Mmm," Mark murmurs. And when I put a hand on his bare hip, he covers mine with his own.

"You do snore," I whisper.

"Do not."

I grin against his shoulder. Then I kiss him slowly right behind his ear. He inches a little closer, his body seeking me out.

"How was your drink with Flip?" he slurs.

Aggravating. I'm not going to share that, though. "We drank a very peaty scotch. I think there might be hair on my chest that wasn't there before. Feel free to check."

"Okay."

I wait for him to roll over.

He doesn't.

"Baby?"

"One sec. I will rally for 33A."

". . . And 33B, and 34A," I tease. "I'm going to make a bar chart with your data, baby."

He doesn't laugh.

"Mark, I just made a spreadsheet joke. A little appreciation, here."

Nothing. He's out again.

I hitch my body closer to his, pressing my chest against his back. And that's when I discover that Mark is starkers under my sheet. He'd set himself up in my bed, naked.

How sexy is that? His confidence just does something to me.

I reach up and run a hand through his hair.

He sighs happily.

Kissing the back of his neck again, I tick through my options.

I could wake him up in the most time-honored way. With a blow job, of course.

Or I could just . . . not. As sexy as Mark's naked body feels pressed to mine, it's comfortable to lie here beside him. It washes away the aggravation. With him right here, I can feel my own annoyance drifting out to sea till it's gone.

My mouth comes to rest against his shoulder, and I take a slow taste of his skin. The soundtrack of the night is his steady breathing.

My heart rate slows. This is nice too.

Nice. It's not something I thought I was looking for. I don't seduce men with the goal of cuddling them at midnight while the bay laps against the beach.

But it's hard to deny the pleasure of this moment. I haven't had a night like this since Garrett—

And, yup. There's a lesson learned. I'm not the kind of guy who can pull off the nice, domestic couple stuff. I'm shit at it.

This is just a stolen moment. An oasis in the disco desert.

I lay my head on the pillow beside Mark's and curl an arm around his waist.

Flip's voice pops back into my head. *What are you doing?*

Shut up, I tell my inner Flip. He can keep his opinions to himself. I'm not bruising Mark's heart. I'm not bruising any part of him. (Unless he asks me to. And these days, the good hand-cuffs are padded.)

I'm a gentleman.

And I'm going to be somebody's godfather. Maybe that's Flip's way of nudging me toward his style of adulthood.

Maybe his comments were more about his big life changes than my shortcomings.

That must be it.

On that thought, I fall asleep snuggled up to Mark Banks.

30

GOOD COP, BAD COP

FRIDAY

MARK

*T*he sun mocks me.

    I mock me.

An hour after the string quartet visit, I'm still kicking myself. Spoiler alert—their instruments are tuned and they're ready to play *Pachelbel's Canon in D* tomorrow.

Hannah's wedding kicks off in twenty-four hours. Another day has been checked off the calendar. And what do I have to show for it? A whole damn night squandered.

"I'm officially putting myself in the doghouse," I tell Asher even as Ramon calls us over to the tent, eager to show us his finished work.

"For being such a naughty dog?" Asher asks with a dirty wink as we walk.

"No, for wasting a night," I mutter again.

"You're still beating yourself up about that?"

"Yes. This is why I can't have nice things," I tell him as we march to the tent.

"Ahh, but who says last night wasn't nice?" He flashes me a look that's not . . . sexy at all.

It's devastating.

His hazel eyes are all dreamy, like he means every single word. My body heats up like the sun, but it's not from desire this time.

"You should have poked me till I woke up," I hiss, trying to escape the way I feel when he looks at me like that—like I can't breathe.

Asher cracks up. "*Sleeping babe*, even my fire pole wasn't getting you up last night. And, like I said, it was still nice."

Nice.

Such a simple, throwaway word.

A word we use for the weather, of all things.

Maybe that's the right usage, since there's a storm brewing inside me from that word and the way he delivers it, like that's all he wanted from me last night.

But possibilities of *nice* are doing all sorts of crazy things to my head, so I slam the drawer on those when we reach Ramon, and he shows us around the tent.

"It's the tent of our dreams," Asher declares after the brief tour.

"Perfect," Ramon says, then tells him the final price.

And it's a bit too high. I'm positive that's not the number Asher agreed to before, though.

I nudge Asher. Just a little. His eyes flick to mine as he chews his lip.

"So, uh, you quoted us a number about ten percent less, man. I could find the email," I say.

Ramon stops. He frowns slightly. And Asher opens his mouth, probably to tell him that it's fine. That it doesn't matter. "We're going to need ten percent off that," he says instead, leaving no room to argue.

"But . . ." Ramon begins.

Asher straightens his spine. "That's what we agreed to, Ramon. This stunning, beautiful tent we're going to post pictures of and rave about . . . at a slightly lower price."

And just like that, Ramon smiles and nods. "Yes, of course. I'll make the correction."

When the man heads off to grab his tablet, I put a hand on Asher's back. "You know what? Negotiation turns me on too."

"Does it now?" he asks in a silky voice. "I think you're *rubbing off* on me."

"Oh, you can bet I'll do that later."

But there's no more time to flirt, because once we finish with Ramon, Hannah scurries over and asks me to help review the reception seating.

I do that poolside for a few hours, stealing glances at the time, hoping I don't miss my last chance tonight.

But this is the world's longest planning session.

It never ends as vendors rush by, as flowers are delivered, as caterers set up for the rehearsal dinner in four hours, as the day thins, and the hours disappear. It continues even as I take a quick dip in the pool with Rosie, then I return right away to the planning table.

As the clock races toward three, Hannah, my mom, and I are knee-deep in seating charts and I want to stab myself in the eyes.

But this is Hannah's one and only wedding, so a man's got to do what a man's got to do.

Including trying to keep my eyes off the guy who thinks last night was *nice*. He's stalking toward the table, phone to his ear. "Yes, Simone. I understand."

That's the wedding photographer, and Asher's voice sounds heavy. "Sure, things come up. But . . ."

His jaw is tight as he paces along the pool.

"And you're good with the Steinbergs here?" my sister asks my mom.

Mom answers but I pay no mind. My ears are on Asher. If the photographer is bailing . . .

My shoulders tighten.

"Your apprentice? Hmm. Well, I'd have to see her work," Asher continues.

I stand, cross over to him. "Have them send a portfolio now," I hiss.

He waves me off. "Right. You're on the road, and she's finishing a shoot. Fine, tell her we'll meet her at the studio in thirty."

Then he hangs up.

"What the hell?" I ask.

He claps a hand on my shoulder. "We need to go see Simone. Evidently, she's double-booked for tomorrow, but she has a backup."

No fucking way. "We didn't pay for her backup. We paid for her. We reserved her. You said everything was fine," I say, my blood starting to boil.

"And it will be. Let's go sort it out," he says, trying to reassure me.

"I'll fix this," I say quickly, because I fucking will.

With concerned eyes, Hannah walks over to us. "What's going on, guys?"

"It's the photographer—"

"—We'll work it out. I've got my pit bull here to handle things," Asher cuts in, squeezing my shoulder. "We're going to see her now."

Hannah's brow knits, her eyes darting from Asher to me. "Good cop, bad cop?"

"It's our thing," Asher says, but he taps his wrist. "Gotta go."

Hannah worries at her lip. "You'll fix this, Mark?"

"Absolutely, and if not, Asher can take the pictures."

He snaps his fingers. "Good thinking."

Then we take off for the Porsche, and the second we're in the car, I huff out an annoyed breath. "I can't believe this is happening the day before the wedding. Hannah loves Simone's shots. You have to take the pics if she can't," I say as Asher backs up the red sports car, then turns onto the street.

He says nothing. Just smirks.

"It's not hard to keep your word," I continue. "It's not rocket science to keep a damn calendar."

His lips twitch wickedly as he flicks the turn signal.

"Aren't you pissed?"

The car slows at the stop sign. He pushes up his shades. His eyes glitter with mischief. "Everything's fine with Simone. We talked and she'll be here tomorrow as planned. That stunt, Captain Filthy Mind, was for you."

My mind is a messy blackboard with numbers in the wrong place. A math problem I can't solve. "What do you mean?"

As the car idles, he curls a hand around the back of my head, drags me close and plants a hot, desperate kiss on my lips.

The world winks off.

I sigh into his mouth, kissing him back hard and relentless as I solve the equation instantly. When he breaks the kiss, I say, with a little more wonder in my tone than I expected, "You did that . . . for me?"

"I needed to get you alone."

"For sex?" I ask, not caring that my voice pitches up with dirty hope.

He scoffs, then plucks at his board shorts. "For the beach, Banks. I'm taking you to the beach in Miami, like I promised. You've never been, and that's a sin. But you can find your absolution with me right now."

Then he reaches for my hand and squeezes it.

I don't even care if we're not going to get it on in the sand.

I. Have. Butterflies.

And I'm going to be okay with that for the rest of the afternoon as Asher St. James takes me on a date to the beach.

AFTERNOON DELIGHT

MARK

*A*sher counts off on his fingers as we walk through the sand. "Let's see. I introduced you to your first time with a dude. To first class on a plane. And now you're, finally, after twenty-seven years, going to the beach."

I shoot him a steely stare. "I've been to the beach before. Just not *this* beach," I say as we trudge through the soft-as-sugar sand, flip-flops in hand, the sun casting rays high above us.

"Exactly. *I* took you to the beach," he says, like he owns the world.

Shaking my head, I laugh. "You love all the credit, don't you?"

"I *deserve* all the credit."

He's not wrong. Asher's specialty is getting me to have a good time, and he's earning top grades. I'm not entirely sure what I do for him, but maybe I'm simply entertainment during this trip—like staging this beach intervention has amused him.

My gaze travels around the sand and the surf. In the waves, a fit old dude tosses a tennis ball to a Border Collie. At the edge of the water, a pack of college-aged kids play volleyball.

And beside me is the guy I won't see much after tomorrow night.

Funny, how on Tuesday morning I was dreading these days with him. Now a part of me dreads leaving Florida.

While we make our way through the sand, I picture another first time. My eyes laser in on his hand.

Ah, what the hell.

I reach for his hand, thread my fingers through his.

Without any hesitation, he curls his fingers tight through mine. I'm holding hands with a guy for the first time. Everything about this moment feels right.

Just right.

Even when Asher says, "Look at you. You've come so far from the day you hid behind the dressing room curtain at Angel Sanjay's showroom."

"I wouldn't say I was hiding."

With a laugh, he squeezes my fingers harder as we reach the surf and walk along the water. "You were. You were hiding and horny at the same time. Such a dangerous combination."

I scoff-laugh. "You will never not mock me."

He rubs his thumb in a circle along my wrist, the motion sending small shock waves of pleasure across my skin. "Truer words."

I laugh, and Asher turns to me, studying my face, his eyes serious.

I school my expression. "What is it?"

We stop walking. He drops my hand, then his shoes. I follow suit, letting mine fall to the sand.

"There's something I want to do," he says, his voice a touch vulnerable, like he's about to take a risk.

That look paired with that tone scrambles my thoughts. "Sex on the beach in the middle of the day might be my *only* line," I tease.

He doesn't laugh. Instead, his eyes pin me, and they glimmer. "You're so fucking fearless, Banks. It's insanely hot. You're kind of wild in bed, and I love that," he says, and my heart tries to destroy my sense of reason.

That dangerous organ wants to slam into Asher. But really, he's making it clear what I do for him—I entertain him in bed.

That works for me *for now.*

I mean . . . it works plain and simple. There's only a now with us. Nothing more, no matter how intensely he looks at me.

"But . . ." Asher drags out the word. "That's not what I want to do right now."

Whatever he wants to do, I want it. "Do it. Whatever it is."

A crooked grin curves his lips. "That's what I mean." His breath comes in a quick huff, like he can't get enough oxygen either.

Then, he threads his fingers through my hair, and my muscles quiver with anticipation.

He draws his hands toward my face again, then gently slides off my shades. He folds them, tucks them into his pocket, and lets out a low, swoony hum of desire.

He curls his hands over my shoulders, and in some kind of voodoo slow-motion move, he dips his face to mine, then brushes his soft lips against my right eyelid.

My insides jump.

Asher murmurs, like he's drifting off to another land as he gives the same treatment to my left eye. A gentle caress of his lips, and like that, my body doubles down on bliss.

But on something else too.

Some strange new sensation that makes my heart thunder.

Then, thump around in my chest when Asher stops just to catch his breath. He presses his forehead to mine. "Wanted to do that for so long," he admits.

I'm so glad he staged a beach escape. I never knew what I was missing. *This feeling* in my body. Like I've escaped from my head, and it's fantastic.

I'm not even sure what to say in response to his confession.

Thank you feels weird, but it's on the tip of my tongue. Except, with the way he touches me, his hands sliding down my arms, the gratitude feels pretty damn mutual.

Maybe that's what he's getting out of this thing with me.

The same thing I get with him.

Want.

A bottomless kind of want that I feel everywhere.

Trouble is, there's a flagpole in my shorts.

So I pull an Asher St. James.

Grabbing my shades from his pocket, I carefully set them down on my flip-flops, then I jerk off my T-shirt, yank off his, and I haul him all the way into the water and fall backwards into the ocean. With a loud, satisfying and salty splash.

"See? I knew you'd like the beach," he says as he sinks into the water too.

A wave rolls over us, and we bob for a few seconds.

"I do, which is why we needed an erection intervention," I tell him. "Or I was at a serious risk of showing the good people of Miami the biggest boner of all time."

He cracks up, dragging both hands through his messy, wet hair. "Thank you for your service."

I tap my temple. "I'm always thinking."

His gaze goes warm and lazy. "Not always. When we're fucking, you stop thinking. And you like it."

"Yes I do. Also, stop talking about fucking right now."

"If I must."

He's quiet for a second. And I'm about to change the subject, when suddenly, Asher grabs my waist in a tackle. I take a gulping breath before he plunges me underwater. And when I almost choke anyway, it's from laughing. "You dick," I say.

"You love my dick."

True. But I fight back anyway, sweeping his feet out from under him.

Although it's hard work horsing around with a professional athlete. He rolls, gaining the upper hand, and I have to take another quick breath before he dunks me again.

I'm outclassed in this wrestling match against all his battle-hardened muscles. But my God, the *view*. I may be losing, but I'm winning at life.

We goof off in the ocean for a long time, and everything about this beach date is perfect.

Including the hammock we find at the edge of the sand when we get out of the water.

"Let's dry off," he says.

"Code for make out in a hammock?" I ask.

He curls his hand over my ass as we walk. "You know me so well."

Maybe I do.

And maybe I like that.

"I think this was made for one person," Asher announces as he sinks down into the hammock, which hangs between two palm trees.

"Then you better get out," I tell him.

He scoffs, then reaches for me. "Get in here and get next to me."

"So bossy," I say, then slide next to him, the woven rope smushing us together, shoulder to crushed shoulder. "This is comfy."

"Do I detect a note of sarcasm, Banks?"

"All the sarcasm." But I'm not going anywhere. This is exactly where I want to be. "I could spend the whole day here."

It comes out like a joke, but it's all true.

"Same here," he says, a dry note in his voice too. And he's not moving either.

Maybe we're both saying the same thing—that we don't want to go.

Or maybe that's wishful thinking on my part.

I'm honestly not sure what's happening in my mind anymore or my dumb heart. Everything just feels good with Asher. Like a drug, a hit of the best stuff.

And all I want is to stay intoxicated.

So I shift my body, a task which isn't the easiest while lazing in a roped swing. But I soldier on, the hooks of the hammock creaking as I turn toward him, then brush my lips along his neck.

"Mmm. Do that again," he rasps out.

"With pleasure," I say, and I rub my jaw across his.

He sighs softly, a throaty rumble finishing off the sound. And for the first time ever, I feel like I'm seducing him.

It's a good feeling, and it drives me on.

I brush another soft kiss to his warm skin, then loop my hands through his damp strands. "Floofy when wet too," I whisper, but he has no time to protest since I nip his earlobe, and the moan that falls from his lips is my reward.

I take my time, coasting lazy kisses along his neck as his hand slides down my side, his leg hooking over mine.

We're not quite indecent, and that feels right too. This afternoon delight. I want to stay here forever—on vacation with him, my body floating in this state of suspended desire, his husky voice gliding over my skin. "I meant what I said about last night, Banks," he says. "I enjoyed it just as much as . . ."

I can't hide my smile even as I deflect. "You did not."

He grabs my hand, threads his fingers through mine. "I did, Banks. Trust me, I did."

And I decide to trust that it's the truth. "Me too. I think," I say. "I remember maybe five seconds."

"You were out of it, and it was still . . . good for me."

My chest squeezes. Why does he have to say those things?

"I liked your text too," I say, pushing the limits with that barest admission. "That was good for me," I add, using his words, since it's easier than coming up with my own right now.

"I'm not always an arrogant dick," Asher says with a naughty hum in his voice, tracing circles on my hip bone with his thumb.

"Every now and then you're not," I tease. "Will you miss Flip when he's busy being a dad?" I ask, since that's got to be on Asher's mind. I called him the wingman for a reason. That's what they are to each other.

He chuckles. "You're so good at switching topics. And to answer your question . . . yes. Everyone's life is changing," Asher says, more pensive than usual.

"True, but you'll still have plenty to keep busy. Work and stuff," I say, since the man likely has a crazy schedule lined up of sexy photo shoots and glamorous parties when we return to New York and go our separate ways.

"I will, but it doesn't mean I won't miss . . . the good times." He punctuates those last words with a sweep of his lips along my neck.

Exactly.

This is *good times*.

This is not anything else.

I'd do well to remember that.

And when I run into him in New York—since that's inevitable—I'll thank myself for sticking to my own rules.

"The good times have been fun. And soon, it's back to reality for this, as you'd probably call me, *nerdy single dad*," I say.

His grin stretches to his eyes. "I do call you that affectionately. You're a good dad, Mark. I admire that," Asher says.

I shouldn't need his compliment on my parenting skills, but I like it all the same. "See? Sometimes you're not an arrogant prick at all," I say drily, then spread my hand across his abs.

Asher laughs. "As long as it's only sometimes. You're impossible to compliment, actually. You hardly ever let down your guard."

"I know." I take a beat then say something hard. "Although I do appreciate the kind words."

He gives me another kiss. Another soft flick of his tongue, and a gentle wave rolls down my body. "You let down your guard in other ways. I don't have to read you with words."

Do I truly want to know how he's reading me? No idea, but mostly, I don't want him to stop reading me. Or touching me.

At least for today.

This is all I want today.

But all good things come to an end, and soon, the sun is sailing toward the sea.

We roll out of the hammock awkwardly, which is pretty much the only way to exit a hammock—tumbling and bumping into each other.

Once we land in the sand, Asher offers me his hand, and I take it. It's time to go.

32

HOMICIDAL MANGOES

ASHER

*W*hen we reach the car, I toss Mark the keys.

He catches them easily, gives me a flirty, dirty look. "So you *do* want me to drive."

I grab Mark's hip. "Yes, I want you to drive tonight. Been wanting that the whole time."

He growls. The look in his eyes is incendiary. "Me too."

I dip my face to his neck, drag my nose along his skin, inhaling Mark. "Mmm. Now you smell like the beach. I like this smell on you."

"Turns out, I like this beach," he says, a little breathy.

I pull back. Meet his eyes. "Is that so?"

Mark doesn't look away. "It is. I like this beach . . . *a lot.*"

My gaze drifts down to his throat. Then back to his dark blue eyes. "I do too," I say.

I don't think he's talking about the beach. I'm not either.

And there's nothing to be done about that, except enjoy the hell out of tonight.

By the time we arrive back on Star Island, I've tucked this after-noon's beach detour—in all its tingly perfection—away in a corner in my mind. Maybe I'll revisit it another time, but we're back to being the best men now, rolling up alongside a restau-rant truck in the driveway.

"That's for dinner on the pool deck?" Mark asks. "Hannah said Flip had called someone."

"That's right," I agree, parking the car in the last available space. "His parents wanted to swoop in for dinner, so he called the Cote d'Azur Bistro and asked them to cater a meal."

"We could have handled that," Mark says.

"No, we could not." I set the parking brake and kill the engine. "You and I are maxed out, Banks. Let's retire from party planning, okay? Let's go eat a meal that we didn't plan, cook, negotiate, or shop for."

Mark blinks. "Sometimes I forget that's even possible."

"Come on." I climb out. "You've never met Flip's parents, right?"

"No. Neither has Hannah, if you can believe it."

"Oh, I can." Just thinking about Mr. and Mrs. Dubois makes me grin. "Monsieur still does some consulting work in Hong Kong. And she insists on spending springtime in their house in the Dordogne. And they go everywhere together, spending the year circling the globe."

"Wow. Sounds intense." Mark follows me to the door of the mansion.

"You have no idea."

The house is quiet. But in the dining room, three strangers are putting the finishing touches on a table set for eleven people.

"Wow. Do we have the timing or what?" Mark asks, eyeing the seafood salads that are landing at each place setting.

"We better have the timing tonight. Ticktock."

Mark snorts and follows me through the open French doors. When we emerge onto the pool deck, we find the whole crew. Flip is chatting up Hannah's college friend Yasmin, who must have arrived while we were gone. Hannah and Bridget—both in sundresses—sit side by side on the edge of the pool, watching

Rosie splash around the shallow end. Mark's parents look on, holding cans of soda.

Flip turns around, squinting at me. His expression says *where have you been?*

"Is everything okay with the photographer?" Hannah asks, rising to come and speak with us.

The photographer?

A beat goes by before I remember my own lie. "All set!" I say quickly. "I'd misunderstood her. She's asked someone to take her other job for tomorrow so she can be here in person. And then she and I got to chatting. You know. Shop talk . . ."

Mark gives me a stare that says maybe I should shut up now.

"So, where's Madame et Monsieur?" That's how Flip and I always refer to his parents.

"I was wondering the same thing," Hannah says with a frown. "Was traffic on the causeway terrible? I don't want to start dinner without them." She drops her voice to a whisper. "The caterer is getting cranky, though. I'm not sure how much longer I can hold them off. Will you say something soothing to them? Use that Asher charm for me?"

"Sure, princess," I say, squeezing her arm. "But I doubt that'll be necessary."

"Why?" Hannah leans to the side to try for a better angle toward the driveway. "Did you hear a car?"

"No, but look." I gently take her shoulders in hand and rotate her until she's looking out at the bay again. An eighty-foot yacht cuts through the water en route to the mansion.

"What the ever-loving . . .?" Hannah breathes as the white vessel aligns with the dock. A sailor, wearing smart navy shorts and a button-down shirt, complete with a white captain's hat, jumps down and secures the boat to the private dock.

"Flip's parents don't do traffic," I explain. "They will pay any amount of money to be conveyed in style and comfort."

The sailor, using practiced, quick motions, ties a fancy knot on the rope before another dude in the same getup lowers a metal ramp between the boat and the dock.

I'm kind of digging the sailor studs. I think I've seen a porno starring guys in those outfits . . . How would Mark look in those shorts? Or ripping off that shirt for me?

I sigh happily. My mind is a wonderful place sometimes.

Mere moments later, Madame Dubois is being helped off the boat by Sailor Stud Number One. And then Monsieur appears, shaking off Sailor Stud Number Two's offer of assistance, and hops down under his own power.

"They sure know how to make an entrance," Hannah says. "Holy moly. I knew they were well off, but this is extreme. Mark, am I underdressed? Wait—you're not the right one to ask. Asher?" She looks down at her dress with a helpless expression.

"You look beautiful," I assure her.

"Besides," Mark hisses. "This is *your* wedding, Hannah. You wear what you want."

"He's right," I add. "Measuring up to Madame's fashion standards is an impossible task. Flip's strategy is just to nod and agree with her, and then do whatever the fuck he wants."

But I don't think Hannah heard me. She's already wearing a sort of starstruck smile as she follows Flip toward her future in-laws.

After introductions have been made, the caterers swoop in to beckon us into the dining room, and ask for everyone's drink order.

"I would like a kir," Madame explains. "But the wine must be dry, not sweet. A Burgundy, perhaps."

"Yes, ma'am," the server says.

Mark asks for a beer, and Flip and I order caipirinhas.

"That is a vulgar drink," Madame says, elbowing her son playfully.

"Yes, *Maman*," he says cheerfully. "But Miami is a vulgar city. And one must embrace the *terroir* of his surroundings."

"Quite," she says. "Now pull out a chair for your Maman. And what is Hannah drinking?"

Hannah's face goes instantly pink. "A ginger shrub. The caterer brought me several nonalcoholic choices."

"Pity." She snaps her fingers at the server. "Bring Hannah a proper glass of pinot noir. It thickens the blood," she explains. "I drank wine all through my pregnancy."

"That must explain Flip's tolerance for liquor," I say under my breath, just to earn a snort of laughter from Mark.

I'm successful, so I count that as a win.

Hannah's face turns even redder. The poor thing will have to pretend to sip it. I make a mental note to steal her wineglass and have a gulp when Madame isn't watching.

One thing I'll say about a party with Flip's parents—it's never dull.

My phone chimes with a call. It's Lucy's ringtone. I pull it out of my pocket as a reflex.

"Asher, darling," Madame says. "It's rude to handle your phone at a soiree."

"Even in a vulgar city?" I try.

"Even then," she insists.

"As you wish," I say to her in French, then tuck my phone back in my pocket.

Mark and I take turns ducking out of the room to change out of our ocean-scented swim trunks, then return to the dining room. The seating arrangements at the table place me at the end, where I have a view of all the drama. All the Duboises are seated on one side of the table, and all the Bankses on the other.

The contrast is like something out of *Schitt's Creek*.

"Does anyone know what these yellow things are in my salad?" Mrs. Banks asks.

"Mangoes," Mark says, patting his mom's hand. "They're delicious."

"Have you never had mango?" Monsieur gasps. "I was once almost killed by a mango. We were biking in Hawaii . . ."

"Fiji," his wife corrects.

". . . And I stopped to fiddle with my backpack . . ."

"Your *shoelace*."

". . . When I heard this whistle near my ear. Like the sound of a mortar shell flying past. Then a loud *smack*, and the biggest, ripest mango I've ever seen had made a crater in the earth right next to my bike. It fell from a fifty-foot tree. I swear, it could have brained me."

"I don't think we have mangoes in Ohio," muses Mrs. Banks.

"At least, not homicidal ones," Mark snickers.

"Did you eat it?" Flip asks. "Five second rule!"

"Of course we didn't eat it," Madame says with a shudder. "But they served lovely local fruit that afternoon at The Ritz."

Hannah nudges her wineglass toward me, and I take another surreptitious gulp.

"Thank you," she whispers.

"It is my absolute pleasure."

Beneath the table, Hannah touches my elbow in gratitude.

And on the other side of me, her brother puts his hand on my thigh.

I fucking love Florida, from the clubs to the beaches to the hammocks. Especially the hammocks. I never want to leave.

33

EVERY CELL OF MY SPREADSHEET

MARK

*H*oly shit, this party is hilarious.

I can't imagine having the Duboises as in-laws. I don't think Hannah can imagine it either. Her wide eyes and rapid glances around the table tell me she's a little freaked out. Luckily for her, they live on another continent, so she won't have to tolerate them for more than a few days a year.

Besides, the *modest* twenty-room country home in the south of France, as Flip's mom just described, doesn't sound like a bad place to visit.

"All escargots are snails," Madame is saying. "But not all snails can be escargots."

"Obviously." Flip says with a grin. He seems to enjoy his mother's wild pronouncements. "Not every living squiggly creature deserves to be bathed in butter and garlic for your pleasure."

"Well, I think that sounds *gross*," my daughter says suddenly. And very loudly.

Beside me, Asher chokes on a sip of my sister's wine.

"Now Rosie," Hannah squeaks, laying a hand on her silky

hair. Rosie loves Aunt Hannah, and never misses a chance to take the seat beside hers. "We don't yuck someone else's yum."

"We do if it's a *snail*," my kid insists. "*Ew*."

Madame Dubois sniffs. "In France, children do not dine with the adults at the table. They dine in the kitchen with the au pair."

At the other end of the table, Bridget clutches the stem of her wineglass. But her eyes are twinkling merrily. She's obviously holding back the same bark of laughter that I am.

Our eyes lock. And by silent, mutual agreement, we each take a sip of our drink instead of saying a damn word to our daughter about this particular culinary opinion.

Because snails *are* gross. And because she's barely six. And because Madame Dubois is a bully in pearls and a diamond brooch.

I catch myself smiling at my ex-wife for the first time in a *long* time. I guess it's hard to stay bitter when you're eating a sumptuous meal in a mansion on the bay. And getting laid on the regular.

Just then, Asher shifts in his chair. He hooks a bare foot under mine and pulls it closer to him.

Then he puts a hand on my knee and strokes.

I don't dare glance at Bridget again, in case she can read the situation from my face. Not that it really matters anymore. My attitude toward her is shifting now that she's not the only one who has a life. In fact, this week has shown me that it's possible I could someday feel grateful about the way our marriage turned out.

For the first time, I'm liking this divorced life. As well as the hand on my leg.

I don't wear a watch, so I don't know what time it is. But I'm still counting down the minutes until everyone turns in for the night.

This time I won't conk out early. There's no chance I'll miss my last night with Asher St. James. We're going to lock the guest house door tonight and have *all the sex*.

Every goddamn cell of that spreadsheet is going to be kissed and licked and boinked into oblivion. The program will probably crash before we're through.

Tomorrow, all hundred thousand employees of the Microsoft Corporation will probably feel strangely horny, and they won't know why.

Asher nudges me with his toe. "You're smirking," he murmurs.

"I don't smirk." A waiter leans in to remove my empty salad plate. "What do you think the main course is? Something with a complicated French name?"

"If you're lucky."

I fake-cough into my napkin. "Posh fucker."

And I don't even have to turn my head to know he's grinning.

After dinner, we all gather in the living room, where I continue my silent countdown till bedtime. Bridget and Rosie are the first to head upstairs. My own parents follow shortly after. Hannah disappears eventually too.

Then Asher gives me a meaningful glance and declares that he needs some sleep before the big day.

Flip actually rolls his eyes as Asher leaves seconds later. Not sure what's up with that. But I dutifully spend ten more minutes on the sofa listening to Mr. Dubois exclaim about elephant polo matches he's seen in India. I make myself wait a few more crucial minutes. But then I've had enough. After making my excuses, I step out into the dark, easing my way around the pool deck, sex already on my brain.

I hope Asher is naked. This is it. We have no more time to waste.

I'm picking up speed when something moves in the dark on the last pool chair.

And I startle like I've just spotted an alligator in the bathtub.

But it's only Hannah sitting there alone in the dark. "Mark, sorry. I didn't mean to scare you."

Reluctantly, I slow my roll toward the guest house. My sister hugs her knees, alone in the dark. And suddenly, I suspect a disturbance in the force. "Is something wrong?"

"You already tried to tell me there was," she says softly. "I should have listened to you."

Oh, hell. I sit down on the end of the chair. Then I reach for my sister's ankles and tug until her feet land in my lap. "Tell me what's the matter, Banana. Tomorrow is your big day. You seemed really happy a few hours ago. What happened?"

"You told me this was too sudden," she whispers. "But I didn't want to hear it. And then . . ." She swallows hard. "And then I met Flip's parents."

"Oh." My mind is spinning. "They're a little much. But they live in Europe, Hannah. It's going to be okay."

"Is it?" She rubs a hand over her small bump. "I don't know, Mark. It's just like you said—I just haven't known Flip very long. What if our values don't line up? I've been so busy admiring his gray eyes and his bright smile and his really big—"

"*Hannah*," I caution.

"*Apartment*," she finishes. "Geez, Mark. I wasn't going there."

"Sorry. Go on. I'm still not hearing a problem."

She exhales. "Tonight, Madame Dubois asked me about my childcare plans. She wants the baby to have an Irish nanny. She said only the Irish girls are any good. And Flip agreed with her."

"Okay, well, that's kind of . . ."

"Racist," Hannah finishes. "Good nannies come in all shapes and colors."

"Hmm," I say, buying time. It's possible that Madame Dubois is a horrible human. But it's also possible that she watches too many BBC period dramas to have a modern opinion on childcare.

"It gets worse," my sister whispers. "After that, she said she hoped we'd have a boy so he could go to the Lucerne boarding school that Flip attended. *At age six.* And Flip said he thought that sounded nice."

"Age six," I repeat stupidly. Do people actually send little kids to boarding school? "Didn't this happen in *The Sound of Music*?"

"Yes!" Hannah wails. "Almost. The marriage didn't happen, because the Captain called it off."

"Oh," I say slowly, processing the extent of her mayday. "But Hannah, come on. This isn't the same."

"Isn't it?" she sniffs. "I screwed up, Mark. I really did. You tried to tell me, and I didn't listen. You said this marriage was the worst idea in the history of bad ideas. It's even worse than Crystal Pepsi. It's more permanent than a mullet. And I laughed it off." She puts her hands in front of her face and sobs.

I've got to help her fix this.

"Hannah. Hey. Oh, hell." My baby sister is *wigging*. And this is partly my fault. "Listen. I need you to listen to me right now. Can you do that?"

She wipes her eyes. "I don't know what you could say that would make this all right."

For once, though, I do. "In the first place, those drunk texts were more about me than you. I was in a lot of pain over my own marriage. I was really bitter about Bridget dumping me—" I stop myself and marvel for a split second. Very recently I'd been drowning in my own misery.

Funny what a few days of good sex can do for a guy's outlook.

"You got married too young," Hannah says glumly. "I get it. But what if I'm making the same mistakes?"

"Look," I argue. "I have a couple of theories. Right over there —" I point at the pool shed "—I've hidden four casserole dishes on a shelf under some chlorine test strips. Because our own mother's horrible impulses need to be managed with cunning and deception."

Hannah smiles through her tears. "And I love you for it. But this is about more than ham casserole, Mark."

I squeeze her ankle to emphasize my point. "I get that. But I think Flip manages his mother by yessing her to death. And then he does what he pleases. If I'm right, we could learn a thing or two from him." That's what Asher had said. And after watching the Dubois family in action, I believe him.

"But what if you're wrong? What if he wants to ship our child off to boarding school before their first visit from the tooth fairy? Does the tooth fairy even visit European boarding schools?" Her lip trembles.

"Hannah, come on, now. Did you *ask* Flip if that's what he wants? Did you pull him aside and tell him that some of the things his mother says scare you to death?"

Slowly, she shakes her head. "Not yet. I'm afraid to hear what he'll say."

"Don't be," I insist, flashing back to the night of the engagement party, the way Flip wrapped a protective arm around my sister—to shield her from *me*.

He'll listen. He cares for her so much. Even if I couldn't admit it then, I see it now.

"Look, you and Flip are not Bridget and me. You're just not. Even though I worry about you—which is basically my job as your older brother—you guys were never like us. I barely knew who I was when I met Bridget. I got myself a wife without ever asking if I wanted one. But you and Flip were both ready to meet your forever partner. You two were practically planning your wedding on date number three. Nothing has changed here. You love each other."

She swipes at her eyes. "I do love Flip."

"Do you trust him too?"

"Yes," she whispers. "I trust him to listen."

"Then just go talk to him."

She draws in a deep breath, swipes away her tears, and nods resolutely. "You're right. My freak-out is unwarranted."

"Yes and no. Your mother-in-law is a category-five hurricane in pearls. But that's just life, and that needs to be managed by you and Flip together."

"Together," she repeats. "I need to speak to him. Right now." She sounds like my strong, determined sister again as she pulls her feet out of my lap and stands. "God, Mark. I'm sorry to be such a drama queen. I'd blame the pregnancy hormones, but that sounds like a cop-out."

"Hey, don't be sorry." I stand up and pull her into my arms. "Commitment is scary. Some people get burned. There are no guarantees. But you can't let his mother throw you off course. She's not the one who matters."

"Okay. I know. I let her scare me."

I give her one more squeeze. "Now go and tell Flip that you are not sending a six-year-old to boarding school. See what he says. I'll bet he already agrees with you. But even if he doesn't, I bet he'll listen."

"He will. You're right." She stands up on her tiptoes and kisses me on the cheek. "I love you. Thank you for being here for me."

"Anytime, Banana. Seriously."

She darts off toward the house. I listen to the door open and then close again. But I'm still standing here by the pool chair, replaying that moment.

Sometimes you just have to go after what you want tenaciously, whether it's your forever, or just one night.

34

GREATEST THEFT OF ALL TIME

MARK

$\mathcal{W}$ith that behind me, I can resume my beeline for the guest house.

And what I want most.

The second the door shuts, I erase the rest of the evening. I turn the lock and I am not opening it for anything less than a five-alarm fire.

"This is your five-second warning!" I announce. "If you're asleep, I am waking you up with my mouth. Five, four, three—"

I turn into Asher's room, and I can't even finish.

My throat goes dry.

He's waiting for me, all tanned and muscled and gloriously naked. Ankles crossed, flipping through a glossy magazine. "It's about time. I was almost going to have to learn how to play beginner's chess since I just read this *Travel & Leisure* cover to cover. But don't ask me a damn thing about traveling to Fiji, because I was thinking about sex on a tropical island the whole time."

He tosses the magazine off the bed, and it skids across the tiles.

My eyes are greedy, and they drink up the sight of Asher

stretched out in bed, his cock half hard, his hair still a little damp.

"I had to . . . talk to . . ." But I don't finish that either. I'm done with words.

I take off my glasses, yank off my shirt, and climb on top of him. And I just start kissing him.

His neck, his jaw, his face.

He's all shower clean and soapy and that drives me wild, since it's mixed with that rainfall and summer breeze scent that is all Asher. Maybe I can bottle it, and inhale a whiff every now and then when I want to remember the good times.

This is it. My last chance to experience Asher St. James. I can't afford to waste one more second.

I loop my hands through his too-long hair, tugging hard, making him groan. Making me instantly hard as granite.

Asher's hands wrap around my back, skating down to my shorts. "Get these off." For the last time, his strong hands undo my clothing.

Seconds later, we crash together. I want to feel him everywhere, his skin against mine, our limbs tangled, our bodies joined.

I kiss him harder, hungrier than I ever have before.

He's right. I don't have to use my words. He can read me in other ways.

And he has to know what's in my head right now.

I didn't know it could be so good.

I'll never forget this.

I'll never forget us.

We grind against each other, and my body lights up like a neon sign at night. I'm so fucking aroused, I'm not sure I can withstand much foreplay.

But I'm willing to try, especially when I slide my hand between us, grip his cock, and swipe a thumb over the tip. Then, I use that liquid arousal, and mine, too, taking us both in hand, spreading it over our lengths.

He shudders from head to toe, and I grin wildly. I did *that*. I made him feel that good. And I want him to feel all the things.

Letting go of our dicks, I break the kiss, rise up to my knees, and reach for the lube. I might be new to this, but I'm a good student, and I've done my homework.

Nudging his legs apart, I settle between them, savoring the view of this gorgeous man under me, his shaft at attention. "I'll get you ready."

Asher's eyes twinkle. "Baby, I'm ready. I took care of that."

My jaw falls open, and my dick twitches at the image of him pre-gaming. "Wish I coulda seen that."

"Another time," he says, and my chest constricts.

Hell. I know it's just a phrase. That it just slipped out. But I can hardly stand the fact that there won't be another time. I want *all* the times.

But the last thing I want is to feel bittersweet, so I laser in on *this* second.

He sits up, reaches for a condom on the nightstand, but before he hands it to me, he grips my jaw. A little rough, a little demanding. Just the way I like it.

"Tell me how you pictured this. When you were fucking your fist back in New York, Mark. How did you imagine fucking me?"

His voice is loaded with raw, unfiltered desire, and the question scorches me. My mind spins with a merry-go-round of images. Positions flip before my eyes, and the erotic carousel is almost too much. My brain might be short-circuiting. I'm nothing but ash as I answer him in a throaty rasp. "Every way. Just every way," I say.

"I know what you want." He growls, then opens the condom, and rolls it down my shaft. Next comes more lube, and I'm vibrating with want, with need.

Then, he hauls me in for one more hot kiss before he gets on his hands and knees.

Yes, this is it—this is the sexiest moment *ever*.

This man offering his body to me for the taking. Reading my thoughts and giving them to me as my reality.

For once in my sorry life, I don't stop to remind myself of the how-tos, or review my homework. I get behind him, rub the head of my cock against his hole, and push in.

The world tunnels away when he unleashes the most carnal groan of all time. A long, feral *fuuuck* that lasts forever as I sink inside him. He stretches a strong arm to reach back, grabbing my ass cheek to pull me deeper.

My body is a torch.

Wild sensations whip through me and I try to take it all in—the sheer heat, the tight grip, the utter intensity of his body welcoming me.

But it's too much to process.

Too many things are happening at once, and all I can do is let instinct take over. I thrust, and soon we find a pace.

I can't stop gazing at the man under me, recording every detail for posterity. The sheen of sweat beading his skin. The muscles in his back, the waves of his hair, those strong shoulders. And most of all, the way he stares at me when he cranes his neck around to watch me with heavy-lidded eyes.

Like he's never seen anything better.

Same here, Asher. Same fucking here.

This is everything, and still, I want *more* of him.

As I pump my hips, I slide a hand along his back, then grip his shoulder hard.

"Yes . . ." he moans.

I move with his sounds, working my hips to the rhythm of his groans. Pretty sure I'm hitting sensory overload, and it won't take me long.

I reach down, grab his cock, and stroke.

But he issues a warning. "Wait . . ."

I go still as he mutters how he wants me next.

Drunk with lust, I pull out as he shifts us around. Somehow—and this may be a new law of physics I just discovered—it's even better lying behind him, my chest against his back. Especially when I return to where I want to be. *Inside my man.*

"That's it," Asher murmurs. "Wanna feel you close to me."

Those last three words send me spiraling in all directions.

This is just sex, that is all, but it's also so much more.

It's a brand-new kind of intimacy that's frying all my neurons.

As I wrap an arm around his chest, hauling him close, my other arm slides down and I grip his dick. There are no more words as we fuck, sweat slick between our bodies, breath coming fast.

We race to the finish line, and when we're close, he turns his face to me, curls a big hand around my head, and fuses his lips to mine.

We kiss like bandits getting away with the greatest theft of all time, stealing these midnight hours to come together.

And when we do, it's nothing like my fantasies.

It's so much better than everything I imagined. That both thrills me and scares me.

Since I know I will miss these good times.

So much that I'm starting to imagine all the things that I can't have.

35

THE SEX FAIRY

ASHER

*F*ive minutes later, I'm still trying to catch my breath. And I'm not sure exertion is to blame. Mark remains pancaked against my back, his palm in the center of my chest, over my thumping heart.

It's a blessing he can't see my face, because I need a minute to myself.

I've had good sex before. Many times. But startling things keep happening in this bed.

Mark's fearlessness is a huge turn-on. There's nothing sexier than a man who knows what he wants and then takes it. Our chemistry is white-hot.

But I *like* the guy. I know I'm not supposed to. He told me he's not looking for a relationship. He told me he can't have one.

And God knows I'm trash at them.

Maybe that's why I can't shake this wistful feeling—like we're supposed to see where this goes. Perhaps we're all programmed to crave the things we can't have.

Behind me, Mark lets out a satisfied groan. And I realize I've gone silent on him. So I try to shake off my deep thoughts with a bit of my typical snark. "Well, Banks, I'm giving you an A plus."

"But . . .?" he asks. "I hear a *but*."

I roll toward him and prop my head in my hand. "But . . ." I run a finger along his hip. "What did *you* think, Mark?"

He grabs my hand and links his fingers through mine. "I can't think at all," he whispers. "I've never had as much fun in bed as I've had with you."

"Yeah?" My smile is dangerously large—dangerous because I'm not quite ready to let him know how much I'll miss this when it's gone.

"Hell yeah." He leans in and kisses my neck. "There's only one thing this weekend is missing."

"Mmm?" I'm distracted by the brush of his lips on my neck. As far as I'm concerned, not a thing is missing.

"Lord Ollie and Sir Trevor. I think we should watch it together. One of these days, Hannah is going to remember to ask me what I thought of the first episode. And I won't be able to keep a straight face."

"Hell yes." I love this idea. "But if there are any hot sex scenes, I might have to pause the show and get you off again."

"I might need that anyway," he says with a devilish smile. "Now let's get comfortable and do this right."

Fast forward a half hour, and we're freshly showered and reclining in Mark's bed while the sheets from my bed spin around in the washer.

We're snuggled close together so we can both see his laptop screen. And we're drinking seltzer water and picking at a bunch of grapes while we watch two Hollywood actors in period costume give each other smoldering looks.

It's so . . . nice. And healthy. Usually I come to Miami for the nightlife. But there's no place else I'd rather be right now. I haven't had a TV buddy in a long time.

"She's going to trick Lord Oliver into signing the marriage banns," Mark says, his wrist grazing my abs as he reaches for a grape. "I called it."

"No way," I say, taking the other side as a reflex. "He's too smart for that."

It may not actually be true. But Lord Oliver is a blond guy with floofy hair. I have to stand up for my people.

Sure enough, the duchess slips a marriage contract into the stack of papers Lord Oliver's secretary placed onto his desk for his signature. "Nooooo," I bellow. "This is a disaster. I want a refund."

And I use the moment to wrap an arm around Mark, because I'm smooth like that.

"Sir Trevor will think of something," he says, relaxing against me.

"He'll make a spreadsheet," I say, stroking Mark's shoulder.

"In 1821?" Mark chuckles.

I lean in and nibble on his ear. Just a little.

"Are we still watching this show?" Mark asks.

"Of course we are." I lick his earlobe. "I'm just pre-gaming. There'd better be a sex scene soon. My patience is not infinite."

Mark leans back a little farther into my embrace, but I try to behave. Meanwhile, Sir Trevor discovers that Lord Oliver's bride is in love with someone else. He writes her a poem so heartbreaking that she breaks down, weeping.

And, even more cleverly, he helps her elope to Scotland with her man.

Then—praise Jesus—Lord Oliver and Sir Trevor meet up in the dead of night for some hot lovin' at a hunting cabin on Ollie's ancestral grounds. "Here we go!" I crow as Sir Trevor bolts the door. "You go get it, man. You know you want him."

"Will Ollie bottom?" Mark asks, eating the last grape.

"Nah, Trevor is a power bottom, and probably a size queen."

Mark snorts out a laugh. "Rip his shirt off, Ollie! Hurry!"

And he does. Our two heroes stumble into the bedroom where the sex fairy has kindly popped by to light about seven hundred candles.

Trevor pushes Ollie onto the giant bed. "We don't have much time."

"We have all night," Ollie argues, gripping Trevor's chin. "Now kiss me with that clever mouth of yours."

"It's more clever even than that, Lord. Would you like a demonstration?"

"Say yes, Ollie!" Mark yells.

Ollie crushes his mouth to Trevor's instead. And then more clothes come off.

Mark's hand lands on my knee and begins to stroke.

Yesss. I put a hand on his abs and spread out my fingers temptingly. "You like this, huh?"

"And you don't?"

"Oh, I do." I kiss his neck. "But I'm really here for the fashion and the British accents."

"Sure you are." He runs a hand up my thigh to tease my bulge. "This semi is for the knee pants, I bet."

"And the waistcoats," I add.

I wait for his snark. After all, *fuck you* is our love language.

But that's not what happens. Instead, he turns around and takes my mouth in a bossy kiss. And with his knee, he closes the laptop.

"I was watching that," I say against his lips.

"But now you're not anymore."

He pushes me back against the pillows, and my temperature jumps a good ten degrees. God help me, but I cannot resist Mark Banks in a bossy mood.

We may never get to the end of the show.

I don't even care.

We do finish the show. Later.

Much later. And then, lying naked in the dark, we debate what might happen in the next episode.

"Lord Ollie will be sent back to the country," Mark says, emphatic. "And Sir Trevor won't chase him."

I scoff. "That bad boy poet is going to be commandeering the next carriage to go after his man."

"Nope." Mark insists he'll be right.

I do the same.

Funny, I can almost see us conducting this same kind of post-mortem when the next episode airs. But I file that under *things that will never happen*, like me driving a minivan, or keeping a spreadsheet.

Just because you can picture something doesn't mean it can or will come true.

When I turn off the light, I kiss the back of his neck, savoring the scent of this well-fucked man. "Hey, Mark?"

"Yeah?"

I kiss him one more time. "Fuck you."

I can feel his smile in the dark when he says, "Fuck you too."

36

NOT SO FLOOFY NOW

MARK

I wake up alone, and my first reaction is surprise.

And isn't that just nuts? I blink up at the ceiling, wondering what's happened to me. For a year, sleeping alone was just fine. It was normal. Now it isn't anymore.

Yet my time in Miami is nearly over. Twelve hours from now, I'll be checking into an Orlando hotel with Rosie.

These four days went so very fast. I can't even stand it.

Can't stand being in this bed alone either. It feels wrong. Tossing off the covers, I get up, eager to inhale my final minutes alone with Asher before our best man duties kick in.

Maybe he's in the living room or kitchen, though I don't hear him.

But I hope I'll find him there.

I pull on clothes and glasses and head into the empty kitchen where Asher has left me a love note on the counter. It's written on crisp white stationery with a palm tree in the corner. Something supplied by the property management company probably. Maybe for secret trysts. I pick it up and read.

Have some coffee, nerd boy.
Your suit is hanging in my bedroom closet. You will look hot in it.
Aren't you glad I didn't make you try on the salmon one?
I will find you later to check for love bites.
Pictures start at 10 a.m.

My heart kicks. No one would ever accuse me of being sentimental, but I fold the letter and tuck it safely into my pocket. This is the kind of note I'll read more than once.

An unformed idea tugs at my mind, and since I'm not quite ready to dress for the wedding, I take the kernel of an idea along with my mug of coffee and head into the mansion to see how my sister is holding up after last night's freak-out.

I find Hannah on the second floor, where Flip has been kicked out of the master suite. Not for bad behavior, though—for wedding preparations.

My sister stands in front of a three-way mirror, trying on her newly fitted dress to show my mother.

Happiness is everything I could want for my baby sister on her wedding day.

"Isn't it beautiful?" Hannah croons. The light in her smile tells me that she and Flip must have had a good talk last night. Hopefully I can get her alone later and ask. "Some women put off their weddings because they don't want to look pregnant when they're walking down the aisle. But I don't care! The baby bump is glorious, and I wouldn't change a *thing!*"

I guess that answers that. And yup, only good things happened here on Star Island last night. There is nothing Titanic-like about Hannah's wedding. Not a damn thing is doomed.

"So what happens now, Banana?" I ask. "You need anything?"

"Not one thing," she says. "Hair and makeup are next, although Asher snuck off with the hairdresser after he checked the wedding cake delivery. You can eat some breakfast and then get dressed before the photos."

"Will do." I step closer and kiss her cheek. "You're beautiful today."

"I know." She beams.

"And humble," I tease. "And—most importantly—happy."

"I am all those things." She squeezes my hand. "Thank you for . . ." She glances at my mother. ". . . chatting with me last night. I needed that."

Funny, but I needed it too. That talk did something for both of us, and now, an idea starts to take shape in my mind. There's room for it at last.

But first, Hannah. "No problem. Glad to help. Are you sure I can't do anything? Like look for the florist?"

"They're already here and decorating the tent. Don't worry, Mark! You did exactly what I asked you to do, and it's going great. I'll never forget this."

"Good," I say, squeezing her hand.

"I know I sprung it on you," she continues. "I asked you to fly twelve hundred miles and collaborate with someone you don't really like."

And now I don't know whether to laugh or cry. Because I do like him.

God, I like him so much. And we're done. As in, finished. Because I wanted it that way.

But now? I don't want that at all.

I take a deep breath and blow it out.

"Are you okay?" my mother asks.

"Yes," I say quickly. But I'm all turmoil inside. I'm going to have to talk to Asher and admit that I want more. That all these ideas forming in my head involve him—another morning, another night, and then the next ones too.

Hell, he probably won't agree. He likes the single life. And lord knows I wouldn't be an obvious choice for him—a guy with long hours and a child. Kids aren't in his future, he'd said.

Shit.

"Mark?" My mother touches my arm. "You look distracted. Did you hear what I was saying?"

"Um, sorry. What was that?"

She puts her hands on her hips. "Can you believe a house this size has not a single casserole dish?"

"That's . . . wow." My poker face comes in handy. "Who knew?"

"I had to prep my casserole in a *skillet*," she says with a sigh. "But it will still taste good. It's not a party without ham casserole and potato chip topping." She turns on her heel and marches out of the room.

"Fuck!" *This outburst brought to you by ham casserole, potato chip topping, and also by some other frustrations.*

How am I going to convince Asher that I'm worth the trouble? It won't be easy. But I'm up for the challenge. I won't back down.

At least Hannah is not at the top of my worry list. She puts a hand over her mouth and giggles. "You tried, Mark. And I do appreciate it."

"I did try. And I failed."

"It's okay," she chirps, her mood bulletproof. "Everything is going to work out."

If only I was sure she was right.

I return to the guest house, which is still empty. I shower and shave. It's nine-thirty, so I've got a half hour until pictures.

Where the hell is Asher?

Leaving the bathroom with a towel around my waist, I go looking for both Asher and my best man suit. But in the doorway to his room, I pull up short.

He's back, standing by the bed, tapping on his phone.

And something is very, very different about him.

"Whoa!" I gasp. "You cut your hair."

He lifts his chin, seeming distracted at first, but that look disappears when he meets my gaze. He holds up his phone. "My PA is trying to reach me on a Saturday morning. I hope it's not another Commando bulge fiasco."

I barely hear him, because I'm still gobsmacked by his new style. "What did you do?"

He lifts a hand and runs it through the short, sandy-colored strands. "I asked the hair and makeup lady to give me a quick cut. Not so floofy now, huh?"

"No . . ." I'm kind of in awe of his shorter style, and how monumentally sexy he is no matter what. "It'll be harder to hold onto now. Harder to *tug* on." Although I'm willing to try right fucking now.

"I suppose it would." He licks his lips. And I'm a hundred percent certain that we're both having exactly the same thought. If he dropped to his knees and loosened my towel, we could test the tuggability of his new short hair.

But I still want to know why he trimmed it this morning. "Why did you cut it?"

"Yeah, about that," he says, taking his time, looking just shy of sheepish as his eyes pin mine. "I did it for you."

My heart flutters. *Fucking flutters.* I no longer care about tuggability. "You did it for me?" I repeat because I can't quite believe it.

"I thought you might . . ." He doesn't have to finish for me to know what he's saying—*like it better.*

I swallow roughly, trying to find words to describe what I'm feeling. *You're superhot by default, and now with that* short *hair, you look like . . . the guy I want to try with.* Nerves thrum through me, but I shove them all the fuck aside, since I feel more certain than I did before.

"Mark? What do you think?" he asks for the second time.

Right. I haven't answered him. "Why don't I show you?"

I close the distance and rope my hands through that short hair. *Jesus.* That feels so good, his soft hair in my fingers. And he did it for me. I can barely handle how much I want a chance with Asher in New York. And I show him how very much I like all his looks as I tug on those strands no problem at all, and bring his lips to mine.

We kiss slowly at first. Deep and wet and full of promise. But it doesn't stay slow for long.

In seconds, we heat up, our bodies slamming together. Our kiss turns urgent, and I swear we're both saying the same thing with our lips.

Let's do this.

Let's try.

Maybe that's wishful thinking, but he cut his hair—his famous hair—for me.

All because I said it was floofy in a drunk text.

I might be smiling ridiculously as we consume each other.

When I break the kiss, we're both panting, chests rising and falling. "Now it's *swoopy. You* . . . with your swoopy hair and your stupid lips," I say, gripping the neck of his shirt, since I just don't want to let go.

"You with your made-up words," he says, and his grin is full of his big charm once more, and all for me.

This haircut is like a sign falling from the sky, telling me to go for it. I don't even know what to say, but I don't care. I'll wing it for once in my life.

I part my lips to speak, but his phone chimes again.

His gaze jerks toward the device.

"Go. Check," I say, since I'm feeling all kinds of magnanimous this morning.

He grabs the phone from the bed and scans the screen. I look out the window at the blue sky and the ocean, taking a few seconds to try to string the right words together.

When our gazes crash together again, his eyes are intense. Because we're out of time. In so many ways. But maybe we don't have to be if I just say what I want—what I hope he wants too.

Dropping the phone, he comes to me, wraps his hands around my hips like he did at the club on the night we ignited.

And like I did that night, I'll go after what I want. *Ask for it.*

But he's faster, jumping in with a barren whisper. "Mark, I have to shower. And get dressed. Your sister doesn't need me to be late for the pictures."

"Right," I say quickly, taking the timeout. "Of course you do. Go on."

He stares at me a moment longer. For a second, I think I'm

about to get one more kiss. "Give me ten," he says. "I'm crap at tying a bow tie. I might need some assistance."

"A posh fucker like you?" I gasp playfully. "Thought you would have been born in one."

He smiles. "You've seen my birthday suit, Banks. No bow tie." With a wink, he heads off to the shower.

I use the time to get dressed. To tie my own bow tie. And to plan the speech I'm about to give him. *Listen, Asher. My life is a little crazy right now. But I'm tired of waiting for the perfect moment. And I think we have something special . . .*

Does that sound cheesy? Maybe I could make it more casual. *Hey, Asher, you have a really nice dick and great hygiene. I'd like to see more of you.*

Nope.

Cheesy it is, then. For once, I'm going to just say all the things I'm feeling. If I don't do it now, I never will.

I can't lose him because I'm afraid to put myself out there.

If he turns me down, he turns me down. It will suck, but I'll get over it.

Like I told Hannah last night . . . life happens, and you deal. There are no guarantees.

But if I took a chance for my list, I can take a chance for what's beyond all the rows, columns, and body parts.

I tuck in my shirt and plan my speech again. *It turns out I have a posh fucker kink, Asher. Let's do this right.*

37

POKER FACE

ASHER

*A*lone in the bathroom, I read Lucy's texts. And I can't believe what she's telling me.

There's no fuck-up. Quite the opposite—FLI wants to give me that job that I was *sure* I'd already lost. But now it's mine. If I want it. Although the details have changed.

I crank on the shower and try to process this development.

The job is still photographing football players. It's still the sport I love. But it's not a month's worth of branding work. They want a *year*.

It's a huge opportunity and one I *should* be thrilled about. Hell, I figured I'd be dancing a jig.

But I'm not. Maybe it's because the details changed. Or maybe it's something else.

Something bigger.

I shower in a state of numbness, briefly surprised at how quick it is to rinse out my short hair. And as I towel off afterwards, I still can't believe I got this plum job—and that it starts in five days. And Lucy says they want to hear from me ASAP.

That's just so typical of FLI. In the world of football, they're all powerful. Every day, they change players' lives with a single phone call. And photographers', I suppose.

Today it's my turn.

But first, a wedding. I try to shrug off my surprise —I did, after all, pitch FLI on the whole idea— as I head to my bedroom. My crisp new shirt waits for me on a hanger. As I get dressed, my mind ricochets like a pinball from one life-changing event to another. Flip is marrying the woman of his dreams in just over an hour. The wedding guests include a number of our prep school friends that I haven't seen in years. They're descending on Star Island imminently.

I need to focus on today's events. I put on socks, and step into the new trousers. Work can wait.

Except it can't.

Because of Mark.

He enters the room carrying my bow tie. And a serious look in his eyes. "Hey," he says, and there's a lot of weight in that one word.

"Hey." My throat is tight all of a sudden. He looks so good in the gray slacks, and the white shirt, and that steely blue jacket. The colors that I put together that afternoon only . . .

That was less than a *week* ago.

But everything has changed in just a few days. Now, when I look into his cool blue eyes, I see so many things that I didn't see before. Passion. Comfort. Humor.

Me.

Fuck.

"Can I talk to you for a second?" he asks.

"Of course." My voice is gravel.

"But first, let's get this over with," he says, coming forward to loop the bow tie around my neck. His hands on me, even through clothes, make my skin sing. It feels wrong to enjoy his touch this much, but still, I savor it as he flips up my collar and adjusts the position of the silk. "God," he rumbles from inches away, and this moment is about as perfect as one could be. "Posh fuckers look good after a few days in the sun. The view from where I'm standing is top notch."

Mark smiles, but his eyes dart up to check mine for a reaction. He seems nervous. Mark is hardly ever nervous. He never was in the bedroom. He hardly was out of it either, except when he was trying to sort me out. And all of a sudden, I have a pretty good idea of what he wants to talk about.

"Mark?" My bones are heavy as I say his name.

"Yeah?" His knuckles graze my jaw as he works. I lean toward him, craving his nearness. And the scent of his crisp aftershave.

And more hours like this, alone with him.

Except that's not fair.

"I think we have—"

"I'm moving to Paris," I cut in, my voice a scrape.

His fingers freeze on the bowtie. "What?"

"The texts from Lucy. It was about this job I've been after. It's . . . overseas. It's in France. I'm moving there," I say, the words spilling out in a messy pile-up.

And Mark's eyes widen.

He gulps in air.

His gaze is pained.

Then, in the span of a heartbeat, his expression goes blank.

Stony.

Everything is erased.

"That's . . . great," he says, and the transformation is so fast, I swear I imagined that hurt look from seconds ago.

"I leave in five days," I add.

He's pure cool now as he nods like he's agreeing to a business deal. "Congrats, man," he says.

Man.

Not *St. James.*

Not *you posh fucker.*

And not even my first name.

The distance between us is miles now, or maybe it's just that way for me. No clue anymore what Mark—the expert poker player—is thinking.

I can't read him at all.

"It all happened quickly," I say. "I didn't even know it was for a year. I thought it was going to be for several weeks. But FLI wants a photog who knows the sport and can craft a new image for the organization. And is free to travel around Europe. That's me."

And I'm not even sure why I'm justifying my choice.

It's my life. This is a huge opportunity—one I pursued. J'adore Paris. I have a ton of friends from boarding school there. Felicity, Oscar, and others.

I'm not going to toss it away just because I want more days and nights with Mark Banks.

"That's perfect for you," he says. He tips his chin to my bow tie. "We're ready for the pics."

This is not the Mark from a few minutes ago, and I can't even sweep my gaze over his throat for a clue. It's covered.

"What were you going to say? *I think we have . . .*" A dangerous spark ignites in my chest but what's the point?

I'm leaving.

Yet I'm dying to know if he was going to say—*I think we have to give this a chance.*

He shrugs casually, shoots me a tight smile. "I was going to say . . . *I think we have* to get out there for the photog. Can't take pics without the two best men."

Then, he turns on his heel and leaves.

Taking a little piece of me with him.

Not that I want to be soaked, but a little courtesy, weather? Some rain clouds would be fitting. Maybe a thunderstorm. A crash of lightning.

Fine, fine. I don't wish that on my bestie and his bride, but it would fit *my* mood.

Instead, as I stand beside the groom at the edge of the lawn, the bay behind us, the emerald grass in front of us, the sun shines, a breeze blows, and it's barely over seventy-five in June.

It's a picture-perfect day for a Miami wedding—more lovely than June in Florida has any right to be.

Good luck, perhaps, and a sign of things to come for a couple who are meant to be.

Hannah practically floats along a white runner, her father's arm hooked through hers, a radiant smile on her face as the bridal march begins.

One glance at Flip is all anyone needs to know that he's besotted with his bride and their baby.

He only has eyes for her.

As for me? I'm fighting like hell to keep my gaze off Mark.

The man merely feet away from me, dressed like me, but who hasn't so much as looked my way since the guest house, when I dropped my *oh, I'm jetting across an ocean* bombshell.

As the cellist plays *Pachelbel's Canon in D* for seventy-five guests, the bride gazes happily at my friend. Everything ought to feel right in the world.

Flip is getting hitched.

I got laid the last few days, many times over.

I have a great gig waiting for me in a city I love.

Friendship, sex, and a fun as fuck career—that's all I've ever wanted.

Yet I can't shake this unsettled feeling. This *what-if-ness* clawing at me.

That's entirely the wrong feeling for today. Wistful might be an okay emotion, but mostly I should be disgustingly happy for the end of the era, since it's the start of a new one for Flip. My bud and I will be friends no matter what. We'll talk and text while I'm on the other side of the world.

We always have.

But that's not the issue, is it? As Hannah arrives under the wedding arch, hands her bouquet to her mother in the front row, then turns to her groom, I steal another glance at the other best man.

A terrible longing gnaws at me. The wish that he'd look my way, toss me a knowing wink.

But that's ridiculous.

This is how we end.

Here in front of Hannah and Flip's closest friends and family, at the edge of Miami.

The officiant clears his throat, takes a step closer to the woman in white and the man in the tux. "We are gathered here today to celebrate one of life's greatest moments . . ."

Yup, this is when Mark and I were always supposed to end.

Today.

But *after* the wedding. Not before.

"The joining of two hearts, and two lives," the officiant continues.

Mark and I could have had a drink at the party, shared a laugh, toasted to strange and fantastic things happening in Florida.

The officiant turns to Hannah. "Do you, Hannah Banks . . ."

Even that last name pierces me.

Mark fucking Banks.

Of all the men in the world.

And I can't help but wish there were a way.

But that's foolish. I'll be an ocean away. It's not like we're going to get together for a Friday night fiesta of fucking and bingeing *An Arranged Marriage,* then get coffee in the morning. Briefly, I close my eyes, lingering on those images.

Hannah's voice cuts into my thoughts as she solemnly says, "I do."

And I return to my own questions.

But what about when the gig is up? Maybe in a year? What if I could see Mark at the same time next year? Have a go at things then?

The officiant looks to Flip. "And do you, Phillipe Dubois, take this woman . . ."

My gaze swings to Mark's blue irises. His attention is lasered in on his sister, with that intensity that he gives to every-thing—to negotiation, to Scrabble, to sparring with me.

To touching, and kissing, and talking, and everything.

And *fuck my life*. This is not okay. I don't linger on men. I don't loll in the past.

But Mark isn't just some guy.

It's so surreal. I finally found someone I want to see for longer than a weekend, and now I'm leaving.

My timing sucks.

There's no future for us. In a year, Mark will be happily attached. Some real estate tycoon will catch his eye, or a chef, or a lawyer. Someone stable, reliable, a guy or a gal with a kid. They'll blend their families and go play chess together on Saturdays while their kids run around on the playground in Central Park.

My stomach twists at the terrible thoughts right as Flip utters the most important words of his life.

"I do."

All around me are tears and joy as the officiant beams and then declares, "You may kiss the bride."

A collective sigh of happiness falls over Star Island as Flip kisses Hannah, and Mark's eyes land on mine for a split second before he looks away once more.

Yeah, he'll be taken in a year, and I'll still be . . . well, just me.

38

SOMETIMES MEN KISS EACH OTHER

MARK

*A*sher and I are at the same table during lunch, but he seems a world away.

He'll be a transatlantic flight away in a few more days.

And I've got to be okay with that.

So I don't try to talk to him at lunch. Just like I didn't look at him during the ceremony. It's too hard. Stirs up too much.

I've scarcely seen him since this morning. Don't want him to know I was about to go full romance flick *will you be mine* on him.

But I'm not pissed. No point in that. I'm just damn glad I reeled in my *hey, let's do this*, since it'll make it possible for me to handle running into him again in New York whenever that next happens.

Lunch is stunning, though, courtesy of Chef Garnier. True to his word, every morsel is terrific. Even the vegetarian option.

Good thing Hannah and Flip elected to have their wedding happen earlier in the day. In deference to Hannah's pregnancy, they deliberately planned an event that's not a booze-soaked late-night fête.

After lunch, we play beach games in the sand—shuffleboard,

cornhole and volleyball—and dance under the tent. I take a spin with Hannah and my mom and Rosie, and wish I could dance with the other best man. DJ Drake shows up on time and performs exactly as I asked. Fruit and cheese are served next, with a coffee service just as the cake is cut.

The wedding goes off without a hitch, from the flowers to the cake to the tent. Never have six hours flown by so swiftly. It's still daylight, but my time in Miami has run out, along with this brief romance.

Guests are leaving. The parking attendants' pockets are full of tips. The music has ended.

And at the edge of the lawn, my daughter tugs on my hand. "Daddy! Is it time?" She has that crazed look in her eye that children get when they're on the brink of a Disney World vacation. "Mommy packed my suitcase! She put it in the car."

"Right." I glance around the grounds, looking for Asher. And, yeah, saying goodbye is going to be hard. But it'll be even harder if I can't find him to do it.

"Daddy, where is your suitcase?"

"In the guest house," I tell her. "Why don't you hang out with Mommy for a few more minutes, and I'll go get it?"

"Hurry, Daddy!"

"I will," I promise.

With a brisk pace, I head for the tiny house where I've had so much fun this week. *Fun*—that's how I'll have to file this away. When I duck inside the front door, I hear the sound of a zipper in Asher's room, followed by the sound of a suitcase handle retracting.

Thank fuck. I've caught him.

"Hey, Asher? I, uh, came to say goodbye." I haven't stumbled on words in days.

A moment later, his face appears in the doorway. He drags his suitcase into the living room with him. "Hell, Banks. I don't even know what to say. It's been . . ." He shakes his head, then smiles at me. "It's been—" He stops. He peers behind me.

"Daddy?"

I whirl around to find Rosie standing in the doorway.

"Are you ready? Is it time for Disney World?"

"In a second," I say, waiting for her to turn around and leave again.

But no. Rosie enters the house and crosses her arms over her chest. And waits.

Asher lets out an awkward chuckle. "Hey, cutie. Are you going to meet Mickey Mouse?"

"No, Ariel." She shakes her head. "Mickey is for old people."

"Ouch," he says with a genuine laugh.

Ouch is right. My adorable six-year-old is cock-blocking my goodbye kiss. I shouldn't even be surprised.

This is my real life—Rosie and Disney and heading home afterwards. This was always the plan. Good thing I didn't get the words out earlier. What was I even thinking?

"So . . ." I clear my throat. "I guess this is it."

Asher lifts his regal chin and watches me for a beat. "I guess it is." He takes a step toward me, like he isn't sure how to proceed either.

We're obviously not going to make out in front of my kid. But even if Rosie weren't standing here, I still don't know what I'd do or say. There's no instruction book for this. No spread-sheet macro to tell me what comes next.

"Have . . . a great time in Paris," I manage.

"I'll try." He takes a step closer, frowning, like he's not sure if he should hug me or what.

And I'm no help. I'm just standing here, half stunned at everything that went on between us.

Then Asher thrusts out a hand.

So that's how this ends—with a goddamn handshake. I don't know whether to laugh or cry. But I grasp his strong hand in mine and squeeze it.

The warmth of his hold only makes me want more. But even that brief touch is over almost immediately. He steps back and sighs. "I'm off, Banks. I'm taking an earlier flight. I have to pack up my life in the next four days."

"Wow, okay." I can't even imagine. "We'll walk you to the car then."

"All right." He gives me a jerky nod.

Barely two minutes later he's seated in the Porsche. The top is up, though. Our convertible days are truly over. He starts the engine and turns to me one last time through the open window. "You take care of yourself, Banks. I'll probably see you around. Maybe when the baby is born."

"Sure," I say stiffly. I can picture it all too clearly—Asher swooping in from Paris to meet his godson or goddaughter. The two of us nodding awkwardly at each other from either end of Flip and Hannah's living room.

Before he returns to his Paris lover. Or lovers.

Hell. That's my new definition of hell.

"Goodbye, Banks." He locks his gaze to mine. "I won't ever forget this week. Just saying."

My stomach does its new fluttering thing again. "Fuck it," I say under my breath. I lean down to peck his golden-hued cheekbone.

He turns his head again, though, finding my mouth with his. And my peck becomes a kiss. A quick one, but a kiss, nonetheless. Soft lips on mine, one more time.

Then it's over, and I'm standing upright again, feeling like someone just stepped on my chest with a steel-toed boot.

I back away, holding Rosie's hand so she isn't anywhere near the red car as he carefully reverses out of the spot before changing direction again and driving slowly off the property.

And then completely out of sight.

I'm probably not a super-fun dad as I hurriedly pack up my own stuff while Rosie paces. She's on a roll about Ariel and Snow White, and I try to nod at all the right moments.

Thirty minutes later, I'm strapping Rosie into the booster seat in the back of the Subaru that Bridget rented. She's handing off the car as well as the kid, and she'll take a Lyft to the airport tomorrow.

"Daddy?"

"Hmm?" I check the straps to see if they have the right tension. That's what dads do.

"You kissed that man goodbye."

Surprised, I lean back and check my daughter's expression. She stares at me with Bridget's wide brown eyes.

"Yes, I did," I say carefully. "Asher and I are close, Rosie. And sometimes men kiss each other. Sometimes men even have boyfriends. A man can have a girlfriend or a boyfriend, just like a woman can have a girlfriend or a boyfriend."

We have a picture book about this at home, of course. Bridget bought it when Rosie asked why Alba had two mommies.

"Mommy kisses Morgan sometimes," Rosie says.

"Yes, I'm sure she does. She loves him. And when you love someone—and you have their permission—you can kiss them."

"Okay," she says.

This is going pretty well, but I brace myself for another question. And then it comes.

"Can I get frozen cheesecake on a stick?"

"Wait, what?" My mind scrambles to make sense of that question. But nope. I got nothing.

"When Darcy went to Disney World, she ate cheesecake on a stick. Are we going to do that?"

"Uh, maybe? If we see it, and if we ate a good lunch."

"Okay," Rosie says simply. "Neat."

I close the door. Then I climb into the car and start up the engine.

See you later, Miami. It was nice knowing you.

39

NEVER SAY NEVER

TUESDAY AND BEYOND

MARK

"*C*an we go back to the pool, Daddy?" Rosie asks as I sign the dinner bill Tuesday night.

"Nope," I say with weary firmness. "It's already past your bedtime." Daddy needs a twelve-dollar beer from the mini bar, a massage, and a break. "Tomorrow we'll hit the pool, though. We'll do all your favorite things one more time."

"Even the teacups? Even if the line is long?"

"Yup. I promise."

I'd bought four-day passes to the parks when three would have been plenty. Disney World is killing me. The lines. The crowds. The heat. But Rosie is having the time of her life. I've taken approximately one thousand photos. And I know I'll look back on this trip fondly.

Someday. After my feet recover.

Rosie is tired, too, and she doesn't put up a fight when I get her into her nightie up in our room. I skip bath time, though, because pool water totally counts, right?

Right.

"Good night, cupcake," I say, kissing her forehead as she snuggles under the comforter.

My phone bleats with a text.

Her head pops off the pillow. "Is that Mommy?"

"No," I answer immediately. Even if it is, this day is done. I'm mentally putting my feet up right now.

"How do you know if you don't check?" my wise daughter wants to know.

Good point. I cross to the console table and peer at the phone. *Asher St. James.*

My stupid heart kicks just seeing his name. The text says: **New episode tonight. Want to watch it together?**

"Is it Mommy?" Rosie asks again.

"No, pumpkin. Just a friend." I set the phone down and give Rosie another goodnight kiss. I turn out all the lights, mute my phone, and climb onto my own bed to contemplate Asher's text. I wasn't expecting to hear from him. Didn't think we'd become text buddies. If that's what this is.

And I haven't reached out to Asher at all. In my defense, I've been busy dragging my ass all over Disney World.

But I also didn't want to come off as clingy. The man is moving to another continent, after all.

I stare at Asher's text, wondering what to say. After way too much thought, I go with: **Hey stranger. Wish I could watch it with you. But I'm in a hotel room with my sleeping kid. You'd better watch without me.**

And do every other thing without me, too. I don't add that, even though it's true. **When do you leave for Paris?** I ask, because I like to torture myself.

He replies immediately. **Tomorrow.**

Well that settles that, doesn't it? **I hope you have an amazing time. Be well and take care of yourself.**

I almost add something flirty about his hair or his lips. God knows all the things I said to him this past week. It was a lot. It was intense.

But maybe every hot fling feels like that. How would I know? Maybe I imagined that we were something special together.

You too, he eventually replies. But that's all I get.

I stare at my phone, wondering if there's anything more I could say that would make a difference. Doubtful. Besides, maybe his watch-party offer is just something he does—staying pals with a hookup. Just like he rents expensive sports cars, flies first class, and knows all the DJs by name.

My phone lights up again, and for a second, joy whips through me. It's scary how much I like being in touch with him. But Hannah's messaging. She's in Hawaii, where it's mid-afternoon. *Can I call you?* she asks.

That gets me off the bed in a flash and tiptoeing into the bathroom, where I shut the door and tap her number. "Is everything okay?" I ask as soon as she answers.

"Just fine. Sorry to make you worry. I'm calling to say thank you again for all you did for my wedding. And also to tell you that Hawaii is amazing and I never want to leave."

"Okay, phew," I say quietly. "I didn't think you'd call me on your honeymoon."

"I wanted to get a mani-pedi, so I sent Flip golfing."

"Ah." It all makes sense now.

"Mark, you were totally right about Flip. He told me that he always nods along with his mom, because it's easier than fighting. And he said that he doesn't want our child to be raised by boarding schools. And that he'd never assume anything without discussing it with me."

"Well, I'm a genius, clearly. But mostly, that's a relief for you."

"Of course it is. You were right. How's life at Disney?"

"Exhausting," I admit. "I'm going to need a vacation after my vacation."

"You get a few more days off after you get back, right?"

"Right," I agree.

"Look, I made a decision—you need a rebound guy or gal."

I snort. Are she and Valencia in cahoots? "That's your decision, huh?"

"Yes," she says, as if this weren't a silly conversation. "Your split with Bridget was a year ago, Marky Mark. So you're not allowed to feel sorry for yourself anymore. It's a rule."

"I don't," I insist. "I'm just too busy in New York to date."

"What about hookups?" she presses.

"Hannah! I'm not going to discuss *any of those* with you."

A sharp intake of breath tells me I've said too much. "Ooh! That means there's something to discuss! Oh my God. This is great. Tell me *everything*."

How the hell do I get into these situations? But my sister will pry it out of me eventually, so it's best to confess. "I had a hookup. But then it ended."

"With who?" she squeals.

"I believe that's with *whom*."

"Mark! Spill."

I sit down on the edge of the tub and sigh. "It's tricky," I say, and then I cringe. Because that makes it sound clandestine. Like my hookup was with a cheater or something.

At least, that's how it sounded to me. But maybe not to Hannah, because she yelps with glee. "Omigod, was it Asher St. James? Omi*god*!"

Is she a mind reader? Hope not. "Now hang on. Why did your mind go straight there?"

"Because he's hot, in the first place. Like, *superhot*. Your words. And because you stared at him during my wedding lunch. And because you came back the other day from an 'errand' looking tousled."

I drag a hand along the back of my neck. "What the hell happened to my poker face?"

She giggles. "Was it amazing? I bet it was. But, wow, did you know he's moving to Paris?"

"I'm aware," I mutter.

Her voice drops. "Uh-oh. It was that good, huh? You sound sad."

"Maybe. A little." It feels good to admit that to her.

"Oh, poor Mark."

"No," I argue. "Don't say *poor Mark*. I'm fine. He doesn't date, and it wouldn't have worked. We're too different."

She's quiet for a moment. "Honestly, I can picture you two

together. You need someone spontaneous in your life. And he could use someone grounded. Someone . . . *real*."

Huh. Is that what Asher got out of our fling? Maybe I wasn't merely amusement.

"You know his ex-boyfriend dumped him, right? He called Asher a hot mess and bailed."

She must mean Garrett. The one who called Asher a bad boyfriend. The dick who left him for another guy. Who'd ever leave Asher? "Yeah. He's the fuckwad who's getting married, right?"

"Someone has a strong opinion on Asher's ex. And so do I. He didn't deserve Asher. But now Asher is convinced that he's not a great boyfriend."

That tracks with what he told me in bed the morning after we slept together for the first time. I file away the added intel about Asher's past to think about later. Or not. Because I don't suspect his past romances even matter. "He lives in Paris now. So I guess we'll never know."

"Never say never. Isn't that job only for a year?"

Like I haven't thought that too. But those thoughts are too risky for a guy who nearly got his heart broken. "A year is a long time, Hannah. He'll probably meet a French guy and they'll go off and eat baguettes and brie together, and drink wine on the Pont des Arts."

"Or not," she says brightly, because she's on her honeymoon, and the whole world is a happy place for her.

As it should be.

"Let's just see what happens," she says. "I have a good feeling about this."

She's the only one who does.

TROUBLE FOR TROLIVER

SEPTEMBER

ASHER

*N*ights like these are one of the *many* reasons I said yes to my dream job. An evening out with old friends, a good meal, a beautiful city.

And a great job. I've taken a million photos of athletes at work. Redefining FLI's audience for a younger generation is our goal. And I can't believe I get to be part of the project.

By all accounts, Paris has been fantastic for the last ten weeks.

And so have England, and Spain, and Germany. I've been all over, shooting right in the thick of the action.

The gig is everything. The lifestyle, even more so.

Truly, I can't complain.

Well, not about much.

And definitely not about the weather, since rain can make for great photos.

With my phone, I snap a shot of my English friends on the other side of the table at the Parisian brasserie while silvery drops of water hit the cobblestone street in a faint drizzle.

"Make sure I look pretty," Felicity chirps, tilting her blonde head next to her husband's.

"You always do, love," he says.

"And Oscar is correct," I say as I set down the phone. "I'll send it your way later."

As we return to the debate on the merits of skiing in Switzerland versus France, my mind meanders to New York. Does Mark ski? No. Too risky. Bet he even has a risk analysis spreadsheet for skiing versus . . . walking in the city.

And why do I find that idea so fucking endearing?

"Should we all go later this year then?"

I snap my attention to my friends. "Name the date," I say, since that's my mantra.

Felicity suggests the first week of December, then goes quiet. "Asher . . ."

The sound of my name is full of import. "Yes?"

"You don't quite seem yourself."

I blink. "What do you mean?"

"You're here, but every now and then you're . . . *not*," she says, far too observant for my own good. "Like, your mind is elsewhere. And I know it's not us, because we're brilliant company." She adds a wink.

"You are." I finish my wine, then wave a hand. "It's nothing."

Oscar arches a bushy brow. "Nothing? Since when do you, mate, ever live in anything but the present?"

That's an excellent question. With a very easy answer.

Since Mark Banks.

I just shrug, but then flash a grin. "Since never."

Felicity taps her chin. "I call bullshit."

Well, then. Maybe serving up the short story will help me forget him. "I met someone. Had a fling. Can't quite get him out of my mind. But don't worry. Soon, he'll be gone from here." I tap my temple.

I'm met with eyebrow arches from both of them. "But what about in here?" Felicity asks, tapping her heart.

That's a question I don't want to contemplate.

I came to Paris for this dream job, not to moon over a man. If there's any place I can get over someone, it ought to be the City of Love.

But I've had no interest in getting on top of or under anyone. Totally fucking annoying.

"Yup, I'm fine there," I say as the rain falls harder.

Oscar cranes his gaze to the sky. "Well, that's a sign," he remarks, giving his wife a naughty look.

His wife laughs. "A sign you want to get home and shag?"

"You know me so well, love," he says.

"And on that note," I say, pushing back in my chair since we've already paid the bill, "I better let you get right to it."

Oscar wraps an arm around her. "Actually, we were going to watch *An Arranged Marriage* first. The final episode runs tonight. Have you been watching this summer?"

Well, well. This just got more interesting than their sex life. "You two like that show?"

Felicity gives a coy shrug. "I like Ollie and Trevor. They get me in the mood."

Join the club.

Oscar squeezes her shoulder. "And I like what she likes," he says, and he sounds like he's already in the mood.

Which is as good a reason as any for me to say goodnight. Not that Englishmen from the Victorian era aren't reason enough. Is Mark still watching? What does he think of the twist last week when Ollie's long-lost brother showed up, the rake who'd lost his fortune and begged his brother for help?

After I say goodnight to my friends, I make my way along Rue Saint-Dominique as the rain patters down. Absently, I run my finger across the phone screen in my pocket, tempted once again to text Mark like I did last month when Lord Ollie was sent back to the country. *You called it, but so did I . . .*

Sir Trevor had indeed chased Ollie down. The poet is mad about his lord, and can't resist the dashing Ollie.

Understandable.

You were right too, Asher, Mark had replied. As I cross the avenue, I swipe my thumb on the text thread, re-reading our last string of messages from August as a few raindrops hit the phone.

That's the last time we texted. I probably shouldn't message him again.

After all, it's nine o'clock in Paris, and I'm heading to my flat to watch my favorite TV show as I re-read old notes from the guy I left behind in New York.

Pretty sure this isn't what I signed up for when I volunteered as tribute.

Forty-five minutes later, I'm perched on the edge of the couch, wanting to reach out to my nerdy banker, and share a play-by-play.

When Ollie pushes Trevor up against the wall in the library at the end of a ball for the duchess, I mutter, *"Get your man."*

"I don't care what my brother says. It is only ever you that I want," Ollie says, all hot and bothered.

Trevor tries to look away, to fight off the desire. "I don't know how to believe you anymore."

"Believe me," Ollie declares, then kisses the hell out of his man.

"That's what I'm talking about," I say to the screen, and my fingers itch to text Mark. To ask if he wants to test out those moves.

Slam me against the wall. Rip off my shirt. Or be slammed. Be stripped.

I start to type a message.

Then stop.

Is this really what I'm going to do? Talk dirty to him about a TV show? On the other hand, I *could* text and ask if he wants to grab a flight this weekend, and we can screw, then walk along the Seine, hit a club, or hell, just get dinner.

But I don't type anything, because what in the holy fuckery of TV twists is happening on my screen right now?

The dastardly—their word—brother broke up Troliver by sending my favorite lord to America! Are you kidding me? I want to throw my laptop into the river.

Good thing I didn't text Mark to tune in. That'd be so fun—watching together as those two guys broke up. *Not.*

I exit out of Webflix and head to my calendar to get my mind off ex-lovers. I vowed to do a better job these days of keeping my schedule.

The next few weeks have me following a dozen teams to a dozen places. The gig is going to vault me to the next level of world-class photogs. Added bonus—another couple weeks of this kind of busy should do the trick in erasing Mark from my mind.

Then I can live in the present again.

I click away from the calendar when an email notification pops up from Hannah for a party. Is it already time for a baby shower?

But when I open it, the invitation makes perfect sense.

The big three-zero for Flip is coming up soon. He's younger than me by nine months, and we always used to joke that we'd go skydiving on his thirtieth.

Instead, Hannah is hosting a party in the city.

Mere miles away from the guy I can't stop thinking of.

Will Mark be there?

No idea, but I know where I'm scheduled to be that weekend.

Barcelona. And that's not anywhere near Manhattan.

41

MANSION KINK

A WEEK LATER

MARK

"*I* have two things to discuss with you," Bridget says as she puts a plate down in front of me on her kitchen table. It contains three tacos, two with carnitas-style pork, lime and radishes, and one stuffed with homemade guacamole.

My mouth waters. But at the same time, I know she's about to ask a favor. That's the only explanation for the feast she's set in front of me. "What did you want to talk about?"

"Rosie's teacher wants her to do math with the second graders instead of the first graders."

I pick up a taco and consider this while I take a bite. "Okay?" I say through crispy pork and crunchy radishes that make me moan in happiness. Let's face it—Bridget's tacos are the closest I've come in months to having a sexual experience.

The summer has been hellaciously busy. Work is nuts, as always. But Bridget has taken five business trips in ten weeks. So I've done a lot of extra parenting, too, including summer T-ball practices that start at eight a.m. on Saturdays and Sundays.

Whoever thought that was a good idea? I haven't slept in

since June. Hell, some days I feel like I haven't slept *at all* since then.

"Are you good with her jumping up a grade in math?" Bridget continues. "The second-grade class does math at the same time as the first graders so she won't miss any other subjects."

"Sure," I agree, since math is awesome. "What else?"

She taps her fingers on the table. "Tomorrow morning— before your tennis game—my book club is throwing a baby shower for Maxine."

I put the taco down on the plate. "Did you say tomorrow morning? During Rosie's T-ball practice?"

Bridget winces. "It's Maxine's first baby. I offered to bring the cupcakes. Rosie and I are making them."

I shove the rest of the taco in my mouth and make her sweat it out. But of course I'm going to say yes. I'll come here tomorrow morning—it's Bridget's weekend and Rosie is coloring in her room right now—and pick my daughter up for T-ball practice like a good dad.

Because I *am* a good dad. And my kid will grow up knowing that both her parents would do anything for her.

Except stay married.

"Fine," I say through a mouthful. "But shockingly I have some plans, so I'll have to cancel tennis with Brett. Someday, if I manage to get a more exciting life, I won't be so easily bought off with guacamole."

I expect her to smile, but she doesn't. "You should have a life, Mark. You should date . . . *whoever* you want."

Thanks, Bridget.

A flame of anger slices through me, since I don't need her permission. But I cool it down with a sip of the iced tea she made just the way I like—with a splash of lemonade. I *should* have a social life. It's just that I don't have any idea how to get one. Last month I downloaded Grindr, spent an hour perfecting a profile I'd started last spring, then spent *another* hour inter-acting with strangers . . . before deleting it again.

I hate dating apps. *Hate.* And I don't have any single guy

friends anymore, either. No wingmen in sight. When I see the odd college friend, I'm usually the third wheel.

It's a problem I don't know how to solve. I might actually let Valencia set me up with her dentist one of these days.

Maybe.

"Is there anything else?" I ask Bridget. "Flip's party starts in half an hour."

"That sounds fun," Bridget says with a cheerful smile. "I like Flip."

"Everybody likes Flip," I point out. I'm not in the mood for his birthday bash, though. Seeing his whole preppy crew will only remind me of Asher.

"Where's the party?" Bridget asks. "Where do multi-million-aires celebrate their thirtieth birthdays?"

I snort. "I swear, this place had a preppy name too. Hang on. It's somewhere on the Upper East Side . . ." I pull my phone out and navigate to my email. I need the address before I hit the number 4 train uptown.

I tap the link to bring me to the party's page. "It's called Downton Club—on Madison and Seventy-Ninth." I roll my eyes. *"Join us at an historic private supper club for finger sandwiches and Pimm's cup cocktails with old man Flip.* Jesus—these people have a kink for mansions."

Bridget's eyes twinkle. "Come on. It sounds like they're being ironic."

"Maybe," I admit. Although I still don't really want to go. I have to, though. It will be nice to see Hannah and her big baby bump, of course.

The wedding was only three months ago. It feels like three years.

"More guacamole?" Bridget asks. At least she feels bad about shanking me with another early T-ball practice.

"No thanks," I sigh. Idly, I scroll down the list of RSVPs, wondering if Asher will be there, though I'm sure he won't.

But then . . .

His name appears on the RSVP list.

And all my blood stops circulating. Wait. Really? I scroll up to make sure that I'm reading the *yeses* and not the *maybes* or the *nos*.

But it's true. His name is there. He RSVPed *yes*.

Holy shit.

I spring out of my chair and pace across Bridget's kitchen, staring at my phone.

"Mark?" my ex-wife asks. "Is something wrong?"

"No," I bark. Although, I'm not sure that's true. Asher's in New York? And he didn't even tell me?

I feel sick.

On the thirty-minute subway trip uptown, I don't feel any better. I knew that someday I'd encounter him again. But I thought I'd have more time to put on my poker face.

Or at least a nicer shirt. As I exit the 4 train on Seventy-Seventh, I actually contemplate looking around for a men's shop and buying something better than the polo shirt I'm wearing.

But I don't do it. A grown man does not have a fashion crisis before confronting the hookup he isn't truly over.

It was never about my wardrobe, either. Asher and I are in different places in life. We need different things and we both knew that. The end of our brief fling was very civilized.

Okay, that may be the *right* word for the last second I saw him, but it's the *wrong* word to describe Asher at all. The fizz of excitement and dread that I feel as I trudge down the street is anything but civilized. And the way I felt when he stripped me down and fucked me hard was anything but civilized.

I can fake it, though. I'm going to have to.

My phone chimes with a text, and suddenly my heart is in my mouth. I pull it out of my pocket, hoping to see Asher's name.

But it's only Hannah. The preview on the lock screen reads:
Mark, before you get here, you should know that Asher . . .

I shove the phone back in my pocket as my stomach bottoms

out. I don't even want to know how that sentence ends. *Asher and his new boyfriend are here.* That's probably it.

Whatever happens, I'm going to be cool-headed tonight. I'll greet him in a friendly way. But not flirty. I'll shake his hand. *Good to see you again,* I'll say, as if it isn't tearing me apart to be in the same room again. *What brings you to New York?*

I already know it isn't me.

The Downton Club is a four-story limestone row house between Madison and Fifth. It has an intricately carved oak door with only a tiny brass sign beside it. You'd never know it was here if you didn't know it was here.

Rich people. They're seriously weird.

I trudge up the limestone staircase and open the door, feeling like a peasant. Inside the marble foyer, a host greets me. "May I help you, sir?"

Holy crap. He's wearing a full livery suit and sports a handlebar mustache. I've stumbled onto a doppelgänger from the set of *An Arranged Marriage.* And he could easily be cast as an extra.

"I'm here for the Flip Dubois birthday party. The name is Mark Banks."

"Of course." He consults a list on a clipboard. Then he makes a check mark next to my name. "The party is straight through, sir. Enjoy your time with us."

"I sure will," I lie.

As I pass through a carved doorway and head towards the party noises in the rear of this place, I realize that Flip's party is a big affair. As the mansion opens out to reveal a large parlor with French doors leading to a garden, the tacos I ate do the samba in my stomach.

I'm in no shape for a party. I'd rather turn around and go home.

But then I spot *him.* He's by the back wall, one hand casually slung on Flip's shoulder. He's holding a martini glass in his other hand, and laughing at something Flip just said. His golden face is split into a smile.

And I ache.

When I look away, I spot my sister waving at me. She smiles and beckons me over.

I hold up a finger in the universal sign for *just a second*. And then I do a one-eighty and locate the open bar. Because this moment requires a beer. Stat.

Later, I won't remember anything I said to the bartender, or anything he said to me. I'm too full of prickly awareness and tension.

I'm in the same room as Asher St. James. He didn't even bother to tell me he was coming. Unbelievable.

Then a hand lands on my shoulder.

42

SKYDIVING

ASHER

*T*he moment he enters the room, I realize some things never change.

Like Mark's fashion.

Like the fact that I don't give a fuck what he's wearing.

Or like the way my pulse spikes the second I lay eyes on my glasses-wearing, dark-haired hot nerd.

"There are many ways to have a midlife crisis," Flip says from his spot next to me as he surveys the scene. "But admit it—this party is so much better than skydiving."

I can barely focus on what my best friend is saying as we shoot the breeze about birthday celebrations. Still, I force out a laugh. "Maybe for your fortieth, I'll finally convince you to bungee jump," I say, but he'll probably have three or four kids by then, and take fewer risks.

But speaking of risks . . .

My Friday night has just narrowed to the guy heading to the open bar.

It's been nearly three months. I thought this summer would erase him. I was wrong.

"How about hang gliding?" Flip offers. "Maybe we can do

that over the summer. Or better yet, I'll strap on a BabyBjörn and cheer you on."

"Sounds great. Excuse me," I say, distantly, not even meeting his gaze. I'm caught in the lure of my Florida fling.

The man who's kept me distracted from a continent away.

I am tired of this empty feeling and not having what I desperately want.

I knock back the last of my martini, set the glass down on the tray of a passing waiter, and then weave through the throng of people, my vision narrowed to that dark hair, those confident shoulders, that strong back.

My entire body tingles.

I dart around some old friends, avoiding hellos, and pass another waiter. When I'm a foot away, I lift a hand, powered by instinct only, and set it on Mark's shoulder.

Contact.

Everything I crave.

But he tenses. Turns into a statue.

"Banks," I say, my tongue thick.

He unfreezes, turns his gaze to me in slow motion, his eyes drifting up to mine. "St. James."

We sound like we're about to duel, and we're both speechless for too many long beats, then Mark rearranges his features, and tips his chin at me. "Hello."

His tone is cooler than ice.

"I've heard warmer greetings from a Beefeater at Buckingham Palace."

His brow pinches, but Mark has always been fast with his mouth. "And do you spend a lot of time with them?"

"What?" My head spins. "No."

"Then how do you know?"

"Because," I stammer, and fuck, I should have planned this moment. I had a whole flight to decide what to say and how to say it.

But I'm not a planner. Especially right now, when I feel like my organs barely fit into my body. I meet the gaze of the man who's been living rent-free in my consciousness for all these weeks. Now he's standing right in front of me. And it's like I'm sixteen again and staring at my crush. I don't know what to say.

"So, you're here," I say. Then I want to kick my own ass for that stupid observation. *Nice, St. James. You're killing it, here.*

He lifts his beer, brings the bottle to his lips, takes a drink. That lucky bottle. When he sets it down, he licks the corner of his mouth, and hell if I can focus now. "So you're back in New York for the party. That . . . makes sense."

"Well, you only turn thirty once."

He practically rolls his eyes. "You wouldn't want to miss a chance to have a good time." Mark glances around like he's looking for someone. "Are you here with . . ."

"With? Who would I be here with? I came for . . ." The word gets lodged in my throat. I'm fucking this up. Big time. "I wouldn't miss this chance for the world. I had a thing that got canceled. I was supposed to be in Barcelona for a FLI event but it was moved."

"Ah," he says, like my answer makes perfect sense. "So, you basically had a free slot in your schedule?"

"Well, yes. But . . ." I hate how awkward this is. This isn't how Mark and I talk. We're not *how's your sked* guys. We poke and spar. So naturally, I say the exact wrong thing as I tug at the sleeve of his maroon polo. "Nice shirt."

His jaw ticks. "Seriously? You don't give me a heads-up you're coming, you show up, say you had a cancelation, and you mock my clothes?"

It's easier.

It's fucking easier than telling you why I'm here.

The words crawl up my throat, but saying *I want you* hardly conveys why I got on that plane ten hours ago.

And saying I'm here for Flip hardly does either.

Lord knows, I'm still trying to sort out this tangled knot of emotions in my chest.

"That's not what I need to say," I try again.

He smiles with his lips closed. "It's all good. We're good. You don't need to think of things to say to me. I'm just . . . some guy you used to know and it's fine. Let's not make a big deal of this.

Now, if you'll excuse me," he says, then threads his way through the crowd at the speed of light, like he did in the club that night, heading toward the hallway. And like that night, I'm not going to let him go.

I follow him, and when he turns the corner, I call his name. "Mark."

He doesn't turn around.

"Wait!" So many words clog my throat.

I was dying to see you.

I was hoping you'd be here.

I had no idea what to say.

But I'd always intended to go skydiving on Flip's thirtieth, so I guess it's time to leap out of this plane. "I was hoping you'd be here," I say to the back of his head.

His entire body goes still. But he says nothing as he turns, stares at me. Our eyes lock, like two fighters.

"Say something." I demand.

He breathes out hard. "Why? So we can catch up on Ollie and Trevor? They broke up, man. It happens. It fucking happens."

Keep falling. Maybe there's a parachute along the way. "I hated that," I say to him.

He crosses his arms. "It's just fiction."

It feels real, though, and it hurt like hell. Like my dumb heart hurts when I look at Mark, those blue eyes, those cheekbones, that hair. That five o'clock shadow.

God . . .

I think I'm . . .

I breathe out hard, scrub a hand along the back of my neck, and try one more time. "I should have told you I was coming," I admit, helpless with all these wild emotions swinging through me.

And Banks, my hardly-ever-lets-down-his-guard, nerdy, hot, gorgeous single dad with the eyes that haunt me, looks at me with resignation. "You don't owe me anything, Asher," he says, like he's forgiving me for *not* wanting more.

But he's wrong.

He's so fucking wrong.

"I know. But I should have texted," I say.

"Because you think I can't handle seeing you? I'm fine, man."

But his Adam's apple throbs. His poker face falters, and longing flashes in his eyes. I recognize it because I feel it in every damn cell in my body too.

I try again. "I know you can handle anything—"

Heels click. A woman sashays toward us. Black, sleek hair. She waggles her fingers at me. "Hey Ash," she calls out.

"Hi Danya," I say, but that's all. I don't meet her gaze. I can't deal with anyone else.

My eyes dart around, scanning the hall. There's an open door a few feet ahead. I step closer to Mark, grab his arm, and pull him into the room.

It's a library, with rich wood shelves lining the walls from floor to ceiling, laden with spines of hardcovers, and the scent of pages filling the room.

It's so fucking fitting.

I kick the door closed.

THIS IS WHAT LIBRARIES ARE FOR

MARK

*N*ot gonna lie. That was a hot move, kicking the door closed. My pulse races. But I'm *not* going to let on how much it affects me.

"You didn't have to do that," I say as I cross my arms, lean against the shelf of tomes.

His hazel eyes are fierce as he stalks over to me, stopping inches away. "I wanted to. Just like I wanted to text you to tell you I was coming."

I swallow roughly. "Yeah. You should have. It's just . . . polite," I say, but I'm not entirely sure what words are coming out of my mouth. Focus is hard with the way he stares at me. Like he wants to lick every inch of my skin.

"Polite is the last thing I feel toward you, Banks," he says, and where he was unsure minutes ago, he's strong now. Determined. "That's why I thought about just showing up and surprising you. But I don't think you like surprises, so I RSVPed."

"I hate surprises," I say, *but I like what you're saying, so keep going. Don't stop talking, please.*

"Yeah, I figured you did," Asher says, his voice going sultry.

"I RSVPed weeks ago. You did . . . maybe today?"

I know because I checked the invitation every damn day for his name. But I keep that to myself.

"Like I said, it was a last-minute thing," he says, stepping closer, so I catch a whiff of his rainfall scent, and it makes my mouth water. "The organization changed my itinerary, and as soon as that happened, I hopped on a last-minute flight, and I swear, the whole time, Mark, the whole fucking time I was flying over the Atlantic, all I was thinking was how much I wanted to see you."

This can't be real.

But it is.

Sometimes you just stop thinking.

You do.

Like right now.

I step away from the wall, spin him around so his back is to it, and shove him against the shelves.

Like magnets, our lips return to each other.

Our mouths crash together in a frenzy. Electricity crackles between us. I swear I can hear the sizzle, feel the snap of the line.

I grab his hands, lift them above his head, and push him rougher against the books. The spines probably dig into his back, and I don't care, and he doesn't either.

The fact that I'm supposed to be at a party just doesn't matter at all.

My hands thread through Asher's, our fingers linking. I devour the man I have missed madly.

It's a greedy kiss. Hot and messy, and I love every single second of the sloppiness. The click of his teeth, the tangle of our tongues. Most of all, the way his fingers curl so tightly around mine. Like he's holding on for dear life. His fingers coil around mine in a possessive grip that makes me feel like he doesn't want to let go of me.

I don't want to let go of him.

The temperature inside me launches like a rocket, shooting to the sky. Sweet, hot tension lashes through my body, and I want to revel in this moment as he sweeps his tongue against mine, and we say hello again.

We say everything with our bodies.

I missed you.

I want you.

I need you.

I don't want to break this kiss for anything in the whole universe, except maybe for this . . .

I wrench away. "Spend the weekend with me."

I blurt it out, and it's not even a spur-of-the-moment request. Well, technically it is, but it's born from months apart, missing this man.

This man who just makes me feel . . . *alive.*

He makes me feel good in a way that's so much more than sexual.

Asher's smile is contagious as his lips twitch, and his eyes glint. "With you, as in at your place?"

I laugh, confused but happy. "Yes. With me. The whole weekend. Can you?" My voice pitches up but I don't care. He's here, he came to see me, and that's literally all I need to know.

He nods in slow motion, like he can't believe his luck. "I was going to stay the night with Flip," he whispers, but the sentence is unfinished when he dips his face to my neck, grabs my hips, and hauls me close as he sweeps his mouth under my chin.

Has anything ever made me weak in the knees?

Nothing except him.

My toes are curling as he kisses me luxuriously, with slow, soft, wet kisses along my jaw, like he's relishing the taste of me.

"Mmm. Missed this," he murmurs.

I groan, running my hands through his hair. "So you have to leave tomorrow?"

Another kiss on my jaw as he nods.

"I'll take tonight, Asher. If it's all I get," I say.

He lifts his face, dusts a soft, tender kiss to my lips. "I'll change my flight. I want to see you, Mark Banks. I want to spend the weekend with you. I want to take you up on the best sleepover offer ever."

The way I felt when I walked in? Sick and nervous?

I'm the opposite. I'm electric and elated. And I never want

this to end. But I'll take two days. I will gladly take two days with Asher St. James.

And make the best of them.

I grab his face again. "So you really came here to see me?"

"I kind of can't stop thinking about you, Banks."

I know he said he can read me in other ways. But sometimes, words matter. I run a hand through that swoopy hair and go for it. "I missed you, Asher St. James," I whisper, feeling a little wobbly as I lay out the truth for him.

"You have no idea," he says.

"I'm pretty sure I have every idea," I whisper. "But I have to tell you something."

"Yeah?"

"You snore too."

44

A MUTUAL MANHANDLING

ASHER

*W*e don't leave yet. I don't want to advertise to all our friends that I mauled the guest of honor's brother-in-law.

Or, wait, did he maul me?

Well, if the way his hair looks is any indication of mine, it was a mutual manhandling. So I stop Mark, before he opens the door.

"One thing," I say. "We can't leave yet. We're not presentable." I step to him, gently smoothing his tousled hair. "There."

He dips his reddening face. "Thanks," he says, while lifting a hand to adjust his glasses. They might have gotten knocked around a bit, and the photographer in me wants to capture this look. I'd call it . . . *relentlessly kissed man.*

That might be my favorite photo ever.

I snap it in my mind's eye, then my gaze drifts down. "Also, we need to wait one more minute."

He laughs. "Yeah, it's good that you do the thinking at times like this."

But I don't let go of his hand. Don't want to stop touching him. I'm tempted to drag him against me one more time, but that won't help us make our great escape. So I keep things chaste as I adjust the collar of his maroon shirt with my free hand.

Which reminds me.

"I know you don't like surprises but I do have a surprise for you tomorrow that I think you'll like," I tell him.

"Is it a sex surprise?"

"No, it's someplace I want to take you in New York. Sort of like an errand."

"I like sex errands."

I run my thumb along his wrist. "Are you always thinking about sex, Captain Filthy Mind?"

He stares at the ceiling. "Not always, but a good ninety-five percent of the time."

"Consider this a five percent errand then."

"And you think that'll get me to agree to a surprise? Making it *not* about sex?"

I picture where I want to take him. Fine, we can squeeze in certain five percent things. "Do you have a spreadsheet for risky places in New York for . . .?" Then I whisper the number in his ear.

A sharp intake of breath comes from my guy. "I might like this surprise now."

I pull back, brush my knuckles along his jaw, smirking at Mark. "Thought you might."

"Dude, stop touching me. We need to go," he says, sounding ornery.

Ornery Mark is hot.

But all Marks are hot to me.

And that makes all the sense in the world.

"By the way, I can't wait to see your place. I bet you have navy sheets and gray pillowcases," I say.

He stares dead-eyed at me. "Why do I like you so much?"

Tossing my head back, I crack up. "That's a very good question."

For a while, I asked myself the same question about him. But I know exactly why Mark Banks does it for me. He's never once tried to change me. He sees exactly who I am. He takes me as I am.

And he's still here.

I squeeze his hand. Check the goods. We're presentable. "I'd say we're ready. Let's go pretend to be social. Ten minutes?"

"Ten minutes tops," he agrees.

I drop his hand, and we leave the library.

I fucking love libraries.

———

As much as I'd like to drink and dash, I can't. After I grab my weekend bag from the coat check, I track down the man of the hour. Flip's holding court with some old friends, entertaining Danya, Jasper, and Archie, so I catch his eye, and nod toward the door.

He lifts a finger to them, then peels away.

As we duck into an alcove, he stares curiously at my weekend bag, slung over my shoulder. "You never leave a party early. Even for jet lag . . . ergo?"

Flip isn't dumb. He's likely done the math since I've been here less than thirty minutes. "Change of plans. For your thirtieth birthday, my present is to give your home all to you and your wife tonight."

"Why do I feel like that's more of a gift to you?"

No point beating around the bush. "I'm staying an extra night, and spending the weekend with Mark." I don't even attempt to joke about it or make it seem light. There's nothing casual about my decision to fly to New York or to take Mark up on his offer.

Flip's gray eyes bore into me. "Let me get this straight. You flew to New York. And you're spending the weekend with my brother-in-law?"

"Correct."

"So this is more"—he stops to sketch air quotes—"*a little harmless fun?*" he asks as he quotes me back to me. "A weekend with bennies?"

Actually, it's not that at all. Not for me.

I wish I could tell him what it is. "I'm not sure what this is. The only thing I know is that I don't want to end things with him," I say, and I'm pretty sure I've shocked my best friend senseless.

Flip blows out a long stream of air. Takes a weighty beat. "Wow. Gotta say, I didn't see that coming."

I chuckle. "That makes two of us."

Flip strokes his chin, eyeing me. "So, you and Mark Banks. I guess stranger things have happened, but not by much."

"I know, but somehow it just kind of works," I say, and I haven't entirely figured out why. I just know that it does. *We fit.*

Flip shrugs, holds out his hands to show he's got nothing. "I can't even give you a hard time. Or a *you better be careful* line."

"Lucky me. I dodged a bullet," I joke.

But his eyes turn serious, and I half expect he's going to issue some kind of growly *if you break my wife's brother's heart, you're dead to me* warning. "So, should I be worried about your heart getting broken now?"

Words I never expected to hear from Flip. But the last few months have been unexpected.

"Maybe," I say, without any pretense.

"I have no idea who you are and what you did with my best friend. But I'll say this—you better not back out of our hang gliding plans for next summer."

"Flip, come on. I'm the one going hang gliding. You're going to watch since you're the guy with a kid on the way and a low tolerance for risk."

He stares at me. "You do know your boyfriend has a kid. That means—"

I wag my finger back and forth. "No one's using the boyfriend word yet."

Emphasis on *yet.*

BETTER THAN TACOS

MARK

"*H*annah, hey." I smile at my sister and try to look casual. But it's possible I have crazy eyes and mussed hair.

My poker face is gone forever, I think. It met its match in the form of Asher St. James.

"Hey to you," my sister says, giving me a funny smile. "Did you read my text?"

"No. Why?" I pull my phone out of my pocket and tap on her name.

That message I didn't want to read about Asher? It says:

Hannah: Mark, before you get here, you should know that Asher is here, and he is watching the door like a lonely dog at the end of the day. I wasn't supposed to say anything, but please show up and put him out of his misery.

I laugh out loud. "You're hilarious."

"Can I assume from the beard-burn on your face that you two got reacquainted?"

"Yeah." My laugh turns embarrassed. "About that . . . We're, uh, leaving. Sorry to take off. But he's going to spend the weekend so . . ." I feel my face burn bright red.

Hannah doubles over laughing. "This is great. I'm going to tease you about this for *years*. Remember when Flip turned thirty and you spent five minutes at his party and then left to have sex?"

"We'll probably go out to dinner first," I sputter.

She laughs harder.

"Weekends are short, and then he'll go back to France." I clear my throat and try to clear my head. "This is our only chance."

"I see how it is." She gives me a little shove toward the door. "Go on. You know you want to."

"Thanks." My face is still aflame. But it's totally worth it. I lean in and kiss her cheek. "Love you."

"Love you too, Marky Mark. Now scram."

I don't make her say it again. With a wave and a smile, I head for the door. On my way I spot Asher, standing beside Flip, the two of them lost in conversation. So I head outside alone to wait for him on the street.

Because, unfortunately, there's someone else I need to talk to.

Bridget answers on the second ring. "Talk fast because I'm frosting cupcakes."

"About that," I say slowly. "I'm sorry, Bridge, but I can't do T-ball tomorrow." I *could* do it. But I don't want to leave Asher in my bed at seven-thirty in the morning to handle something that's Bridget's problem. Not this time. Not when I have less than forty-eight hours with him.

"Mark! I'm literally frosting the cupcakes."

I take a deep, slow breath so I don't explode. "Look. Earlier I said I could do it. I was wrong. You can find a way. Ask Valencia. Ask Morgan. There's a friend in town that I never get to see, and I'm going to do that. I'm going to live my damn life."

"A friend in town? At seven-thirty tomorrow morning?"

Clearly, she doesn't think I deserve a life if she can't do the math here. My silence fills in the blanks for her.

"Oh," she says, with a sigh. "Well, look, like I said earlier. I'm glad you're doing your thing. That's great. But what if you swung by the ball field later? At nine? We could do a handoff."

"No," I say immediately. "We're not negotiating right now. I *never* say no to you. Never. I've spent the last year terrified that Rosie would think I don't care about her. But you take advantage of that, Bridge."

She makes an irritated squeak. "I do *not.*"

"Not intentionally," I concede. "But you never hesitate to ask me to step in. And for once in my life, I'm saying no."

"Fine," she snaps. "Fine. I'll figure something out."

"I'm sure you will," I say softly.

She hangs up.

Huh. I guess I won't be getting any more of those tacos anytime soon. But damn, that felt good. A whole lot better than tacos. I take another deep, cleansing breath and wait for my *weekend surprise*—yes, I like the surprise of Asher very much—to emerge from the preppy mansion.

He doesn't make me wait too long, either. Only two minutes have passed when the door opens for the man who's got a weekend bag slung over his shoulder. "All right, Banks. Where to?"

"Let's see . . ." I check the time. "It's barely past seven, and you've been on a plane all day. Want to walk a bit in Central Park?"

"That sounds great," he says. "Although, you're probably hungry. I could find us somewhere to have dinner."

"Actually . . ." I eye the V of golden skin that's visible in the open collar of his shirt. "I already ate."

"Did you?" His gaze travels to my mouth. And he licks his lips. "I took a nice long walk already too. I asked the cab driver to drop me at the corner of Sixtieth, so I could wake up a little before walking into that party."

"Interesting," I say.

"Mmm," he agrees. "So what's your next idea?"

I stick my hand in the air. "Taxi!"

"More," Asher growls. "Yes. Harder."

I look down at the muscular Adonis that I'm currently drilling into my bed. He's on his back, strong arms braced against the headboard, staring up at me with lust-filled hazel eyes. His chest is flushed and his lips are swollen from our make-out session in the taxi.

Barely twenty minutes have passed since we stumbled into my apartment and began shedding our clothes in a breadcrumb trail from the entrance, through the living room, down the hall, and into my bed.

We'd communicated in only one-word commands, like *yes*, *more*, *baby*.

Except for when Asher managed to string four words together at once: *fuck me right now*.

Yessir. So here we are, with me groaning through ragged thrusts, losing my ever-loving mind. "Fuck." I'm valiantly trying to stave off the inevitable. "Close," I warn.

The problem is made worse by Asher's big hands that wander along my bare chest, lighting me up wherever they land. And then there's the view of his flexing pecs, dusted with honey-toned hair. The six pack makes me drool, too.

But the thing that's got me hanging by a thread is the look of ownership in his sex-darkened eyes. Like he needs me as much as I need him right now. Like he's burning up for it.

"Fuck," he moans with all the eloquence the moment calls for. "Roll."

"What?"

He doesn't explain. He takes action instead, wrapping his legs around my ass, grabbing my shoulders and rolling me underneath him. In the time it takes me to do a slow blink, I'm on my back while Asher rides my dick with athletic finesse.

And, *whoa*. If I thought the view was good before, now it's mind-shattering. Asher's pistoning body rocks over mine in a feral swagger as he takes me deep. Those bright eyes roam my frame with an intensity that I can feel almost like a sunburn.

The change in position has done good things for my stamina,

too. I reach for his cock and give it a lazy stroke, his hot girth sliding against my palm.

He groans, a vein in his neck pulsing. "So. Good." He locks his arms against the headboard and stares into my eyes. I'm so turned on, but I'm also completely at peace with this man and his warm gaze and the sound of our skin slapping in a naughty rhythm.

This moment is *everything*. I've missed him so much.

But then Asher does something that blows up my self-control once again. He leans down to kiss me.

I have to crane my neck to meet him. But the moment our tongues touch, I let out a moan. Because it's all too much. His taste and his skin and the scent of sex.

"Come," he whispers against my lips. "Do it."

And, yup. I'm done just like that—pouring my entire soul into the condom with a teeth-rattling groan.

"Baby, yesssss," Asher says, the words a scrape against my lips. Then he shudders and paints my chest as he slows down the pump of his hips. Like a wind-up toy winding down, he slows to a stop before collapsing in a sweaty mess on my chest.

Everything is silent except for the thump of my heart against his. We're still in the midst of a long, slow kiss that eventually ends with a wet *snick*.

After a long moment of stillness, I realize I'm clutching his body to my chest, as if afraid that he'll get away from me. I relax my grip, and Asher eases off with a quiet moan. "Wow."

"Wow."

He flops onto the bed beside me, and neither of us says a word for a few minutes. My thoughts are billowing around the room. I wonder briefly what I did to deserve this bliss.

"So this is your place," Asher says in a gruff, blissed-out voice.

"Yup," is all I can manage.

"You have navy sheets and a one-eyed cat."

I pick up my head just a few degrees and spot Blackbeard licking his paw on top of my dresser. "Yup."

"I think he's plotting to kill me."

"He is. But I'll save you."

Asher laughs. He reaches for my hand, lifts it to his mouth, and kisses my knuckles.

This small maneuver makes me unreasonably happy. "So, what do you want to do this weekend?"

"I just did it," he says. "And as soon as I'm able, we'll do it again."

46

MORE THAN HANDCUFFS

ASHER

J am facedown on Mark's couch, recovering from round number . . . actually, I've lost track at this point. We just can't keep our hands off each other. On and off, all night long. In his bed, in his shower. This last time, I bent him over his own couch and held him tightly until I made him shout.

Now it's about eleven a.m. New York time on Saturday. That means it's five p.m. in Paris. I've barely had four hours sleep in the last day and a half, but I couldn't be happier. I guess I'll sleep when I'm dead. And now he's making coffee, so that will probably help.

I doze.

The couch depresses with Mark's weight. At least, I hope it's him and not that freaky cat. That cat is proof that Mark Banks is full of surprises—I never expected him to have a pet. And one who's a pirate.

A warm hand lands on my back and then travels up to sift through my hair. "Have I finished you off? Or do you have enough strength left to drink this coffee?"

"I can't wait to drink that coffee." With a yawn, I push myself up to a seated position.

Mark puts his feet onto the coffee table. He hands me a steaming mug, keeping one for himself.

I prop my feet up right beside his. And then I rub his instep with my foot while we silently sip our coffee.

This is so . . . nice. A Saturday at home with Mark. I want all the Saturdays, damn it. I don't know what it is about Mark, but he makes me want things I don't usually crave.

My hand finds its way onto his thigh. I'm not putting the moves on him. I just want to touch him.

His hand slides over mine. "I stirred up some pancake batter. And I also put some bacon in the oven. How do you feel about bananas in pancakes?"

Maybe the jet lag is getting to me, because the idea that Mark is making us breakfast almost makes me want to cry. "I feel great about it," I rasp. "Feed me all the things."

I take a big breath and, yup, the air is bacon-scented. I'm basically in heaven right now.

Then the door buzzer rings. Apparently there are visitors in heaven.

"Fuck," Mark says. He gets up.

"What's the matter?"

"I forgot about Brett."

"Brett from work?"

"Yeah. We were going to play tennis." He walks over to the vestibule and lifts a phone that's attached to the wall. "Yes, thanks. Send him up." Then he glances down at his gym shorts and threadbare T-shirt before turning to give me a head-to-toe sweep, and then a smile. "Just making sure we're both decent."

"Are we?" I glance down at my joggers and my FLI T-shirt. "I haven't looked this shabby in ages. We both look recently fucked."

Mark just shrugs. Then he pulls the door open to reveal another dude. This one is wearing . . . a polo shirt. Carefully trimmed hair and pressed khaki shorts complete the look.

I suppress a smile. Mark's work husband is cut from the same cloth.

"Dude, I'm so sorry," Mark says. "I spaced on tennis. Come in, will you?"

"Whoa," Brett says with a chuckle, entering as he takes in Mark's ragged appearance. "Did you get drunk last night? I've never seen you looking so wrecked."

"Um . . ."

I laugh from the sofa. Can't help it. Wrecked is one way to put it.

". . . Not exactly," Mark says as Brett's gaze swings toward me. "I have company this weekend."

"Hi," I say, giving Brett a little wave. "I'm Asher."

Brett tips his head to the side, and I can practically see the equations working behind his eyes. "You look familiar. Do you play soccer?"

"I used to. We call it football, though. Now I'm a photographer."

"Huh," Brett says slowly. "Nice to meet you."

I stand up and offer my hand. "It's a pleasure to meet you, Brett. I've heard a lot about your prowess at the chess board."

"That's interesting," he says, shaking my hand. "Because I haven't heard the first *word* about you."

Uh-oh.

"It's complicated," Mark says at the exact moment that I say, "It's new."

Then we both turn and gaze at each other with wonder and amusement. Because it is, in fact, both complicated and new.

Brett chuckles uncomfortably. "Mark? Is this part of the reason you got divorced?" He's still doing the math apparently.

"Nope," he says, popping the P at the end of the word. "But it's the reason I'm finally enjoying being divorced. I'm bisexual."

"Oh. Cool."

"Want some pancakes and bacon?" Mark asks.

"Sure." Brett shrugs easily, and I see that he finally understands the equation. "Is there more of that coffee?"

"You bet. Let's eat."

We crowd into Mark's smallish kitchen. He shoos us both to the table with our mugs of coffee. "Do you do . . . whatever Mark does?" I ask him.

He laughs loudly. "Yeah, but I'll spare you the details."

"Good. Because dumb jocks are Mark's type. I don't really understand finance. Although I do enjoy spreadsheets."

Mark snorts from the stove.

"Eh. Finance can be a drag. But it pays the bills. Do you at least play chess?" Brett wants to know.

"Sorry, no."

"Ah, well." He sips his coffee. "Nobody's perfect."

"I like tennis, though."

"Good to know," he says.

I'm a lucky man.

I've lived a charmed life. No great childhood drama, no traumatic coming out story. I'm only thirty, and I've already had two fantastic careers. The first one on the pitch, the second behind the lens.

It's very good to be me.

But right now, on a Saturday in September in Manhattan, as I walk through Greenwich Village with Mark, this is the day I want to bottle up.

From the sex marathon, to the pancakes, to meeting his nerdy banker friend.

Every second is perfect.

"And we're almost there. The five percent errand," I say, waving to the end of the block.

"Ah, so the sex dungeon you're taking me to is up ahead?" Mark asks, swinging his gaze around the street.

Reasonable question, since we've passed leather shops and sex toy stores, all adorned with rainbow flags.

"That's for later, pet," I tease him.

Mark laughs. Something he's been doing a lot of this weekend. He has a great laugh, dry and full of genuine humor. The man has a fantastic smile too. And I can't help feeling like a king since I'm the guy who brings it out in him. I'm also the *only* guy who's brought out this side of him. I don't have a virgin kink, but I definitely have a Mark Banks one. Being his first for all the good stuff in bed only makes me want to experience *more* good stuff with him.

Every single night.

I drape an arm around his shoulders. "We can have a whole night of sex dungeon spreadsheets at your place any time you want."

"Good thing I stocked up on handcuffs, then," he says, offhand.

I stop in my tracks, and he pulls up short. "Do not tease me about handcuffs," I say, in a deep, low voice.

Mark grins wickedly. "You kinky fucker. Are you into handcuffs, Asher?"

I'm into you. "I had a dirty daydream about you in handcuffs once."

"Guess you can come play with mine tonight then," he says, and yup, this is officially the best day ever.

I grab his face, give him a quick peck.

When I break the kiss, we walk the last several feet to one of my favorite clothing shops. Sexy music filters out, and a tall woman with short white hair and stern glasses glances up at us from the stark white counter.

"We're going . . . shopping?" Mark asks, brow creased. "That's your surprise?"

Oh, shit.

"Yes," I say, and my heart skitters. Now that I'm here, it hits me—he's going to think I'm trying to change him and I'm not really. This is just fun. "I thought maybe I'd get you some new shirts, but let's forget it."

"You really do hate my clothes." He sounds amused.

But I feel like a jackass. "Actually, I don't."

"I'm so confused. You want to take me shopping. Get me some new clothes, but now you don't?"

I had this idea to buy him some stylish new shirts that I'd want to rip off him, and it felt brilliant at the time. Now, it seems like an insult. "You don't have to change a single thing for me," I tell him. "I don't need to take you shopping."

"Dude, you're seriously fucking confusing," he says with a laugh. "Do you honestly think I care if you want me to wear something different? Because I don't."

I jerk my head back. "You don't?"

He plucks at his gray T-shirt. "Clothes are whatever. They're not my thing. But if they're your thing, and it makes you happy, then it's cool. Did you think I was going to be offended that you dislike my clothes so much you want to take me shopping for something new?"

Shit, I did. "At first I just wanted to take you because I thought it would be fun."

"Because shopping is fun to you," he supplies, like he's trying to understand me.

"Yeah, it is," I say, but that's not what this is about. But fuck it. I rip off the Band-Aid and tell him where this idea came from. "The day I met your parents? I had this image flash before me of taking you shopping in New York."

A grin spreads on his face. "You had a fantasy in Florida about what we're doing today?"

"Now who's mocking who?"

"I'm just processing this. So, let me see if I got this right. While we were in Miami, you were picturing doing something with me in New York?" he asks, and he's so restrained as he adds up the evidence, but I can hear the sliver of the smile in his voice, and I can see the delight in his blue eyes.

"I was," I admit.

"And that made you happy? This image? This fantasy?"

I nibble on the corner of my lips, then admit the truth. "It did at the time."

"And now?"

"Everything kind of does," I blurt out.

"Jesus," he mutters, but he's laughing.

And I feel like all the tables have been turned on me by this man.

Especially when Mark invades my space completely and roams a hand up my back. He whispers against my lips. "I don't care about polo shirts or designer shirts. I don't care if you want to change my style or not change my style. Literally none of that bothers me. The only thing I take away from this is that you wanted to do this with me . . . and you wanted it back then. So right now, you should take me shopping, then take your reward."

Somehow, my day just got even better.

This isn't a rom-com shopping montage. We're not living in *Pretty Woman*. Mark tries on three shirts, and I wait outside the dressing room with the full-length door, giving him my opinion on each item.

"How's this one, honey?" he asks in a playful voice, as he swings open the door.

And fuck me.

I whistle my appreciation.

I was right.

My guy is a smoke show in a tight, sky-blue short-sleeve button-down that hugs his biceps and pecs, and makes me think dirty thoughts.

Not that that's hard with him.

Not that anything is hard with him.

Except for the ocean that separates us, come tomorrow.

This shopping excursion is another stolen moment. Like when Miami ended and we went our separate ways.

That's what'll happen tomorrow night when I catch the six-thirty flight to Charles de Gaulle, and return to a punishing schedule of games, events, shoots, and back-breaking but wonderful work. And when he returns to Wall Street, and parenting, and living his life far, far away from me.

Which means I should just make the most of this weekend in New York.

I glance around the shop. The woman is busy with another customer. The music is just the right volume. I step into the dressing room, close the door quietly, and dip my face to his ear. "Don't make a sound."

"Actually, I was going to say that to you."

Then he gets down on his knees and gives me the rest of my shopping fantasy.

After dinner that night, we walk past a bank. A clock flashes the time in red digits in the ATM lobby.

I look away from the reminder of passing days. So many more months till next summer. Are we doing this for that long? And what is *this* even? I have no idea if he's going to miss me in the same big way I'll miss him.

Except, he told me as much last night. He took that risk, and he's been taking risks left and right with me from the start. "Funny, when I first met you, I thought you weren't a guy who took risks, but I was wrong about you."

"You think I take risks?" Mark's eyes twinkle.

I give him a pointed stare. "You're here with me. I'd say yes."

He smiles, like that pleases him. "Maybe I'm learning things about myself with you. But I think you're wrong about yourself."

My brow creases. "In what way?"

"You seem to think you're bad at . . ." He stops, waves a hand from him to me. Maybe he doesn't want to define us either.

"Right."

"But really, you're not, Asher. I mean, I'm no expert at . . ." He trails off again. Neither one of us is using labels. "But you rented that hot car, you took me clubbing in Florida, and you stole me away to the beach, and you made a fun thing out of everything. I think you're pretty good at this . . ."

Fuck labels.

I just want Mark, whatever we are.

But I have no idea how to have him. And we're both shit at discussing it. So we don't.

Instead, I handcuff him to the bed later that night and torture him with my tongue until he's begging for release. And I still want more. More than handcuffs. More than sex.

Just more Mark.

47

MY LIFE IS A FRENCH FILM

MARK

*W*e trudge up the steps to my building on Sunday afternoon.

"Thank you for taking me to the Statue of Liberty, and the Empire State building. But I'd have to say my favorite part of my forty-eight hours in New York has got to be the M&M shop in Times Square. It was a lifelong dream to go there," Asher replies as we reach the top step.

"Had a feeling you'd love all the tourist traps."

We did none of those things today. Which made this Sunday another perfect day—filled with sleep, sex, coffee, walking around Manhattan, and Asher.

My . . .

As I unlock the door to my building I wonder once again—what is Asher to me after this weekend? Because *lover* is a weird fucking word to use in any situation except for a French film.

As I wander down the hallway, my chest hollows. Tomorrow, I won't see him. Or the next day or the next. But I want this life. Hell, I want a weeknight life with him too—seeing him after work, or after Rosie goes to bed. I never thought I'd want that at all.

But now I want that so much I can taste the possibility. The last day we were in Miami, this was what I imagined having with him, but it's going to vanish in mere hours, when he walks down those steps and gets on that plane. And, holy fuck, my head *is* a French film.

I hate foreign films. I'm not broody.

Except when it comes to Asher St. James.

"Next time, will you take me to a show and on a carriage ride?" Asher asks, deadpan.

"Count on it . . ." But the sentence dies as I stick on *next time.* How the hell do we get to a next time?

A door creaks open at the end of the hall. "Yes, I know, Zoe. Sprinkles. Get sprinkles. It's one of the four basic food groups."

"Wine, sprinkles, cake, and sushi," Zoe calls out to her wife.

Shutting the green door, Valencia comes into view, all olive skin, waves of chestnut hair, and big eyes that fire questions at me when she acquires the target—me with a man.

"Hello there, *friend*," she says, pointedly, then gestures from Asher to me, then back.

"You mean *bad friend*, I believe, Valencia. And to answer your unsaid question, this is Asher."

"Who can only be the smug *and* hot one?" she asks with a too-big smile.

And for the fiftieth time, my face flames red.

Asher loops an arm around me, cracking up. "Aww, fuck you, Mark."

I laugh too. "Yes, the smug best man." *My . . .*

Why does a label even matter?

Valencia strides forward, grabs Asher's hand, and says, "I had a feeling about you two." Then she gives me Robert De Niro *I'm watching you* eyes. "And I expect a full report later."

She heads out the door as we hit the stairs, Asher behind me.

"She knows you wanted to fuck me?" Asher asks.

This guy. Laughing, I answer. "Yes. She's a good friend. She wants to set me up with her dentist. And before then, it was her creative director," I mention casually, catching him up on my friendship with Valencia.

"And you said . . .?" Asher's voice is stripped of all fun. It's intense. Commanding even.

I turn to him on the steps. There's no humor in his eyes. Only possession. "I said no. And I'll still say no."

He doesn't even smile. He just nods crisply. "Good answer, Banks."

I keep walking up, a smile teasing at my lips as I look ahead. With that understanding—*this is exclusive*—the stranglehold on my emotions loosens slightly. But only slightly.

That means I need to say more.

Thirty minutes later, Asher is packed and ready to go, his car arriving within the hour.

I flash back to Florida, to the morning in the guest house when I was rehearsing how to ask him for more. I swallowed my words then. I won't do that now.

I gesture to his suitcase. "Funny, how much I was dreading the first flight with you back in June."

Way to go, Banks. Start it off by telling him you hated him.

But isn't that how our story began?

"You seemed pretty miserable, even though you were undressing me with your eyes all the time," Asher quips.

I smile faintly, but I can't hold onto the grin, because honestly, I'm fucking sad that he's leaving. He sits on the edge of my bed with my navy sheets and gray pillowcases. The man knows me so well.

I soldier on. "But then," I say, rubbing my hands along the comforter. "I was dreading leaving Florida without saying . . ." I stop to swallow, then meet his gaze.

I expect his eyes to drift down to my throat, checking for the truth. But they stay locked on mine patiently.

"Saying what, Mark?" he asks softly.

I scrub a hand across my jaw. Fuck, why is this so hard?

Oh, right. Because you're falling for the guy next to you.

"Without telling you how much I wanted to see you again," I say, and it's more than a weight lifting.

It's a door opening. Maybe into a whole new future.

Asher's grin is buoyant. "I had a feeling you were going to then. Or maybe just a hope. Even though I was leaving the country."

I stare down at my hand on the navy comforter, then at his in his lap. The man does know me. He called it last night—when I really want something, I take the risk. He's the reward. I reach for his hand. "I want us to try this out. Just you and me. I don't want you to date anyone else. I'm not going to. I want to do this, whatever *this* is," I say, and my fingers clasp his so tightly as I put my heart on the line for the first time in a long time. Maybe ever.

With astonishing speed, an answer flies from his lush lips. "Yes."

That's it. I don't even have to speak the word that's been forming on my tongue.

His lips are on mine, and he's kissing me. It's a soft, poignant kiss that tastes far too much like goodbye. But also like the start of something new and complicated and so very big.

When he breaks the kiss, his eyes gleam wickedly. "Is this on your spreadsheet?"

"What?" I ask, still a little dazed from everything.

"Asking me to be your boyfriend?" he goads.

"You're such an arrogant prick."

"But now I'm *your* arrogant prick," he says, and the man is far too pleased in this moment.

Or really, maybe as pleased as I hoped he'd be.

"Yes, you are. So let's do this." Leaving the bedroom, and the scene of the best weekend ever in my life, we move to the living room and compare schedules.

It's not the least bit romantic or sexy, and it's the only thing I want to do with my boyfriend.

48

LIKE DRACULA

ASHER

I'm not a planner, but I will definitely plan for Mark Banks.

Worth it.

"I have some three-day weekends coming up." Mark scrolls through his phone. "There's a bank holiday the second Monday of October."

"Yeah?" I flip to that date and find . . . "Shit. That's no good. I'm in Monaco for Saturday and Italy on Sunday."

"Posh fucker." Mark gives me a grin. "Fine. There're two bank holidays in November—Veteran's Day is the second Monday. And then there's Thanksgiving. But I have Rosie for the holiday, and we're supposed to go to a parade party. So you could come here?"

I click through November. "Thanksgiving is no good because there's an awards ceremony I'm supposed to attend. I could cancel? But Veteran's Day is a real possibility."

When I look up, Mark seems more hesitant than I'd hoped he would. "Wow, November . . ." He sighs.

"I know."

He drops his gaze to his phone again. "Maybe I could come

295

just for an ordinary weekend? The risk is getting delayed, though, and not showing up for work on Monday."

"Well, a five-thirty flight after work on Friday gets you to Paris early in the morning on Saturday. So you'd get all of Saturday and most of Sunday."

"Right," he says.

But the paucity of that timing sits heavily between us. A transatlantic flight for a day and a half of togetherness. Fuck.

"Okay." He reaches a hand across the sofa cushion and squeezes my thigh muscle. "November for sure. And hopefully another weekend before then."

That's when the door buzzer rings. "That will be Rosie." Mark lets go of me and heads to the vestibule.

A moment later, his kiddo comes tearing through the apartment, followed slowly by Bridget. "Hi," she says to Mark, her tone curt. Then she spots me and does an actual double take. She notes my weekend bag at my feet, and her mouth forms a straight line.

An awkward silence hangs between Mark and Bridget.

But Rosie doesn't notice. "Asher! Hi! You're here."

"Hey, girl." I hold up a palm for a high five as her parents head to the kitchen. "How was your weekend?"

"Fine," she says, slapping my hand. "We went to the zoo in Central Park, but the line was too long for the penguins."

"Bummer. Who did you see instead?"

"There are these super-creepy bats, like a foot long . . ." She holds her hands twice that far apart. "They hang upside down from the ceiling of the tropical room! And sometimes they fold and unfold their wings in their sleep."

She mimes a gesture like Dracula opening and closing his cape, and I crack up. "Wow. But how do they poop if they're upside down?"

She frowns deeply. "I don't know. They don't poop on *themselves*, right? Gross."

"Gross," I agree.

We both get distracted, though, by the muffled arguing coming from the kitchen.

"That is not what happened," Mark's voice says. "If you want to stay mad at me for something you did because you wanted to go to a baby shower, that's on you."

I look away from the kitchen door, as if I could silence them by ignoring them.

"Mommy is mad at Daddy," Rosie says in a low voice. "I don't like it when they yell."

"All parents yell sometimes," I point out. "Then they stop."

She doesn't seem convinced.

"You want to see a video on my phone? It shows a bunch of times that animals ran onto football fields in the middle of a game, and none of the players knew what to do."

She perks up. "What kind of animals?"

"All kinds." I open YouTube. "The bull is my favorite. I was there for that one. But the dogs are pretty funny too."

She moves closer to me on the sofa until her little body is tucked right up next to mine. So I press *play* and then put an arm around her so we can both see the screen. We watch a bunch of athletes run around like nutters after various panting dogs. And the silly music drowns out the sound of her parents arguing in the next room about schedules.

But better schedules than . . . lifestyle choices.

Since ten minutes later, as Bridget leaves, she stops in front of the couch, then says through thin lips to us, "Good luck, you two."

"Thanks," I say, since Mark doesn't say a word.

I remember what he told me in Miami about their marriage—the end of it was never about his orientation. But it's always good to know the mother of your kid isn't a homophobic selfish jerk. Maybe just a selfish jerk.

Sometimes, that's all you can ask for, so I'm glad she gave that much to him.

Besides, Mark seems more interested in the two people on the couch. I catch him watching Rosie and me with a soft look on his face. He seats himself on his daughter's other side and watches a Barcelona player catch a chicken in front of the goal.

When the video finally ends, he looks over Rosie's head at

me. "It's four. Isn't your car downstairs? Aren't you worried about traffic?"

Holding his gaze, I slowly shake my head. "I *should* be, though. I suppose."

"Is Asher going?" Rosie looks up from the phone. "*Now?*"

That's as good a cue as any. "I have a plane to catch."

"You could stay for dinner," she says as I tuck my phone back into my shirt pocket.

I wish I could. "Maybe another time," I say gently. I rise from the sofa and reluctantly grab my bag and head for the door.

Mark follows me. The vestibule is tiny, and not at all private. It's just as well, or I'd probably maul the guy again and miss my flight.

"Take care of yourself," Mark says, his voice like gravel.

"You too," I whisper.

From the sofa comes a question. "Are you going to kiss him again, Daddy?"

I find this query startling, but Mark does not. He holds my gaze, his eyes warming. "I am, cupcake."

Then he lifts a hand to my chin, steps closer, and gives me a kiss so sweet and tender that I have to close my eyes and just experience it.

It's over way too soon. "Goodbye, Ash," he whispers. "Talk soon."

"I can't wait," I whisper. Then I wave goodbye to Rosie and leave the apartment, before I lose my nerve.

49

I HATE TIME

MARK

*T*he next three months are heaven and hell.

Asher carves out two days in October to get away, and we spend an autumn weekend in the city that makes me want to stop time. We go to bed together, we wake up together, and we visit Caroline—*my* niece, *his* goddaughter—since Hannah and Flip had a little girl. In November, I fly to Paris for Veteran's Day, and the capital of France is better than I imagined, especially since my tour guide speaks French.

In my ear.

My favorite French words are the ones he mutters in that husky voice he uses when we're naked, grinding together. He could be telling me to do the laundry or wash his socks and it'd still make me shudder.

Problem is, those weekends are like a rich cognac.

One small pour and then you're done.

Long-distance sucks big time. The pain of separation pounds through me every day like a dull headache.

I have to live with it, and there's no aspirin to take away the sting.

But December has coasted into Manhattan and that means in

299

one week, I'll fly to Paris for Asher's birthday. That's what he wants as a gift, he said.

Me.

Change is a funny thing. My sister is right about life's moments. A year ago this month, I met the guy at one of her game nights. If you'd asked me then if I'd be planning a birthday trip to France to see the superhot wingman who'd become my boyfriend, I'd have said that was as likely as Warren Buffett investing in GameStop.

Now, I'm counting down the days.

And he knows it, evidently. "Are you doing that thing where you're crossing the days off on your wall calendar with a big marker?" The question comes from Asher on the phone.

I keep my eye on Rosie as she clambers up the monkey bars in Chelsea Green park after school on a brisk December day.

"I do not keep a paper calendar."

"I meant the digital one in your head, nerd boy."

"Yes, and I presume you're also counting down, since I know how much you like gifts."

"Obviously. I require several blow jobs for my birthday," he says as Rosie climbs her way to the top of the blue and orange bars.

"Daddy, I'm a spider monkey," she shouts.

"And spider monkeys are very careful," I tell her as I pace the edge of the structure, craning my neck to watch my kiddo.

Asher laughs. "Your multi-tasking skills never cease to amaze me."

"Yes, I'm kind of blowing my own mind too."

He laughs. "Speaking of multi-tasking and blowing, this blow job requirement—that's giving and receiving."

"Obviously. And I think thirty-one is a good goal."

"Yes! What more could a man ask for on his thirty-first birthday. I call first dibs on the terrace."

Yeah, we've enjoyed tradesies on his terrace overlooking the Seine. "It's your birthday so you deserve it, birthday boy."

Rosie scrambles back down, then runs to the other side of

the jungle gym. "Daddy, take a picture of me and send it to Asher."

"Of course, cupcake," I say.

"What is she doing right now?" Asher asks, and my heart warms, like it does nearly every time he asks about her, or talks to her during our regular phone chats—the PG ones, that is. I never imagined my guy and my kid would have any connection. Why would I? But they do, and at first I thought it was the sporty thing—Rosie is an active girl. But that's not why they like each other. Asher talks to her like she's a person, with thoughts and feelings, not like a little alien doll from another planet. In Miami, I was so sure the kid thing would be a big issue for him. Turns out, it's not. I don't question it anymore. Maybe because Asher and I just work, and he knows I'm a package deal.

"She's showing me one of the many ways she plans to strike fear into me for the next several years of my life. By doing daredevil stunts on the jungle gym. I'll show you." I say, then snap a quick pic of her racing up the jungle gym again and send it to him.

"Aww," he says, and I picture him on his couch looking at the shot. "I did that, too, as a kid. And I'm no worse for wear."

"Well, my heart is beating crazy fast and I'm standing five feet away from her," I say.

"Go for it, Rosie! Climb all the way to the top," Asher says, even though I'm the only one on the phone.

"Don't encourage her," I say, but I love seeing her happy, and she's been having a blast lately. I'm still doing the bulk of the parenting and that still works for me and for Rosie too. We've all adjusted and settled into our post-divorce routine.

"Do you want me to take you on a tour of the Louvre for my B-day?" Asher asks. "Go to Versailles? We could even take the elevator all the way to the top of the Eiffel Tower. I know you *love* touristy things," he says, since we never do any of those things. I've seen very little of the city beyond a few blocks in the Seventh where he lives, and I'm more than fine with that.

I cup my mouth, speaking just for him. "All I want is the terrace and the food and the wine and . . ." I trail off because I'm not romantic with words. That hasn't changed. All I want is just to be with him. Spend time with him. That is literally all I crave.

"C'mon, Mark. You can say it. You just want . . ."

I roll my eyes as Rosie waves to me on her way down. "I see you, cupcake," I shout, then into the phone, I dip my voice. "Fine," I groan begrudgingly, but I like telling him. He deserves to know. "I just want you."

"Daddy!"

When Rosie grabs the bar again, she misses the metal and loses her grip. Without thinking, I rush toward the bars right as she topples to the ground. My heart crawls up my throat as she lets out a shriek of pain.

Four hours later, Rosie is conked out, her right arm in a pink cast stretched out on her twin bed, the orange cat draped around her head.

My heart rate has slowed, but only slightly.

Pretty sure I won't forget the sound of that fall for a long time.

Turns out it's *only* a forearm fracture, and the doc said she could play on the monkey bars as soon as three to four weeks after the cast comes off.

Tell that to the gray hairs I probably have.

There is nothing—nothing in the whole world—as harrowing as witnessing your kid fall. I head to the kitchen, grab a beer, and text Asher again. I texted him when I left the ER in one piece. But he asked me to text him, too, when we returned home, even though it's the middle of the night. I send him a quick note letting him know that Rosie's sound asleep.

His reply is instantaneous. *If you're not asleep, FaceTime me. Want to see your face.*

I dial him, stat.

The second his handsome profile fills the screen, my pulse calms. Crazy, how one person can both get you going and settle you down. "Hey," I say.

With a red pillow behind him, Asher stretches on his side in bed, propping his head in his hand. His hair is shaggy again. No scissors have touched his locks since the wedding. "How is she?"

I give him the details. ". . . and she'll have it on for four weeks. Through Christmas."

"Was she bummed about that?"

"Not at all," I say, laughing for the first time in hours. "She was more concerned with when she could have it signed."

"And the verdict?"

"Monday. So tomorrow, guess who's taking her marker shopping?"

He chuckles softly, then yawns. "Sounds like fun."

I roll my eyes. "Yeah, sure."

"I mean it, Mark. It does sound like fun. Wish I could go with you two."

That sounds like a perfect Saturday. I take a swig of the beer. "Me too."

"She's going to be fine, though. I've broken plenty of bones. I bet you were way more freaked out than she was."

"I think I aged ten years, Ash," I say, leaning against the counter.

He yawns once more, and I really need to let him go. But talking to him is my favorite part of every day.

"Listen, Mark," Asher says, sitting up in bed.

For a second, I tense. Hardly anything good starts with *listen*. But I don't have a single reason to suspect anything bad is coming so I decide not to worry. "What is it?"

"I hate to say this, but I don't think you should come next weekend for my birthday. It seems silly when you have a kid in a cast. She needs you. And I don't want you to have the added stress of worrying about letting me down. I'm a big boy. I'll be fine. Your little girl needs you."

My brow creases as I stare at my sleepy boyfriend who's impossibly sexy in his Parisian bed, and incredibly thoughtful too. He's so fucking good to me.

"I think you're right," I say, relieved.

"And trust me, I want to see you so much I could chew my leg off."

I crack up. "I like your legs. Keep them on."

"That's pretty much the only reason I haven't chewed off the right one. Anyway, we'll see each other at Christmas. Tomorrow, when you go shopping, get an advent calendar, to pass the days. Think of it as twenty-five days of dick."

I laugh harder. "And I better get a double dicking on Christmas," I tell him.

"Count on it. But I do want a naked striptease on Facetime on my birthday," Asher says. His smile makes me want to crawl through the phone to Paris.

"And you'll get one," I say, then sigh. "I really want to see you, Asher. Can it be June?"

"July, baby. That's when I started."

"I hate time."

"Me too," he says, then we say goodnight, and I cancel my trip.

Too bad. I had so many birthday plans for him, including telling him exactly how I feel about him.

But that'll have to wait till Christmas now.

50

PROPERTY OF MARK BANKS

ONE WEEK LATER

ASHER

I'm too old to care about birthdays, right? That's the reason I didn't tell anyone here that I'm having one tomorrow. And why I'm not allowed to be sad about spending it alone.

That's what I'm telling myself, anyway, as I lie on my bed, unable to sleep, staring up at the trompe l'oeil ceiling of my cute little furnished Parisian apartment.

It's not like I didn't get any presents. Flip sent me a pair of noise-canceling headphones that he describes as "sick." Lucy—who is still working for me part-time in New York—sent me a box of exquisite chocolates and a card that sings a song: "Happy Birthday, Sexy Beast."

She gets me. Also, she's still grateful that I flew her to Paris for a week of "business" that mostly involved her sightseeing and shopping between our "meetings."

Only Mark's gift is still waiting for me on the kitchen counter. I told myself I wouldn't open it before my birthday. It should cheer me up the day that he was supposed to arrive.

LAUREN BLAKELY & SARINA BOWEN

But it's already past midnight and it's starting to sink in that today is going to be a lonely day. I'd cleared my schedule in order to spend time with Mark. Oscar and Felicity and my other friends have made plans without me.

Hell, my birthday isn't really the problem. I was already lonely. I miss Mark all the time, except when we're yammering on the phone. But the six-hour time difference is killing me. I've sat up way too late so many nights just to hear his voice. Last month, I even nodded off in the middle of one of our calls and woke a few hours later with the imprint of my phone on my face.

I'd blearily taken a selfie of that for Mark's amusement. But then I didn't hit send, and not because I'm too vain to send him a photo where I look, like, super *not* hot. But the symptoms of our separation are depressing.

So I try not to dwell on it. I try not to point out that we've got six more months to go. And I love our phone conversations. I know more about Mark now than I ever knew about Garrett. My boyfriend is a great listener, and a thoughtful conversationalist.

Some nights, it seems like enough. But some nights, I miss him so fucking much that it hurts.

And then? Some nights his daughter breaks her arm because I'm bending his ear about my stupid birthday.

So that was a low point. If he hadn't been on the phone with me, snapping pics to send my way, she might not have fallen off those monkey bars. My long-distance relationship is actually a danger to children. Yay me.

It's possible that I'm slightly depressed.

Is thirty-one too young to have a mid-life crisis?

My phone chimes with a text, and I snatch it up, even though it's early evening in New York, and Mark told me he's making cookies with the kid, so I doubt it's him.

The message is a birthday greeting from . . . my New York dentist? Well, that gives me the warm fuzzies. He's throwing in a twenty-five percent discount on whitening too.

I roll off the bed with a groan, and pad into the kitchen. I grab a knife out of the block and use it to slit the tape on Mark's present. I'm opening this sucker right now. Maybe it will cheer me up.

Inside the box I peel back some tissue paper decorated with . . . are those eggplants? I let out a snort of laughter. See? Mark is already lifting my spirits.

There's a card on top of the gift, with Mark's handwriting on it: *Can't wait to be there with you. Please wear these.* I lift the card to find a pair of boxer briefs in cerulean blue. They're knit from something soft. Is that silk?

And the waistband says PROPERTY OF MARK BANKS in a continuous loop.

Hilarious! I'm definitely taking a thirst-trap selfie with these on. And underneath the briefs there's something in crisp white cotton. When I unfold it I find . . .

A polo shirt. I laugh again, and when I shake out the shirt, another little card falls out. *Laugh if you want, but you'll look hot in this too. Besides, what else would you wear when we play tennis this summer?*

That's when the ache hits me hard—right in the center of the chest. I miss him. I miss his kiss. I miss hearing him tell me that I snore. I miss *his* snore. I even miss his most boring gray polo shirt.

And the navy one too.

Fuck my life. Why am I in Paris when Mark is in New York?

What am I even doing?

I know there are rational answers. I wanted this job. Our relationship is still new. Blah, blah, blah. But those things just don't seem important enough tonight.

Alone in my kitchen, I drop my jeans and my underwear and put on the silky briefs. Then I shed my shirt and pull on the polo.

There's one more thing in the box. A bottle of Glen Scotia 15. *Nice, Mark.* That's a real treat. So I find a glass and pour myself two fingers of scotch. No, three fingers. I barely ate dinner, but who cares.

I take my phone into the bedroom. Time for a little photo

shoot. And an hour or so from now, I can call my man and tell him how much I miss him.

51

THE ECLAIRS ARE REALLY GOOD HERE

MARK

*H*ere's something nobody ever tells you about childrearing—kids turn into psychos in December. There should be a whole parenting book just about surviving a month of sugar cookies, Santa cravings, and Christmas break.

There could be an entire chapter just for advice on how to get the song "Jingle Bells" out of a guy's head.

My kitchen is trashed. Bits of cookie dough are everywhere. But at least the last cookies are out of the oven, so I can leave Rosie and Alba at the kitchen table with their sticky tubes of icing and their sprinkles.

"No sprinkles on the floor, girls," I beg.

"Sorry, Daddy," Rosie says. "The cast makes me clumsy."

"Does it hurt?" I ask for the millionth time this week.

"Nope," she says. "But Blackbeard just stepped on my pinky toe."

"Ah." My tone is dry. "Another trip to the ER then?"

"No, Daddy. His feet are soft."

Alba giggles.

"Good to know. I'll be in the living room if anybody needs

LAUREN BLAKELY & SARINA BOWEN

me." But I sure hope they don't. It's been a rough week. Bridget hasn't said she blames me for Rosie's broken arm.

But I know she totally blames me. Heck, I blame myself.

I head into the living room, where Valencia has just poured us each a glass of red wine. Zoe dashed out to pick up sushi for dinner from the Japanese restaurant around the corner. "Better your kitchen than mine," Valencia says.

"Gee, thanks." I take the wine and we both line up our feet on my coffee table.

"Your tree looks great, though. At least you have that."

"It's nice, right?" I gaze at the colored lights and wish that Asher were here to see it in person. It's almost eight o'clock, and he's probably asleep already. An hour ago, I had to tell him that I was elbows deep in cookie dough and unable to sneak away for our usual phone call. And I feel terrible about it too. His birthday is tomorrow. I was supposed to be on a plane tonight.

"Stay with us, Mark," Valencia says softly. "Don't go towards the light."

I turn back to her quickly. "Sorry."

"I bet I can guess who you're thinking about right now."

"Doesn't make you a genius."

She laughs and touches her wine glass to mine. "Does he still feel guilty about Rosie?"

"Yup. Even though I told him it was actually your fault for taking the girls to see Cirque du Soleil."

"That was a year ago!" she says, scandalized.

"No kidding, but he doesn't know that."

"Aw, Mark." She clutches her chest. "You're such a softy."

"Never call a man a softy. That's mean."

She chokes on her sip of wine and then howls with laughter.

My phone buzzes with a text in my pocket. I ignore it. Asher is asleep, and there's nobody else I want to hear from right now. Bridget actually decided to capitalize on my canceled trip by getting tickets to a Broadway show for tonight, since we switched weekends with Rosie.

I'm not even surprised.

"Mommy?" calls Alba from the kitchen. "Can Rosie sleep over?"

Valencia gives me a sideways glance. "You know, her arm does seem fine," she whispers.

"It's still broken, though," I whisper back. "You don't need to deal with that."

"Not this time!" Valencia calls to the girls.

My phone vibrates again. And again. And then two more times.

Hmm.

With a lazy sigh, I pull it out of my pocket. The texts are from Asher? It's two in the morning in Paris. What's that about? I open the first one and gasp.

The first message is a picture of Asher wearing nothing but the unbuttoned white polo and the briefs I sent him. Plus, an unfocused smile.

The second is a picture of him without the polo. And the smile is downright blurry.

And then the texts start.

MARK HONEY THE ECLAIRS ARE REALLY GOOD HERE IN PARIS. THERE IS ONE BAKERY THAT PUTS GOLD LEAF ON TOP. I WANTED TO TAKE YOU THERE TOMORROW.

I DON'T KNOW WHY EATING GOLD IS COOL. IT JUST IS.

I'M SAD AND A LITTLE DRUNK BECAUSE PARIS IS AMAZING BUT YOU AREN'T HERE AND I DON'T LIKE IT AS MUCH AS I THINK I SHOULD.

THIS JOB ISN'T EVERYTHING AND I MISS YOU ALL THE TIME AND I LOVE YOUUUUUUUUUU.

"Holy shit," I whisper.

"What's the matter?"

"My superhot wingman is drunk texting me." And I love every single word. Especially that last part.

Valencia gasps. "Did he say anything mean? Isn't that a thing with you guys?"

"He told me he loves me." I don't want to look away from the screen. I can't actually. I just stare at those three words. And I *feel* them too. Everywhere.

"Oh!" She covers her mouth with her hand. Then she scoots closer on the sofa to read over my shoulder.

OH SHIT I DIDN'T MEAN TO SAY THAT IN A TEXT I WANTED TO SAY IT IN PERSON. I WAS TRYING TO WAIT.

AND YOU WAIT TOO MUCH TOO. YOU WAIT FOR ME ALL THE TIME. BUT I DON'T KNOW WHY. I SNORE AND MY HAIR IS FLOOFY.

YOU NEVER COMPLAIN ABOUT MY STINKY FEET BUT IT'S ONLY A MATTER OF TIME.

TONIGHT I'M LISTENING TO MAROON 5'S DAYLIGHT ON A CONTINUOUS LOOP, LIKE AN EMO LOSER. BUT IT HURTS SO GOOD.

"Oh, that poor, sweet summer child," Valencia says as the texts roll on. "Your man needs you."

"I know," I groan. "But there's not enough of me to go around right now. This is the worst."

"Mommmmyyyyy!" Alba calls. "Can Rosie sleep over tomorrow night instead?"

"Does Rosie want to?" Valencia yells back.

"Yes!" my daughter shouts. "Duh!"

"I should just text him back," I say.

Valencia pokes me in the ribs. "No, Mark, please go into your super-tidy bedroom and throw a few things into a bag. Get your passport. Go to France. That's what you *should* do." She locks eyes with me. "*Tonight. Now.*"

Wow. The moment she says this, I can actually picture stepping off that jet at Charles de Gaulle, hurrying towards the immigration line to see my man, kissing the hell out of him on his birthday.

But it's just not practical. I have to work on Monday morning. It's already eight on Friday. Plus, I have my kid. "I couldn't do that," I say, even as the image of Asher's smile flashes before my eyes. "I can't just walk out on you and Rosie."

"You're not," she says firmly. "The person who needs you right now is Asher, not Rosie. She can spend the whole weekend with us, and she'll have a great time. You need to be in France. *Now*. Go get your man. I'll hold down the fort here. Seriously. How hard could it be?"

"Daddy!" Rosie yells. "I got icing on the pirate cat!"

"F-fiddlesticks," I say, setting my wine down on the table in preparation for cleaning that up.

Valencia holds out a hand. "No. I got this. I got tonight and tomorrow night, too, if Bridget decides to go to the opera or the damn symphony. Go, Mark. It's hard work finding your special someone. If you love Asher, go tell him so in person, and when you get your butt in a cab in ten minutes, text him that you're on the way."

She's completely right. My guy needs me. My friends have my back. My kid is doing great. There's only one place I need to be right now, and it's not here.

My chest squeezes with gratitude for Valencia. I'm lucky to have this life. "Are you a hundred percent serious?"

"A hundred and ten percent."

I meet her warm brown eyes. "Okay. I'm really going to do this crazy thing."

Holy shit. I am.

"Hurry," she says, then wags her phone as the door swings open, and Valencia's wife strolls into the vestibule.

"Who has yellowtail rolls and mackerel? This girl," she calls out.

Valencia nods in the direction of her wife. "I'll look up flights, and Zoe will handle the kitchen. Pack a bag and talk to Rosie. Quick!"

"Talk about what?" My daughter comes around the corner, probably to beg for a sleepover. Her hair is in a messy ponytail and red icing lines her cheekbone. I look at her—*my baby girl*.

And my heart tugs in another direction.

Rosie has always been my number one. From the very first time I held her, I knew I'd never let her down if I could help it.

"What, Daddy?" she asks, cocking her head. "What's wrong."

"Nothing. Everything is fine." I sit back down as Zoe crosses into the kitchen with a wave. "It's just that Asher is sad, baby. I was supposed to go to Paris for the weekend to see him."

She marches into the room and slides onto my knee. "Why don't you go?"

"Because you needed me too." I give a little tug on her ponytail. "And you're my number one. Always."

"I know *that*." She shrugs her narrow shoulders. "But maybe Asher needs you a little. He's your number two, right? You could go and I could stay with Alba."

"Only if you're sure," I say, wrapping my arms around her. "I'd come home on Sunday night, or maybe Monday. But no later."

"And you'll call me from Paris?"

"Of course."

She looks me right in the eye. "And you'll bring me those chocolates from the airport? In the shape of the Eiffel Tower?"

Valencia snorts. "Work it, girl. Work it."

"I'll take some macarons," Zoe calls out.

"Possibly," I hedge to Rosie. "That was a lot of chocolate. I might have to choose a smaller treat."

"Fine." She gives me a cherubic smile. "Bring one for Alba too."

And now, I can go. "It's a deal." I set her on the couch, kiss her on the head, and run to my room to pack.

Ten minutes later, I'm in a cab.

52

SEX, LOVE, AND CAMEMBERT

ASHER

*I*t's. Just. Too. Bright.

The sun aims its morning death rays my way, blaring at fifty thousand watts through the bedroom window.

That's . . . weird.

I always shut the drapes at night since, well, sleep is my second-favorite activity, after sex.

I rub my eyes, push up on my elbows.

Must be early, but I can't find my phone to check the time. Yawning, I stretch my arms over my head as I sit up, then get out of bed to shut the curtains so I can sleep some more.

Maybe I could sleep the whole day away. What better way to spend my lonely birthday? As I trudge to the window, I glance down.

Whoa.

Property of Mark Banks is stamped on my briefs.

Oh shiiiiit.

Last night slams into me, and I groan so loud they can hear me at Notre Dame.

I pulled a Mark Banks, didn't I?

I got *intexticated.*

315

But what the hell did I say? Spinning around, I race to the bed, hunting for my phone. Is it between the sheets? Grabbing the covers, I haul them off. It's not there.

A search between couch cushions, on the coffee table, and in the nightstand comes up empty.

Wait.

Maybe I showered with the phone, shot him a very sexy selfie. Yup. Sounds totally stupid and totally like me. Bet I did that instead of spilling my love guts via SMS.

But my phone's not in the bathroom, so I march to the kitchen, where the charger lies unattached on the counter next to a bottle of scotch.

And that's a lot less full than it would have been when I opened it.

My mouth is sandpaper, so I yank open the fridge to grab the water pitcher.

What the . . .?

My phone is perched on top of the camembert, dying at two percent.

With a groan, I jam it onto the charger for juice, where it takes one hundred years for my texts to open.

Clicking on the text string, I scroll up right away, embarrassed as I re-read every single sappy message. This is a disaster. I told Mark that I love him. I do, of course. But you're not supposed to wail it at your true love when you're wasted. Gawd, this is ugly. Now if I repeat it, he won't even believe me.

I feel sick as I scroll through all the crazy things I said. I'm thirty-one years old today and still incapable of adulthood. Example—the last text I sent before I passed out:

AND NOW I'M PUTTING THE PHONE IN THE FRIDGE WITH THE CAMEMBERT SO I'M NOT TEMPTED TO TEXT YOU LOVE NOTES ANYMORE TONIGHT

But there's a reply blinking up at me. Sent nearly ten hours ago.

Mark: I'm on my way to JFK right now to catch the 10:20 p.m. flight. The details are in your email. Pick me up at CDG at 12:20 p.m. at international arrivals. I need to have eclairs with you in Paris on your birthday. Clearly, you need me, too, since Maroon 5 sucks.

Is this real?

But Mark Banks is not a prankster. And the email from Delta serves up the absolutely spectacular news that my save-the-day boyfriend is traveling coach on a flight that lands in one hour and fifteen minutes.

He's flying *coach* for me.

I smell like the sewer, but feel like a rock star.

Leaving the phone to charge, I take the world's fastest shower, brush my teeth, pull on clothes, and run a hand through my wet hair. I grab my cell and bound down the creaky staircase in my building to hail a taxi.

It's Saturday morning, and I'm totally sober again, but buzzed in a whole new way—with joy.

"Charles de Gaulle, *s'il vous plaît*," I tell the man at the wheel.

Then I go to the airport to pick up the only gift I want—the man I love.

———

I feel sheepish as I stand outside of the secure area, waiting for Mark. The app on my phone shows me that his flight landed safely, right on time. But what the hell am I going to say to him?

Hey, honey, thanks for leaving your injured daughter in New York after I got drunk and lost my mind last night. I really do love you, but you don't have to say it back if you're not feeling it for this man who smells like a distillery. It's too soon, and I'm kind of a mess, but maybe I can feed you some eclairs and change the subject to blow jobs? After all, your name is on my underwear. What do you say?

I'm still working on this little speech when another group of passengers streams through the doors. And, like magic, my gaze goes *right* to Mark. He's walking confidently through the crowd, weekend bag slung over his shoulder, hair tidy in spite of the overnight flight.

He's wearing a blue cashmere sweater that I sent him as a gift. The color makes his eyes pop just as I knew it would.

And he's smiling at me from behind those sexy glasses. In spite of every inconvenience I've caused him. In spite of my pathetic drunk texts, he's smiling like he's won the lottery.

He looks just how I feel.

Finally he's here, and I'm pulling him into my arms. His bag hits the floor with a slap, and we kiss like we haven't seen each other in a year instead of a month.

"I love you," he says against my lips.

"I love you more," I argue. And it's probably true. I wasn't looking for love when I offered to work through Mark's spread-sheet with him.

But that's what I found, and I'll do whatever I can to keep it. And I'm pretty sure I know exactly what I can do for him—*for us*. But, first things first. "There are things I need to explain," I say, forcing myself to break our kiss. "I'm sorry I got all broody last night."

"I'm not," he says, his blue eyes taking me in. "Happy birth-day, hot stuff."

"Thank you. But I'm serious. There are lots of things I need to say to you."

He tips his head to the side. "What things?"

Things like . . . *let me show you how fucking happy I am that you're here.* And *get naked right now and fuck my mouth.*

And now, *this* . . .

"God. Yes. Get there," I pant, letting him fall from my lips for a second.

"Babe," Mark groans, his tongue on my cock.

Our heart-to-heart took a sudden turn with Mark pushing me down on my bed the moment we arrived back at the flat.

Now we're communicating mostly in moans as he draws me

back into his throat, and I give his cock the same mind-bending treatment. He thrusts faster, pushes deeper, signs he's close. His hums around my shaft intensify, but so does his sloppiness, and that flips the switch in me—him losing control. My whole body flashes with heat, and the world blurs deliciously out of focus as we hit the end together. Happy birthday to me, indeed.

Neither one of us moves for several, long, lust-drenched seconds.

"Two down, twenty-nine to go," I say when I pop off his dick.

"We'll hit your birthday requirement, especially if we go hard on the sixty-nines," Mark says.

I roll onto my back. "Holy hell, I've missed you."

He snickers from somewhere near my feet. "I can tell."

"No, honey. I really miss you. Not just your impressive technique." I prop myself up on an elbow and run a hand along his strong leg.

"I miss you too. Every day. In case that wasn't clear from the last-minute, overnight flight."

Yup. Time to tell him. I may not be a planner, but I have a plan for us. Since I do have a lot of things to say to Mark. Things well beyond *get on my dick*.

"We're going to eat eclairs, and then I have a surprise."

"I hate surprises," he grumbles, but he doesn't sound annoyed. Maybe he's come around to my kind of surprises.

"This is a good surprise, and I don't just mean the gold in the eclair," I say, since I think he'll like my idea. At least, I hope so. But he flew across an ocean to tell me he loved me, and that's all I need to know to skydive once again.

We're at the bakery, sitting inside at a tiny table, sharing a plate of two of the most amazing eclairs, and it's almost time to tell him my plan.

"So, eating gold is kind of weird," he says. "Because I suppose you poop gold afterward."

"The French are so decadent," I say, then take a sip of strong espresso and gather my courage. My plan crystallized during the hungover cab ride to the airport. Then, when I saw him, I knew for certain that I was about to do something big. I'm the only one of the two of us who can take this step.

He can't make this leap for us, but I can.

"Babe," I begin, "I want to talk about the next six months. I want to move back to New York. Right away."

Mark freezes with the eclair in hand, a serious expression on his face. "Seriously? But what about your job here?"

I shrug. "It's just a job. It was a passion project. But lately, all the passion in my life is reserved for *you*." I reach across the table and squeeze his arm. "Unless I'm terrifying you right now and you don't want a mess of a boyfriend parachuting back into your life."

"Hey." Mark grabs my hand and holds it. "Don't say that. You're not a mess. Except for that hair." He winks. "But I like it floofy, and I like it swoopy. And if I ever meet this asshole Garrett, I'm going to tell him he's nuts."

Warmth blooms in the center of my chest. Does it make me an asshole that I totally want to see him do it?

"No—wait." Mark sets down his eclair. "I actually don't want him to know he passed on the best guy in New York." He raises his cool blue eyes to mine. "You are always there when I need you, Asher. I'm dead serious. You're the best guy I know. I love you, and Rosie and I will be lucky to have you close by. This is a very good surprise."

Everything inside me finally relaxes. This decision feels so right, it isn't even funny. I let out a whoop of joyful laughter. "Then I can't wait to get started on the logistics. It's a shame I sublet my apartment. I'll have to find a short-term rental. Or—wait. I could find a different place altogether. Maybe I don't want to live in Brooklyn if you guys are in Manhattan. I should start researching neighborhoods."

Mark frowns. "Look, don't let real estate rule your life either way. Figure out when you're ready to come home. And then get on a plane. You can stay with me and Rosie while you decide where you want to live."

"Really?" I breathe.

"Really." He covers his hand with mine. "I'll move some polo shirts to make space for you. We're doing this, Asher St. James. I'm not scared. I don't do things half-assed."

My inner superhot wingman wants to make a joke about asses right now, but I rein it in. "That's an incredible offer, Banks. Will Rosie be okay with it?"

He threads his fingers through mine. "I think so. I spent the last year worrying about Rosie all the time, and never worrying about myself. But you helped me get past that . . ."

My heart thumps with happiness. I don't think I realized until this very minute that I was as good for Mark as he is for me.

". . . And the truth is simple: Rosie is a happy kid who'll be lucky to have you in her life. I would do anything for her. But setting aside my own needs doesn't seem like the right call anymore."

I might actually burst now. "Continuing to make you happy in New York would be an honor, Mark. I don't even know what else to say." He's the only person who's ever made me speechless.

"Good. Then I'll say something else. You're mine, wingman. So let's go home and make this work. I love you, and I'm ready when you are."

That's when I run out of words completely. I lean over and kiss him on the lips instead.

EPILOGUE

SIX MONTHS LATER

YOU TWO LOOK FAMILIAR

MARK

I'm sitting on the sofa, eavesdropping, while Rosie manipulates my live-in boyfriend.

"That was a short chapter," she says. "We could read another one real quick."

My hands go still on the corkscrew, waiting to hear whether he gives in or does the hard thing and gets his gorgeous ass out here so we can watch TV together. It's not like I've been waiting a whole damn year for the conclusion of *An Arranged Marriage*. Tonight we're finally getting the finale to season two.

"Well . . ." Asher hedges.

I clear my throat. Loudly.

". . . Not this time," he says, his voice colored by regret.

Honestly, Asher and Rosie are a great team. When he came to stay with us last winter, I'd had no idea how easily my boyfriend would slip into the role of becoming another parent to Rosie.

They have a whole set of jokes and hobbies together. He's teaching her to play soccer. And lately, they've been reading a British series of children's books I'd never heard of before.

It's magic. *Usually*. But tonight, I'm impatient.

I hear the low sound of Asher's goodnight to my daughter. And the click of the lamp. Now it's quiet, and I can picture him passing a hand over her hair, and giving her a last kiss on the crown of her head.

Asher never moved out of my apartment. He flew home for Christmas after our Paris weekend and never left. Next month, he's selling his Brooklyn place to the subletter. We're going to look around this neighborhood for a bigger place to buy together. But we'll take our time until the right apartment comes along.

The door closes with a soft click, and Asher emerges from Rosie's room.

"Finally!" I hiss. "I'm dying here."

"Simmer down, nerd boy. Ooh, wine?" He seats himself on the couch beside me and I pass him a glass.

I press *play*.

The theme music kicks in, and Asher wraps an arm around me. "C'mon, Webflix. Give us a happy ending. And if that's too much to ask for, at least give us a good make-out scene."

"It's not too much to ask for," I argue. "They can tell the duchess where to shove it, and settle down to manage Ollie's place in the country. His people need him."

"Hmm." Asher sips his wine. "But will the bad boy poet be content in the country? He's a man of action and sin. What if he loses his muse? What if all his poems start to rhyme? There was an old git from Nantucket . . ."

I snort. "I'll admit that Sir Trevor has been slutting it up during season two. But it's all an act. He's trying to convince himself that he doesn't need true love."

"He does, though," Asher says, turning to kiss my neck. "He really does."

An hour later, the show ends more or less how I called it—in a swell of orchestra music and a hot, steamy kiss. Troliver have kept a pied-à-terre in London—to keep Trevor up on the latest gossip. But they spend much of their time frolicking around Ollie's estate and modernizing the agricultural technology.

Or something. I'm a little unclear on the details, because Asher has been sucking gently on my neck for the last twenty minutes.

The cat slinks by, heading into the bedroom. He has the right idea. "Should we move this to the bed?" I ask, palming the bulge in Asher's pajama pants. "You shouldn't stay up too late, though. Aren't you playing tennis with Brett tomorrow?"

"Pfft," Asher says, running his hand beneath my T-shirt. "You think I can't beat Brett at tennis after a late night with you? What do I get if I win?"

I mull that over, but his hands turn wicked, which makes thinking hard. "You have to win all the sets, or I get first dibs on our rental car in Italy."

"Ooh, good one, Banks." He chuckles. "It's on."

Then his hand creeps into my briefs, and it so is.

ASHER

I'm wearing a white polo shirt.

Stranger things have happened.

Like falling in love with a hot, nerdy, single dad banker who is not boring; Mark Banks is an adventure every single day.

And like me living happily with that guy and his seven-year-old daughter. Who I took to a softball game last week, since my guy had to work late. Something about the inflation index or the CPI blah, blah, blah. It didn't make much sense, so I shut him up with my mouth when he told me all about it.

Then he said much more interesting things like *yes, more, deeper.*

So yeah, life is strange and good. Imagine that. Single, globetrotting, former-athlete-now-photographer settles down with a Wall Streeter and his kid. And he loves every single second of it.

But I'm really going to relish destroying Mark's work husband at tennis.

"Hope you lose today," Mark tells me when I leave *our* home the next morning.

"No, you don't. You love it when I drive," I say with a wink.

"You love it when *I* drive," he counters as he pours his coffee.

But I plan to win. There's an Alfa Romeo in Tuscany calling my name.

Well, I still love fast cars. Some things never change. That means I have to beat Brett in a shutout today.

Which I do a few hours later, when Brett misses the final ball by miles and I clean up.

"Rematch. Can we play again?" he asks.

"'Fraid not, Brett," I say, then I look at my watch. "I have to collect on a bet. Another time."

"Another time," he says with a nod as we shake at the net.

I leave and return to Sixteenth Street. As soon as the door unlocks, I call out, "Honey, I'm home, and I'll be driving first."

"Dammit," Mark curses from the bedroom.

I sweep into our room where he's tossing T-shirts into a suit-case. I grab him, yank him up, and kiss him hard. "I'm sweaty," I rasp out.

He growls. "And I like it."

"I know you do," I say, then I glance at the clock. We have to meet Hannah, Flip, and Caroline for fro-yo to celebrate Rosie's last day of first grade, then in the evening, we'll take off.

"There's just enough time for . . ."

Ten minutes later, we're gasping and panting.

Life is very, very good.

Later that night, we settle into the second row on our transatlantic flight.

"May you never fly coach again," I say, as I squeeze his hand.

"We're posh fuckers all the way," he says, and when we're airborne, a statuesque flight attendant does a double take.

"You two look familiar."

So does she—the Gisele Bündchen ringer. "We flew to Miami together a year ago and you were on our flight," I say.

"Right," she says, wagging a finger. "You called yourselves . . . what was it? *The best men.*"

Mark looks at me as he answers. "That's us, and he's all mine."

That's all the label I'll ever need.

His.

THE
END

Made in United States
Cleveland, OH
24 November 2024

10888695R00192